"All this information ma... ...y ... ... to Agnes Tufverson. She had been heavily drugged with sleeping pills when she had been carried on board in the trunk—Poderjay would not have risked killing her in case the trunk was opened before the ship set sail. He had then murdered her, probably by suffocation, and spent the voyage slicing the flesh from her bones with razor blades and feeding it to the fish. Finally, the skeleton, greased with cold cream, had also been pushed through the porthole. And when it vanished below the waves, Poderjay must have sighed with relief, and made sure that there was not the slightest sign of blood in the cabin or in the trunk—he had probably dissected the body on a sheet of rubber, after draining it of blood."

How was this heinous murderer brought to justice?

It's all in...

WRITTEN IN BLOOD
THE TRAIL & THE HUNT

"A sprawling history of the evolution of forensic science....A writer who has spent so much time pondering violent crime is well placed to celebrate the meticulous scientific sleuths who help bring criminals to book."

—*The Observer*

Also by Colin Wilson
Written in Blood: Detectives and Detection
Written in Blood: The Criminal Mind and Method*

Published by
WARNER BOOKS   *forthcoming

WRITTEN IN BLOOD

THE TRAIL & THE HUNT

COLIN WILSON

Robert Christiansen Jr.
TRUE CRIME

WARNER BOOKS

A Time Warner Company

This work is volume two in a trilogy first published in hardcover in Great Britain in one volume entitled WRITTEN IN BLOOD.

WARNER BOOKS EDITION

Cover design by Don Puckey
Cover photos by AP/Wide World and Popperphoto

This Warner Books Edition is published by arrangement with Thorsons UK, Denington Estate, Wellingborough, Northants NN8 2RQ, England

Warner Books, Inc.
666 Fifth Avenue
New York, N.Y. 10103

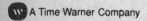 A Time Warner Company

Printed in the United States of America

First Warner Books Printing: September 1991

10 9 8 7 6 5 4 3 2 1

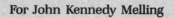
For John Kennedy Melling

ACKNOWLEDGMENTS

This book owes an immense debt of gratitude to two friends: John Kennedy Melling and Stuart Kind, both of whom have provided me with so much material that they are virtually the co-authors. I was also fortunate enough to secure the co-operation of many other experts in various fields, including Dr. Mike Sayce, Dr. Alf Faragher, Dr. Denis Hocking, and Candice Skrapec, one of America's leading authorities on serial killers. Other American friends who provided information are June O'Shea, Stephen Spickard, Dennis Stacy, Denis Rickard, Michael Flanagin, and Ann Rule. As usual, access to the immense library of my friend Joe Gaute was invaluable, as was the help of the crime-specialist bookseller Camille Wolfe. Two skilled crime writers, Brian Marriner and John Dunning, also provided invaluable information on many cases. Others to whom I owe a debt of gratitude are Paul Williams, Donald Rumbelow (both of the Metropolitan Police), Robin Odell, James Rentoul, D. J. Werrett, and Ian Kimber.

ANALYTICAL TABLE OF CONTENTS

1
Whose Body?

"To write the history of identification is to write the history of criminology," says Edmond Locard in his classic *Traité de criminalistique*. And the reader of the two volumes entitled *Proofs of Identity* can sense the author's almost obsessive involvement in the subject. For Locard, the question of identification is indeed the essence of criminology.

Locard's account of the famous case of Lesurques and Dubosq offers a key to his attitude. It began on the evening of 27 April 1796, when the Lyon mail-coach failed to arrive at the village of Melun, just south of Paris. Early the next morning, a search party found the abandoned coach near the Pouilly bridge. The driver and post boy had been brutally hacked to death, and more than five million francs was missing. One of the horses had also been taken, and it became clear that the wine merchant who had been the sole passenger had actually been a member of a gang of highwaymen. He had carried a large cavalry sword, and this had probably been the murder weapon. The other members of the gang, it soon became clear, were four heavily armed horsemen who had dined in the nearby village of Montgeron a few hours before the mail-coach went through.

The police picked up the trail remarkably quickly. The missing horse was found in Paris the next day. Then a stable-keeper reported that four sweating horses had been returned to his stable in the early hours of the morning by a man named Couriol. With luck and patience, the police traced Couriol to a village north of Paris and arrested him; he was found to be in possession of over a million francs, obviously his share of the booty.

On the morning Couriol was due to appear in court at the Palais de Justice, a man called Charles Guénot went to the Palais to collect some papers the police had taken from him—they had found him in the same house as Couriol, but he was not suspected of being one of the gang. With Guénot was a friend called Joseph Lesurques, a well-to-do business-man from Douai, who had bumped into Guénot by accident that morning. Also in the Palais were two barmaids from Montgeron, who had served dinner to the highway robbers. When they saw Guénot and Lesurques, they became excited and told an usher that they recognized them as two of the robbers. Geúnot and Lesurques were arrested. In due course, they were tried, together with Couriol and three other men who were accused of being accomplices. Guénot was ac-quitted; Lesurques and Couriol were among those condemned to death.

Couriol immediately declared that Lesurques was completely innocent. And the judge who had ordered Lesurques's arrest—a man named Daubanton—was so disturbed by this that he went to see Couriol in prison. Couriol repeated that Lesurques was innocent. The barmaids, he said, had mistak-en Lesurques for the real culprit, a man named Dubosq. It was true that Dubosq, unlike Lesurques, had dark hair, but he had worn a blond wig to take part in the robbery.

Daubanton had the case reopened. A commission was set up to re-examine the evidence against Lesurques. It was pointed out to them that Lesurques had no possible motive to get involved in highway robbery; he was already well off. Unfortunately, this piece of information backfired. The com-mission decided that perhaps Lesurques's relatives had offered to bribe Dubosq's relatives if he would declare Lesurques innocent. The Minister of Justice agreed with them. And the unfortunate Lesurques took a tearful farewell of his wife and children and went to the guillotine with Couriol.

But the police evidently believed Couriol. They went to considerable trouble to arrest four men named by Couriol, including the fake wine merchant, and these men were also condemned and executed. Judge Daubanton's campaign to have Lesurques declared innocent only damaged his own career.

Obviously, this is a classic case of mistaken identity, like that of Adolf Beck and Oscar Slater. Yet we can see why Edmond Locard thought it so important. The brutality of the crime aroused a determination to punish it at all costs. When the barmaids identified Guénot and Lesurques as two of the highwaymen, everyone was understandably delighted. But when Guénot was found innocent, it should have been obvious that Lesurques was also innocent. Unfortunately, the authorities were so anxious to see justice done at any cost that Lesurques was executed. Identification, which Locard defined as the center of any criminal inquiry, had failed utterly.

For Locard, this represented the greatest challenge for the science of criminology. This is why his two volumes on the proofs of identity are the very heart of his great *Traité de criminalistique*. Dozens of pages are devoted to case after case of mistaken or doubtful identity, and again and again he points out the unreliability of eye witnesses. He is obviously fascinated by the controversial case of Anastasia, the woman who claimed to be the last survivor of the Russian Royal Family. On 16 July 1918, the Grand Duchess Anastasia, together with her parents—the Tsar and Tsarina—and her three sisters and brother, was taken down to a cellar in Ekaterinburg and shot. The bodies were destroyed by acid and thrown down a mineshaft. In February 1920 a girl tried to commit suicide in Berlin. A fellow patient in hospital declared that she recognized her as the Grand Duchess Anastasia. The girl herself later declared that this was true, and that she had escaped the massacre with the aid of a soldier named Tchaikovsky, whom she later married. After his death, she attempted to kill herself . . .

Various people who had known Anastasia went to see Mme. Tchaikovsky. Her tutor, Pierre Gilliard, was at first convinced, but later changed his mind; Anastasia's uncle, the Grand Duke Andrei, was totally convinced; so was an officer who knew her well, when she addressed him by his old nickname. Soon, "Anastasia" had hosts of people who thought her genuine, and hosts who were convinced she was a fraud. In 1938, she allowed a German lawyer to try to obtain for her a share of the Tsar's fortune lodged in foreign banks. The case dragged on for 20 years, but Mme. Tchaikovsky never established her legal right to call herself the Grand Duchess Anastasia.

Locard's *Proofs of Identity* appeared in 1932, long before the law case; but the 20 pages he devotes to the identity of Mme. Tchaikovsky leave very little doubt that "Anastasia" was a fraud. Two photographs alone—one superimposing Anastasia's profile on Mme. Tchaikovsky, the other superimposing Mme. Tchaikovsky's profile on Anastasia—make it obvious that they are not the same person. The Grand Duchess has a smaller mouth, a smaller nose, a smaller ear; moreover, her nose is straight, while Mme. Tchaikovsky's is "tipped." Even the fact that the photograph of the Grand Duchess Anastasia was taken at the age of 17, while that of Mme. Tchaikovsky is taken two years later, cannot account for the difference; faces do not change so much in two years. Moreover, Locard shows that two photographs published in the *New York Evening Post*, purporting to be those of Mme. Tchaikovsky and of the Grand Duchess Anastasia, and showing an astonishing resemblance are, in fact, both of Anastasia, one of them slightly retouched. Locard's analysis makes it clear beyond all doubt that Anna Anderson (as Mme. Tchaikovsky later called herself) and Anastasia were two different people.

The riddle remains: how could a number of people who knew Anastasia intimately, like her uncle, have made such an extraordinary mistake? The answer is obviously that Anna Anderson *did* bear a close resemblance to Anastasia, and that people who had not seen Anastasia for several years were taken in by the resemblance. Locard also cites the extraordinary Tichborne case of the 1860s, in which a grotesque impostor was accepted by an English lady as her dead son. Roger Charles Tichborne was lost at sea off Brazil in 1854. Twelve years later, his mother, Lady Félicité Tichborne, received a badly spelled letter purporting to come from her long-lost son in Wagga-Wagga, Australia, asking her to send the money so he could come home. When Lady Tichborne finally went to see her son in his hotel in Paris, she was startled to see a vast whale of a man, weighing 26 stone, lying in a darkened room with his face to the wall—the son she remembered had been thin. Yet, incredibly, she accepted him as the missing Sir Roger (the son would have inherited his father's title) and allowed him a £1,000 a year until he could legally establish his claim. In due course, "Sir Roger" became chief mourner at his mother's funeral. Like "Anastasia," he aroused widespread support, and large sums were donated to prosecute his claim on the understanding that these supporters would be richly repaid when he won his case. This ended by costing £200,000 and dragged on for nearly a year. A commission that visited Australia had little trouble in showing that the claimant to the Tichborne millions was actually a butcher called Arthur Orton, also known as Castro. A pocket-book was found, which the claimant admitted to be his property, in which he had written: "Some men has plenty money and no brains, and some men has plenty brains and no money. Surely men with plenty money and no brains were made for men with plenty brains and no money." The jury had no difficulty in deciding that Arthur Orton and Sir Roger Tichborne were not the same person, and Orton was later sentenced to 14 years' imprisonment for perjury, of which he served 10. Here is a case in which there can be no possible doubt that the fraud was made possible only through the obsession of a half-blind old lady who refused to accept that her son was dead.

Far more baffling in every way is the case of the "second Joan of Arc." In May 1436, five years after Joan of Arc had been burnt at the stake by the English, her two brothers heard that she had returned and was taking part in a jousting

tournament at Vaucouleurs, near Metz. They hurried along
to denounce the impostor, but when a woman dressed in
armour raised her visor, both of them greeted her as their
sister Joan. In Metz, many people who had known her well
in her days as a soldier accepted her as "the Maid." She
returned to her home village of Domrémy, where her relatives, and apparently her mother, accepted her as Joan. Her
brothers went to tell the king—whom Joan had crowned—
that their sister was still alive, and in 1440, she went to the
court. The king tried to deceive her by asking one of his
men to impersonate him, but Joan was not deceived, and
went and knelt at his feet, whereupon Charles VII said:
"Pucelle, my dear, you are welcome in the name of God."
Yet after this meeting, the king denounced her as an impostor.
In spite of this, Joan returned to Metz and continued to be
accepted as La Pucelle, the Maid. She married a knight and,
as the Dames des Armoires, lived to an advanced age.

The greatest mystery that remains is: if Joan was not
executed at Rouen in 1431, then who *was*? The crowd that
witnessed her death was kept at a distance by 800 English
soldiers. It is just conceivable that the English connived at
her escape; she was a person who could command astonishing
affection and loyalty, and when she complained to the Earl
of Warwick that her two guards treated her disrespectfully,
he was furious and immediately changed them. But if she
was allowed to escape, we can only assume that some
unfortunate woman—perhaps some derelict from the Rouen
jail—was burned in her place. At this distance in time the
mystery is clearly insoluble, but Locard's criteria of identification seem to suggest that the Dame des Armoires was
Joan of Arc.*

Locard proceeds from problems of the identification of
the living to the—criminologically speaking—more interesting problem of identifying the dead. Here he was able to
draw upon the work of the greatest pioneers in this field, his

---

*For a more detailed account of the case see *The Encyclopedia of Unsolved
Mysteries,* by Colin and Damon Wilson, Harrap, London 1987.

friend and mentor Professor Alexandre Lacassagne, who, in a celebrated case of 1889, had demonstrated the techniques of identifying an unknown corpse.

_____ 2 _____

In earlier centuries, the methods had been crude, and often ineffectual. A rare exception was the case of Catherine Hayes, which took place during the "crime wave" in early eighteenth-century London. At daybreak on 2 March 1725, a watchman named Robinson saw a head lying on the muddy foreshore of the Thames at Westminster. Fortunately, the features were still intact, and the local magistrates ordered that it should be washed and have its hair combed, after which it should be placed on a pole in the local St Margaret's churchyard. Parish officers were ordered to place themselves around the churchyard, and be prepared to take into custody anyone "who might discover signs of guilt on the sight of it." (A footnote to the case in *The Newgate Calendar* of 1774 describes how the wounds of a corpse will bleed profusely if it is touched by the murderer.) But the head soon began to decay, whereupon the parish officers ordered that it should be preserved in a jar of spirits (probably gin).

Meanwhile, an organ-builder's apprentice named Bennet called on a woman called Catherine Hayes, who lived in Tyburn Road (now Oxford Street) and told her that he thought the head was that of her husband John. Catherine Hayes, a dominant, rather attractive woman in her mid-30s, assured him that her husband was perfectly well, and warned him against spreading false rumors. The same day, a Mr. Patrick went into a pub called the Dog and Dial and remarked that the head looked like John Hayes. A youth named Billings was drinking in the pub; he told Mr. Patrick that he was lodging with John Hayes, and that Hayes had been lying in bed when he left that morning. But some of Hayes's close friends were more persistent. When a man called Ashby asked her outright what had happened to her husband,

Catherine Hayes told him in confidence that he had been forced to flee to Portugal, having killed a man in a quarrel. Ashby was unconvinced; he went to another friend of Hayes called Longmore, and asked him to go and put the same question. Mrs. Hayes told him the same story—except that this time she claimed that the husband had fled to Hertfordshire. When the two men compared notes, they decided to go and tell their story to a magistrate. And the magistrate, a Mr. Lambert, agreed that it all looked highly suspicious, and issued a warrant for the arrest of Catherine Hayes. Catherine Hayes had recently changed her lodgings, but was easily located. The officers found her in bed with the lodger, Thomas Billings. She and Billings were both arrested. So were two more lodgers called Thomas Wood—who was even younger than Billings—and a Mrs. Springate.

Catherine Hayes now demanded to see the head, and was taken to the house where it was kept. On beings shown the jar, she cried dramatically: "Oh, it is my dear husband's head!", and proceeded to kiss the jar. The man in charge of the head lifted it out of the jar by the hair, whereupon Catherine, declining to be unnerved, kissed it passionately and asked if she could have a lock of the hair. The custodian replied drily that it was bloody, and she had already had enough blood, at which the widow fainted away.

The young man Wood proved to be a weaker spirit. On being confronted with the evidence, he made a full confession. He and Billings were both Catherine's lovers. Catherine Hayes was a dominant, quarrelsome woman, and she was tired of her husband's meanness. So she persuaded her lovers to murder him. They had made John Hayes drunk on six pints of wine, and when he fell asleep, Billings had hit him on the head with a coal-hatchet; Wood completed the job with two more blows. Then they placed the neck above a bucket, and sawed off the head with a carving knife. Catherine wanted to boil it to make it unrecognizable, but the killers were too unnerved. They took the head away in a pail, and threw it on the foreshore of the river. Then they returned to the house and dismembered the body; the following night they tossed the pieces into a pond at Marylebone, where they were found just after Catherine's arrest. Mrs. Springate, it seemed, had been unaware of the murder, and she was duly discharged.

Catherine Hayes was shocked when she learned that the charge against her would not be murder, but "petty treason" —her husband was supposed to be her lord and master and she had rebelled against him. The penalty for this was to be burned alive. This finally led her to "confess" that the other two had committed the murder. But it did no good. After she was condemned to be burned, she screamed all the way back to Newgate prison. Billings, with whom she was undoubtedly in love, was hanged. Wood died in jail of fever. And Catherine was duly burned alive—the executioner was trying to strangle her when the flames licked his hands and he was forced to jump back. The chronicle comments that she survived for a considerable time, trying to kick the burning faggots away, and that it was three hours before her body was reduced to ashes.

More than a century later, the science of identification was still in a primitive state when a tailor of Norwich called William Sheward had a furious quarrel with his wife about money matters, and slashed her throat with a razor. Sheward was not a violent man—he was, in fact, a rather inadequate alcoholic—and the realization of what he had done overwhelmed him with horror. But the thought of the hangman made him bold. He and his wife Martha had never got on together—she was a shrew, and many years his senior—and he was determined not to swing for her. Unlike Billings and Wood, he did not make the mistake of losing his nerve, but spent several days carefully dismembering the body, boiling the head to reduce the stench of decay. Then he proceeded to distribute the pieces in ditches around the area. He burned all the bloodstained nightclothes—he killed her in bed—as well as the mattress. Six days after the murder, a man who was out for a country walk wondered what his dog was chewing in a ditch; he called it, and the dog ran towards him with a human hand in its mouth. And for the next few weeks, other parts of the body were found in different places around Norwich.

The chief problem of murderers who kill their wives is to account for her sudden disappearance. Sheward told his neighbors that his wife had left him and gone to London. It was an unimaginative invention and hardly deserved to succeed. But luck was on Sheward's side. Doctors who examined the remains agreed that they were those of a woman in her 20s—Martha Sheward had been 56. She had taken good care of her hands, and Sheward had unintentionally created further confusion by boiling most of the members to reduce the smell. He also avoided another mistake made by Catherine Hayes, and cut up the head into small pieces. A magistrate ordered that the unidentified remains should be pickled in spirit, and kept in the Guildhall, and there they remained undisturbed for the next 18 years.

Sheward was a haunted man; he even gave up alcohol in case he betrayed his secret in his cups. But in 1862, 11 years after the murder, he felt sufficiently relaxed to marry again—this time to a lady of a less quarrelsome disposition, by whom he had two children. Oddly enough, he frequently tried his wife's patience by extravagantly praising the virtues of the deceased Martha; now she was gone, he allowed himself to indulge in sentimental reminiscences.

By 1869, his conscience was troubling him so much that he decided to commit suicide. For some reason, he chose to do it in London, where he had met his wife when he was a young man. On New Year's Day, he took a steamboat to Chelsea, and tried to nerve himself to cut his throat. "But the Almighty would not let him do it." Instead, he went and stood in front of the house in Walworth, where he had first seen his wife, then went up to a policeman standing on the corner, and declared that he wanted to confess to the murder of his wife. He was taken to the police station, and told the story in detail.

The remains in the Guildhall were now re-examined, and the doctor who had originally identified them as those of a young girl agreed that the hands could have been those of an older woman who had done little housework. By now,

Sheward had regretted his confession and retracted it, realizing that there was no evidence against him but his own admissions. But the jury preferred to believe the original confession, and he was sentenced to death. And Britain's best-known pathologist, Alfred Swain Taylor (who had been asked to look at the pickled remains) remarked: "The case shows the necessity of using extreme caution in giving an opinion respecting the age of bones, and of allowing sufficient latitude in years for the bones of adults." But Taylor's own record as a forensic pathologist leaves some doubt as to whether he would have been any more successful in assessing the age of the dismembered corpse.

———————————— 3 ————————————

It was in 1889, 20 years after Sheward had been hanged, that a great pathologist transformed the identification of corpses into an exact science. His name was Jean Alexandre Eugéne Lacassagne, and he was the Professor of Forensic Medicine at the University of Lyon. Lacassagne was an obsessive collector of facts. In 1885, an old man had been found dead in a locked bedroom in Savoy; he had been shot through the head, and a revolver in his hand seemed to indicate suicide. But there was one odd circumstance. The arms were under the bedclothes, which had been pulled up under the chin. Could a man blow out his brains, and then pull up the bedclothes under his chin? Called to examine the body, Lacassagne found other suspicious circumstances. There were no powder burns on the dead man's forehead, no powder grains embedded in the skin. Most people who shoot themselves in the head place the muzzle of the revolver against the skin; it is exceedingly rare for the suicide to hold the revolver at a distance. Nevertheless, the two doctors who had first examined the corpse had diagnosed suicide.

The eyes of the corpse were closed. Lacassagne now spoke to a number of nurses, and asked them for their

observation of the eyes of corpses. He was told that
when people die naturally, their eyes are usually closed. But
people who die suddenly—of suicide, or of a heart attack—
have their eyes open. In the case of violence, they may be
staring. Lacassagne reasoned that, whether the old man
committed suicide or was murdered, his eyes should have
remained open. Therefore someone had closed them after
death.

But what of the revolver clutched in the hand? Current
medical wisdom insisted that this was a sure indication of
sudden violent death. A French soldier killed at Sedan
continued to hold his rifle with one hand while the other
pulled back the ejector. Another whose head had been
blown off by a shell sat with a cup half raised to his lips.
So if the old man was holding the revolver, he must have
shot himself. A gun placed in the hand after death will not
be gripped.

Again Lacassagne decided that the only way to find out
was by experiment. When he was in the hospital in Lyon or
Paris, he asked to be instantly notified when anyone died,
and then tried closing the hands of the corpse around any
convenient object. He discovered that the hand *could* be
made to grasp a revolver after death—at least enough not to
drop it. And if the corpse was found after rigor mortis had
set in, usually around two or three hours, then the gun
would be difficult to remove from the hand, producing the
impression that it was tightly gripped.

These facts, taken in association with the pulled-up bedclothes and the lack of powder burns, led Lacassagne to
assert that the old man had been murdered. The old man's
son, who was under suspicion, was arrested and convicted
of the crime. He had shot his father, placed the revolver in
the hand, locked the door and then escaped through the
window. He had made the obvious mistake of closing the
eyes and pulling the bedclothes up under the chin; but these
facts had escaped the attention of the local doctors, who had
supported the suicide verdict. Only Lacassagne's obsession
with experimental evidence revealed that a murder had
taken place.

In 1889, Lacassagne was 45 years old. He had been an army doctor in North Africa in his youth, and had written a treatise on tattoos as a method of identifying corpses. It was in November of that year that he was asked to undertake the most unpleasant task of his career.

Three months earlier, a roadmender had discovered a canvas sack hidden in some bushes by the riverbank at Millery, 10 miles from Lyon; it proved to contain the decomposing naked body of a dark-haired man. Dr. Paul Bernard, one of Lacassagne's pupils, directed the police to take the corpse to the morgue in Lyon. There he examined the body, which had been wrapped in oilcloth and tied round with string. Bernard concluded that the man had been strangled. Meanwhile, another important piece of evidence had been found—the remains of a wooden trunk, which stank of rotting flesh. Fragments of labels indicated that it had been sent from Paris to Perrache, in Lyon, on 27 July.

Now on that date, a man had gone to the Paris police to report the disappearance of his brother-in-law, a bailiff called Toussaint-Augssent Gouffé. Gouffé was a 49-year-old widower who lived with his three daughters and had an office in the rue Montmartre. But he was a man of powerful sex drive, and spent most of his evenings pursuing the opposite sex in the cafés and night-clubs of Paris. He had last been seen on Friday 27 July. He was accustomed to spend Friday nights in beds other than his own, and as a result of this habit, he usually left the day's takings in his office overnight. The porter had heard a man go upstairs to Gouffé's office at nine o'clock on Friday evening, and assumed it was the bailiff. But when the man came downstairs, he realized it was a stranger. He had started to ask the stranger his business, but the man hurried away. The next morning, the porter looked in Gouffé's office, half expecting to discover a robbery. But everything was in perfect order, and a sum of 14,000 francs was found lying behind some papers.

The disappearance of Gouffé became something of a sensation in Paris, particularly when police investigation uncovered his fascinating love life. The detective in charge of the case was Assistant Superintendent Marie-François Goron, the man who had followed Pranzini's trail all over Europe two years earlier. When, one morning, Goron found two provincial newspapers on his desk, with accounts of the Lyon discovery, he lost no time in telegraphing Lyon for a fuller version of the events. Then he despatched the brother-in-law, a man named Landry, to Lyon, to see if he could identify the corpse. Lacassagne has an amusing account of the Lyon morgue, which was housed on an obnoxious barge on the river, and which, in mid-August, smelt like an open grave. His eyes watering with retching, Landry cast a swift glance at the corpse and fled back to the riverbank. His brother-in-law had chestnut hair, he said, and that of the corpse was black.

Goron was a stubborn man; he made his own way down to Lyon. This was against the advice of the examining magistrate, who assured him that the Lyon case was solved. A cabman had told the police that three men had unloaded a heavy trunk off the Paris train and driven off with it to a spot near Millery; there they had unloaded the trunk and thrown it into the bushes. The cabmen had identified three convicts by their photographs in the rogues' gallery, and both he and they were now under arrest. But the cabman claimed this had happened on 6 July, before Gouffé had vanished. When Goron saw the label on the remains of the trunk, proving it had been despatched from Paris the day after Gouffé's disappearance, he sent for the cabman and asked him what he was playing at. The cabman admitted that his story had been an attempt to "get in well" with the authorities, since he was in danger of losing his license. It is not recorded whether he was charged with wasting the time of the police.

Goron interviewed Dr. Bernard, who told him that the corpse could not possibly be that of Gouffé, since the hair was the wrong color. He produced a test tube with some hair taken from the head of the unknown man. Goron asked for some distilled water, and immersed the hair in it. To Bernard's embarrassment, this had the effect of removing caked dust and blood, and revealing that the hair was, in fact, auburn in color . . . Goron lost no time in ordering the exhumation of the corpse.

The body was in an advanced state of decomposition when it finally arrived in Lacassagne's laboratory at the University. The genital organs had entirely rotted away, most of the hair and beard had also vanished. Parts of the skull were missing. There was little to do but concentrate on the bones and the hair. Lacassagne had some irritable things to say to Bernard about the previous autopsy.

He spent days removing the maggoty flesh until he finally had a skeleton; formaldehyde lessened but could not drown the stench. And when the skeleton finally lay on the dissecting bench, and Lacassagne could study it in detail, he observed that there had been something wrong with the man's right leg. The knee was slightly deformed, and the parts of the bones to which the muscles are attached revealed that the muscles must have been undeveloped. Lascassagne was able to tell Goron that the man had a limp, and had probably suffered from a tubercular infection of the leg in his youth. Checks with Gouffé's relatives in Paris, as well as with his doctor and shoemaker, revealed that he *had* limped. Breaks in the thyroid cartilage convinced Lacassagne that he had been correct in believing that the man had been strangled, but Lacassagne thought the signs were consistent with manual strangulation rather than strangulation with a cord. Close examination of the state of the teeth led Lacassagne to conclude that Bernard had also been mistaken about the age of the corpse; Bernard had guessed 35 or so; Lacassagne decided he was closer to 50. Gouffé had been 49. Some of Gouffé's hair, found on his hairbrush, was compared under the microscope with the hair of the corpse; again, Lacassagne concluded that Gouffé and the unknown man were the same person. In fact, when Goron came to the laboratory, Lacassagne turned to him with a flourish. "Messieurs, I present you with Monsieur Gouffé."

But who had murdered him? A friend of Gouffé's had been suspected and placed under arrest, but released for lack of evidence. But by now, Goron had another possible suspect. Another friend of Gouffé's had told him that Gouffé

had been seen drinking in a bar with a man called Michel
Eyraud two days before the murder; also present was Eyraud's
attractive young mistress Gabrielle Bompard. The mention
of a pretty girl had aroused Goron's interest; by now he
knew that the missing bailiff was the sort of man whose
mouth watered at the sight of any attractive, or for that
matter unattractive, girl. He tried to find Eyraud, without
success. Eyraud sounded as if he might be in need of
money. He was a married man of 46, but was separated
from his wife; he had been a distiller in Sèvres, then
become a salesman for a firm that went bankrupt; he was
ugly and pockmarked, but apparently attractive to women.
His 20-year-old mistress Gabrielle had been a prostitute—
she claimed she had been raped under hypnosis as a child.
Eyraud, like Pranzini, had been something of an adventurer,
and some of his business deals had been distinctly unsavoury.

Back in Paris, Goron decided on a rather desperate
expedient, a thousand-to-one chance. There was enough of
the trunk left to have a copy made; this Goron had exhibited
in the morgue, and begged the public to go and look at it.
They did, in their thousands, since the Gouffé case was still
discussed avidly. A trunk-maker ventured the opinion that it
looked as if it had been manufactured in England. And a
few days later, Goron received a letter from a Frenchman
living in London, who had read about the case in French
newspapers sold there. The previous June, an ugly, balding
man named Michel had taken lodgings with him; he was
accompanied by his daughter. They had bought a trunk from
Zwanziger's in Euston Road, and departed for Paris with it.
When her landlord had remarked that it seemed a large
trunk for her possessions, the girl had laughed and answered
that they would have plenty to put in it in Paris.

The hunt was now on for Eyraud and Gabrielle Bompard.
The newspapers publicized the search. And, at this point,
Eyraud virtually gave himself up. He wrote Goron a long
letter, from New York, asking why he was being slandered
in this way. He had nothing to do with the disappearance of
his friend Gouffé. Perhaps Gabrielle had persuaded one of

her lovers to murder him . . . He would, he promised, return to Paris soon and hand himself over to Goron.

A few days later, Goron was startled when Gabrielle herself came to see him. She was small and pretty, with grey eyes, good teeth and a large head. "Corruption literally oozed from her," said Goron later in his memoirs. She was accompanied by a middle-aged man who seemed to be infatuated with her. And her purpose, incredibly, was to denounce Michel Eyraud as the killer of Gouffé, and to admit that she had been his willing accomplice. The crime ·had been committed in a room at 3 rue Tronson-Decoudray, but she had not been present. She had travelled with Eyraud to America, where she had met the gentleman who now accompanied her. Eyraud had planned to murder and rob him too, she had informed the proposed victim, and together they had fled back to France. Now her lover had persuaded her to go to the police and tell them everything. They were both obviously upset when the prefect, M. Lozé, told them that he was compelled to place Gabrielle under arrest.

The hunting down of Eyraud is another classic example of the needle-in-the-haystack method. Two detectives travelled around America and Canada searching for him, followed by enthusiastic pressmen whose stories gave Eyraud prior warning whenever the hunters came within 500 miles. But people who had been swindled and robbed by the fugitive kept the trail alive. In New York he had persuaded a Turk to lend him a costly oriental robe, claiming he wanted to be photographed in it; that was the last the Turk saw of Eyraud or the robe. And an American actor who is called by Goron "Sir Stout" had been touched by Eyraud's account of how his wife had deserted him, and lent the distracted husband $80. Sir Stout was of the opinion that Eyraud was a great actor. In March 1890, the disgruntled detectives returned to Paris without their quarry. But in Havana, Cuba, a French dressmaker was offered a rich oriental robe by a pockmarked Frenchman, and a few weeks later, she read a newspaper description of the Turkish robe "borrowed" by Eyraud. That day she saw the Frenchman standing before her shop and asked him if he still had the robe. Eyraud said no. The dressmaker then engaged him in conversation, and brought up the name of the assassin Eyraud. "You look rather like him, you know." The next day, the Frenchman came back to her shop with a newspaper that contained a poor photograph of Eyraud. "Look, he's nothing like me." But when he left, the dressmaker contacted the French consul. Now by an extraordinary coincidence too preposterous for a detective novel, one of Eyraud's former employees from the distillery happened to be in Havana at the time. The consul sent for him and told him that he thought Eyraud was in town. And as the man left the consulate, he bumped into Eyraud, who had been keeping the dressmaker under observation. There was no point in trying to disguise his identity, so Eyraud invited his former employee for a drink, and begged him not to betray him. But late that evening, when Eyraud tried to lead him down a darkened alleyway, the man suspected that Eyraud was contemplating a more certain method of ensuring his silence, and leapt into a passing taxi. The next day, the search was on; in Eyraud's room in the Hotel Roma, the police found his baggage packed, but learned that Eyraud had preferred to sleep at a seedy hotel opposite. That night, Eyraud tried to get into a brothel, but the Madame was suspicious of his down-at-heel appearance, and sent him packing. By chance, he again ran into his former employee, and remarked: "It's all up with me now." He was right. Half an hour later, a policeman saw the solitary wanderer, who looked aimless and tired, and took him back to the station. In the night, the man made an unsuccessful attempt at suicide, confirming the opinion of the Spanish police that they had captured the assassin of Gouffé.

Goron had already obtained an account—or rather, several accounts—of the murder from Gabrielle Bompard, but she was such a pathological liar that it was impossible to be sure of how much was true. Now Eyraud was back in Paris, it was at least possible to construct an accurate account of the crime. When they had bought the trunk in London, they had intended to use it to conceal a corpse, but had not yet chosen the victim. Eyraud had learned of Gouffé's existence only two days before the murder; a mutual friend had described the bailiff who was reputed to be rich, and who left a large sum of money in his office before he went off for a Friday night's debauchery. It was Gabrielle who accosted Gouffé, and made an appointment with him for Thursday evening. This was the evening when Gouffé, Eyraud, and Bompard had been seen in the Brasserie Gutenberg. She had then succeeded in making a "secret" appointment with him for the following evening. Gouffé needed no persuading to go to her room; as they went in he commented: "A nice little place you've got here," and Gabrielle replied that Eyraud knew nothing about it. In fact, Eyraud was hiding behind a curtain. Gabrielle lost no time in retiring to an alcove, stripping naked, and donning a silk dressing-gown given her by an admirer. Then they lay on the couch— Eyraud's confession says she sat on Gouffé's knee in an armchair, but he may have been trying to mitigate the circumstances—and Gouffé soon had the dressing-gown open. Gabrielle showed him the sash, and told him that the gown had been a present; then, jokingly, she passed it around his neck and tied it, saying: "What a nice necktie." At the same time, she slipped it over the hook of a pulley suspended from an overhead beam. Alerted by the signal, Eyraud heaved on the other end of the rope; Gabrielle leapt to her feet, and Gouffé soared into the air. But Gabrielle had failed to tie a slip knot, and Gouffé began to scream. Eyraud let him fall, knelt on his chest, and strangled him with his powerful hands.

After that, Michel Eyraud hurried to Gouffé's office. But he was in such a hurry that he overlooked the large sum of money—around $1,000—that lay behind some papers. In a state of raging frustration, he rushed back to Gabrielle's room and beat her. Then, with the body lying a few feet away in the trunk, he insisted on having sexual intercourse. After that he left her alone with the corpse. Gabrielle does not seem to have been unusually disturbed; she later admitted that she had been struck with a humorous idea: to go on the street and pick up some middle-aged bourgeois, then take him back to her room. And "just as he was beginning to enjoy himself" she would say "Would you like to see a bailiff?'' and open the trunk. Then she would run out and fetch the police. ''Just think what a fool he would have looked . . .''

The next day they took the trunk down to Lyon. It was a bad choice; if they had taken it elsewhere, the corpse would not have been examined by the great Lacassagne and its identity confirmed. Without the confirmation of its identity, Goron would not have put out the alert for Eyraud and Bompard—for there would have been no proof of murder— and the case would have remained on the unsolved file of the Sûreté. As it was, Goron's already distinguished reputation with the French public was considerably enhanced, and Eyraud went to the guillotine after a trial that lasted only four days. Unwilling to sentence a young woman to death, the jury found extenuating circumstances, and Bompard received only 20 years in prison.

-------------------------- 4 --------------------------

Seven years after Michel Eyraud's execution, New York was to experience its own sensational equivalent of the Gouffé case. On 26 June 1897, two teenagers, James McKenna and John McGuire, were swimming in the East River near the foot of 11th Street when they found a floating parcel that proved to contain human remains. The headless torso was wrapped in a red and gold oilcloth with a cabbage rose pattern, and the hairy chest had a patch of skin missing, suggesting that a tattoo had been removed; the mutilations seemd to indicate surgical skill. The next day, the lower half of the body, minus the legs, was found in woods near 176th Street—the legs were later found by another two boys swimming off the Brooklyn shore.

The newspaper magnate William Randolph Hearst, virtually the inventor of the ''Yellow Press,'' saw an opportunity to sell more of his newspapers, and assigned a ''murder squad'' of reporters to the case. One of these, George Arnold, was inspecting the remains (now complete except for the head) in the city morgue when he observed that the hands and the fingers were heavily calloused. Arnold was a devotee of the Turkish baths, and he knew that masseurs develop the same kind of callouses. Since the big man on the slab looked vaguely familiar, he hurried down to his favorite establishment in Murray Hill and asked if any of the masseurs had failed to report for duty. The answer was that a man called Willie Guldensuppe had not been in for two days. And he had a tattoo on his chest. Guldensuppe had lived at a boarding-house at 439 Ninth Avenue, which was run by an unlicensed midwife called Augusta Nack.

Hearst's "murder squad" now set out to trace the distinctive oilcloth in which the remains had been wrapped, and the newspaper, the *Journal*, published appeals for information, and a colored reproduction of the oilcloth. It was a Hearst reporter who was making a round of dry goods stores on Long Island who found the dealer who had sold the oilcloth; the mans' name was Max Riger, and he described the woman who had purchased it as a well-built but not unattractive lady. Since this description fitted Augusta Nack— who had the dimensions of an opera singer—Hearst reporters galloped off to the Ninth Street boarding-house, narrowly forestalling those of a rival newspaper, the *World*, and persuaded Augusta Nack to accompany them to the police headquarters. To keep rival reporters away, Hearst rented the whole boarding-house and placed guards on the door; they even severed the telephone wires.

The police decided on shock tactics, and took Mrs. Nack to view the remains. Pointing to the legs, the detective asked: "Are those Willie's?"

Mrs. Nack looked at him haughtily. "I would not know, as I never saw the gentleman naked."

But the *Journal* reporters had heard another story from the inhabitants of the boarding-house and from neighbors. They asserted that Mrs. Nack and Willie Guldensuppe had been lovers for years. But they had quarrelled recently, the cause apparently being a fellow lodger, a young barber named Martin Thorn.

The police managed to forestall the *Journal* reporters at

the barber shop where Thorn worked. There another barber
named John Gotha told them that Thorn had confessed
the murder of Willie Guldensuppe to him. Thorn's story was
that Mrs. Nack had seduced him when her regular lover,
Guldensuppe, was away. But when Guldensuppe had found
them in bed together, the brawny masseur had beaten Thorn
so badly that the barber had to go into the hospital. And
when he reported for work with two black eyes, he was
dismissed. Thorn decided to change his lodgings. But Mrs.
Nack had continued to visit him there. And Thorn had
purchased a stiletto and a pistol, determined to revenge
himself . . .

Martin Thorn was arrested, and the *Journal* headline
declared: MURDER MYSTERY SOLVED BY JOURNAL.
By now, both the *Journal* and the police had located the spot
where the murder took place. It was in a pleasantly rural
area on Long Island called Woodside, not far from the store
where the oilcloth had been purchased. A farm stood next to
the cottage, and on the day Willie Guldensuppe's torso had
been recovered from the river, the farmer had been puzzled
to see that his ducks had turned a pink color. The reason, he
soon discovered, was that they had been bathing in a large
pool of pink-colored water, which had issued from the
bathroom drainage pipe of the cottage next door. But it was
not until the farmer read of the arrest of Martin Thorn and
Augusta Nack that he connected this event with a couple
who had rented the cottage two weeks earlier. They had
called themselves Mr. and Mrs. Braun, and had paid $15
rent in advance. But they had only visited the cottage on
two occasions, the second on the day of the disappearance
of Willie Guldensuppe . . . Belatedly, the farmer decided to
pass on his suspicions to the police.

A revolver, a carving knife and a saw were found in the
cottage; but, advised by their respective lawyers, the two
declined to confess. Thorn succeeded in escaping to Canada
and was brought back; yet even when shown the "confession"
he had allegedly made to John Gotha, he continued to insist
on his total innocence.

The difference between the Nack–Thorn trial and that of

Eyraud and Bompard is a measure of the difference between Paris and New York in the *fin de siècle* period; the French would have been horrified by the carelessness and levity of the American courtroom. Thorn was represented by a brilliant but not over-scrupulous lawyer named Howe, whose line of defense was simply that the two defendants were unacquainted with one another, and that neither of them knew the victim anyway. What evidence was there, asked Howe, that the assorted arms and legs belonged to Willie Goldensoup? (On other occasions he pronounced it Gludensop, Gildersleeve, Goldylocks and Silverslipper.) They might belong to any corpse. What evidence was there that the victim had ever existed?

This audacious line of defense might well have succeeded— New York jurors liked to be amused, and Howe had talked innumerable clients out of the electric chair—except that Mrs. Nack decided to confess. Hearst had sent a Presbyterian minister to see her in prison every day, and one day he had brought his son, a curly-haired child of 4, who climbed on to her lap and begged her to clear her conscience; Hearst naturally printed the story a day ahead of his rivals. And on the second day of the trial, Mrs. Nack declared that she had seen the light, and gave a gruesomely detailed account of the crime. On the day before the murder, she and Martin Thorn had rented the cottage on Long Island. She then told Willie Guldensuppe that she had decided to run it as a baby farm, and asked him to come and give his opinion. When Willie entered the building, Thorn was waiting behind a door, and shot him in the back of the head. Then they threw him into the empty bathtub and, while he still breathed stertorously, Thorn sawed off his head. While Mrs. Nack went out to buy oilcloth, Thorn dismembered the body—he had once been a medical student, which explained the surgical skill noticed by the police surgeon. He left the taps running, under the impression that the water would run down a drain and into the sewers; in fact, there was no drain, and it formed a pool in the farmyard, where the ducks were delighted at the opportunity of a midsummer bath.

Thorn then encased the head in plaster of Paris, and threw it in the river . . .

The narrative so upset one of the jurors that he fainted and had to be carried out of court. This caused a mistrial, and when the case was resumed, Thorn had changed his story. He now declared that the cottage had been rented only as a love nest, and that on the day of the murder, he had arrived to find Mrs. Nack already there. "Willie's upstairs. I've just killed him." Once again, Howe rested his defense upon the assertion that there was no proof that the corpse was that of Willie Guldensuppe, and for a while it looked as if the absence of an American Lacassagne might sway the issue in favor of the accused. But the jury chose to be convinced by the negative evidence of the missing tattoo, and found them both guilty. Martin Thorn went to the electric chair; Mrs. Nack was sentenced to 20 years. The *Journal* was jubilant, but the *World* took the view that Thorn was the victim of a scheming woman.

Mrs. Nack was apparently an exemplary prisoner, and was paroled after 10 years; she returned to her old neighborhood on Ninth Avenue and opened a delicatessen shop; but for some reason, the neighbors found her cooked meats unattractive, and she retired into obscurity.

_____ 5 _____

In the same year, a Chicago businessman named Adolph Louis Luetgart decided to dispose of his wife's body by a method that showed startling originality.

Luetgart seems to have been what is clinically known as a satyr—a man whose sexual appetites are insatiable. When his first wife died, he decided to marry again—a curiously ill-judged decision in view of his obsessive need for new mistresses. Louise Bicknese had been a maid in their home, and had probably been his mistress. And after he married her, he lost no time in according Louise's maid, Mary Simering, the same status. He also slept regularly with

Mrs. Christine Feldt, and with a saloon-keeper's wife named Agathia Tosch. His love life, which included regular visits to prostitutes, impaired his business efficiency, and by 1897 he was on the verge of bankruptcy.

His domestic relations had been strained for many years. On one occasion, he told a mistress that his wife had been seriously ill and he had sent for a doctor. "If I had waited a little longer, the dead, rotten beast would have croaked." Neighbors who heard her screaming one day looked through the parlour window and saw that her husband had her by the throat; when he realized he was observed, he released her. A few days later he was seen chasing her down the street with a revolver.

On 11 March 1897, Luetgart ordered 325 lb of caustic potash from a wholesale drugs firm—he explained he needed it to make soap. It was delivered to his business address, a sausage factory on Hermitage and Diversey, the next day. More than a month later, on 24 April, he ordered an employee known as Smokehouse Frank to take the metal drums of potash to the basement and crush it up with an axe. Then he and Frank placed the crushed potash in the middle of three vats, used for boiling the sausage meat. Luetgart turned on the steam, and the vat was soon full of boiling caustic potash, a liquid strong enough to dissolve flesh on contact.

At about 10:30 on the night of Friday 1 May, a young German girl who was passing the factory saw Luetgart and his wife going down an alley near the building. The night-watchman, Frank Bialk, was sent out on an errand, and when he came back, found the factory door was now closed. Luetgart told him to go to the engine room, which was apart from the factory. Later the watchman was sent on another errand. The next morning, the man found Luetgart fully dressed in his office at an early hour. When he asked if the fire should be allowed to go out, Luetgart told him to bank it up. In the basement, the watchman noticed a gluey substance on the floor, with some flakes of bone in it. But since the vats were used for boiling meat, he thought nothing of it. On the following Monday morning, Smokehouse Frank was told to scrape up the gluey substance and flush it down the drain; whatever would not go down the drain should be scattered on the railroad tracks.

On 4 May, Mrs. Bicknese's brother Diedrich came from out of town to see his sister; on being told she was not at home, he went away and returned in the evening. Luetgart then explained that he had not seen her since the previous Saturday—she had walked out of the house with about $18 in her handbag. He was convinced that she had simply left him.

Diedrich spent the next two days calling on relatives and friends looking for his sister; then he went to the police. Summoned before Police Captain Schuettler, Luetgart explained that he had not notified the authorities of his wife's disappearance because he was a respectable businessman and wanted to avoid scandal. Schuettler decided that Louise Luetgart had probably committed suicide, and began dragging the river. A week after her disappearance, they interrogated Smokehouse Frank and the night-watchman, and heard about the slimy substance on the basement floor.

The middle vat was still two-thirds full of a brown liquid like soft soap. Schuettler, now reasonably certain that he was looking at all that remained of Louise Luetgart, decided to drain it, using gunny sacks as filters.

Adolph Luetgart had been correct in his assumption that boiling caustic potash would turn a body into soap. But he had forgotten to remove his wife's rings. Two of these were found in the filters, one with the initials "L.L." engraved on it.

Even with this evidence, the outcome of the trial was by no means a foregone conclusion. The defense argued that the evidence was entirely circumstantial, and that Mrs. Luetgart was probably still alive. In fact, she had been seen in New York by a man who had known her well. She had also been seen in Kenosha, Wisconsin, by several witnesses two or three days after the murder. Luetgart's 12-year-old son Louis insisted that he had heard his mother in the house after his father had left for the factory. The young German girl, Emma Schmiemicke, who claimed to have seen Luetgart and his wife going towards the factory, proved to be weak minded, and her testimony was discredited. Perhaps the most convincing argument of the defense was to point out that if Luetgart had dissolved his wife in caustic potash, he would hardly be likely to leave the incriminating evidence in the vat when he could pour it down the drain—many people felt that this was self-evidently true. They were forgetting that Luetgart believed that nothing of his wife remained in the vat, and that if he had poured the "soft soap" down the drain, it would have been practically an admission of guilt.

The prosecution evidence was, admittedly, mostly circumstantial, but as such it was very convincing. Fifty years later, the medical evidence alone would have convinced any jury. Many experts identified the fragments of bone taken from the vat as human. Professor George Dorsey, an archaeologist from the Field Columbian Museum, testified that one of the bones found in a pile of animal bones in the basement was the left thigh bone of a woman. Other experts testified that fragments of bone found in the drain pipes leading from the vat were human: part of the humerus (or great bone from an arm), a fourth toe of the right foot, ear bones, a palm bone, fragments of a temporal bone, and a sesamoid bone from the right foot. (This as discussed with some passion, with the result that the sesamoid bone, which no one had heard of before the Luetgart trial, became part of normal conversation.) Mrs. Luetgart had had false teeth, and part of an artificial tooth had also been discovered. Dr. Charles Gibson and Professor de la Fontaine testified that the soapy substance was human flesh that had been boiled in caustic potash. All this should have been quite conclusive, but in 1897, American juries were as suspicious of experts as a British jury had been in 1832, when it rejected James Marsh's evidence that Farmer Bodle had been poisoned with arsenic, and set the murderer free.

The prosecution had no difficulty in demonstrating that Luetgart had behaved like a man with something on his conscience. When Mrs. Tosch, the saloon-keeper's wife, inquired as to the whereabouts of his wife, Luetgart blenched and replied: "I am as innocent as the southern skies'

—recalling Hélène Jegado's protestation "I am innocent" before anyone accused her. And a detective had hidden under the bed of the night-watchman Bialk when Luetgart came to visit him, and overheard Luetgart ask nervously whether the police had found anything incriminating in the factory; when Bialk replied in the negative, Luetgart sighed "That's good." The large quantities of hunyadi water that Bialk had been sent out to purchase on the night Mrs. Luetgart disappeared had later been purchased by a druggist, who testified to the sale, demonstrating that Luetgart had no genuine need for the "nerve medicine."

Luetgart's defense was simple; he had decided to make a large quantity of soft soap to give his factory a thorough cleaning, his aim being to persuade investors to provide more capital. The potash was not the only thing he had bought; there was also a quantity of grease—and a defense witness swore that he had delivered the grease. But the prosecution pointed out that it was absurd to spend $40 on potash to make soft soap when he could have bought enough soft soap to clean the factory for $1. And if he was really inspired with a desire to make soft soap, why spend all night doing it instead of paying one of his workmen to do it by day?

The jury was divided; when they failed to agree at the end of three days and nights, the judge discharged them. But at his second trial, they were able to reach a unanimous verdict of guilty. Luetgart escaped the death sentence; instead, he was sent to prison for life (where he eventually died, still protesting his innocence). The verdict reflected the doubt felt by the judge and jury that Mrs. Luetgart just *might* still be alive. The defense in the Guldensuppe case relied on the same shadow of a doubt. In retrospect, the notion strikes us as preposterous. Yet in a missing body case, no jury has the right to make an absolute assumption of guilt, in case "circumstantial evidence" happens to point in the wrong direction.

The classic case of such a miscarriage of justice occurred in 1660, at Chipping Campden in Gloucestershire, and because the mystery is still unsolved, has become known as the "Campden Wonder." On 16 August 1660, a 70-year-old steward named William Harrison disappeared while collecting rents, and his wife sent a servant named John Perry out to look for him. Perry did not return that night, and when a bloodstained hat was found on the road, Perry was suspected of murdering his master. Under interrogation, Perry declared that Harrison had been murdered by his mother and brother, Joan and Richard Perry, and that Richard had strangled Harrison with a hair net. All three were indicted, but one judge declined to try them because no body had been found. When he was finally tried, John Perry withdrew his confession, declaring that he was "mad and knew not what he said." But it was too late, and all three were hanged, and their bodies hung in chains. But two years later, William Harrison had reappeared, and described how he had been "shanghaied" and taken to Smyrna, where he was purchased as a slave by an old Turkish doctor. When the old man died, he succeeded in getting a ship back to London. This extraordinary story was widely believed at the time, but everyone who has examined the case since then has pointed out its various absurdities and inconsistencies. The mystery remains insoluble: why William Harrison chose to disappear, why John Perry chose to hang his mother and brother as well as himself. All that *is* perfectly clear is that if the judge, Sir Robert Hyde, had chosen to sentence them to life imprisonment, a great injustice would have been avoided. The Campden Wonder remains a warning against the dangers of circumstantial evidence.

6

In England at the turn of the century, the science of forensic medicine had not yet recovered from the conspicuous misjudgements of Alfred Swain Taylor, particularly the Smethurst case. Smethurst's conviction and subsequent pardon caused widespread concern about the accuracy of medical experts, for it was clear that he could have gone to the gallows. Where laboratories and institutes of forensic medicine were concerned, England continued to lag far behind the Continent. France had its Institute of Legal Science at Lyon; Scotland Yard made do with Home Office pathologists and toxicologists who could be called upon when needed. Among the best of these were Dr. A. P. Luff, Dr. William (later Sir William) Willcox, and Dr. Augustus Joseph Pepper, all three of St. Mary's Hospital in Paddington.

Pepper's name came to the attention of the wider public in 1903, when he figured in one of the most sensational murder trials of the year, that of Samuel Herbert Dougal, the "Moat Farm murderer." Dougal had spent most of his life in the army, and attained the rank of sergeant; during that time, two of his wives died under curious circumstances— according to Dougal, both of oyster poisoning. Discharged after he had spent a year in jail for forgery, Dougal paid court to a cultured and romantic spinster, Camille Holland, and induced her to elope with him; it was Miss Holland who purchased Moat House Farm in Essex in 1899. But when Dougal made an attempt to climb into the maidservant's bed, Miss Holland ordered him to leave. A few days later, she vanished; Dougal simply announced that she had taken a holiday. And for four years he lived at the farm and seduced a succession of maidservants, meanwhile gaining access to Miss Holland's bank account and securities by means of forgery. In March 1904 the police came to call to inquire about Miss Holland, and Dougal decided to flee. He was caught in London and charged with forgery. Meanwhile the police had succeeded in locating a ditch which had existed in 1899, and eventually uncovered a greatly decomposed female corpse. But could it be proved to be that of Camille Holland? It was Pepper who examined the remains, and established that it was that of a middle-aged woman who had been shot below the ear. Unfortunately, Miss Holland had no distinguishing marks, and the utmost forensic skill could not prove the identity of the corpse. This was finally accomplished by Miss Holland's shoe-maker, who identified the boots he had made for her by his own initials, worked into the heel in brass tacks. Dougal confessed to the murder as he stood on the scaffold.

Later that year, 1903, Pepper figured in another case involving identification—the Druce affair. Thomas Charles Druce died in 1864 and was buried in a vault in Highgate cemetery. In 1898, the wife of one of his sons, Anna Maria Druce, created a sensation by asserting that Druce had not been the prosperous draper everyone assumed, but the highly eccentric Duke of Portland, John Bentinck, who had died in 1879. According to Anna Maria, the duke had lost his reason because he had killed his younger brother George Bentinck, after a quarrel about a woman—George Bentinck had been found dead in a field, apparently having succumbed to heart disease. Anna Maria's contention was that the coffin in Highgate contained lead taken from a roof. She wanted the coffin opened to prove her contention. Thomas Druce's son Herbert opposed the exhumation, inevitably producing the impression that he had something to hide. A court supported his decision. The dispute dragged on for nine years and, as in the Tichborne case, many "shareholders" were persuaded to contribute to the legal costs, on a promise of receiving a share of the Portland fortune. Several apparently credible witnesses testified that Thomas Druce and the Duke of Portland were the same person, and eventually, on 30 December 1907, the Highgate vault was opened, with Dr. Pepper in attendance. Pepper was assisted by Sir Thomas Stevenson, the toxicologist who had figured in the Lamson case, and whose position as Home Office toxicologist Pepper had taken over in 1900. They were able to prove, on the medical evidence given by the doctor who had attended Thomas Druce in 1864, that the bearded man in the coffin was undoubtedly Druce, and not the Duke of Portland or a quantity of lead. Two witnesses were imprisoned for perjury, and the most sensational "identification" drama since Tichborne ended in anticlimax.

Pepper had also figured in the prosecution of Arthur Devereux, a chemist's assistant who, in 1905, had poisoned his wife and twin sons with morphine, then concealed their bodies in a trunk, which he placed in storage. His motive was poverty, and the desire to devote himself completely to his eldest son, whom he adored. His mother-in-law revealed unusual talents as a detective, and tracked down the trunk to a Kilburn warehouse, where it was opened by the police. In this case, Pepper could only confirm that the victims had been poisoned with morphine; he was unable to combat Devereux's assertion that his wife had committed suicide. But Devereux had made the mistake of describing himself as a widower when he applied for a new job—some weeks before the death of his wife. This convinced the jury of his guilt, and he was hanged in August 1905.

So by the year 1907, Pepper was England's best-known pathologist—at least in his own narrow world of hospitals and police courts—a kind of Anglo-Saxon equivalent of Lacassagne. And, like Lacassagne, Pepper's reputation would be eclipsed by that of his most brilliant pupil. By 1905, Pepper had acquired himself a protégé, an earnest young medical student named Bernard Spilsbury. In fact, Spilsbury was not so young; he had become a medical student at the relatively late age of 22, in 1899, after three years at Magdalen College, Oxford. Son of a wholesale chemist who had wanted to be a doctor, Spilsbury was a quiet, introverted young man who gave his contemporaries the impression of being a mere plodder. Pathology was not the most popular subject at St. Mary's, being known as "the beastly science." But Spilsbury was soon fascinated by it. No one has ever said so, but it is impossible not to suspect that Spilsbury was a devotee of the Sherlock Holmes stories, which had made Conan Doyle so famous in the 1890s; one merely has to look at a picture of Spilsbury looking down a microscope, with his serious, intellectual face, to be reminded of Holmes. By 1904, as his biographers Douglas Browne and E. V. Tullet remark, Spilsbury had been a medical student far longer than modern standards allow, and he would be almost 28 before he became a qualified doctor. He became Pepper's assistant at St. Mary's, and married on a salary of £200 a year. When Pepper retired in 1908, Spilsbury was appointed to succeed him as pathologist. He was often called to give evidence in criminal cases, many involving death during abortion. But it was in 1910, when he was 33, that Bernard Spilsbury became a household word.

The Crippen case has been written about so often that it is difficult to discern the underlying reality. In his novel *We the Accused*, Ernest Raymond presented the story in a way that is sympathetic to the little doctor; since then, the case has been dramatized, filmed, even turned into a musical. The basic outline of the drama has the simplicity of a folk tale. The kindly, mild-mannered doctor is married to an aggressive and hysterical female who bullies him. He falls in love with his quiet, womanly little secretary, and is finally driven to murdering his wife—or, in other versions, kills her accidentally in the course of administering a drug to lessen her sexual demands. His dismemberment of her body so horrifies public opinion that he goes to the gallows, possibly innocent, certainly deserving of mercy.

The truth is rather more complex. Crippen was an American whose medical degrees, if they existed, would not have allowed him to practice in England; his diploma came from a college of homoeopathy, still regarded by many members of the medical profession as a crank aberration. He was a 30-year-old widower when he met a 19-year-old Polish girl who had Anglicized her name to Cora Turner. She was the mistress of a stove manufacturer, who had set her up in a flat and was paying for her singing lessons—Cora was convinced she would become a great singer. The notion of being a doctor's wife appealed to her, and she induced Crippen to propose by telling him her lover wanted her to run away with him. The great depression of 1893 made life difficult; when they were forced to move in with Cora's parents, she told him it was time to forget general practice and become a quack. Crippen remained, basically, a quack and a confidence man for the rest of his life. He worked as a salesman for a patent medicine company, and in 1897, became manager of its London office. His employer called himself Professor Munyon, and his cure for piles, advertised by a picture of himself with an upraised finger, gave rise to many ribald jokes. But Munyon fired Crippen when he found he was the ''manager'' of a music-hall singer—Cora was now calling herself Belle Elmore and was on the stage—and from then on, Crippen was forced to struggle on as a low-grade quack selling worthless nostrums. He became a consultant to a firm of dubious ear specialists, Drovet's, and a magazine editor who called on Crippen had his ears examined with a filthy speculum which he made no attempt to disinfect. He was also startled by Crippen's flamboyant dress—the loud shirt and yellow bow tie, the enormous diamond stick-pin. For a quiet, unassuming little man, Crippen had an odd taste in clothes. He also had a reputation for meanness—he made a habit of offering to buy a drink, then discovering he had left his money at home, and borrowing half a crown. The editor commented on Crippen's "flabby gills and shifty eyes."

The "ear specialist" Drovet went bankrupt when the firm was convicted of gross negligence in the death of a locksmith and other examples of what amounted to medical homicide. But it was there that Crippen met a 17-year-old typist named Ethel LeNeve (whose real name was Neave). She was a moaning hypochondriac whose endless complaints of headache and catarrh had earned her the nickname "Not very well thank you." She had been a miserable child, painfully conscious of a deformed foot, and hating her father because he insisted that it would cure itself if she walked properly. (He proved to be right.) She was also jealous of her vivacious younger sister. Yet underneath these unpleasant traits, she had a highly dominant character, and this is undoubtedly what attracted Crippen to her. Crippen was something of a masochist in his relations with women. This is presumably why he did not divorce Cora when he found she had taken an ex-prize-fighter as a lover, and why he put up with a series of lodgers who shared his wife's bed. With bankrupt stock purchased from Drovet's, Crippen set up his own business, with Ethel as his bookkeeper.

As Belle Elmore, Mrs. Crippen became a moderate success in the London music-halls. The British liked American acts, and Belle seems to have been the sort of person that everyone liked anyway—immensely vital, good natured, embarrassingly frank. She earned the enduring friendship of

Marie Lloyd and many other music-hall artists. But at home, she became inclined to bouts of screaming temper. And most of her friends detested her husband, regarding him as a sponger.

Ethel was in love with her employer, and in some ways they were well suited. Crippen was a crook, although as a result of weakness rather than moral delinquency, and Ethel was a pathological liar, whose biographer Tom Cullen writes that she "lied from sheer perversity—in fact she seemed incapable of telling the truth." But she was also determined not to yield her virginity until they were legally married. It was not until Crippen discovered his wife in bed with the German lodger—and Ethel, presumably, had reason to feel that his marriage was at an end—that she consented to become his wife in the physical sense of the term; the date was 6 December 1906, seven years after their first meeting. It seems to have happened in a hired hotel room during the day, as did their subsequent intimacies—Crippen continued to return home at night.

Crippen became a dentist, and Ethel his assistant. At one point, Ethel became pregnant; she was determined to have the baby, and for a while it looked as if it might transform their lives, and bring about the inevitable break with Belle. Then she had a miscarriage. And to make things worse, Belle went around telling the Music Hall Ladies' Guild members that no one was sure which of Ethel's many lovers was responsible. This may well have been the last straw. Instead of leaving her, which would have been the obviously sensible course, Crippen decided to murder her. On 17 January 1910, he bought no fewer than 17 grains of hyoscine, a vegetable poison that he had seen administered to calm the violently insane at London's Royal Bethlehem Hospital. There is a strong probability that Ethel knew that her lover intended to kill his wife—she may even have planned it. On the evening of 31 January 1910, two of Belle's music-hall friends came to dinner at the Crippens' house at 39 Hilldrop Crescent, Camden Town. They said goodbye to Belle at 1:30 the next morning; it was the last time Belle was seen alive. The following day, Crippen pawned Belle's diamond ring and ear-rings, and Ethel slept at Hilldrop Crescent. The following day, letters were received by the Secretary of the Music Hall Guild, signed Belle Elmore and resigning her membership; they explained she was leaving for America to nurse a sick relative. Just before Easter, in the third week of March, Crippen told his friends that Belle was dangerously ill in Los Angeles; soon after, he announced her death.

Belle's friends were suspicious. Someone checked with the shipping lines, and discovered that no one of that name had sailed for America in February. A music-hall performer called Lil Hawthorne paid a visit to New York with her husband John Nash, and they also made inquiries, which achieved no positive result. Back in London, they talked to Crippen, who sobbed convincingly, but told contradictory stories about precisely where Belle had died. The Nashes decided to go to Scotland Yard. There they spoke to Chief Inspector Walter Dew of the CID, who agreed to go and talk to Crippen. And Crippen smoothly admitted that his wife was still alive. She had simply walked out on him and gone to join her former prize-fighter lover in Chicago. Dew was completely taken in. A thorough search of the house convinced him that there were no suspicious circumstances. When Dew left the house, he was more than half convinced that Belle was alive.

Then Crippen made his greatest mistake; he decided to flee. He and Ethel left for Antwerp, and took a ship for Canada. Ethel was dressed as a boy. When Dew returned two days later, and found the house deserted, he called in his team of diggers. Beneath the coal cellar floor, buried in quicklime, he found the remains of Mrs. Crippen.

On board the *SS Montrose*, Crippen's secret had already been discovered by Captain Henry Kendal, who quickly realized that "Mr. Robinson's" son was a girl in disguise. In a copy of the *Daily Mail* which he had taken on board, the captain found a picture of the wanted "cellar murderer" Crippen. He handed his radio operator a message that began: "Have strong suspicion that Crippen London cellar murderer and accomplice are among saloon passengers." So it came about that Crippen was the first murderer to be caught by means of wireless telegraphy, for which Marconi had received the Nobel prize in the previous year. On the morning of 31 July 1910, as the ship lay off the mouth of the St. Lawrence river, Crippen went on deck, and was greeted by Dew, who greeted him with "Good morning, Dr. Crippen."

On the morning Cora Crippen's remains were found, Bernard Spilsbury was preparing to leave for a holiday in Minehead with his wife and child. Then he received a summons from his eminent colleagues Drs. Pepper, Willcox, and Luff, to go and view the body. Richard Muir, who had prosecuted the Stratton brothers, was in charge of the prosecution. (When Crippen heard this, he remarked dolefully, "I fear the worst.")

Crippen was defended by the brilliant but unscrupulous Arthur Newton, who would later go to prison for forging Crippen's "Confession" and selling it to a newspaper. As a defendant, Crippen was certainly his own worst enemy. His only chance of escaping the rope was to admit everything except intent to kill. But if Crippen pleaded guilty, the whole sordid story about Belle and Ethel would emerge. Crippen chose to protect Ethel and enter a plea of innocence. His defense was that Belle had left him, just as he said, so the body in the cellar must be that of some other woman, buried by some previous tenant, or hidden there during his tenancy. It was obviously an absurd story, and it amounted to suicide. And, of course, it left to the prosecution the fairly light task of proving that the corpse *was* that of Cora Crippen. So the forensic evidence lay at the heart of the case. On one side was the formidable team of Pepper, Willcox, Luff, and Spilsbury, on the other, Drs. Turnbull, Wall, and Blyth. Turnbull had been accosted by the defense at a bridge party, and had casually agreed to give his opinion as to whether a piece of skin was from the stomach, and contained an operation scar; he decided it was from a thigh, and that the scar was merely a fold. Since the operation scar was almost enough in itself to identify Mrs. Crippen, the defense was delighted. When Arthur Newton broke his promise not to call Turnbull as a witness, the doctor was horrified and tried to change his mind. But unless he was willing to make a public confession of error, it was too late.

Willcox had found hyoscine in the remains, and Crippen was proved to have bought 17 grains of the drug not long before his wife's disappearance. Spilsbury, an expert on scar tissues, had no doubt whatsoever that the fragment of skin was from a stomach, not a thigh. And when they found part of a rectus muscle of the abdominal wall attached to the skin, the identification was proved beyond doubt. In court, Turnbull identified the skin as coming from the thigh, and the scar as a fold. Spilsbury, with the calm, grave manner that later led juries to think him infallible, pointed out the older man's errors with a pair of forceps, and the harassed Turnbull left the box with an embarrassed flush. He was followed by Dr. Wall, who admitted that he had changed his mind about the piece of skin, and that it came from the abdomen. Dr. Blyth disputed the presence of hyoscine in the body, but made a poor showing. It was Pepper's team that carried the day, and it was the junior member of that team who made the most powerful impression in court.

Crippen's downfall was not due entirely to this medical team. Part of the body had been wrapped in a piece of pyjama jacket, and it contained the maker's name. One pair of Crippen's pyjamas had a missing jacket, but Crippen insisted that these had been purchased years before, in 1905 or 1906—the intervening years would explain why the jacket was now missing. But Muir was able to establish that the pyjamas to which the jacket belonged had been purchased in 1909. Crippen was caught out in a direct lie, and this did as much as anything to convince the jury of his guilt. It took them only 27 minutes to reach their verdict. Crippen was hanged on 23 November 1910. Ethel was tried separately, but acquitted.

Ethel LeNeve emigrated to Canada, but she returned to England in 1916, took a job in a furniture store in Trafalgar Square, and married an accountant there. Her husband is said to have borne a strong resemblance to Crippen. They lived in East Croydon, and in 1954, she revealed her identity to the novelist Ursula Bloom, who had written a novel called *The Girl Who Loved Crippen*. Miss Bloom became a close friend, and it was to her that Ethel LeNeve remarked one day that she had never ceased to love Crippen. She died in 1967, at the age of 84.

Many writers have pointed out that the great mystery remains: why did Crippen kill his wife when he could simply have walked out of her life? In his novel, *Dr. Crippen's Diary,* Emlyn Williams settles for the explanation that Crippen gave her hyoscine tablets in mistake for aspirin. Dr. Ingleby Oddie, who worked with Muir for the prosecution, had a more plausible theory. It was his belief that Crippen intended to kill his wife with hyoscine, convinced that her death would be ascribed to a heart attack—which is highly likely. What Crippen did not realize is that a large dose of hyoscine does not invariably act as a sedative, but can have the opposite effect. Witnesses claim to have heard screams coming from 39 Hilldrop Crescent on the morning of the murder, and another neighbor heard a loud bang. Crippen possessed a pistol and ammunition. Oddie speculates that the dose of hyoscine, given in a "night cap," caused her to become hysterical and start screaming. If neighbors rushed in, all Crippen's plans would collapse; there would be an inquest, and hyoscine would be discovered. Crippen salvaged what he could of the murder plan, and shot her through the head—the skull was never found. Then he had no alternative but to dismember the body and seek a place to hide it . . .

<hr>

7

Pepper, Willcox, Luff, and Spilsbury were mainly responsible for changing the attitude of British juries to "expert evidence." Yet two years after the Crippen trial, Spilsbury witnessed a courtroom scene that made him aware just how easy it could be for an intelligent counsel to discredit the expert. The case centered around Frederick Henry Seddon, a

50-year-old insurance agent, who was accused, together
with his wife, of poisoning his lodger, Miss Eliza Barrow,
by the administration of arsenic. Seddon was a miser in the
classic sense of the word; he was obsessed by pounds,
shillings, and pence. The overweight lodger who came to
live with the Seddons in 1910 was just as miserly, and her
habits more insanitary. But Seddon could be charming and
persuasive, and soon induced Miss Barrow to transfer
£1,600-worth of India Stock to him in exchange for an
annuity of about £2 a week; when she assigned some
leasehold property to Seddon, he raised it to £3 a week. In
August 1911 she became ill; she was subject to asthma, and
there was danger of heart failure. In September, she died of
an illness that her doctor diagnosed as heart failure due to
epidemic diarrhoea. Her cash, £700, simply vanished.

When her cousin, a Mr. Vonderahe, heard (accidentally)
about her death, he wanted to know what had happened to
the money, and when Seddon assured him there had been no
money, he flew into a state of furious resentment and went
to the police. Two months after her trial, Miss Barrow was
exhumed.

Scotland Yard asked Spilsbury to examine the body. His
conclusion was that her inner organs seemed to be sound,
and her death was not due to heart failure. Then Willcox
took over, and soon discovered that her stomach and other
vital organs contained a quantity of arsenic. But Willcox
was not content with that discovery; he wanted to be able to
state precisely how much arsenic had been administered. He
was one of the most brilliant toxicologists since Orfila, and
had demonstrated this in the Crippen case when he had
identified the poison as an alkaloid by dropping it into the
eye of the hospital cat—it caused a contraction—then
gone on to demonstrate that it was hyoscine by a new
method involving the type of crystal it formed. Now he
decided to try and determine the amount of arsenic in Miss
Barrow's body by weighing the "mirrors" it formed in the
Marsh test. It required immense precision, but was not in
itself a complicated operation. He first had to experiment
with hundreds of samples of arsenic, and construct a table

telling him what weight of "mirror" corresponded to what weight of pure arsenic. (The mirror could be weighed by weighing the glass tube before and after.) He then assumed that the arsenic had become evenly distributed in Miss Barrow's stomach, and tested a piece of the stomach whose weight was exactly one two-hundredth of its weight. Having obtained his arsenic mirror from this piece, he multiplied its weight by 200. And the same procedure was applied to the rest of the body. His final figure was about 131 milligrams of arsenic, or more than two grains. The fatal dose (according to Taylor) is between two and three grains. This much had been absorbed by the vital organs; Willcox did not bother to try and establish how much arsenic had been absorbed by other parts of the body and by the bones. He had established the presence of the fatal dose.

But in court, a brilliant defense attorney, Edward Marshall Hall, came close to overturning his calculations. Eliza Barrow had originally weighed 10 stone (140 lb) but when she was exhumed, evaporation of water from the tissues (the human body is more than 50 per cent water) had reduced her weight to 60 lb, less than half. This weight loss meant that the remaining arsenic was far more concentrated than it had been at the time of death. And, with some embarrassment, Willcox admitted that he had left this out of account. And if his 131 milligrams of arsenic was halved, then it was less than the fatal dose . . . In fact, if Willcox had extended his examination to other parts of the body, the total might have been as much as six grains, three times the fatal dose. Of course, the precise dose was not really the issue; the major question was how arsenic had got into Miss Barrow's stomach in the first place. But Marshall Hall had scored a good point. And he went on to score another that almost destroyed the prosecution case. The questioning turned on the amount of arsenic found in Miss Barrow's hair; Willcox had found one-eightieth of a milligram next to the scalp, and about a quarter of that amount at the far end. But for arsenic to reach the end of the hair, it must have been administered about a year earlier. And Miss Barrow had certainly shown no signs of discomfort at that period—the prosecution case was that the Seddons had administered the poison within two weeks of her death. It was a good point, for it seemed to suggest that Miss Barrow had been absorbing arsenic from some other source. Miss Barrow's room had been full of flies, and Seddon himself had pointed out that an old-fashioned arsenic flypaper, soaked in water, was on the mantelpiece in her room.

Again, Willcox was taken off guard, and had to admit that Hall had a point. But then, as the cross-examination continued, he suddenly saw the answer. After the autopsy, Miss Barrow's body had lain in the coffin in a certain amount of bloodstained fluid, and this fluid had contained arsenic. The hair had absorbed the arsenic from the fluid. Willcox took the opportunity to introduce this explanation, and Hall—predictably—looked skeptical and implied that it was just an excuse. But Willcox proved his point by taking some hair from one of his patients and soaking it in the same fluid; at the end of three days, it had absorbed enough arsenic to indicate that the patient had also been poisoned.

In the end, it was Seddon himself who caused his own downfall. One of the major arguments of the defense was that Seddon had no need of Miss Barrow's money; he was quite adequately well-off already. But Seddon's performance in the witness box made it clear that he was an obsessional miser, and that £700 in cash was a more than sufficient motive for murder. Seddon was found guilty and sentenced to death; his wife was acquitted. The obsession with money stayed with him to the end; when, after his appeal had been dismissed, he heard of the poor price his property had fetched, he snorted: "Well, that finishes it!"

Spilsbury's next major case was that of George Joseph Smith, the "Brides in the Bath" murderer. Smith was a confidence man who made a habit of marrying susceptible spinsters, then drowning them in a zinc bath. The verdict was always death by misadventure. Earlier victims were merely deserted, but when a lady named Bessie Munday declined to part with her money or property, Smith persuaded her to make a will in his favor and drowned her. This was in July 1912, and in 1913 he made £600 from the death of a nurse named Alice Burnham. The third and last victim, Margaret Lofty, was found dead in her bath on 18 December 1914, Smith (who was calling himself Lloyd) meanwhile playing the organ to establish an alibi. When the death was reported in the newspapers, a relative of his second victim read the report, and was struck by the similarity of the circumstances; she went to the police.

The Director of Public Prosecutions, Sir Charles Mathews, agreed that the circumstances looked incredibly suspicious, but pointed out that it would be extremely difficult to drown someone in a bath—they would fight and struggle.

Examining the corpse of Margaret Lofty, Spilsbury was inclined to agree; there was no sign of violence, except a small bruise on the elbow. That she had died of drowning was obvious—there was foam in the lungs. (As incredible as it sounds, it was not until the 1890s that it was finally established that drowning was due to water entering the lungs—an observation that seems self-evident to anyone who has ever swallowed a mouthful of tea the wrong way.) But if force had been used, how had it been applied? Spilsbury and Detective Inspector Arthur Neil decided to conduct experiments to find out. Young women in bathing dress were persuaded to sit in a bath of water while Spilsbury and Neil tried to drown them. It seemed impossible; even if the victim's head could be forced, her hands could still grip the sides and prevent further immersion while she turned over on to all fours. Then Neil saw the answer; he grabbed the girl by the knees, and raised them in the air. Her head slipped under immediately, too quickly for her hands to grab the sides. And, to Neil's alarm, she immediately became unconscious—the rush of water into the mouth and nose had caused an instant blackout. It took some minutes to revive her. But Spilsbury and Neil now knew how Smith had killed his bride.

In fact, the medical evidence played little part in convicting Smith; it was obvious to the jury that when three wives die in bathtubs in three years, coincidence may be ruled out. Smith was executed in a state of collapse, still protesting his innocence.

Two years later, in November 1917, the discovery of the torso and arms of a woman in Regent Square, Bloomsbury, looked as if it might provide Spilsbury with an interesting problem in identification. The remains were in a meat sack, and some brown paper scrawled with the words "Blodie Belgiam" were also found. In fact, the body was quickly traced through laundry marks on the sheet in which it was wrapped: it was a Frenchwoman named Émilienne Gérard, aged 32, who had been missing for three days. An IOU found in her flat led the police to her lover, Louis Voisin, who was sitting in a bloodstained kitchen in Charlotte Street, Soho, with his latest mistress. In his cellar, the police found the victim's head and hands. Asked to write "Bloody Belgium," Voisin wrote "Blodie Belgiam." Voisin was a butcher by trade, and Spilsbury noted that the mutilations had been performed by a skilled hand.

Voisin's defense was that he had found the dismembered body in Émilienne Gérard's flat in Munster Square, and had only tried to get rid of them. His story was apparently supported by bloodstains in the flat. But Spilsbury's examination soon established what had really happened. The blows that had battered the victim unconscious had been struck by a woman's hand; if the powerful Voisin had struck them, the skull would have been shattered. Then Voisin had dismembered the body, and gone back to the Munster Square flat to spread blood around and support his story of finding her there. Apparently unaware that medical science had now learned to distinguish human from animal blood, he insisted that the bloodstains in his own basement were those of a calf; Spilsbury had no difficulty disproving this. It finally became clear that the murder had been due to a quarrel between the two women, and that the new mistress, Bertha Roche, had battered the old one unconscious, after which Voisin had completed the job by strangling her with his bare hands. Voisin was sentenced to death. At the later trial of Bertha Roche, Spilsbury had to accompany the jury to the Charlotte Street basement and demonstrate—in dumb show—how the murder had been done. (His comments might have prejudiced the jury and caused a mistrial.)

Bertha Roche was sentenced to seven years, but went insane after two, confirming the impression of the investigators that she had been mentally unstable at the time of the murder.

Asked at a banquet which of his cases he regarded as his most difficult, Spilsbury mentioned the Crumbles murder of Emily Beilby Kaye by her lover Patrick Mahon. A Liverpool Irishman with an abundance of good looks and charm, Mahon had been to prison for embezzlement and for breaking into a bank and knocking the charlady unconscious. He was also a philanderer with an impressive string of successful seductions. In 1923 he had seduced a 34-year-old secretary named Emily Kaye, and in 1924 she became pregnant. On the weekend of 12 April 1924, Mahon invited her to a bungalow on a desolate stretch of shingle known as the Crumbles, Eastbourne, and at some time during the weekend, murdered her—probably with a blow on the head—and then dismembered the body. At this point he recollected that he had a date with a young lady called Ethel Duncan, whom he had picked up just before the murder by offering to share his umbrella in a rainstorm; he hastened back to London and persuaded her to come down for the weekend. Emily Kaye's dismembered body was at this time in a trunk in a locked bedroom. When Ethel Duncan showed curiosity about the locked bedroom, Mahon sent himself a telegram recalling himself to London on business. There he deposited a Gladstone bag at the Waterloo station left-luggage office, and went back to his wife. But before returning to Crumbles to continue the task of disposing of the body, he decided to spend a day at Plumpton races. A friend saw him there and mentioned it to his wife. Mrs. Mahon was already worried about her husband's mysterious movements, and now went carefully through his pockets; in one of them she found the ticket from the left-luggage office. She asked a friend who had been a member of the railway police to investigate. She probably suspected that the bag contained love letters or other proofs of infidelity; what the friend discovered was some bloodstained ladies' underwear and a carving knife.

He went to the police. The next day, Mahon was arrested as he went to recover the bag.

His story was that Emily Kaye had died as a result of an accident; she had attacked him with a hatchet during a quarrel, and they had wrestled. She had fallen backwards, and he had lost consciousness. When he recovered, he found that she was dead—her head had struck against the coal bucket . . . In a panic, he decided to get rid of the body, and went out to purchase a saw and a knife.

Spilsbury was called down to the Eastbourne bungalow. He found a rusty tenon saw that was covered with grease and had a piece of flesh adhering to it. On the fire there was a 2-gallon saucepan half full of a reddish liquid, and covered with a coating of solid fat; this proved to contain a piece of boiled human flesh. The trunk contained four segments of a body, and a hatbox another 37 pieces of flesh. A biscuit tin contained various inner organs.

Spilsbury took the pieces back to St. Bartholomew's Hospital, and set about reconstructing the body. There were hundreds of fragments and Spilsbury's task was to recognize each and assign it to its proper place. And when it was finally reassembled, he discovered that the head and right leg were missing. (Mahon later admitted that he had taken parts of the body in the Gladstone bag, and scattered them out of the window on the train *en route* to London.) Apart from a heavy bruise on the left shoulder, there was no evidence to indicate how Emily Kaye had died. But Spilsbury's discoveries were enough to wreck Mahon's defense. The breasts told him that Emily Kaye had been pregnant; but the uterus, which would have shown the same thing, was missing. The inference was that Mahon had destroyed it for that reason, unaware that the breasts would tell the same story. As to the coal bucket, it was obvious to Spilsbury that if a head had struck it with sufficient force to cause death, it would have been badly dented; but it showed no sign of a blow.

The missing head was a problem. Mahon claimed that he had burnt it on the fire; but was that possible? The question was worth answering, for it if had not been destroyed, then it might be buried somewhere. And it would almost certainly reveal the manner by which Emily Kaye met her death. With his usual thoroughness, Spilsbury procured a sheep's head, and tried burning it on an open kitchen fire. In four hours, it was a charred remnant that could be smashed to pieces with a poker.

Mahon himself gave evidence in court, and turned on all his Irish charm. He had bought himself a new suit, and used some artificial sun tan to darken his skin. His story of the "accident" was told with the skill of an actor. One part of his story caused a stir in the courtroom; he described how, when he had placed Emily Kaye's head on the fire, the heat had caused the dead eyes to open. This, and a crash of thunder from outside, so unnerved him that he rushed out into the storm. By an odd coincidence, a thunderstorm was taking place as Mahon recounted this incident in court, and he was clearly not acting when he went pale and stammered.

It was not entirely Spilsbury's evidence that convinced the jury of Mahon's guilt. Even if, as Spilsbury stated, it would be virtually impossible for Emily Kaye to have died by falling against the coal scuttle, it was still possible that she died accidentally, in the course of a quarrel. Here the crucial evidence was uncovered by the police. Mahon claimed that he went out and bought the chef's knife and saw four days after her death, on 17 April 1924. But the carbon of the receipt in the hardware store showed that he had bought them on 12 April, before her death. The inference was clear: the murder was premeditated. Mahon realized the seriousness of this piece of evidence, and summoned all his open-faced plausibility. He had, he admitted, made a mistake about the date. But the purchase had still been unpremeditated. He had gone into the shop to buy a lock for the bungalow, but found the saw and the carving knife so attractive that he bought them on the spot. However, he had not used the chef's knife to slice up Miss Kaye's body' she had handled the knife, and for sentimental reasons, he did not feel he could use it for such a purpose. So he had used the ordinary carving knife from the bungalow... But, as Spilsbury had pointed out, the ordinary carving knife would not have done the job; the chef's knife was specially designed to cut raw flesh.

It took the jury only 40 minutes to reach a guilty verdict; Mahon was hanged on 9 September 1924.

———————————— 8 ————————————

Later that same year, another pregnant mistress met her end in a lonely cottage, and once again, it was Spilsbury who conclusively disproved the murderer's story of how it came about.

Norman Thorne was a Sunday school teacher and an unsuccessful chicken farmer; his fiancée, a bespectacled 23-year-old typist named Elsie Cameron, was tired of waiting for marriage, and by the autumn of 1924, was ruefully aware that, in yielding her virginity, she had thrown away her trump card. On the late afternoon of 5 December, she made her way from Kensal Green down to Thorne's smallholding near Crowborough, Sussex, and was seen, attaché case in hand, by two farm-workers. She had told Thorne, untruthfully, that she was pregnant, and Thorne had countered with the equally untrue assertion that he was having a love affair with a girl called Elizabeth Coldicott. This is why Elsie was rushing down to see him on that dark December afternoon.

Five days later, Elsie Cameron's father sent Thorne a telegram asking for news of his daughter; Thorne replied by letter that he had been expecting Elsie, but she had failed to arrive. Mr. Cameron went to the police, who called on Thorne and asked if they could look over the farm. He agreed willingly, and when they left, they were apparently satisfied. The press heard of Elsie's disappearance, and descended in multitudes on the farm; Thorne allowed one photographer to take his picture feeding the chickens in the poultry run.

In the second week of January, a woman came forward to say that she had seen Elsie Cameron walking towards the farm on the afternoon of 5 December 1924. She only confirmed what the two previous witnesses had said, but this time the local police decided to take the sighting seriously, and Scotland Yard was called in. They arrived with picks and shovels, and soon found Elsie Cameron's dressing-case in a potato plot. Thorne was told that he would be charged with her murder, and replied with a line that has been used by many other murderers: "I want to tell you the truth about what happened." The truth, he claimed, was that he had stormed out of the hut that constituted the farmhouse after a quarrel about the "other woman", and had returned to find that Elsie had committed suicide by hanging herself from a beam. He had panicked, and spent the night dismembering the body with a hacksaw. Then, in the dim light of dawn, he had buried it in the poultry run—in the exact spot where he had been photographed by the Press. That afternoon, he had taken Elizabeth Coldicott out to the local cinema. And for the next six weeks, he had behaved with a beaming self-confidence that hardly suggested a man who had panicked on discovering that his mistress had committed suicide.

The dismembered body was recovered from the poultry run, and taken to the Crowborough mortuary, where Spilsbury examined it. The head had been forced into a biscuit tin, so that it was difficult to remove. Spilsbury found several bruises on the body, but none of the marks on the neck that would have pointed to hanging—the extravasation (breaking of blood vessels)—due to the pressure of a rope.

Elsie Cameron's remains were buried at Willesden; but four weeks later they were exhumed for another examination. This was by the pathologist Patrick Bronte, an Irishman who had left for England after the establishment of the Irish Free State in 1922. By now the remains were badly decomposed; nevertheless, Bronte concluded that Elsie Cameron's throat *did* show signs of a rope mark.

But, like Mahon, Thorne had chosen the wrong defense.

Police discovered that the dust on the upper half of the beam was undisturbed, but a rope would have made a mark in the dust. He had claimed that he left the hut after a quarrel, but denied striking the girl; but the heavy bruising on her body showed this to be untrue.

At Lewes Assizes, on 4 March 1925, it soon became apparent that the case would turn upon the medical evidence. Spilsbury's opinion was that the bruising—on the back of the head and on both temples, as well as on the legs—indicated that Elsie Cameron had been attacked with considerable violence, probably with some heavy instrument with a smooth surface. (Thorne possessed a pair of Indian clubs.) All this suggested that she had been thrown to the ground and beaten with a club. Dr. Bronte produced slides which, he insisted, showed the extravasation characteristic of hanging, and mentioned creases or grooves on Elsie Cameron's throat. Spilsbury replied that these were the creases that could be found on anyone's throat. Bronte argued that some of the bruises could have been caused after death; Spilsbury replied that it is impossible to bruise a corpse. And although five other doctors supported Bronte's view that the signs were consistent with suicide by hanging, the jury remained unconvinced, and sentenced Norman Thorne to death.

The case nevertheless marked the beginning of a certain revolt against the tendency to regard Sir Bernard Spilsbury— he had been knighted in 1923—as a kind of infallible Sherlock Holmes. One letter to a newspaper began: "For some reason or other, Sir Bernard Spilsbury had now arrived at a position where his utterances in the witness box commonly receive unquestioning acceptance . . . But a reputation for infallibility . . . is quite out of place in medical and surgical matters."

In fact, Spilsbury's evidence in the Thorne case raises a number of unsettling questions. He believed that the blows would have been sufficient to cause death from shock. But most young women can probably sustain a beating without dying from shock. Spilsbury might have been expected to point to some particular blow—perhaps to the back of the head—as cause of death, and support it with the evidence of injury to the skull or brain; but he did not do so. Therefore, in an important sense, the case against Thorne was incomplete. Now in fact, we know that Elsie Cameron was a highly neurotic woman, who had been out of work for six months before her death through "neurasthenia." On a visit to Thorne's parents she had become hysterical and difficult. All this suggests that when she went to Thorne's cottage with a false story about pregnancy to blackmail him into marriage, there was a violent quarrel with a great deal of screaming, and that Elsie Cameron's death took place as a result of this quarrel. The bruises of the legs support this view; a man who intends to murder an unwanted mistress does not cover her in bruises; he strikes a single blow. Thorne's fatal mistake was to choose a defense of suicide. But Spilsbury's disproving of the suicide defense should have made it obvious to the jury that Thorne had killed her during a quarrel, and allowed him a certain benefit of the doubt. Unfortunately, Spilsbury's quietly confident manner of giving evidence tended to leave the jury feeling slightly cowed. So in a sense, Thorne was not hanged by the medical evidence, but by Spilsbury's reputation. It was for this reason, rather than professional jealousy, that a certain resistance to Spilsbury began to build up during his later years.

There was another drawback to Spilsbury's world-wide fame; it made the criminal aware of the skills of the forensic scientist, and led him to take redoubled precautions—one result being that few burglaries were now solved by fingerprint evidence. And those who contemplated solving their problems by murder also became aware that a single hair or fiber could lead to their downfall, and planned with increased subtlety. At least one murderer of the 1930s demonstrated that he had learned his lesson.

On 17 June 1934, the Brighton cloakroom attendants noticed an unpleasant smell in the office. The police traced it to a cheap-looking trunk, and it was opened in the police station. It was found to contain the torso of a woman, wrapped in brown paper and tied with window cord. A word written on the paper had been half obliterated by a blood-stain, but its second half read: "ford."

Where was the rest of the body? Cloakroom attendants all over the country were asked to report suspicious packages, and the result was that a pair of legs was found in a suitcase at King's cross.

The trunk and the suitcase had both been deposited on Derby Day, 6 June, between six and seven in the evening; the person responsible had estimated correctly that the cloakroom attendants would be too busy to remember who left any particular item. The Brighton attendant could only recollect that the trunk had been left by a man.

Spilsbury verified that the legs and the trunk belonged to the same body. She had been a woman in her mid-20s, and had been five months' pregnant. Various clues suggested that she had belonged to a reasonable income group: the hairs on the legs were bleached with sunbathing, and some light brown head-hairs found on the body suggested a permanent wave. The hands and feet were well kept, and the armpits were shaved; lack of callouses on the feet indicated well-fitting shoes. The brown paper in which the torso was wrapped had been soaked in olive oil—sometimes used by surgeons to stop heavy bleeding, and this might have suggested a restaurateur or some fairly well-to-do household. On the whole, it seemed likely that the victim's identity should be fairly easy to establish. Newspaper and wireless reports made certain that every adult in the British Isles knew about the crime. Yet although 700 women were traced, none proved to be the victim. The maker of the trunk was found, in Leyton, but he had no record of where it had been sold, or to whom; one of his employees had written the word "ford" on the paper. Five thousand prenatal cases were traced and eliminated. At one point it seemed to the people of Brighton that the whole of Scotland Yard had moved into their hotels; the Royal Pavilion was used as a search head-quarters. When eventually the trunk was traced to a big shop in Brighton, it looked as if all this effort was at last yielding some result; but once again, the trail petered out. The "Brighton trunk murderer" had proved that it *was* possible to commit a perfect crime.

———————————— 9 ————————————

Oddly enough, one of the men who was questioned and then released was a certain Captain Ivan Poderjay, whose name also survives in the annals of crime for having committed a "perfect murder." In 1933, Captain Poderjay—a small, dapper, bald-headed man—was on a cross-channel steamer when he observed a tall, attractive blonde lady suffering from incipient sea-sickness; he ushered her onto the deck, where she soon made a recovery. He introduced himself as an ex-army intelligence officer from Yugoslavia; he also mentioned that he was a millionaire inventor. If the lady, Miss Agnes Tufverson, a New York attorney, had happened to see the magazine *John Bull* for 12 March 1933, she would have discovered an article pointing out that Poderjay was a confidence swindler who preyed on rich women. As it was, the 40-year-old Miss Tufverson became the latest of Poderjay's dupes, and by the time he saw her off to New York, she was hopelessly in love. She had given him $5,000 to invest for her, although he had certainly spent half that sum entertaining her in London.

A few days after her return to New York, she received a love letter enclosing a draft of $500, a first return on her investment, and suggesting that she should send him another $5,000 to invest. Miss Tufverson was tempted—she entertained no suspicions about her new business adviser—but she urgently wanted to see him again. And, as she explained to her closest friend Julia Tilinghast, if she played hard to get, Poderjay would come to New York all the sooner. She was right. In November 1933, Poderjay arrived accompanied by an incredible quantity of flowers. On 4 December they were married, Poderjay wearing a full dress uniform. The fact that the top of his head scarcely came up to her breasts seems to have worried neither of them. On 20 December, they sailed off to England for their honeymoon on the SS *Hamburg*. Mrs. Poderjay had sold off $38,000 worth of stocks and shares, since her husband had told her he could invest the money at a far higher rate in interest in Europe.

But the *Hamburg* left without them. Two hours after they had set out for the dock, they were back at her apartment, with Agnes in tears. No one saw her again. The next day, Poderjay went out and purchased a large trunk, as well as 800 razor blades and an immense quantity of vanishing cream. He told Agnes's friends that she had left on the *Hamburg*, and that he would follow on the *Olympic* after transacting some urgent business. The trunk, now a great deal heavier, was transported to the ship, with Poderjay sitting on top of it, and was placed in his cabin.

In January, Agnes's family received a cable stating that she loathed the British climate and was on her way to India. When they heard nothing more of her for another five months, her sister Sally came from Montreal to the Missing Persons Bureau in New York to ask for help. The bureau went to work, and traced Mr. and Mrs. Poderjay to the Hinterstrasse in Vienna. But Mrs. Poderjay was not Agnes Tufverson, but a Frenchwoman whose unmarried name had been Marguerite Suzanne Ferrand. She and Poderjay had been married since 1931. A check with the *Hamburg* revealed that Mr. and Mrs. Poderjay had never been booked on board; but Captain Ivan Poderjay had booked his own passage a week earlier on the *Olympic*. Furthermore, the shipping company was able to tell them that Poderjay had insisted on a cabin just above the waterline. His cabin steward added that Poderjay had allowed no one to touch the heavy trunk, and that when the ship arrived at Southhampton, he had caught a glimpse inside it and been surprised to discover that it was only half full.

All this information made very clear what had happened to Agnes Tufverson. She had been heavily drugged with sleeping pills when she had been carried on board in the trunk—Poderjay would not have risked killing her in case the trunk was opened before the ship set sail. He had then murdered her, probably by suffocation, and spent the voyage slicing the flesh from her bones with razor blades and feeding it to the fish. Finally, the skeleton, greased with cold cream, had also been pushed through the porthole. And when it vanished below the waves, Poderjay must have sighed with relief, and made sure that there was not the slightest sign of blood in the cabin or in the trunk—he had probably dissected the body on a sheet of rubber, after draining it of blood.

When the Vienna police arrested Poderjay, they discovered that his home contained a room full of every conceivable instrument of torture and sexual perversion. The most eminent Viennese psychiatrist, Sigmund Freud, was called in to report on the case. He diagnosed Mr. and Mrs. Poderjay as polymorphous perverts whose sex life together was one continuous fantasy. Poderjay was basically a female personality; his wife was male. As "Count John" she treated her mistress "Ita" with appalling savagery; Poderjay was Ita, who was having a lesbian affair with two of his wife's female personalities, Sonja and Jeanitason, as well as being Vanchette, who was flogged by Count John. Freud found it one of the most complex cases of sexual perversion he had ever studied. Now, at least, it was clear why Ivan Poderjay had chosen such an original method of disposing of the body; it had not been a gruesome chore, but a continuous delight.

Poderjay's arrest corresponded with the finding of the torso in the Brighton left-luggage office; it can be seen why the British police wished to question him on his way back to New York. But it was fairly clear that a man who has just acquired a fortune in dollars and is hastening back to the delights of the torture chamber would have no time or inclination to dissect a pregnant mistress in Brighton; besides, the girl in the trunk must have become pregnant in early January, at which time Ivan Poderjay was still on his way across the Atlantic.

Back in New York, Poderjay seemed to enjoy his days of intensive questioning by the police, and remained irritatingly bland—he was probably trying to provoke them to complete his happiness by administering third degree. His story was that Agnes had walked out on him, probably with another man; beyond that he refused to make any admissions. Poderjay's case history, forwarded by the Vienna police, revealed only that he had been born in Serbia in a poor family, had started life as a fortune-teller, joined and deserted the French foreign legion, then taken up his true calling as a confidence man. He had swindled at least two women out of their fortunes before he met his wife, Marguerite Ferrand, in 1931, and his interest in her fortune had swiftly deepened into warmer feeling when he learned of her desire to flog him. None of this brought the New York police any closer to provoking a confession of murder, and they relieved their frustration by charging him with bigamy. He emerged after a five-year prison sentence with only one eye and half his teeth, having infuriated a fellow convict with some unmentionable proposition. He remained cheerfully uncommunicative under further police questioning, and was deported back to Serbia. Some time after, he wrote to a New York newspaper from Belgrade insisting that Agnes Tufverson was still alive, and would probably reappear one day...

10

It was another Derby Day killing, that of Agnes Kesson, that inspired one of the most ruthless and ingenious murder schemes of the early 1930s. The body of Agnes Kesson was found in a ditch near Epsom, where the Derby is held, on 7 June 1930. She had been strangled with a cord, and her murderer was never found. A 36-year-old commercial traveller named Alfred Arthur Rouse, whose personal life had reached crisis point, found himself reflecting on how easy it seemed to be to get away with murder.

Ever since a head injury, caused by a shell splinter during the First World War, Rouse had been a changed man. He had been a sober and conscientious character; now he became an obsessive seducer of women. As a commercial traveller, working for a garter manufacturer, he was earning £500 a year—a comfortable income in days when farm laborers earned £2 a week. But part of this had to be paid in maintenance to a French girl who had borne his child during the war, and part went to supporting other illegitimate children all over the south of England. It was later calculated that he had seduced about 80 women by posing as a carefree bachelor; in act, he was married, and his wife was taking care of an illegitimate child of a servant girl named Helen Campbell, who was one of many that Rouse had married bigamously. By Derby Day 1930, his wife was threatening to leave him, one mistress was having her second baby in a London hospital, and another in Wales had announced that she was pregnant. She was a nurse from a middle-class family, and Rouse had persuaded her to pretend they were married when he visited her home; he had also told her family that they were about to move into a luxury home at Kingston upon Thames, and had invited her sister to come and stay.

Rouse decided that the solution to these problems was to vanish—in fact, to die. And as he meditated on the Agnes Kesson murder, he began to see how this might be done. She was a waitress who had probably been lured into a car by a customer, then strangled. And during the depression years, England was full of down-and-outs who could be lured into a car.

He put his plan into effect on Bonfire Night, 1930. On the Great North Road, near St. Albans, he picked up a hitch-hiker, a man who, he noted, was of roughly the same build as himself. Toward two o'clock the following morning, Rouse stopped the car near Hardingstone, Northampton, and told his passenger he wanted to relieve himself. What happened next is not certain; but a mallet with hairs on it, found near the car, suggests that he knocked his passenger unconscious. Then he poured petrol over the body—which was stretched across the front seats, with the legs sticking out of the open door—and lit a trail of petrol leading to the car. As it exploded into flame, Rouse ran and hid in the nearest ditch. Then, when he felt the coast was clear, he climbed out and began to walk down the road. But within a few yards, he encountered two young men who were returning from a dance in Northampton. He hurried on past them, and when they asked what had happened, called back "It looks as if somebody's got a bonfire up there."

Rouse's perfect murder plan had failed, and he knew it. There was now no point in "vanishing." Instead, he went on to the home of the pregnant nurse, Ivy Jenkins, at Gelligaer in Wales. As soon as he arrived, he was shown a photograph of the burnt-out car in the evening newspaper, and it stunned him. The next day, the newspapers mentioned his name—and, worse still, his wife. But by now Rouse was on his way back to London, where the police met him off the bus at Hammersmith Bridge.

His story was that the death of his passenger had been an accident. He had asked the man to fill the petrol tank while he climbed over a hedge to relieve himself; the man must have lit a cigarette, for the car burst into flames . . .

What was obviously more difficult to explain was why he had walked away from the blaze without seeking help. His explanation was feeble; his shock had caused him to "lose his head."

Spilsbury was called in to examine the charred remains. The first thing he discovered was a scrap of rag between the legs, still smelling of petrol—the tremendous heat had caused one of the legs to bend, trapping the rag. It had also caused the skull to explode, and destroyed all indications of the victim's sex, with the exception of part of the flies trapped between the thigh and the stomach. To Spilsbury, the position of the body indicated that the victim had been alive when the fire started. And the rag, and the smell of petrol on the trapped fly, showed beyond all doubt that the man had been soaked in petrol before his death. It was Spilsbury's evidence that destroyed Rouse's defense that the fire had started by accident. To the suggestion that the victim had kicked his way through the badly burnt door, Spilsbury replied: "He would have been dead long before that."

The jury took over an hour to find Rouse guilty of murder. His counsel appealed, on the grounds that newspaper publicity about Rouse's "harem" could have influenced the jury. (All evidence about Rouse's sexual life was excluded from the courtroom.) The appeal failed. Just before his execution, Rouse confessed to the murder. But the identity of his victim was never established.

———————————— 11 ————————————

A week after Rouse was hanged at Bedford jail, another commercial traveller stood in the dock at Ratisbon charged with an almost identical murder. His name was Kurt Erich Tetzner, and he was accused of burning to death an unknown tramp in his car.

For Professor Richard Kockel of the University of Leipzig, a man who had established his right to be regarded as the German Spilsbury, the case began when he was asked to inspect a charred body that was about to be buried. The man, identified as Tetzner, had been found burnt to death in his car, which had apparently struck a milestone. What bothered the insurance agent who approached Kockel was that Tetzner had insured his life with three different companies, for the vast sum of 145,000 marks. His death seemed a little too convenient. Kockel performed an autopsy on the body, and quickly concluded it was that of a youth—he found a particular piece of cartilage that usually vanishes by the age of 20. But Tetzner was 26 years old. Moreover, the corpse had no soot in the mouth or windpipe, which argued that he was not breathing when he was burnt. Finally, microscopic examination of a section of the lung showed fatty embolisms blocking the blood vessels. This was a sign of death by sudden violence; a violent blow or injury drives fat from the tissues into the blood vessels, and they may be carried to the heart, causing a blockage. (This is what Spilsbury meant when he diagnosed Elsie Cameron's death as being due to shock.)

Kockel's conclusion was that the body was that of someone who had been murdered by Tetzner to perpetrate an insurance fraud. In which case, Tetzner must still be alive, and would probably be in contact with his wife. Accordingly, the police tapped Emma Tetzner's telephone, or rather, her neighbor's, for she had no telephone of her own. On 4 December 1929, a week after "Tetzner's" death, a man who called himself Sranelli rang Frau Tetzner from Strasbourg; the policeman, posing as the neighbor, replied that Frau Tetzner was not at home, and asked Herr Sranelli to ring back that evening at six. Chief Superintendent Kriegern, who was in charge of the case, flew off to Strasbourg, and was there in time to arrest the suspect himself. Sranelli was obviously shocked. He was a fat, unhealthy-looking man with beady eyes, and he soon admitted that he was Erich Tetzner. And, still demoralized by the collapse of his foolproof plan, he made a confession to the murder. He had, he said, planned the insurance fraud some time ago, and advertised for a companion to travel with him. One young man had agreed to go, but become suspicious at the last minute. Then, on 21 November 1929, Tetzner had picked up a hitch-hiker named Alois Ortner, who was in search of work. Tetzner persuaded him to crawl under the car to look for some imaginary fault, then attacked him as he emerged with a heavy spanner and an ether pad. But Ortner had fought back, and escaped into the woods. He had, in fact, collapsed unconscious almost immediately, but fortunately, Tetzner had given up the chase and driven off. The Ingolstadt police, to whom this had been reported, dismissed the story as fantastic—they suspected Ortner of an unsuccessful attempt to rob a motorist.

On 27 November 1929, Tetzner had picked up another hitch-hiker, a young man of slight build. When the man was asleep, said Tetzner, he had poured petrol in the car, then tossed in a match and run away, burning the man alive.

The German legal system is more ponderous than the

British one; by the following April, Tetzner's trial had still not begun, and he had decided to change his story. The victim, he said, was a man whom he had accidentally knocked down and killed. He had then decided that it was a heaven-sent opportunity to go ahead with his insurance fraud plan...

This story struck Kockel as altogether more plausible than the previous version, for no soot had been found in the victim's lungs. And at the trial of Erich and Emma Tetzner, which began on 17 March 1931, Kockel gave it as his opinion that the second of the two stories was more likely to be true, although it probably fell short of the horror of what actually happened. But if Tetzner thought that this support for his second story would influence the jury towards mercy, he was mistaken. What emerged in court was a nightmarish tale of greed and brutality that almost defied belief. Tetzner admitted that when he had learned that his mother-in-law was about to have an operation for cancer, he had dissuaded her for just long enough to insure her life for 10,000 marks, then suggested that she should go ahead after all; she died a few days after the operation, and the insurance company paid up. This easy profit led Tetzner to meditate on how he might make an immense fortune from the insurance companies. When he told his wife of his plan of killing a hitch-hiker, she suggested that it would be easier to dig up a newly buried corpse. Tetzner shook his head. "No, there has to be blood around." But after the fiasco with Alois Ortner, he changed his mind; now he thought that it would be easier to blind the victim with pepper, then set him on fire. But then, said Tetzner, the accidental killing of the hiker had enabled him to carry out his scheme without the need for murder...

It was clear that his brutal frankness was an attempt to convince the jury that he had decided to tell the whole truth. They declined to believe him, and he was sentenced to death. Shortly before his execution, he confessed to what had really happened. The thinly clad youth had complained of feeling cold, and Tetzner had wrapped a rug around him, immobilizing his arms. Then he strangled him with a piece of rope. Even this version was probably less than the truth. Kockel was convinced that Tetzner had hacked off the top of the man's skull, to conceal heavy blows (which would still be visible even on a charred skull), and perhaps even his legs, which might have provided some clue—possibly the hiker was crippled. Tetzner was executed on 2 June 1931.

Yet his example had already inspired another "insurance murder." Some time during the summer of 1930, when the Tetzner case was being discussed in German newspapers, a young furniture store manager named Fritz Saffran walked into the store brandishing a newspaper, and exclaimed to his mistress, the bookkeeper Ella Augustin, "Have you read about this man Tetzner? That's how we'll do it . . ."

The Platz Store, in the little town of Rastenburg, was apparently doing excellent business, and its friendly young manager, a former schoolteacher, was universally liked and admired. He had married the store-owner's daughter and taken over his father-in-law's business. The books showed large profits—but only because the plain but determined Ella was willing to falsify them on a massive scale. In fact, Saffran had sold far too much furniture on hire-purchase, and the recession was preventing his customers from keeping their side of the deal. It was then that he read about the Tetzner case, and saw a way out. His first step was to insure his life for 140,000 marks. His next was to take Ella Augustin and the store's chief clerk, Erich Kipnis, into his confidence, and explain that they had to find a body that could be destroyed in a fire. Like Tetzner, they decided that a corpse from a graveyard would not serve their purpose—to begin with, it would be too hard to obtain. Instead, they set up a "murder camp" in the Nicolai forest. Every evening, Saffran and Kipnis drove off in the car, looking for a victim. They proved unexpectedly hard to find. One evening, near the village of Sorquitten, a man accepted a lift. But when Kipnis began hitting him with a life-preserver, Ella became hysterical and held him back; the man escaped, and apparently failed to report the incident. On another occasion, according to Kipnis's later confession, a hitch-hiker told them that he had six children, and they decided to let him go. But finally, on 12 September 1930, they passed a pedestrian near Luisenhof, and Kipnis got out of the car with his life-preserver and a revolver. When the car returned a few minutes later, Kipnis was waiting for them. "He's there in the ditch—give me a hand."

Saffran's original plan was to burn the body in the car, but he then had a better idea: burn it in the store, and also collect insurance for the building. So now they took the body back to the store, dressed it in Saffran's clothes, placed his rings on the man's fingers and his watch in the waistcoat pocket, and doused the place in petrol. Then, leaving a trail, they hurried out of the store, and lit the end of the trail. Minutes later, there was a tremendous explosion. There were 30 people working in other parts of the building, and all managed to escape. And Erich Kipnis rushed to the home of Herr Platz, the store's owner, and babbled that Fritz Saffran had died in the fire. They had been passing the store after an evening in a café when they saw smoke, and Saffran had rushed into the building seconds before the explosion . . .

During the next 48 hours, it looked as if the plan had succeeded. Ella collapsed in a faint in the street, and everyone sympathized with her state of shock, for it was generally known that she cherished a hopeless passion for her employer. But a few days after the fire, the police began to hear curious rumors, to the effect that Fritz Saffran was still alive. A local doctor was asked to take a closer look at the charred corpse found in the store. He found traces of earth on the body, and concluded that it had been buried for some time before being burnt. The police began to make inquires to find if any local graveyard had been robbed. (This is an aspect of the case that remained obscure—three days elapsed between the murder of the pedestrian and the explosion in the store, and it seems probable that the corpse was meanwhile buried in the forest.) Pictures of the teeth were also published in a dental journal, and they eventually led to the identification of the corpse. He was a 25-year-old dairyman named Friedrich Dahl, and he had been cycling home on the night he disappeared.

But by that time, the police were on Saffran's trail. Ella
Augustin was arrested on a charge of falsifying accounts.
She tried to smuggle a note to Saffran; it was intercepted, and
told the police that he was staying with a relative of Ella's, a
carpenter who lived in Berlin; Saffran had been there for
seven weeks. But by the time the police arrived, Saffran had
left. He had decided to escape abroad, via Hamburg. Stealing his host's identity papers, he boarded a train at Spandau,
then a suburb of Berlin. By the kind of incredible bad luck
that seems to dog so many killers, he was recognized by a
guard who had once served with him in the local rifle
brigade at Rastenburg. The guard telephoned the police, and
the police telegraphed Wittenberg, the next station down the
line, where Saffran was drinking coffee in the waiting-room
as the police entered.

At the trial, Saffran and Kipnis tried to throw the blame
on one another. When Frau Dahl, the wife of the murdered
dairyman, appeared in court, both of them fell on their
knees and tearfully begged her forgiveness until the public
prosecutor snapped: "Enough of this play acting."

The police had also considered charging a chauffeur
named Reck with complicity. It had been Reck who had
unintentionally alerted the police by talking about a curious
event that had occurred two days after Saffran's "death."
Ella Augustin had asked him to drive her ailing mother to
Königsberg, but when the chauffeur arrived at her house, it
had been Fritz Saffran who had climbed into the car. Reck
had taken him as far as the village of Gerdauen, then
refused to go further, afraid of being implicated in the fraud.
But he had agreed not to notify the police. He had, in fact,
mentioned to friends that Saffran was still alive, and this is
how the police had eventually heard about it. The chauffeur
was charged with aiding and abetting, but the conspiracy
charge was eventually dropped.

Saffran and Kipnis were condemned to death, Ella to five
years' imprisonment. But an appeal was successful, and the
two "manhunters" spent the rest of their lives in prison.

————————————— **12** —————————————

The most remarkable feat of forensic reconstruction of the 1930s was not performed by Sir Bernard Spilsbury, but by Professor John Glaister of the University of Glasgow.

29 September 1935, was a cool autumn day; a young lady had paused in her afternoon walk to lean on the parapet of a bridge across a pretty stream called the Gardenholme Linn. As she stared at the narrow, rocky stream, she noticed some kind of bundle that had jammed against a boulder. Something that looked unpleasantly like a human hand was sticking out of it.

The police were on the scene by mid-afternoon, and had soon discovered two human heads on the bank of the Linn, as well as four bundles, each containing human remains— thigh bones, legs, pieces of flesh, and an armless torso. One piece of newspaper wrapped round two upper arms proved to be the *Sunday Graphic* for 15 September 1935.

When, the following day, Professor John Glaister—author of a classic *Medical Jurisprudence and Toxicology*—arrived with his colleague Dr. Gilbert Millar, he quickly realized that this killing was not the work of some terrified amateur; he had taken care to cover his tracks. He had not only dismembered the bodies, but removed the skin from the heads, to make the faces unrecognizable, and cut off the fingertips to make fingerprint identification impossible. He had made only one mistake: instead of tossing the remains into the River Annan, a few hundred yards downstream, he had tossed them into its tributary, the Linn, which had been swollen with heavy rains at the time. If the rain had continued, the parcels would have ended up in the Solway Firth. But there were a few days of fine weather; the stream dwindled to its usual trickle, and the parcels caught in the rocks.

The remains were sent to the Anatomy Department of the University of Edinburgh, and there treated with ether to prevent further decomposition and destroy maggots; then they were "pickled" in a formalin solution. Glaister and

Millar found themselves confronted with a human jigsaw puzzle of 70 pieces.

The first task was to sort the pieces into two separate bodies, and this was made easier by the fact that one was six inches shorter than the other. And when it was finally done, Glaister and his team found that they had one almost complete body, the taller one, and one body minus a trunk. there was also an item that caused much bafflement—an enormous single eye, which certainly did not belong to either of the bodies; by some odd chance, this eye, probably from an animal, had also found its way into the Linn.

What could be deduced about the murderer? First, that he was almost certainly a medical man. He had used a knife, not a saw, to dismember the body, and a human body is almost impossible to dismember with a knife without detailed knowledge of the joints. He had also removed the teeth, recognizing that they could lead to identification by a dentist.

Fortunately, the murderer had either lost his nerve or been interrupted, for he had left some of the hair on the smaller body—which, at first, Glaister thought to be that of a man. And when more parcels were found in the river, Glaister found that he had a pair of hands that still had fingertips. After soaking them in hot water, he was able to get an excellent set of fingerprints. And the discovery that the assorted pieces of flesh included three breasts also made it clear that both bodies were of women.

The next problem was the age of the bodies. Glaister determined this by means of the skull sutures. Sutures are "joining lines" in the skull, and they seal themselves over the years; they are usually closed completely by the age of 40. In one of the two skulls, the smaller of the two, the sutures were unclosed; in the other, they were almost closed. This indicated that one body was that of a woman of about 40; the other was certainly under 30. X-rays of the jaw-bone of the younger woman showed that the wisdom teeth had still not pushed through, which meant she was probably in her early 20s. The cartilage, the soft material of which bones are originally made, gradually changes into "caps," called "epiphyses," and the age can also be estimated from how far this change has taken place. The epiphyses of the smaller body confirmed that this was a girl of 20 or so; the other of a woman approaching middle age.

As to the cause of death, this was fairly clear. The taller woman had five stab wounds in the chest, several broken bones, and many bruises. The hyoid bone in the neck was broken, indicating strangulation before the other injuries had been inflicted. The swollen and bruised tongue confirmed this inference. Glaister reasoned that a murderer who strangled and beat his victim before stabbing her would probably be in the grip of jealous rage. As to the other body, the signs were that she had been battered with some blunt instrument. It hardly needed a Sherlock Holmes to infer that she had been killed as an afterthought, probably to keep her silent. The fact that the murderer had taken less trouble to conceal her identity pointed to the same conclusion.

Meanwhile, the police were working on their own clues. The *Sunday Graphic* was a special local edition, printed for the Morecambe and Lancaster area. And the clothes in which some of the remains had been wrapped were also distinctive: the head of the younger woman had been wrapped in a pair of child's rompers, and another bundle had been wrapped in a blouse with a patch under the arm...

And in Lancaster, a Persian doctor named Buck Ruxton had already attracted the suspicions of the local police. Five days before the remains were found in the Linn, Ruxton—a small, rather good-looking man with a wildly excitable manner—had called on the police and mentioned that his wife had deserted him. The police were investigating the murder of a lady called Mrs. Smalley, whose body had been found a year earlier, and in the course of routine investigations, had questioned a domestic in Ruxton's household; he wanted to protest about this harassment. And when he spoke of his wife's disappearance, they were not in the least surprised; they knew that the relations between the two were stormy. Two years before, Mrs. Isabella Ruxton had come to the police station to protest that her husband was beating her, and Ruxton had made wild accusations of infidelity against her; however, he had calmed down, and 24 hours later the two were apparently again on the best of terms.

The parents of Mrs. Ruxton's maid, Mary Rogerson, were not only surprised but incredulous when Ruxton came and told them that their daughter had got herself pregnant by the laundry boy, and that his wife had taken her away for an abortion. Nothing was less likely; Mary was a plain girl, with a cast in one eye, who loved her home and her parents, and spent all her spare time with them; she was as unlikely to get herself pregnant as to rob a bank. In spite of Ruxton's feverish protests, they reported it to the police. On the evening of 9 October 1935, 10 days after the remains had been found in the Linn, Ruxton came to the police and burst into tears. People were saying that he had murdered his wife and thrown her into the Linn; they must help him find her. They soothed him and sent him away. But, in fact, Ruxton had been the chief suspect since earlier that day. The Scottish police had been to see the Rogersons, and had shown them the patched blouse. As soon as they saw it, they knew their daughter was dead; Mary had bought it at a jumble sale and patched it under the arm. They were unable to identify the rompers, but suggested that the police should try a Mrs. Holme, with whom Millar and the three Ruxton children had spent a holiday earlier that year. And Mrs. Holme recognized the rompers as a pair she had given Mary for the children.

The police spoke to the Ruxtons' charlady, Mrs. Oxley. She told them that on the day Mrs. Ruxton and Mary Rogerson had disappeared, Sunday 15 September 1935, Ruxton had arrived early at her house and explained that it was unnecessary for her to come to work that day—he was taking the children to Morecambe, and his wife had gone to Edinburgh. The following morning, she found the Ruxtons' house—at 2 Dalton Square—in a state of chaos, with carpets removed, the bath full of yellow stains, and a pile of burnt material in the yard. A neighbor told the police that Ruxton had persuaded her to come and clean up his house to prepare it for the decorators, claiming that he had cut his hand badly on a tin of peaches. She and her husband had obligingly scrubbed out the house. And Ruxton had given them some bloodstained carpets and a blue suit that was also stained with blood.

On 12 October, the police questioned Ruxton all night, and at 7:20 the next morning he was charged with the murder of Mary Rogerson.

In spite of Ruxton's attempts to cover his tracks, and to persuade various witnesses to offer him false alibis, the truth about the murders soon became plain. Ruxton was pathologically jealous, although there was no evidence that his "wife"—they were in fact unmarried—had ever been unfaithful. A week before the murder, Mrs. Ruxton had gone to Edinburgh, where she had a sister, with a family named Edmondson, who were close friends of the Ruxtons. The Edmondsons and Mrs. Ruxton had all booked into separate rooms; nevertheless, Ruxton was convinced that she had spent the night in the bed of Robert Edmondson, an assistant solicitor in the Town Hall. Ruxton had driven to Edinburgh to spy on them. The following Saturday, Isabella Ruxton had gone to spend the afternoon and evening with two of her sisters in Blackpool. Convinced that she was in a hotel room with a man, Ruxton had worked himself into a jealous frenzy, and when she came back far later than expected, he began to beat her—probably in an attempt to make her confess her infidelities—then throttled her unconscious and stabbed her. Mary Rogerson had probably heard the screams and come in to see what was happening; Ruxton believed she was his wife's confidant in her infidelities, and killed her too. He had spent the next day dismembering the bodies and packing them in straw; that night, he made his first trip north to dispose of the bodies . . .

Ruxton's counsel, Norman Birkett, must have known that his client did not stand a ghost of a chance. His line of defense was that the bodies found in the Linn were not those of Isabella Ruxton and Mary Rogerson, but of some other persons. But when the medical experts—Glaister, Millar, and Professor Sydney Smith—gave their evidence, it was obvious that the identity of the bodies had been established beyond all possible doubt. One photograph, which had subsequently been used in every account of the case, super-imposed the larger of the two skulls on a photograph of Mrs. Ruxton. She had a rather long, horsy face, and it was obvious that the two fitted together with gruesome exacti-tude. Ruxton seemed determined to trap himself in a web of lies and evasions. The result was a unanimous verdict of guilty, arrived at in only one hour. He was hanged at Strangeways jail, Manchester, on 12 May 1936.

Yet examination of the evidence—and of Glaister's famous book *Medico–legal Aspects of the Ruxton Case* (1937)—makes it clear that Ruxton came very close indeed to getting away with murder. If he had taken the trouble to remove Mary Rogerson's fingertips, and destroyed the tell-tale breast tissue as well as the trunk (which was never found), the evidence against him would have remained purely circumstantial; and since British juries are unwilling to convict on circumstantial evidence, he might well have been given the benefit of the doubt. Glaister's forensic skill and Ruxton's failure of nerve played an equal part in bringing him to the gallows.

13

In 1940, Sir Bernard Spilsbury suffered a stroke—partly as a result of shock at the death of his son Peter, a house surgeon who was killed in the blitz. He lived on for another seven years, and continued to perform 1,000 post-mortems a year; but it was obvious that the Sherlock Holmes of forensic medicine was slowing down. He had often talked of retire-ment during the 1930s, but was always dissuaded on the grounds that there was no one to take his place. But in the early 1940s, the British public began to hear about another rising star, Professor Cedric Keith Simpson, of Guy's Medical School. No two personalities could have been less alike. Simpson, like many pathologists, derived a certain macabre amusement from his gruesome trade, and when lecturing on murder enjoyed trying to make his students feel sick. But apart from Spilsbury, there was no pathologist in London of comparable brilliance during the 1940s.

Simpson had been 33 at the time of the Crippen trial; Simpson was 35 when he suddenly stepped into the limelight with the curious case of the body in the church basement, which he later described as "the case of a lifetime."

On 17 January 1942, workmen had started to demolish a bombed Baptist church in Vauxhall Road, south London, and one of them prised up a heavy stone slab in the cellar. Underneath, he found a skeleton with a few shreds of flesh clinging to it, and when he lifted the skeleton with his spade, the skull remained where it was. It looked as if this was another victim of German air raids; yet the fact that the body was lying under a slab raised some doubts. When Simpson inspected the remains in Southwark mortuary the next day, he noted the remains of a womb. It told him not only that this was a woman, but that she had been buried in the past year or so; flesh would not survive much longer.

With the skeleton back in his laboratory at Guy's, Simpson could see plainly that this was a case of murder. The head had been severed, and both legs were severed at the knee. A yellowish powder clinging to parts of the skeleton proved to be slaked lime—calcium hydroxide. More was found in the hole in which she had been buried.

Simpson was able to determine the age of the dead woman from the skull sutures; the brow plates were completely fused and fusion was in progress between the top plates; that placed her age between 40 and 50. The uterus proved to be enlarged, but not due to pregnancy; an X-ray showed a fibroid growth. The lower jaw was missing, but the upper jaw was complete, and fillings and the marks of a dental plate told Simpson that it should not be difficult to identify her if her dentist could be found.

This proved to be unexpectedly easy. Detective Inspector Keeling studied a list of missing persons, and noted that Rachel Dobkin, wife of a fire-watcher at the Baptist church, had been reported missing since Good Friday 1941. Her sister told the police that she had gone to collect arrears of maintenance from her husband, Harry Dobkin, and had not been seen since. Over the years, Dobkin had been in prison several times for failing to pay her maintenance. Mrs. Dobkin's sister was also able to tell them that Rachel's dentist was Mr. Barnett Kopkin of Stoke Newington. And Mr. Kopkin was able to confirm that the photograph of the upper jaw was that of his patient. The doctor who had diagnosed a fibroid growth of the uterus was also found. There could be no reasonable doubt that the body was that of Rachel Dobkin. And a tiny blood clot on the voice box revealed that she had died by strangulation. Simpson completed the identification by imposing a photograph of Rachel Dobkin on the skull, the technique Glaister had used in the Ruxton case; the fit was perfect.

The defense did its best, trying hard to throw doubt on Simpson's findings, and then suggesting that, if the victim was Mrs. Dobkin, she could have died naturally through a bomb blast. The jury declined to consider either possibility, and Dobkin was condemned to death.

Even before the trial of Harry Dobkin in November 1942, Simpson was deeply absorbed in an equally strange murder case. On 7 October 1942, marines exercising on Hankley Common, near Godalming, saw a mummified hand sticking out of the earth. The following day, Simpson was there, carefully digging the body out of the earth to ensure that it remained undamaged. It was a woman, lying face downwards, the legs apart, one arm outstretched. She was fully clothed, and the back of the skull was shattered.

The body was moved back to Guy's, and placed in a carbolic tank; Simpson devoted all his spare time to it. "Spare time" was usually tea time, when he and his secretary Molly Lefebure would sit beside the tank with their tea and sandwiches, and she would take notes at his dictation. Simpson's associate Dr. Eric Gardner often came to help. Their conclusion was that the dead girl had received stab wounds to the left top side of the head. And some of the smaller indentations revealed that a knife with a hook-like point had been used—neither Simpson nor Gardner had ever seen anything of the sort. The girl had apparently fallen heavily on her face, knocking out some of her front teeth. Then there had been a tremendous blow to the back of the head with some blunt instrument, shattering the skull. When Simpson and Miss Lefebure had finished wiring together the skull fragments, they could see a depressed fracture across the back of the head—it could have been made with a stake or a bough. This is what had killed the girl. Her teeth and bones put her age in her late teens.

The task of discovering the girl's identity was less complicated. Detective Inspector Ted Greeno of Scotland Yard made inquiries at Godalming about a blonde teenager who wore a green and white summer dress with a lace collar, and learned that a girl called Joan Pearl Wolfe was known to the local police—she lived like a tramp, and was often seen with soldiers from a nearby camp. She was not a prostitute, but had apparently run away from home. A search of the area where the body was found revealed Joan Wolfe's identity card, her rosary (she was a Roman Catholic) and a letter to a Canadian private called August Sangret, telling him she was pregnant. A few more inquires revealed that Sangret had been spending his weekend leaves with her in home-made "wigwams" made of branches, which he built for her—Sangret was half Cree-Indian, half French Canadian.

Interviewed at the Canadian army camp, Sangret told Greeno that he had not see Joan for more than three weeks, and had reported her disappearance to his provost sergeant. But a little further inquiry revealed that Sangret had told contradictory stories about her disappearance to various friends. And the police search revealed new evidence that made it clear that Sangret was the man they were looking for—a bloodstained army blanket and battle dress, both of which had been ineffectually washed, a birch stake with bloodstains and blonde hairs on it, and finally, a clasp knife with a "hooked" point, which was found obstructing a washhouse pipe—someone recollected that Sangret had excused himself to go to the washhouse while he was waiting for his first interview with Greeno. What had happened was clear. Joan Wolfe and August Sangret had met on Hankley Common on the afternoon of 14 August 1942, and she had pressed him about marriage. They had quarrelled, and Sangret had attacked her with the knife—the point of the clasp knife fitted the indentations in the skull. She had fled and tripped over a military trip-wire, knocking out her teeth, and Sangret had smashed in her skull with a blow of the birch stake as she lay there. Then he had wrapped her body in a blanket, hidden it under bushes for 24 hours or so, then dragged it to the top of the ridge to bury it—possibly following some burial ritual of his Red Indian ancestors.

In court, Simpson produced the skull and the knife, and the jury took them with them when they retired. It took them two hours to find Sangret guilty, with a strong recommendation to mercy, but he was hanged in Wandsworth jail.

While he was still working on the "wigwam case" (as it came to be known), Simpson was called to view the body of an unknown woman found in some reeds by the River Lea, near Luton. The body was trussed up in four potato sacks, the knees against the chest. In the mortuary, Simpson quickly diagnosed the cause of death as strangulation, followed by a blow to the side of the face from a heavy blunt instrument. Bruises caused by the ropes indicated that she had still been alive when trussed up. The woman was in her mid-30s, had had at least one child, and was again pregnant.

Since she had been dead only about 24 hours, the face still looked virtually as it had when she was alive; it was photographed, and the result exhibited in local shops and cinemas. Yet no one seemed to recognize her. There was nothing for it but to apply the "needle-in-the-haystack" method. The police traced 404 missing women, went to all dry cleaners to check on women's clothing that had been left uncollected, and searched rubbish dumps for discarded female clothes. A cast of the dead woman's remaining teeth was taken—she had also worn dentures, which had been removed by her killer—and the photograph published in the *British Dental Journal*. And when, after three months, all this activity had brought no result, Chief Inspector Chapman, who was in charge of the case, decided once more to study all the evidence collected so far. This included a piece of black coat found on a rubbish dump; a piece of attached tape indicated that it had at some time been sent to the local Sketchley dry cleaners. From the tag, the dry cleaner was able to tell Chapman that the coat had been brought in by Mrs. Rene Manton of Regent Street, Luton. The 8-year-old girl who opened the door bore a strong resemblance to the unidentified corpse; she explained that her mother had left home. A photograph of Rene Manton supplied by the child left no doubt in Chapman's mind that the victim was Rene Manton, who had been missing since 18 November 1942.

Chapman's next call was on Mrs. Manton's mother. When she told him that she had received several letters from her daughter, who was living in Hampstead, Chapman wondered for a moment if he was pursuing a false lead. But the old lady was half blind, and hardly able to read the handwriting. He noted that "Hampstead" was spelt without the "p."

His next call was on Rene Manton's husband, Bertie, who was in the National Fire Service, at the Luton station. Manton told him that his wife had left him on 25 November, a week after the discovery of the body, after a quarrel about her association with soldiers. Shown letters to his mother-in-law, Manton identified the handwriting as that of his wife. Asked to write a sentence containing the word "Hampstead," he spelt it "Hamstead."

Manton told the detective the name of his wife's dentist, and the dentist provided the final piece of evidence—the teeth left no doubt that the victim was his patient Rene Manton.

Confronted with this evidence, Manton confessed. He and his wife had quarrelled about soldiers, and she had thrown a cup of tea in his face. He had then struck her to the ground with a footstool. Convinced she was dead, he had stripped the body and hidden it in the cellar, then cleared up the blood before his children returned from school for their tea. Later, he tied it in the sacks, and wheeled it to the river on the handlebars of his bicycle.

Mrs. Manton's 17-year-old daughter had seen the photograph of her mother flashed on to the screen at the local cinema, but the swelling due to bruises had prevented her from recognizing it. The two sons, aged 14 and 15, had also seen the photograph in a local tobacconist's window and told their father they thought it looked like their mother; he said their mother had gone away to Grantham and they believed him.

The final piece of identification evidence was collected by Fred Cherrill, of Scotland Yard's fingerprint department. Going over the Manton house, Cherrill found a thumbprint on a pickle jar which matched that of the dead woman.

Manton's defense was that he had killed his wife in a fit of fury with a single blow, and that it was therefore manslaughter. But Simpson pointed out that marks on her throat showed that he had throttled her—not once, but twice. Moreover, Manton had struck her twice with the stool. All this seemed to indicate a deliberate intention of killing her rather than a single blow struck in a rage. Manton was found guilty and sentenced to death.

Simpson's most famous murder case was still to come. By the late 1940s, he was known to the general public largely as the pathologist who had figured in the most widely publicized murder trial since the war, that of the sadist Neville George Clevely Heath. The 29-year-old ex-Borstal boy was an incorrigible fantasist who loved to pose as a colonel or group captain. On the evening of 20 June 1946, Heath booked into the Pembridge Court Hotel, Notting Hill, with an amateur artist named Margery Gardner, who also happened to be a masochist. Her naked body was found the next day, apparently suffocated accidentally by a gag, the flesh covered with distinctive whiplash marks; her nipples had been bitten off, and her vagina was torn from the insertion of some blunt instrument. When Simpson examined the body he remarked to Detective Chief Inspector Barratt: "If you find that whip you've found your man." The hotel register had been signed "Col. and Mrs. G. C. Heath." Heath meanwhile had gone to the Tollard Royal Hotel in Bournemouth, and booked in under the name "Group Captain Rupert Brooke." There he met a pretty ex-WRNS named Doreen Marshall, and persuaded her to have dinner with him, then to allow him to walk her back to her own hotel. Heath returned alone. Five days later, a swarm of flies alerted a passer-by to her naked body lying in some bushes; like Margery Gardner, she had been sexually mutilated—this time with a knife. The manager of the Tollard Royal told the police she had dined with "Group Captain Brooke." The detective constable who questioned "Brooke" recognized him as the man wanted by Scotland Yard for the murder of Margery Gardner. In Heath's pocket they found a cloakroom ticket, which led them to an attaché case containing the riding whip of distinctive pattern. Heath was found guilty of the murder of Margery Gardner—a curious verdict since her death was obviously accidental—and he was executed at Pentonville on 16 October 1946.

The sensation caused by the Heath murders was eclipsed three years later by the case of the "vampire murderer" John George Haigh. On Sunday 20 February 1949, a man and a woman arrived at the Chelsea police station and explained that they wanted to report the disappearance of an elderly lady, Mrs. Durand-Deacon, who was a fellow guest at the Onslow Court Hotel in South Kensington. The man—dapper and well-dressed, with a neat moustache—explained that he had arranged to meet Mrs. Olivier Durand-Deacon two days earlier, to take her to his place of business in Sussex, but she failed to keep the appointment; now, with her friend Mrs. Constance Lane, he had come to alert the police. When the police checked on him at the Criminal Records Office, they discovered that John Haigh had been in prison for swindling.

Crime reporters flocked to the Onslow Court Hotel, and Haigh gave a kind of impromptu press conference, emphasizing his own concern for the missing woman. But the West Sussex Constabulary was already looking at Haigh's "place of business," Hurstlea Products, at Crawley. He rented a two-storey brick-built storehouse from the firm, using it for "experimental work." The police broke in, and found a revolver, and a receipt for a Persian lamb coat from a firm of cleaners. The coat proved to belong to Mrs. Durand-Deacon, and further inquires revealed that her jewelery had been sold by Haigh to a jewelers in Horsham. Haigh was arrested and taken to the police station. At first he told obviously concocted lies about his relationship with Mrs. Durand-Deacon, hinting at blackmail. Then he suddenly asked the police inspector what the chances were of anyone being released from Broadmoor, the criminal lunatic asylum. Inspector Webb was non-committal. "Well," said Haigh, "if I told you the truth you wouldn't believe me . . . Mrs. Durand-Deacon no longer exists . . . I have destroyed her with acid!" He gazed at the incredulous policeman with a bland smile. "How can you prove murder if there is no body?" Like many murderers, Haigh made the mistake of believing that the phrase *corpus delicti* means the corpse, without which murder cannot be proved; in fact, it means the body of the offense or crime. Fellow convicts who knew Haigh in his earlier days in Dartmoor had nicknamed him "old *corpus delicti*" because he liked to expound his view that a killer could not be convicted so long as there was no body.

Haigh added: "You'll find the sludge that remains at Leopold Road [Crawley]. I did the same with the Hendersons and the McSwanns."

Haigh had decided that his best means of escaping justice was a defense of insanity; he continued to pursue this objective by telling the police that the motive for the killings had been a desire to drink the blood of his victims; he had an insatiable lust for blood, and after each murder, filled a glass with his victim's blood and drained it. (In fact, blood is an emetic, and a glassful would undoubtedly have made him vomit.)

Haigh had embarked on his career of mass murder with the deliberation of a businessman. After a number of spells in jail for petty fraud, he decided that the best way to avoid being caught was to kill his victims and dispose of their bodies. In 1936 he had been employed by an amusement arcade owner named McSwann; after coming out of prison in 1943, he had met their son Donald again, and proposed a business partnership. Donald was lured to Haigh's basement "workshop" at Gloucester Road in September 1944 and bludgeoned to death; then Haigh dissolved his body in a vat of concentrated sulphuric acid—he had already experimented on mice in the prison workshop and decided that this was the perfect method of destroying his corpses. He emptied the "sludge" down the drain. McSwann's parents were told he had gone off to Scotland on business. Ten months later, the elder McSwanns were lured separately to the basement and disposed of in the same way. Haigh then disposed of their considerable property, forging the necessary documents, for about £4,000.

By September 1947, Haigh had spent the £4,000, and looked around for more victims. He saw an advertisement for a house, and introduced himself to its owners, Archie and Rose Henderson, and offered them £10,500 for it. The deal "fell through," but Haigh continued to see the Hendersons, posing as a rich businessman. On 12 February 1948, Archie Henderson accompanied Haigh to his "workshop" at Leopold Road, Crawley, and was shot in the back of the head. Haigh then went and collected Rose Henderson, telling her that her husband was ill, and killed her in the same way. Various letters were despatched to relatives of the dead couple, explaining that they had been close to a "bust-up," and were traveling while their relationship was repaired. Haigh forged these letters so expertly that all suspicion was finally allayed. Then he disposed of their property, collecting some £7,700.

Other possible victims—including the widow of a Wakefield businessman—slipped through the net. By February 1949, Haigh was again in debt, and realized that he had to find a victim within the next week or so. To Mrs. Durand-Deacon, who always dined at the next table at the Onslow Court Hotel, Haigh suggested a business deal involving the manufacture of plastic fingernails. And on 18 February 1949, Mrs. Durand-Deacon made her fatal visit to the Crawley workshop. Twelve days later, on 2 March, Haigh was charged with her murder.

When Professor Keith Simpson traveled down to the Crawley workshop on 1 March, he had little hope of finding evidence of murder; Haigh had already told the police that he had poured the "sludge" over the ground several days earlier. The sludge was lying on an area of ground about six feet by four, and was about three inches deep. Simpson was staring intently at this sludge when he exclaimed: "Aha, gall-stones." He had seen an object about the size of a cherry, lying among some pebbles that were, to the inexpert eye, indistinguishable from it. After this find, the police carefully shoveled the sludge into boxes, to be removed to the Scotland Yard laboratory. There it was searched by spreading it thinly in steel trays; because the acid was so strong, the searchers had to wear rubber gloves. But the effort was worthwhile: the sludge proved to contain a partially dissolved left foot, an intact upper plastic denture, a lower denture, three gall-stones (easy to distinguish at close quarters by their facets), 28 lb of greasy substance, 18 fragments of human bone, the handle of a red plastic handbag and a lipstick container. Haigh had left more than enough of Mrs. Durand-Deacon to hang him.

Simpson took the bones to his laboratory at Guy's. He discovered the presence of osteo-arthritis in some of the joints—Mrs. Durand-Deacon suffered from osteo-arthritis—and was able to identify most of the bone fragments as human. Meanwhile, the police had made a plaster cast of the left foot, and checked it against Mrs. Durand-Deacon's left shoe; the fit was perfect. The plastic dentures were identified by Mrs. Durand-Deacon's dental surgeon as having been supplied to her two years earlier. Haigh had no way of knowing that the false teeth were of plastic, and therefore would not dissolve in acid, nor of knowing that gall-stones cannot be dissolved in acid.

Bloodstains found on the whitewash of the storeroom were tested and found to be human. Bloodstains were also found on the Persian lamb coat, and on the cuff of one of Haigh's shirts. The handbag strap was identified as belonging to the handbag Mrs. Durand-Deacon had carried when she drove with Haigh down to Crawley.

Haigh's major mistake had been in confessing to the murders, and trusting to a defense of insanity. If he had said nothing about the "acid bath," the sludge might not have been examined for many weeks, and Simpson later admitted that by that time, the acid might have consumed everything but the gall-stones and the human fat. And in themselves, these would not have constituted sufficient evidence of identity.

In prison, Haigh continued to build up the notion that he was insane, claiming that there had been three more victims—all penniless—whom he had killed for their blood alone. He explained that the urge to drink blood developed after an accident with a lorry in 1944, when his car overturned. After this, he said, he began to have a recurrent dream of a forest of crucifixes which turned into trees that dripped blood . . . He also claimed that the murders were divinely inspired. When aware of being observed, he drank his own urine.

All this was useless. A number of doctors and psychiatrists examined Haigh, and all but one concluded that he was perfectly sane. A woman friend who visited him in prison observed that he was playing the role of mass murderer with tremendous gusto, delighting in his belated "fame." The newspapers were full of accounts of the "vampire murderer"—probably no case of the century has received so much publicity—and one of them, the *Daily Mirror*, went too far and was fined £10,000, while its editor was sentenced to three months in prison. But at the trial, which began on 18 July 1949 at Lewes Assizes, all the evidence revealed Haigh as a calculating killer who had murdered for gain, and who was shamming insanity. Dr. Henry Yellowlees, for the defense, argued that Haigh was genuinely paranoid, but the jury was so unimpressed that they took only 15 minutes to bring in a guilty verdict. Haigh was executed at Wandsworth on 6 August 1949.

Simpson, who was responsible for the medical evidence that convicted Haigh, later commented on the absurdly small profits that Haigh had made from five years of murder—a mere £12,000. The last murder, of Mrs. Durand-Deacon, would have brought him only about £150 for the coat and the jewelery. He could have made more money in almost any honest occupation.

Keith Simpson died in 1985, at the age of 78. Like

Spilsbury, he was inclined to overwork, and his publisher J.
H. H. Gaute remarked in an obituary that this was the cause
of his death. But his enthusiasm for his gruesome occupation was so great that he was unable to stay away from the
morgue and the "path lab." Gaute recalls how, after lunching
with Simpson at Guy's, Simpson asked him if he would like
to come down to the mortuary, and seemed surprised when
the publisher declined. "Not the keen type, eh?" he remarked
drily.

The present writer did not decline a similar invitation,
and was taken into the mortuary to view the body of a male
child of about 7, who had—according to a teenage baby-
sitter—died after a fall downstairs. Simpson expertly opened
the body in a few minutes, then, as if he knew exactly what
he was looking for, plunged in his hand and drew out the
liver, which was broken in half. "That wasn't caused by a
fall downstairs. It's an impossibility. He must have been
kicked in the stomach." Since the baby-sitter had been
alone with the child at the time of the "accident," the
evidence suggested that he was the culprit. I never found
out the sequel to the story. But I retained the impression that
Simpson had known intuitively that he was looking at a case
of murder.

_____ 14 _____

Since Lacassagne and Locard initiated the science of identification in the late nineteenth century, forensic pathology
had again and again demonstrated its ability to identify
human remains from even the smallest clue. But a case in
Chicago in 1945 demonstrated that a prosecution for murder
can be successful even without the slightest trace of the
"*corpus delicti*," as Haigh would have said.

On 28 February 1945, a man who identified himself as
Milton Michaelis, of Clyde Avenue, Chicago, rang the
Woodlawn police station to report that his wife had been
missing for several hours. It was the first time in their 36

years of married life that she had gone off without telling him. When the police made a routine call, the anxious husband showed them some house keys and the heel of a shoe that he had found in a nearby alleyway since making the call. The police looked in the alleyway, which was beside the apartment building, but could find nothing more. The door to the basement proved to be unlocked, and the janitor, Joe Nischt, told them that he had seen nothing. He had been to collect his pay, stopped for a few beers, and now—towards midnight—was completing various tasks he should have finished earlier. When the police asked him if they could search his furnace room, he agreed immediately. One of the officers even glanced into the furnace, but the glowing coals made it impossible to see anything.

Working on the assumption that Rose Michaelis might have been the victim of a hit-and-run driver, the police again searched the alleyway at first daylight. This time they found some ominous clues: hairpins, fragments of broken glass, and some bloodstains on a telephone pole. Milton Michaelis thought that his wife might have gone out to get water from a nearby filtration plant; she disliked the Chicago tap-water. The broken fragments looked very like those of the type of bottle she used to collect the water. If Mrs. Michaelis had been struck by a hit-and-run driver, then he must have dragged her into his car.

Investigations of the janitor's alibi revealed that he was telling the truth; he had collected his pay, then stopped at a few bars on the way back to the apartment building. A check of the criminal record files revealed that he had been arrested twice for assaulting women in bar-room brawls. On both occasions he had been released with a caution; but it was clear that he was likely to become aggressive towards women when drunk. The police asked him to come in for questioning. And when he seemed sullen and uncooperative, they decided to book him on suspicion of murder. But his union promptly filed a writ of *habeus corpus,* and he was released the next day.

That same evening, a woman called at the police station; she was carrying a copy of the evening paper, which contained a photograph of the janitor. "This man knocked on my door three nights ago and asked if he could see my husband. I told him my husband wasn't at home, and asked if I could help. And he put his hands over his face and said: 'No one can help me. I just killed a woman.' Then he went away. I thought he was drunk..."

Once again the police called in Joe Nischt for questioning. And when they told him of the woman's story, he covered his face with his hands and began sobbing. He described how he had approached the attractive, middle-aged housewife and tried to pick her up. When he became too suggestive, she lost her temper. He struck her so hard that he knocked her head against the telephone pole. Then he dragged her into the basement... He was not specific about what happened next, but he confessed that he had pushed her body into the furnace, and that she was probably still alive. He signed a statement to this effect.

He was held in a cell while the police doused the furnace, then sent the ashes to the laboratory for examination. The results were disappointing. There was not the slightest trace of a human body—not even the tiniest bone fragment. The police were in the position that Keith Simpson might have found himself in if Haigh had not told the police about the acid "sludge"—in fact, worse, since they could not even offer a single gall-stone in evidence. And, like Simpson, they were aware that juries are highly suspicious of murder cases in which there is no trace of the body. The Assistant State Attorney Blair Varnes realized that, in spite of the confession, his case was almost non-existent. Nischt only had to repudiate his confession, claiming that it had been obtained under duress, and the state would have no case. And this is, in fact, precisely what happened. Moreover, Nischt's lawyers declared that it was impossible to destroy a body totally, and that this would be the line of their defense.

This, at least, offered the prosecutor a possible line of attack. He decided to consult Professor Wilton Krogman, an anthropologist at the University of Chicago, who was often consulted by the FBI as an expert witness on bodies. Varnes and Krogman visited various crematoria to find out just how long it took a human body to turn to ashes, and at what temperature. They learned that, at a temperature of around 3000° Fahrenheit, it took an hour or so to reduce a body to ashes. The temperature in an ordinary furnace would be far lower than that, but the one in the Clyde Avenue basement had had three days to do its work. If the prosecution could prove beyond all doubt that the furnace could destroy a body in that time, then they had a reply to the main defense argument.

From the Chicago morgue, Krogman obtained the unclaimed body of a woman of about the same age and weight as Rose Michaelis. Then he staged a gruesome reconstruction—placing it in the furnace of an apartment building, and raising the temperature to its maximum. The furnace achieved very nearly the same temperature as a crematorium, and the unknown body was reduced to ashes in three and a half hours. At the end of that time, not a single identifiable fragment remained. When this evidence was presented to the grand jury—whose business was to decide whether there was a case to prosecute—the janitor was indicted on a murder charge.

In court the case attracted nation-wide attention—since it was the general belief that it was impossible to prove a murder without a body. Many newspapers recalled the parallel case of the other Chicago killer, Adolf Luetgart, and pointed out that the few bone fragments and the initialed ring had proved his undoing. Nischt's attorneys argued that it was impossible to destroy a body so completely that no fragment remained. And when Professor Krogman produced his triumphant refutation, they were obviously shaken. Suddenly, Nischt announced that he wanted to change his plea to guilty. The defense offered to do a deal—life imprisonment in exchange for a guilty plea. And although Varnes felt that he had won his case, he realized that a jury of laymen might still be swayed by the "no body" argument. He accepted, and Joe Nischt was sentenced to life imprisonment in the State Penitentiary at Joliet.

As a Frenchman, Locard would have recognized Krogman's method as the ultimate logical application of his theory of identification.

2
If Blood Could Speak...

The science of bloodstains is probably the most important single advance in the history of crime detection. "For at least as long as recorded history, man has been interested in and mystified by blood," remarks Addine G. Erskine in his standard textbook *The Principles and Practice of Blood Grouping*. Yet until the early twentieth century, there was no reliable way of distinguishing a human bloodstain from an animal bloodstain. This is the reason that bloodstains seldom played a central role in early criminal investigation. And a Scottish case of 1721 served as a warning against placing too much reliance on this type of evidence. William Shaw, a native of Edinburgh, was known to be on bad terms with his daughter Catherine because of her association with a man he disliked. One day, neighbors in the same tenement heard a violent quarrel, followed by groans, and the slamming of the door. When this was succeeded by silence, someone went to the door and knocked. It was locked, and there was no reply. The neighbors sent for the police, who broke in, and found Catherine lying in a pool of blood, with a knife beside her. She was still alive, but unable to speak. Asked about the quarrel with her father, she nodded her head; asked if he was responsible for her present condition, she nodded again. Soon after, she died. William Shaw was taken into custody as soon as he returned, and he was obviously badly shaken when taken into the presence of his daughter's body. The police noted the bloodstains on his clothing, and he was arrested and charged with her murder.

The defense was that she had committed suicide. The accused man insisted that he had not even struck his daughter, but left the room in a rage. He claimed that the blood on his clothing was his own—he had been bled a few days earlier, and the bandage had worked loose. But the jury was particularly impressed by the evidence of a neighbor who had heard the girl scream that her father was the cause of her death. Shaw was condemned to death, and executed in November 1721, continuing to protest his innocence.

The next tenant of the room discovered a letter in an opening near the chimney; it was a suicide note from Catherine Shaw, stating that she intended to kill herself because her father would not allow her to marry the man she loved. The letter ended by stating that her father was the cause of death.

When the handwriting was proved to be that of the dead girl, the authorities realized they had hanged an innocent man. Orders were given for Shaw's body to be taken down from the chains in which it had been hung, and given a decent burial, with semi-military honors—no doubt as a kind of belated apology.

There is one impressive exception to the statement about the role of bloodstains in early criminal investigations. Gustave Macé, one of the most remarkable of Vidocq's successors, solved his first murder case through the discovery of a bloodstain. We have already encountered Macé in an earlier chapter—he was one of the senior policemen who opposed Bertillon's early experiments with anthropometry. But this, perhaps, should not be held against him, for Macé was one of the greatest exponents of the old-fashioned school of ''needle-in-the-haystack'' detection.

In late January 1869, a restaurateur of the rue Princesse, off the boulevard St-Germaine in Paris, received protests from customers about the quality of his water, and decided to investigate the well in the basement. It was 60 feet deep, and covered with a kind of grill within a few feet of the surface of the water. Floating on the surface was a parcel wrapped in cloth, and its stench left no doubt that it was the cause of the trouble. With some difficulty, the man fished it out, and was horrified to discover that it contained the lower half of a human leg. He reported it to the Sûreté, and a new recruit named Gustave Macé was sent to investigate. Macé was not simply a policeman, but a lawyer whose duties included crime investigation and prosecution—an "investigating magistrate." He soon realized that there was another parcel floating just below the surface. It proved to contain another leg, encased in part of a stocking.

The doctors who examined the legs concluded that they were those of a woman. Macé noted that both legs had originally been tied in a piece of black glazed calico, about a yard square, tied at either end; this, he remarked in his first report, was a method in use among tailors and seamstresses. With marvelous thoroughness, he checked on the way seamstresses tied parcels, and observed that it was slightly different—they folded the corners inward in the shape of a cross. And so, concluded this remarkable fore-bear of Sherlock Holmes, it seemed to him probable that the parcel had been tied by a journeyman tailor. The "journey-man" inference arose from the fact that the material was cheaper than the kind that would be used in a first-class establishment. There was an odd mark on the stocking: " + B + ," which Macé soon discovered was not a laundry mark. He began checking the file of missing women, 122 in all, a number he was able to reduce to 84. But at this point, the great doctor Ambroise Tardieu, author of the earliest treatise on hanging, examined the legs, and declared that they belonged to a man. All Macé's labors so far had been wasted. With a sigh, he prepared to start all over again.

The state of decay of the legs suggested that their owner had been dead a fairly long time—perhaps six weeks. A few days before Christmas, a human thigh wrapped in a blue jersey had been taken from the river and deposited in the morgue. A human thigh bone had been found in the rue

Jacob at about the same time. Two days later, a laundry proprietor had seen a man scattering pieces of meat from a basket into the river; he explained that he was baiting the fish. But since then, some fairly large chunks of flesh had been pulled out of the river and the St-Martin canal. On 22 December two policemen had seen a man wandering in the early hours of the morning with a parcel in one hand and a hamper in the other; they had questioned him in case he was a robber, and the man had explained that he had just arrived in the capital by train, and been unable to find a cab. The parcels, he explained, contained hams. He looked so honest that they let him go. They described him to Macé as short, plump, round-faced, with a black moustache and confident manner. The laundry proprietor gave the same description of the "fisherman."

Macé felt he was not on the right track. Why had the murderer deposited the lower limbs in the well? Almost certainly because being stopped by the policemen had given him a nasty shock, and he was unwilling to take further risks. He had been stopped close to the rue Princesse, not far from the restaurant. That argued that he lived close by, or at least knew the place well.

Macé had a conversation with the old and inefficient concierge of the restaurant building. No, she said, there was no tailor living there. But there had been a tailoress—a waistcoat-maker known as Mathilde Dard (her real name was Gaupe)—who worked for a little tailor. He used to annoy the concierge by fetching water from the well and making splashes on the stairs . . . Mathilde had had many male friends (said the old lady with disapproval) but she had now left—the concierge had no idea where she had gone. But she was able to tell Macé that one of the girl's male callers was a chemist's assistant who worked nearby, and the assistant was able to tell Macé that the girl was now a café *chanteuse*. The police made inquiries around the cafés, and soon traced a singer named Mlle Gaupe, who came willingly to the police station. She told Macé that half a dozen tailors had given her work. But the one who had annoyed the concierge by spilling water was called Voirbo. Yes, she cheerfully acknowledged, she had been his mistress. But now he was married. He used to live in the rue Mazarin, but she had no idea where he lived now. She went on to say that he was a strange man who seemed to do very little work, yet he always seemed to have money.

"Did he have any special friends?" asked Macé. The girl recalled a little old man Voirbo often drank with. He introduced him as Père Desiré. And on another occasion, Voirbo had introduced her to Père Desiré's aunt, "Mother Bandage," who lived in the rue de Nesle.

Mother Bandage proved easy to trace. Père Desiré, she said, was her nephew Desiré Bodasse, an upholsterer of mean habits, whose investments brought him an income of 1,800 francs a year—not a fortune, but ample for a man with such niggardly temperament.

Macé recalled the " + B + " mark on the stocking—"B" might stand for "Bodasse"—and took Mother Bandage to the morgue to see the remnants in which the limbs had been wrapped. She immediately identified the " + B + " mark—she had sewn it on herself. She was also able to identify the jersey and a part of her nephew's trousers.

Why had no one missed the old man? Because, said Mother Bandage, he was an eccentric recluse who liked to be alone. On one occasion he had vanished for six weeks; it turned out that he had spent that time in hospital, masquerading under another name, so the hospital authorities could not trace him and make him pay for his treatment.

They went to call at Bodasse's apartment in the rue Dauphin. Here Macé met with a surprise. The concierge was certain Bodasse was still alive. She had seen him in the street that morning, and on the previous evening, they had seen his shadow on the blind of his room.

It looked as if the whole investigation had collapsed again. Macé left a note for Bodasse, and decided to go and interview Voirbo, who certainly sounded like the man with the hamper.

But, as Mathilde Gaupe had said, Voirbo was no longer at his old apartment in the rue Mazarin. From the landlady,

Macé learned that Pierre Voirbo was a man of dissipated habits who was also a police spy. He pretended to be an anarchist, and made rabid anti-authoritarian speeches, when all the time he was reporting the activities of the comrades to the police. He had recently married for the second time, but his old friend Bodasse had not attended the wedding. Voirbo said they had quarrelled because the old miser had refused to lend him 10,000 francs to begin housekeeping.

When Mother Bandage insisted that the articles of clothing *were* the property of her nephew, Macé decided to break into Bodasse's apartment. The place proved to be in perfect order. The clock was ticking. And on the mantelpiece, there were two candle holders, each holding eight candles. These contained 15 stumps and one complete candle, while in the grate were 17 used matches. Macé inferred that someone had been visiting the apartment for the past 15 days, lighting one candle per evening to give the impression that Bodasse was still there.

Mother Bandage was able to show Macé the secret drawer where Bodasse had kept his wallet and his securities. It was, as Macé expected, empty. But when Macé opened the case of a watch hanging over the bed, a slip of red paper fell out. It contained a list of numbers of Italian Government stock. The stock were pay-to-bearer securities, which could be negotiated like banknotes.

Back at Voirbo's lodgings, Macé confirmed that the landlady had heard nothing more from him. He asked about rent, and learned that Voirbo had paid up his arrears when he left. He had paid with an Italian Government security, and the landlady directed Macé to the money changer she had used to cash it. This man had kept a record of its number. It was one of the securities listed in the back of the watch. Voirbo had, at last, connected himself to the disappearance of Desiré Bodasse.

The charlady of Voirbo's flat also had an interesting story. He was usually the laziest and most untidy of men. But one morning in mid-December—she thought it was the 17th— she had found Voirbo already up when she arrived, and the whole place scrubbed. He had explained that he had dropped a bottle of cleaning fluid, which had made such a smell that he had to clean out the whole place. The charlady thought this was an unlikely story—why should he clean the place up himself when she was coming the next day?

Macé was hoping to catch Voirbo red-handed in Bodasse's lodgings, and placed two plain-clothed policemen on guard. But after a week, Voirbo had still not appeared. Then Macé learned that Voirbo had approached the building, seen the detective, who was an old acquaintance, and asked him what he was doing there. And the detective, without dreaming that he was talking to the man they wanted to trap, told him the whole story... So Voirbo now knew the police were after him. And Macé knew he still had no case. Even the evidence of the Italian security could be discounted, for Voirbo would undoubtedly say that it was a loan.

It was time for Macé to confront his quarry. Voirbo was asked to call at the police station. Face to face with him at last, Macé summed him up as a highly dominant and energetic individual, although he described his slightly hang-dog manner as that of a broken-down stockbroker or a commercial traveller who adulterated his wines. Thirty years of age, round faced, with dark eyes and a dark complexion, he was obviously a man of considerable physical strength. He talked to Macé as if they were colleagues—which was, in a sense, true—and remarked blandly that he had thought of offering his services to Macé, but had been told that, due to Macé's youth and inexperience, this would be pointless. Macé declined to take offense. Instead, he told Voirbo that he heard his name mentioned favorably and thought of asking for his help in trying to find Bodasse. Voirbo, no doubt wondering what kind of fool Macé took him for, said he would be glad to offer his assistance. His own theory, he said, was that Bodasse had been killed out of jealousy, and that the killer was a butcher named Rifer, a heavy drinker. He also mentioned that he thought Rifer had three accomplices. Then he took his leave, accepting 100 francs for expenses. Macé immediately set out to learn what he could about Rifer and his "accomplices." Two of them had perfect alibis—they were in jail throughout most of December.

Macé now saw that Voirbo was spending his expenses on drinking with the chief suspect, Rifer, and plying him with so much drink that Rifer could hardly walk. There was nothing Macé could do about it. One morning, Rifer had DTs and was dragged off to an asylum, where he died that night. The next morning, Macé found Voirbo seated in his office when he arrived, asking whether Macé meant to drop the case now Rifer was dead.

Macé was determined that the time had come to arrest Voirbo and put an end to the farce. But he was a small man, and no match for Voirbo. So he excused himself, explaining that he had to write a letter, and offering Voirbo the morning papers. Then he wrote instructions to his subordinates to surround Voirbo and arrest him. He also ordered all exits to be closed, and instructed a messenger to remove the fire irons on the pretext of replenishing the coal bucket. As Voirbo was expounding his latest theory about a girl who had helped Rifer to kill Bodasse, he fumbled in his pocket for an address, and a card fell out. Macé handed it to him politely—noting as he did so that it contained the address of a shipping agent. His bird was intending to fly.

The precautions proved unnecessary. As the policemen came into arrest him, Voirbo went pale, but made no resistance. He insisted that he knew nothing whatever about Bodasse's death, and skillfully parried all the questions. His demeanor showed that he felt that Macé had no evidence. And he was right. As an examining magistrate, Macé knew he lacked proof that Voirbo was a murderer. Voirbo was searched, and in his pocket, Macé found a ticket from Le Havre to New York in a false name—Saba.

In front of an instructing judge, Voirbo sullenly refused to answer questions. Meanwhile, Macé went to Voirbo's present apartment at 26 rue Lamartine. Voirbo's wife was there, a fragile little creature, who obviously had no idea of the true character of her husband. She told Macé that she had brought Voirbo a dowry of 15,000 francs, and that he had brought 10,000 francs to the marriage—the precise amount of Bodasse's securities. But when they forced the box that should have held the securities, it was empty.

A side table contained a pile of newspapers. Macé found these intriguing. Several were about the mystery of the legs found in the well in the rue Princesse. Others were about the murder of a man called Bernard at Aubervilliers. Voirbo also seemed extremely interested in the murder of a servant girl called Marie Carton in the rue Placide. Finally, there were a number of newspapers about a recently executed killer called Charles Avinain, who had intercepted farmers on their way to market with loads of hay, and offered them a better price than they could normally expect. The farmer was invited back to Avinain's hut near the river at Clichy and murdered with a hammer blow; the dismembered body was then thrown into the river, and the hay sold. But finally one of the victims escaped, and the police called at the riverside hut, and caught Avinain as he tried to escape through a trapdoor into the cellar. Avinain's last words from the steps of the guillotine had been: "Never confess." Obviously, Voirbo felt he had something to learn from Avinain.

The search for the missing bonds continued. In the cellar there were two barrels of wine. Macé's keen eye noted that the bung of one of them was slightly higher than the other, suggesting that it fitted less tightly. Closer examination showed that it held a piece of string. When Macé pulled on the string, a soldered tin cylinder came out. It proved to contain the missing securities.

Back at the commissary, Macé told Voirbo he wanted to have him photographed.

"Why this additional outrage?" asked Voirbo angrily.

Macé replied: "So I can show it in Aubervilliers and in the rue Placide." Voirbo indicated, with some strong language, that nothing would induce him to hold still long enough for a photograph to be taken—evidently he had good reason to avoid being recognized.

The next day, Macé decided to make one more attempt to extort a confession. He took Voirbo back to his former lodgings in the rue Mazarin, now occupied by a young couple. His first task was to discover precisely where the furniture had been during Voirbo's tenancy. This convinced Macé that there was only one spot in the room where Voirbo could have dismembered the body—on a round table in the center. Macé had also noted that the tiled floor sloped down towards a bed in a recess. If Macé's own account is to be believed, he then proceeded to make the kind of speech that fictional detectives make in the final scene when all the suspects have been gathered together in the same room. "You are now going to see how very important an accessory may be in a criminal case and how the most trifling detail may enable us to complete an inquiry..." And after five minutes or so of this sort of thing, he concluded: "In short, in this very room which was once Voirbo's, an accessory is going to reveal to us the name of the murderer..."

He then took in his hand a carafe of water, and raised it in the air. "You observe a perceptible slope down towards the bed. If a body was dismembered in this room, the blood must have run down like this...", and Macé poured the water. Voirbo watched with horror as it flowed across the floor, to form... to form a pool under the bed. Then a workman was brought in, and ordered to remove the tiles. As each tile came up, dried bloodstains could be clearly seen on the sides and underneath. Voirbo was now trembling, and when Macé asked him to hold a candle while a cupboard was searched, he burst out: "Don't continue. I am guilty. I will tell you everything. But take me away from this accursed place."

Voirbo's confession, cited at length in Macé's *My First Crime*, is one of the most fascinating documents in criminological history. He admits that his real name is not Voirbo, but says he prefers to be regarded as an orphan, since he hated his father, who often screamed at him: "You shall perish by my hand." "Perhaps he is the cause of all my misfortunes" says Voirbo, and for once this sounds like something more than the usual self-pitying rationalization so typical of criminals. Voirbo was determined to achieve success and security, by fair means or foul. Marriage to Mlle Rémondé seemed the answer; but he had told her parents that he possessed 10,000 francs in securities, and he had to produce it. The miserly Bodasse refused to lend him the money, so Voirbo decided that he had to die. Bodasse often went to Voirbo's room, in the hope of meeting some of his workgirls. (In those days—the 1860s—most workgirls would accompany a gentleman for 10 francs, which was a day's wages.) Voirbo lured him there on 14 December 1868, telling him that his fiancée would be spending the evening there. Then he struck him a tremendous blow from behind with a flat iron. And when Bodasse still moved, Voirbo slit his throat with a razor. After that, he undressed down to his underwear and chopped up the body—not hacking at it with a cleaver, which would have made too much noise, but placing the sharp edge against the flesh, then striking it with a metal bobbin.

And, just as Macé had supposed, it had been the encounter with two gendarmes when he was carrying parts of the body to the river that decided Voirbo to dispose of the remaining limbs down the well in the rue Princesse—a decision that eventually cost him his life. Voirbo did not die on the guillotine, but cut his throat with a razor smuggled in a loaf of bread.

2

But Voirbo had made an even more serious mistake: failing to pay heed to the advice of the murderer Charles Avinain: never confess. In 1869, and for many decades afterwards, there was no method of discovering whether a bloodstain was animal or human. Microscopic examination could distinguish a bloodstain from an iron stain or fruit juice, by showing the corpuscles, but only if the blood was fresh, or clotted; once blood dries, the corpuscles become indistinguishable. As early as 1841, a French doctor named Barruel believed he had found a method of determining whether blood was animal or human, by heating it with sulphuric acid; he claimed that human blood gave off a sweat-like odor. But, as far as is known, this absurd claim was never tested in court. Around 1850, Ludwig Teichmann had developed a test based upon the shape of blood crystals; the suspected blood was mixed with acetic acid on a microscope slide, and a grain of salt added; then if heated delicately over a bunsen burner, haematin (or haemin) crystals would form. But it needed a highly skilled analyst to distinguish between, say, human blood and bullock's blood; moreover, if he was not careful, he burnt his fingers, and the slide shattered. Voirbo *could* possibly have been convicted by this test, but it is doubtful—even if the blood had been proved to be human, he could have protested that it might be due to some previous tenant giving himself a bad cut . . .

After 1859, the invention of the spectroscope (by Bunsen and Kirchhoff) provided an infallible test for haemoglobin (the red coloring matter in blood) by its characteristic spectral lines; but this could still not distinguish between animal and human blood. But science was taking some slow and cautious steps in the right direction. It had started in the 1650s when young Dr. Christopher Wren—later the architect of St. Paul's—invented what was basically the first hypodermic syringe—a slender quill with a pointed tip, attached to a bladder. By 1667, Jean Denys, a professor of mathematics at Montpellier, was curing some of his patients with injections of lamb's blood. But in the following year, a patient died, and he was ordered to stop. Why had the patient died? Herein lay the secret forensic scientists were still seeking two centuries later. Around 1814, Dr. James Blundell, whose specialty was midwifery, began experiments in blood transfusion, and discovered that a dog could be virtually drained of blood, and then revived by the blood from another dog. But if he used sheep's blood, the dog died. By 1818, Blundell was ready to try human blood transfusions. And, like Jean Denys, he was baffled by the fact that they were sometimes triumphantly successful, and sometimes the patient died. When this happened, the first symptom was pain in the arm and rapid heart rate, then back pains, vomiting, diarrhoea, and black urine. The answer was not discovered until 1875, when the German physiologist Leonard Landois noticed that if red blood cells from one animal were mixed with the serum—the blood's basic liquid—of an animal of a different species, the red cells "clumped" together like lumps in porridge; sometimes they even burst, which seemed to account for the black urine. But how could this explain why human blood sometimes caused human blood to react in the same way? There could be only one answer: there must be several types of human blood.

By the end of the nineteenth century, blood transfusions were still being attempted by many enterprising doctors, but the patient's chances were only 50:50. It was obviously of immense importance to discover why. The Viennese surgeon Theodore Billroth had theorized that there must be different types of blood that were incompatible; but how did one go about identifying them? In 1900 a young doctor named Karl Landsteiner, Assistant Professor at the Institute of Pathology and Anatomy in Vienna, asked five of his colleagues to give him samples of their blood, and also took a sample of his own. In each of these, he separated the colorless serum from the red blood cells (he did it with a centrifuge machine, but it works just as well if the blood is simply left exposed in a test tube), then put serum from one of the participants, Dr. Stork, into six test tubes. Then he mixed red blood cells from the six participants into each test tube. In four out of six cases, it "clumped" (or agglutinated, to use the correct scientific term). He took six test tubes of another lot of serum, and repeated the experiment—this time only two lots clumped. And when this had been repeated six times over, Landsteiner had an interesting table that told him something quite new: that there were not just two different human blood types, but three. It was a matter of simple mathematical reasoning. Landsteiner could see that there must be something in the serum which "opposed" certain blood cells, and he called this something agglutinin, while the factors they seemed to dislike he called agglutinogens. If there were only two types of blood, it should have been quickly possible to predict each reaction in advance, as he dropped one lot of blood cells into another lot of serum. But it proved to be more complicated than that, and he had to assume that blood came in three types, A, B, and C (C was later called O). Two years later, one of Landsteiner's do-nors, Dr. Adriano Sturli, discovered a type of blood serum that did not clump A or B—which meant that it must have characteristics of both. This "typeless" blood group became known as AB.

In the year after Landsteiner's experiment, a young doc-tor named Paul Uhlenhuth, another assistant professor—this time at the Institute of Hygiene in Greifswald—announced an equally important discovery: he had learned how to distinguish between animal and human blood. His insight derived from Pasteur's tremendous discovery of the princi-ples of vaccination in the late 1870s. Pasteur had been studying a new treatment, invented by a doctor named Louvrier, for the deadly disease anthrax. The treatment did not work; but two of the cows Pasteur had injected with anthrax recovered on their own. And when he tried injecting them with an even more virulent dose of anthrax, it had no effect at all; the cows had developed "resistance" to an-thrax. Pasteur discovered that he could "weaken" germs by subjecting them to heat, and that these "attenuated" germs could be injected into animals, or humans, without endangering life. Moreover, the result was a "resistance" that brought immunity from more powerful forms of the same germ. Pasteur demonstrated his method triumphantly by injecting a small boy who had been bitten by a mad dog with a weakened version of the rabies virus; it took 14 injections, which set up an immune reaction before the original virus could do its deadly work, and the boy recovered.

What was actually happening was discovered in 1890 by Emil von Behring, the assistant of Pasteur's great rival Koch, the man who isolated the germs of tuberculosis and cholera. Von Behring realized that when the blood is invad-ed by a toxin—a protein poison—the serum develops an anti-toxin to resist it. Five years later, the Belgian Jules Bordet, working at the Pasteur Institute in Paris, tried to understand the basic principles of "immunity," and founded the science of serology—the study of body fluids, such as blood. (*Sera* is a Sanskirt word meaning "to flow.") He first identified the factors of blood serum that destroy bacteria by causing the cell wall to rupture, then went on to discover that these same factors will also destroy foreign blood cells. Moreover, if milk or egg-white was injected into guinea pigs, their blood developed the same defensive reaction against it. And if a few drops of milk or egg-white was then mixed with the guinea pig's blood serum, their protein came under attack, and was deposited as a white precipitate. The defensive substances became known as precipitins.

It was the Viennese doctor Paul Uhlenhuth who saw the consequences of this discovery. If proteins produce these defensive reactions in blood serum, then presumably one type of blood—say, a goat's—will produce an immune reaction in another type—say, a rabbit's. In fact, Bordet had already shown this by his experiment in which "foreign" blood cells were ruptured in serum. Uhlenhuth tried injecting chicken blood into a rabbit. It worked like Bordet's egg-white in guinea pigs and produced a defensive reaction. Then he took a test tube of the immunized rabbit's serum and introduced a drop of chicken blood; it instantly turned cloudy. And when a rabbit was injected with human blood, its serum would react just as readily to a drop of human blood. And not only to blood; it would react just as well to a bloodstain dissolved in salt water.

To us, it is obvious that these two discoveries—of human blood groups and of the precipitin test—were among the most important advances ever made in forensic science. Yet the contemporaries of Landsteiner and Uhlenhuth showed themselves curiously unappreciative of their achievement— Landsteiner had to wait until 1930 before his discovery was rewarded with the Nobel prize. The French were quicker to grasp the importance of Bordet's discovery, and in 1902, a French murderer was sent to the guillotine by the precipitin test, when it proved that the blood on his clothes was human, and not, as he claimed, the result of skinning a rabbit. As a consequence, the precipitin test generally became known in Europe as the Bordet test—and this in spite of the fact that Uhlenhuth had already used his test to establish the guilt of a murderer in 1901.

3

Around 1 p.m., on 9 September 1898, the mothers of two small girls in the village of Lechtingen, near Osnabrück, became worried when they failed to return home. And when Jadwiga Heidemann and her neighbor Irmgard Langmeier called at the school, they learned that their children had not been to classes that day. The whole village joined in the search, and at dusk, the dismembered body of 7-year-old Hannelore Heidemann was found in nearby woods—some parts had been scattered among the trees. An hour or so later, the remains of 8-year-old Else Langmeier were found hidden in bushes; she had also been mutilated and dismembered.

The police learned that a journeyman carpenter named Ludwig Tessnow had been seen entering Lechtingen from the direction of the woods, and that his clothes seemed to be bloodstained. Tessnow was soon arrested, but insisted that the stains on his clothes were of brown woodstain. A powerful microscope would have revealed that this was a lie, but the Osnabrück police knew nothing of forensic science, and let him go for lack of evidence. But a policeman visited Tessnow in his workshop, and contrived to knock over a tin of woodstain so that it ran down Tessnow's trousers. In fact, it dried exactly like the other stains. And since Tessnow continued to work in the village, his neighbors concluded that he must be innocent. He remained until January 1899, when he went to work elsewhere.

Two and a half years later, a frighteningly similar crime occurred near the village of Göhren, on the Baltic island of Rügen. On Sunday 1 July 1901, two brothers named Peter and Hermann Stubbe, aged 6 and 8, failed to return home for supper, and parties went into the nearby woods, carrying burning torches and shouting. Shortly after sunrise, the bodies of both children were found in some bushes, their skulls crushed in with a rock and their limbs amputated. Hermann's heart had been removed, and was never found.

The police interviewed a fruit seller who had seen the two

boys in the late afternoon; they were talking to a carpenter named Tessnow. Tessnow had recently returned to Rügen, after traveling around Germany, and was regarded as an eccentric recluse. Another neighbor recollected seeing Tessnow returning home in the evening, with dark spots on his Sunday clothes.

Tessnow was arrested and his home searched. Some garments had been thoroughly washed, and were still wet. And a stained pair of boots lay under the stone kitchen sink. Tessnow remained calm under questioning, and seemed to be able to account satisfactorily for his movements on the previous Sunday. Again, he insisted that stains on his clothing were of woodstain.

Three weeks before the murders, seven sheep had been mutilated and disemboweled in a field near Göhren, and their owner had arrived in time to see a man running away; he swore he could recognize him if he saw him again. Brought to the prison yard at Greifswald, the man immediately picked out Tessnow as the butcher of his sheep. Tessnow steadfastly denied it—he was not the sort of man, he said, to kill either sheep or children . . .

The examining magistrate, Johann-Klaus Schmidt, now recalled a case in Osnabrück three years before, and contacted the police there. When they told him that the name of their suspect was Ludwig Tessnow, Schmidt had no doubt that Tessnow was the killer. But how to prove it? At this point, his friend Prosecutor Ernst Hubschmann of Greifswald recollected reading about a new test for human bloodstains. And at the end of July, Uhlenhuth received two parcels containing Tessnow's Sunday clothes, brown-stained working overalls, and various other items, including a bloodstained rock, probably the murder weapon. It took Uhlenhuth and his assistants four days to examine over a hundred spots and stains, dissolving them in distilled water or salt solution. The overalls were, as Tessnow had claimed, stained with wood dye. But they also found 17 stains of human blood and nine of sheep's blood. It took the Rügen prosecutor a long time to bring Tessnow to trial—German justice was extremely slow-moving—but when he eventually appeared in court, Uhlenhuth was there to give evidence and explain his methods. Ludwig Tessnow was found guilty of murder and sentenced to death.

—————————————————— 4 ——————————————————

England, as usual, was far behind the Continent in making use of the new discoveries. Spilsbury's mentor Dr. William Willcox—who gave evidence at the Crippen trial—was the expert the Home Office called upon when the evidence concerned identification of bloodstains. Around the turn of the century, the chief methods in use depended on the power of haemoglobin to attract oxygen. When hydrogen peroxide was poured on a bloodstain, it foamed. A West Indian shrub called guiaiac produced an extract that turned blue in the presence of oxygen; when mixed with turpentine and blood, it turned blue because the haemoglobin extracted oxygen from the turpentine. The same thing happened with a substance called benzidine, developed at the turn of the century; this also turned blue in the presence of blood. These were the tests known to Dr. Willcox, although he became aware of the "Bordet test" (which, as we know, is basically identical to the Uhlenhuth test) at about the time it became known to French criminologists.

The first British murder case in which the identification of blood played a crucial role occurred in 1910 in Slough. A 70-year-old widow, Isabella Wilson, was discovered in the back room of her second-hand clothes shop in the High Street with a cushion tied over her face with a scarf; she had died of suffocation. Marks on the side of her head indicated that someone had given her two or three violent blows, perhaps with a blunt instrument. Mrs. Wilson was known to carry a purse in the pocket underneath her apron, sometimes with as much as 20 gold sovereigns in it. The purse was now empty, so it was obvious that the motive for the attack had been robbery. On the table there was a piece of brown paper with circular marks on it, and Mrs. Wilson had been known to keep her sovereigns wrapped in brown paper inside her purse; the murderer had left it behind.

Police investigations soon pointed towards a man called
William Broome, a 25-year-old unemployed motor mechanic. Until recently his family had lived next door to the dead
woman's shop, but they had now moved. But on the day of
the murder, several local people had recognized Broome
walking around Slough. Two days after the murder, patient
sleuthing tracked down Broome in Harlesden, and he was
asked to go to the police station and make a statement. As
soon as Broome insisted that he had been in London all day
on Friday 15 July—the day of the murder—the police must
have known they had their man; they had a dozen witnesses
to say he had been in Slough. Asked if he had any money,
Broome produced a few shillings, and said that he had 20
sovereigns back in his room in Albany Street, Regent's
park—the exact amount the dead woman usually carried on
her.

The dead woman's fingernails were long, and one of
them was broken—it looked as if she had scratched her
assailant. Broome had two scratch marks on his face, and
several people had asked him about them. Broome had told
each of them a different story; now he told the police that
the scratches had occurred during his fight with a bookmaker about money he had won on a race—an obvious attempt
to account for the 20 guineas.

In court in Aylesbury on 22 October 1910, it soon became
obvious that Broome's major mistake was in claiming that
he had not been in Slough on the day of the murder—the
prosecution was able to produce witness after witness who
had seen him.

But the part of the trial that excited most interest was
what the local newspaper, the *Bucks Herald*, called "the
sensational evidence of Dr. Willcox," "fresh from his part
in the sensational Crippen trial." Scotland Yard had asked
Dr. Willcox to examine various items, including a pair of
the prisoner's boots—worn on the day of the murder—and
fingernails snipped from the dead woman, as well as some
of Broome's clothing. Broome had carefully cleaned and
polished the boots after the murder, but had failed to notice
a bloodstain on the instep. Willcox had tested this blood-

stain and found it to be "mammalian." Asked if this meant it could be human, Willcox replied yes. He was also able to say that there was human skin on one of the victim's nails, and that it had blood in it. A German or French pathologist would have taken pride in determining whether the blood was human, and whether it was of the same blood group as the murderer or victim. Willcox had evidently decided that it was not worth so much trouble. To do the doctor justice, he may have felt that the evidence against Broome was so conclusive that his work would have been wasted. He himself made it more conclusive by describing how he had examined the brown paper under a microscope, and found minute specks of gold, proof that it had wrapped gold sovereigns. Other pieces of brown paper made it clear that the number of sovereigns had been exactly 20—the number found in Broome's lodgings.

The outline of the crime was now clear. Broome had obviously gone to Slough that day with the specific intention of robbing Isabella Wilson; and since she knew him well, he must also have intended to kill her. The blood on his instep indicated that, after knocking her to the ground, he must have stamped on her head—if he had merely stepped in her blood, the bloodstain would have been on the sole or the heel. Then he went into a nearby pub for a pint of beer, and caught the next train back to London. After the judge had summarized this evidence, the jury took only 13 minutes to find him guilty and he was sentenced to death.

A few days after Broome had been found guilty, Willcox gave evidence at another murder trial. The name of the accused was Mark Wilde, and he was charged with the murder of a rich industrialist named George Henry Storrs. The "Gorse Hall murder" has become known as one of the strangest mysteries of the century. On the evening of 1 November 1909, a slightly built man with a blond moustache broke into Gorse Hall—situated on a lonely moor in Cheshire—and threatened the cook with a revolver. Storrs grappled with him while his niece and some servants ran for help; but when they returned to the house, Storrs was dying from 15 stab wounds, and the intruder had escaped. But he had left the revolver behind. It proved to have no firing pin, but was of a peculiar type known as a "Bulldog."

A man named Cornelius Howard, a cousin of Storrs, was arrested and charged with the murder. The evidence against him looked black, but it was entirely circumstantial, and when he produced a strong alibi, the jury acquitted him.

Five months later, the police made another arrest, this time a man named Mark Wilde. They had found several witnesses who swore that the Bulldog revolver belonged to Wilde. On the night of the murder, Wilde had returned home with bloodstains on his clothes, and told his mother that he had been in a fight. Police also discovered that he had owned two more revolvers, but that he had dismantled them and disposed of the pieces—he admitted that this was in case he was suspected of the Gorse Hall murder. Wilde was charged with killing Storrs, and his bloodstained jacket and trousers were sent to Willcox for examination.

What Willcox did was to apply the Uhlenhuth test to the bloodstains; he discovered that they were human blood. But since Wilde had already admitted this, it made no real difference to the outcome. Once again the jury decided that the evidence was inconclusive. Mark Wilde was acquitted, and the Gorse Hall mystery remains unsolved.

In fact, it seems fairly certain that Storrs knew the identity of the man who stabbed him, although he denied it as he lay dying. Seven weeks earlier, in September 1909, Storrs had asked the local police for protection. He claimed that, on the previous evening, as they were sitting at dinner behind drawn blinds, a man's voice had shouted: "Hold up your hands or I'll shoot," and that a shot had then broken the window. Storrs claimed that he raised the blind, and saw a revolver pointing at him. He wanted to run outside to tackle the man, but his wife prevented him . . .

This story sounds highly unlikely. Would the man shout "Hold up your hands" when he could not see the family behind the drawn blind? Would Storrs have raised the blind after a shot had been fired through the window? If the man intended to kill Storrs, why did he not then fire a second shot? It sounds as if Storrs made up the story—and fired a shot through his own window—to provide a plausible reason for asking for police protection. Why did he not tell them the true reason? Presumably because he preferred to keep it to himself. Did his wife and niece know the true reason? That also seems unlikely; but they probably believed whatever Storrs chose to tell them.

During the next seven weeks there was a police guard at Gorse Hall, and an alarm bell was installed which could be heard in the neighboring town of Stalybridge. On the night of the murder the guard was withdrawn because there was a local election, and all police were required for keeping order. Whoever killed Storrs knew this, and chose his opportunity. As he burst into the dining-room, he shouted: "Now I've got you." He was a man with a grudge, and most writers on the case seem to agree that the likeliest reason for the grudge was that Storrs had seduced some mill-girl—perhaps the man's wife or sister. Whatever the reason, Storrs chose to die without naming his assailant.

Could Willcox have done more to solve the mystery? There was one possibility that he overlooked: to test the stains for their blood group. In 1902, Uhlenhuth's colleague Max Richter had tried testing dried bloodstains to ascertain their blood group, and discovered that the reaction was weak if the stains were more than a few weeks old. Yet there were abundant bloodstains on Wilde's jacket and trousers, and there must have been bloodstains at Gorse Hall—made when Storrs was dying—to compare them with. The reason that he did not do so is almost certainly, as incredible as this sounds, that he had never heard of Landsteiner's discovery of blood groups.

5

For, in fact, Landsteiner's achievement remained virtually unknown for many years. The man who first grasped the significance of his discoveries for criminology was not an Austrian or a German, but an Italian lecturer on forensic medicine in Turin, Dr. Leone Lattes. During his postgraduate studies, Lattes had met Max Richter, and learned of his experiments with bloodstains. He also learned of Richter's conclusion that it is not easy to determine the group of a bloodstain once it is more than a few weeks old.

In 1915, Lattes proved him wrong. An absurd domestic drama was brought to his attention by a local doctor. A construction worker named Renzo Girardi was being tormented to death by his wife's insane jealousy. And three months earlier, he had provided her with reasons for a particularly violent outbreak; he had returned home unusually late one Saturday night, and the next morning his wife had discovered bloodstains on his front shirt-tail. She was quite convinced that Girardi had been consorting with a woman, and had made his life a misery ever since. He asked Dr. Lattes to help him prove his innocence.

If Richter was correct, the case was hopeless, for the bloodstain was now three months old. But Lattes was willing to try. First, he took a blood sample from Girardi, and ascertained that it was group A. Girardi's wife Andrea was persuaded to give a blood sample: she was group O. And a friend of Andrea Girardi's who had been in the house at the time was also persuaded to give a sample—she had been menstruating, and it was just conceivable—although she indignantly denied it—that she might have wiped herself on the shirt-tail after Girardi had removed the shirt. She also proved to be blood group A, like Girardi.

Lattes became fascinated by this ridiculous little problem, and went to immense pains to solve it. First he soaked the bloodstains out of the cloth with distilled water, going to extraordinary lengths to determine their exact weight. (All this care was to avoid "pseudo-agglutination," an apparent "clumping" which appears when the serum is too strong or there are too many red blood cells in the test solution.) And in spite of the age of the stains, he succeeded in manufacturing several drops of liquid blood. And when the blood was placed in tiny "wells" on dimpled microscope slides, and drops of fresh blood—both A and B—were added, he observed that the unknown blood "clumped" with group B. That meant it had to be group A. So it could have been

Girardi's own, or that of the family friend. But examination under a microscope revealed none of the epithelial (skin or mucus) cells that would be present in menstrual blood. (If Lattes had merely wished to disprove that Girardi had picked up the bloodstains from a menstruating mistress, he could have confined his efforts to this test alone.) A medical examination of Girardi revealed that he suffered from prostate trouble which caused occasional bleeding. Mme Girardi was convinced, and her husband's domestic life became, for the time being, more peaceful.

Lattes had shown that even three-month-old bloodstains can reveal the group to which they belong (which suggests that the Gorse Hall case could probably have been solved by the same method). And he was so delighted with his triumph that he went on to a systematic study of serology—all bodily fluids—and its application to crime detection. His enthusiasm increased when, soon after the Girardi case, he was able to prove the innocence of a man accused of murder by demonstrating that the bloodstains on the man's coat were of his own group, and not that of the victim. Of course, it would have been unfortunate for the suspected murderer if he and the victim had shared the same blood group—by now, it had been established that 40 per cent of people are group A, 40 percent cent group O, 15 per cent group B, and 5 per cent AB. But it was clear that, while blood grouping could not finally establish the guilt of a suspected killer, it could sometimes establish his innocence. Lattes went on to invent a greatly simplified method of testing, placing tiny flakes of blood on the microscope slide, adding fresh blood, and placing another slide on top. The serum in the fresh blood would do all the work of dissolving the suspect blood cells and, where the blood was of another group, produce clumping.

In 1922, Lattes gained some of the recognition he deserved when he published a treatise on *The Individuality of Blood*, which soon became a criminological classic. (One of its incidental effects was to bring Landsteiner, who had now emigrated to America, some of the recognition that had long been his due.) And in 1926, his intervention in a preposterous *cause célèbre* of mistaken identity momentarily made the Italian public aware of the importance of the new science of blood grouping.

The Bruneri–Canella Affair is virtually an Italian version of the Anastasia controversy, but with distinctly comic overtones. In March 1926, the caretaker of the cemetery in Turin saw a man apparently praying, but when he looked more closely, noticed that he was stealing a bronze vase from a grave, and trying to conceal it under his coat. The man was chased into the church, and attempted suicide. When he was caught, he insisted that he had lost his memory, and was confined in the asylum at Collegno. Whether the doctors believed his story of amnesia is unclear, but some Italian newspapers printed the man's photograph, asking if anyone knew his identity. In Verona, a certain Professor Canella thought he recognized the photograph as that of his brother, who had been a headmaster until he vanished during the Macedonian campaign in the First World War. The professor hastened to the asylum, and was convinced that he had found his long-lost brother. His parents and friends had mixed opinions about the man's identity, but when the man's wife came, she instantly declared that the amnesiac was her missing husband. The ex-headmaster was released and he and his ''wife'' went off for a second honeymoon.

Soon after, the Préfecture in Turin received an anonymous letter declaring that Canella was an impostor named Mario Bruneri, a printer of Turin who was wanted for fraud. Bruneri had a criminal record, and when the police finally checked his fingerprints with those of the amnesiac (taken in the asylum) they were found to be identical. That obviously settled it—except that Italian public opinion remained unconvinced. An inquiry instituted by Professor Mario Carrara, using the identification techniques described by Locard, also concluded that ''Canella'' was a fraud. But ''Canella's'' family insisted that he was the missing headmaster, and his wife seemed contented to accept him as her long-lost husband.

Now the highly respected Professor Lattes intervened. We

can almost certainly establish the truth, he declared, by simply examining the blood of "Canella," and of his parents and children. Blood groups are hereditary, and if both parents turned out to be group A, and "Canella" was B, then he would certainly not be their son. If Canella was O, and his children were A or B, the same would apply. I need, said Lattes, merely one tiny drop of the blood of each individual concerned, and I can almost certainly establish beyond all doubt whether "Canella" is really the thief Bruneri.

It would be highly satisfactory to record that Lattes carried out his test, and settled the question once and for all. Unfortunately, he was flying in the face of human nature. "Canella" did not want the test; neither did his wife or family. Like the Tichborne claimant, Canella continued to play his game of evasion, frequently infuriating the magistrates with barefaced effrontery. When one of Bruneri's own children ran towards him crying "Papa, papa!" "Canella" replied: "Go, little one, and find your family as I have found mine." Someone asked him: "Why deny that your son recognizes you?", and "Canella" replied with a wink: "It's not for the son to recognize the father, but for the father to recognize his son." And since Mme Canella remained convinced that she had regained her husband, the science of blood grouping was as helpless as the science of fingerprinting to dislodge the impostor.

In the autumn of 1928, the problem of human blood grouping became the central issue in a German murder case, and suddenly made forensic experts aware of the importance of the "Lattes test". (The case may also have been instrumental in securing Landsteiner the Nobel prize in 1930.) On the morning of 23 March 1928, a 19-year-old student, Helmuth Daube, was found dead in the street outside the family home in Gladbeck, in the Ruhr—his father was a school principal. The student's throat had been cut from ear to ear, and at first, suicide was suspected. But when a doctor began to undress the corpse, he realized that the genitals had been mutilated with a knife. This was murder, probably with sexual overtones. On the previous evening,

Daube had been to a neighboring town to a students'
fraternity meeting, and he had walked back home with
another student called Karl Hussmann. Hussmann was fetched
from his home nearby, and asked to account for his movements; he claimed that Daube had walked him home to his
front door, then left him. But the police inspector investigating the death noticed that Hussmann's shoes were heavily
bloodstained. And when it emerged that Hussmann was a
homosexual with sadistic tendencies, and that he and Daube
had at one time been sexually involved, the inspector
became fairly certain that Hussmann was the killer. Inquiries
among their fellow students indicated that Hussmann liked
to dominate Daube, even to the point of causing him
physical pain, and that Daube had recently worked up the
determination to make a break.

Hussmann's first excuse was that the blood on his shoes
came from a cat that he had killed when he caught it
"poaching". Then he remembered that he had found a frog
and torn it to pieces on his way home the night before. The
Uhlenhuth test soon disproved both these stories, revealing
that the blood was human. Even faced with this evidence,
Hussmann maintained his innocence. Now, finally, the shoes
and other bloodstained items of wearing apparel were sent
to the Institute of Forensic Medicine in Bonn, and tested by
its director, Dr. Viktor Müller-Hess. He discovered that
there were two sets of bloodstains on the clothing, group A
and group O. Hussmann was type O, while Daube was A.
This evidence should have convicted Hussmann of murder.
But, as in so many other cases involving "expert evidence," the jury was skeptical, and returned an acquittal
verdict. From the point of view of justice, the case was a
failure. But it had the effect of making forensic scientists
aware of the importance of Landsteiner's discoveries, and
the methods that Leone Lattes had developed to apply them
to criminal investigation.

The next important step forward was taken by Fritz
Schiff, the Berlin serologist who had arranged the transla-
tion of Lattes's book *The Individuality of Blood* in German.
Like many fellow serologists, he was troubled by certain

shortcomings in the Lattes method. This, as we have seen, depended on Landsteiner's discovery of "agglutinins" in the serum and "agglutinogens" in the red blood cells. In the red blood cells, the agglutinogens can be of two types, antigen A and antigen B. The corresponding bodies in the serum are called antibody α and antibody β. In the various blood groups, these are distributed as follows:

Group A: Antigen A in the cells, antibody β in the serum.

Group B. Antigen B in the cells, antibody α in the serum.

Group O: No antigens in the cells, antibodies α and β in the serum.

Group AB: Antigens A and B in the cells, no antibody α or β in the serum.

So cells of type A showed clumping when mixed with B serum, because B serum contained antibody α. They also clumped in O serum, which also contains antibody α. But type O blood cells could be mixed with all three other sera without clumping—as can be seen from the table above. So in theory, it was easy for a serologist to determine the group of an unknown sample by a simple process of elimination.

Unfortunately, experience showed that the β antibody in type O lost its strength much quicker than the α antibody, so type O could easily be mistaken for type B. The β antibody might vanish from a group A bloodstain, so it appeared to be type AB. Such a complication might seem to make the blood test virtually useless. But Fritz Schiff saw that there was a solution. Fortunately, the antigens in the red blood cells retain their strength. So if the cells from an old dried bloodstain were added to a fresh serum they ought to produce *some* effect, even if they have lost their ability to "clump." They ought, in fact, to attract and absorb some of the serum's antibodies. And if a method could be discovered of measuring *exactly how much* of the antibody was absorbed, then the group of the old bloodstain could still be determined. It was a matter of measuring the effectiveness of the serum before and after the cells had been added to it. But although Schiff worked hard at this problem, he was unable to solve it. The method was discovered by a young forensic scientist named Franz Josef Holzer. He used a "dimpled" microscope slide—a glass slide into which a number of tiny wells have been drilled. Into each of eight "wells" he dropped group O serum, diluted with salt solution. Each well contained a solution twice as dilute as that in the previous one. Now he dropped fresh blood cells into each—exactly the same quantity—and examined each well to find out how much each serum had agglutinated the red blood cells. This allowed him to determine how much each serum would "clump" the red cells. He then repeated the same test with his unknown bloodstain, and then re-checked each serum to see how far it had lost strength. It was then again a simple matter of elimination. (A type O bloodstain would produce no clumping at all; AB would produce twice as much as A or B, since it contained both antigens, and so on.)

In 1931, Holzer demonstrated the effectiveness of his method in a rural murder case. A farmer named Franz Mair was found dying in his own barn, his skull split open with several blows of a sharp weapon like an axe; he was inclined to carry his money and his bank-book in his pocket, and these were now missing. The dead man's stepbrother Karl summoned the police. Karl's story was that he had been asleep when awakened by the screams of Franz Mair's mistress-housekeeper. Blood on the toe of Karl's slipper made him a leading suspect. Holzer, who was an assistant at the Forensic Institute at Innsbruck, not far from the murder site, was summoned to examine the scene of the crime. He took the slippers, and a pair of Karl's trousers with a small bloodstain, back to his laboratory. To his disappointment, he obtained no result with the ordinary Lattes test for blood groups. The slipper stains had been absorbed into the leather, and for some reason, the dried blood on the trousers proved equally difficult. He then turned to his own more delicate method, using his dimpled slides, and was delighted when this yielded unmistakable results; the blood was group O, the dead man's blood group. Karl Mair had allowed his own blood to be tested; this proved to be group A. Faced with the evidence, Karl Mair finally broke down, and confessed to attacking his stepbrother with a hoe, which he afterwards cleaned thoroughly. He had taken Franz's money and bank-book and hidden them in the hay, where they were subsequently found. Holzer's evidence led to a guilty verdict against Karl Mair.

One obvious problem was that if Karl Mair and his stepbrother had both been group O, then Karl would probably have got away with the murder. And since A and O are the major bloodgroups, the possibility that murderer and victim happen to share it is obviously great. So considerable relief was felt in forensic circles as researchers began to discover other substances that made one lot of blood different from another. Group A was made up of two different strengths labeled A1 and A2. Then, in the mid-1920s, Landsteiner and his assistant Philip Levine discovered another blood group system by injecting rabbits with human blood. The consonants of the words "immune" suggested calling these new groups M and N. A person could be either M, N or a combination of the two, MN. The M group was found to have various other properties (or "specificities"), given such labels as Mv and MA, all of which are found in all humans, but only some of which are found in apes (whose blood is otherwise very similar to that of human beings). Experiments with rhesus monkeys in 1940 by Landsteiner and Alexander S. Weiner led to the discovery of another M factor which was labeled rhesus, or Rh. In 1927, Landsteiner and Weiner had identified yet another factor labeled P. And so the discoveries continued: the "Lutheran" factor in 1945, the Kell factor the following year, then the Lewis, Kidd, Duffy, and Diego factors, named after their discoverers in 1946, 1950, 1951, and 1955, and Yt, I, Xg, and Dombrock in 1956, 1956, 1962, and 1965.

Obviously, all these additional discoveries made it increasingly simple to identify the blood of a certain individual, just as Bertillon's 11 measurements each helped to pin down a particular individual. What was emerging was, in effect, a kind of "blood fingerprinting."

Yet even more exciting was Landsteiner's realization that "serology" literally applies to all the secretions of the human body, such as saliva, mucus, tears, semen, and sweat. All this culminated in the discovery in 1984 of "genetic fingerprinting," the ability to identify an individual by his sperm—or by a hair follicle—as precisely as by his fingerprints—a subject we shall discuss at the end of this chapter.

———————————— 6 ————————————

In Great Britain, the first major case solved by forensic serology occurred in 1934. The pathologist involved was one of Spilsbury's most active contemporaries, Dr. (later Sir) Sydney Smith. Born in Roxburgh, New Zealand, in 1883, Smith studied medicine at Edinburgh, and was greatly intrigued by stories of the late Dr. Joseph Bell, the man on whom Conan Doyle based Sherlock Holmes; Bell often astonished his students by deducing the occupation of his patients from their appearances. When serving in Egypt as the principal medico-legal expert of the Egyptian government, Smith was asked to report on the body of a British official who had been found shot through the head. It could have been suicide, but there was no suicide note. Smith observed a small nick on one of the fingers of the right hand, and noticed that the man's shirt and waistcoat were unbuttoned. He deduced that the nick had been made when pulling back the bolt of the pistol, and that the only reason for unbuttoning the waistcoat and the shirt must have been that he had originally intended to shoot himself in the heart, then changed his mind. The result of these observations was a verdict of suicide.

The case of the murder of 8-year-old Helen Priestly in Aberdeen called upon Smith's powers of deduction. The child lived with her parents in a tenement in Urquhart Road, and on the afternoon of Friday 20 April 1934, her mother sent her to the local Co-operative store to buy a loaf of bread. When Helen failed to return after a quarter of an hour or so, her mother went out to look for her. A search was instituted, which became more frantic when a local boy said he had seen Helen being dragged up the street by a man.

Late in the afternoon, a man noticed a sack sticking out from a recess under the stairs. It contained Helen's body, and her bloomers were missing. Blood trickling between her thighs suggested that this was a sex crime. The child had been strangled.

Everyone in the tenement building was questioned. But when the police doctor discovered that there was no sperm on the child's combinations or in her vagina (semen stains show up blue under ultraviolet light, and sperm can be clearly seen under the microscope), and that the injuries seemed to have been inflicted with some instrument like a poker or a pudding spoon handle, they realized that the killer could have been a woman.

Next to the stairwell where the body had been found lived a family named Donald: the husband, John, was a hairdresser. He had been at work at the time Helen had disappeared. The wife, Jeannie, had a reputation as a woman of violent temper. Her daughter, also called Jeannie, had once been a friend of Helen Priestly, but they had quarrelled, and the two families were not on speaking terms. Jeannie Donald was known to dislike Helen, because the child used to run past her door shouting the nickname "Coconut." The Donalds were the only family in the tenement who had not taken part in the search for Helen.

Questioned routinely by the police, Jeannie Donald seemed to have an excellent alibi; she had been out shopping for food, and also called at a shop to buy some fabric. On her way back, she said, she had seen a crowd of women standing at the street corner, and Mrs. Priestly crying. But when examined more closely, the alibi began to seem less convincing. She had named the prices she had paid for various items, such as eggs, but had given the prices charged the *previous* Friday. The shop where she claimed she had searched for fabric had been closed that afternoon. The group of women had not seen her pass them, but she could have seen them from a tenement window. Now the police searched the Donalds' flat, and found some stains in a cupboard that might be blood. A police doctor said they *were* bloodstains, and the Donalds were both arrested. In fact, laboratory examination showed that the stains were not of blood. But by now, the police were reasonably certain that Jeannie Donald had killed Helen Priestly.

Sydney Smith was then Professor of Forensic Medicine at Edinburgh, inheritor of Britain's first chair in legal medicine. Regarded by many as one of Spilsbury's chief rivals, he was now asked to see what he could make of the Helen Priestly case. If Jeannie Donald had murdered Helen in a fit of temper, then the evidence had to be sought in the Donalds' flat. Like Sherlock Holmes, Smith studied the clues. First, there was the sack; it was made of jute, had contained cereals, and had a hole in the corner. In the sack there was a double handful of washed cinders, some human and animal hairs, and a little household fluff. Most working-class families reused their cinders on the fire, but Jeannie Donald was the only housewife in the tenement who got rid of the ash by washing them. In the "trap" in Jeannie Donald's sink wastepipe, the police found cinders similar to those in the sack. The sack had come from Canada filled with cereals, and had arrived in Aberdeen via London and Glasgow. Jeannie Donald's brother worked near a farm, and often brought her potatoes in a sack. Sacks such as this one were found on the farm. The hole in the corner had apparently been made when the sack had been hung on a hook; in the Donalds' flat there were other sacks with similar holes.

The human hairs in the sack were not from Helen Priestly's head, and they showed signs of having been "permed". Smith managed to obtain samples of Jeannie Donald's hair from a hairbrush; it had the same signs of artificial waving. Under a comparison microscope, the fluff—made up of around 200 types of fiber—proved to be similar to that found in the Donalds' flat, and not in any other flat in the tenement.

But most significant were a number of small bloodstains found on such items as newspapers (dating from the day before the crime), linoleum, washing clothes, and a scrubbing brush. Smith's laboratory tests found them to be type O, the same as that of Helen Priestly; but could it also be that of Jeannie Donald? Mrs. Donald refused to have a blood sample taken (which was her legal right), but Smith managed to obtain one of her used sanitary towels; it revealed that she was of a different blood group. (In his account in his autobiography *Mostly Murder,* Smith does not specify which.)

But the clinching evidence came from blood on the dead child's combinations. The article that had been used to simulate rape had ruptured her intestinal canal, releasing bacteria. Smith sent samples of the child's bloodstains, and those on articles from the Donalds' flat, to the bacteriology laboratory at the university. The Professor of Bacteriology, Thomas Mackie, discovered that Helen's intestines had contained a rare bacterium that he had never seen before. And the same bacteria were found in the bloodstains on the kitchen floorcloths. It was irrefutable evidence that the cloth had been used to mop up Helen's blood.

Smith was not inclined to believe that Jeannie Donald intended to kill Helen Priestly. He had learned that Helen had an enlarged thymus, and that this gave her a low resistance to various infections; it also meant that Helen would be more prone to fainting than a normal child. Smith theorized that Helen had run past the Donalds' flat chanting "Coconut", and that on her way back, Jeannie Donald had been waiting for her, prepared to chastise her. She was a vengeful woman—the police learned that she had once wrung the necks of all the chickens in a hotel because the chef had reprimanded her—and probably grabbed Helen by the throat or shoulders. Helen fainted. Believing her dead, Jeannie Donald decided to simulate a rape murder, and rammed some hard object into her vagina. The child woke and began to scream (a slater working next door said he had heard a scream at about the correct time) and Jeannie Donald tried to silence her by throttling. In fact, the pressure caused the child to vomit, and it was probably the vomit in her windpipe that caused her to suffocate.

If Smith was correct , Jeannie Donald was not guilty of murder but of manslaughter. He suggested this to the defense. But they underestimated the strength of the scientific evidence, and decided to plead not guilty. It took the jury only 18 minutes to find Jeannie Donald guilty of murder, and she collapsed in the dock—the first sign of emotion she had shown during the trial. Her death sentence was later commuted to life imprisonment, of which she served 10 years.

7

It must be admitted that the latest discovery in serology—that bodily fluids like saliva and semen also contain the "blood fingerprint"—proved to be less successful in practice than the scientists had hoped. It is true that the Japanese solved a rape murder by this method in 1928, but this was largely because the murderer confessed. The victim was a 16-year-old itinerant fortune-teller named Yoshiki Hirai; she had been killed not far from the town of Niigata, and two suspects were arrested. One of them, a mentally defective beggar, confessed to the crime; but Dr. K. Fujiwara, director of the Forensic Medicine Institute in Niigata, soon ascertained, from the rapist's sperm, that his blood group was A, and that the beggar's was O. But that of the other suspect, Iba Hoshi, was A, and when confronted with this evidence, he confessed. Without this confession, there would have been no case against him, for Yoshiki Hirai might have been raped by any number of men with A-type blood. In a sense, it was a new version of the old medieval problem: that the only evidence that would finally convince a jury was a confession.

And this, as Jügen Thorwald points out in *Crime and Science,* was the major problem confronting the forensic serologist in the mid-twentieth century. One of Spilsbury's best-known cases of 1939 concerned the murder of a 9-year-old schoolgirl named Pamela Coventry, who disappeared on her way back to school on the afternoon of 18 January. Her naked body was found in a ditch near the Hornchurch aerodrome the following morning, her knees bound against her chest with insulated wire. A bruise on her chin suggested that she had been knocked to the ground with a blow, then she had been strangled manually. But either the rape had not been completed, or there was not enough sperm for a determination of blood group. However, as the limbs were straightened out, the butt of a home-rolled cigarette fell out—the murderer had evidently been smoking as he bound her.

The police inferred that the girl had been dragged into some house or out-building after being knocked unconscious; there was snow on the ground, and the killer would not have risked a sexual assault outdoors in the early afternoon.

Spilsbury's colleague Dr. Roche Lynch, director of the Department of Pathological Chemistry at St. Mary's, decided to try to determine the killer's blood group from his saliva on the cigarette butt. This depended on whether the man was a "secretor"—that is, whether his bodily fluids contained blood antigens. Fortunately, only 14 per cent of the human race are non-secretors. But unfortunately, the killer of Pamela Coventry proved to be one of these non-secretors.

Police suspicions now centered on a factory worker named Leonard Richardson, who had been away from work on the afternoon of Pamela's murder; his wife was in hospital having a baby, so he was alone in the house. Richardson was a non-stop smoker who rolled his own cigarettes. Tiny blood spots were found on his raincoat, and the precipitin test showed them to be of human blood; but determination of blood group then required a fairly large stain, and there was simply not enough. By examining some dirty handkerchiefs belonging to Richardson, Lynch was able to determine that, like the killer, he was a non-secretor. But although laboratory tests showed that the tobacco and cigarette paper were of the same type used by Richardson, the jury found the evidence unconvincing; the trial was stopped on its fifth day, and Richardson allowed to go free.

A second case of the same year proved to be equally frustrating for the police and the forensic experts. On the evening of 21 May 1939, a well-to-do businessman named Walter Dinivan was battered unconscious at his villa in Bournemouth, and died later the same night. On the table in his sitting-room there were two glasses, suggesting that Dinivan had been offering a drink to someone he knew during the course of the evening. The safe had been opened with his own keys, and emptied. Police inquiries showed that Dinivan sometimes entertained prostitutes in his home, and it was one of these who led them to a man called Joseph Williams, a cantankerous old man who knew Dinivan.

The police had two promising clues: a thumbprint on a glass that had contained beer, and a number of cigarette butts. Chief Inspector Leonard Burt of Scotland Yard was able to identify the thumbprint as that of Williams. By stealthily abstracting a cigarette butt that Williams had smoked while being interrogated, Burt was able to provide Roche Lynch with material for a blood group test. Williams proved to be a secretor whose group was AB—the smallest of the blood groups—which proved to be the same as that on cigarette butts found in Dinivan's sitting-room. Circumstantial evidence was also strong: Williams had been broke up to the time of the murder, and had since apparently had plenty of money—he claimed he had won it on a racehorse.

The case against him seemed watertight. Yet the jury ignored the fingerprint evidence, ignored the blood group evidence, and returned a verdict of not guilty. The same night, in a fit of alcoholic remorse, Williams admitted to *News of the World* reporter Norman Rae that he had murdered Walter Dinivan. But it was too late. The reporter revealed his secret only after Williams's death in March 1951.

Yet it could be argued that the skepticism of the jury in these two cases was not entirely unjustified, for the techniques of blood testing have never been as straightforward—and therefore as reliable—as fingerprint evidence. In 1948, in a brilliant piece of investigation, the fingerprint expert Superintendent Fred Cherrill, was able to identify a killer who had left no other clue than two partial fingerprints. The victim was an old lady called Mrs. Freeman Lee, who lived alone in a house in Maidenhead. When she failed to take in her milk for two days, police broke in and found her body in a chest in the hall; she had died of suffocation. The killer was evidently an intruder who had taken care to leave no fingerprints. But Cherrill found the lid of a tiny cardboard box under the bed, with two faint partial fingerprints on its sides which were only five-sixteenths of an inch in width. They were nevertheless enough to identify a housebreaker named George Russell, who lived in the area and who was duly hanged for the murder.

Yet eight years later, in 1956, German forensic science came close to convicting the wrong man on bloodstain evidence. In the first six months of 1956, there occurred a horrific series of apparently motiveless murders around Düsseldorf—the city that, in the late 1920s, had been terrorized by the sadistic murders committed by the sexual pervert Peter Kürten. On 31 October 1955, two lovers, Friedhelm Behre and Thea Kürmann, had vanished after an evening out. A month later, a car was found submerged in a pond near Düsseldorf, and the bodies of the lovers were found in the back seat. They had apparently been battered into unconsciousness while love-making, and the killer had then driven the car into the pond, jumping clear when it reached the edge.

On 7 January 1956, two men were seated in a car in a secluded spot on the bank of the Rhine when a man wearing a stocking mask wrenched open the door and shot one of them, a homosexual lawyer named Servé, through the head. Another man climbed into the car and struck the other man—a young workman with whom Servé was having an affair—on the head, at the same time whispering to him to sham dead. This saved the workman's life. After an unsuccessful attempt to start the car, the man in the mask took Servé's wallet and vanished.

On 7 February 1956, another car vanished, and its owner reported that his chauffeur, a young man named Peter Falkenberg, had vanished with it. At the same time, a Frau Wassing reported that her daughter Hildegard had not returned from a date with a chauffeur named Peter. It was found parked with its headlights on, and pools of blood inside indicated that some violence had taken place. Later, two bodies were found in a burnt-out haystack; both had been battered unconscious, and the man had also been shot.

It looked as if a sexual pervert who preyed on courting couples was responsible for all five murders. In the town of Büderich, detectives heard of a young man called Erich von der Leyen, who lived close to the burnt-out haystack, and who had a reputation for oddity—he was said to have attacked children with a hayfork. Von der Leyen proved to be a traveling salesman for an agriculture firm, and his alibi for the night of the murder—that he had been at home—was uncorroborated. The entry in his log-book for the night of the murder also seemed implausible. Finally, spots like bloodstains were found in his Volkswagen. When these were examined by the Forensic Institute, they were reported to be human bloodstains. The Institute also said that stains on von der Leyen's trousers were human blood. Some of the spots were blood group A, others AB. Von der Leyen's bloodgroup was A_2. But the victims Friedhelm Behre and Thea Kürmann had both been group B; so had the chauffeur Falkenberg. The police asked a forensic expert to see if he could determine the age of the bloodstains on the trousers. In the course of examining them, he came upon more stains which were undoubtedly blood—but blood which showed epithelial cells under the microscope, indicating that it was menstrual blood. Further tests showed that it was the blood of a dog. In fact, von der Leyen had insisted that the only way he might account for the blood in his car was that a girlfriend's dachshund had leapt into the car when it was in heat. Following this discovery, the police asked the Forensic Institute to re-check the bloodstains on the seat covers. With embarrassment, the Institute admitted that a mistake had been made. Their Uhlenhuth test had indicated that the blood was human, but when tested again, it proved to be dog's blood. The Institute blamed the company that had supplied the serum. Erich von der Leyen was immediately released—he had been intensively interrogated for many days, on the assumption that he was the killer, and would eventually confess.

On 6 June 1956, a forester named Spath was patrolling woods near Büderich. When he saw a courting couple embracing in a parked car, he stood still; at the same time, he realized that a man was creeping towards the car holding a revolver. Spath ran towards him, and the man fled, throwing away the gun. He caught up with him in a hollow, and told the man he was under arrest. At the police station in Büderich, the man identified himself as Werner Boost, a 28-year-old mechanic from Düsseldorf; he protested that he was married and the father of two children, and hardly the type of man to attack courting couples. But his police record showed that he had started life as a juvenile delinquent, had been in prison for robbing cemeteries, and fined for possessing firearms without a permit. Confronted with the evidence of the revolver, Boost explained that he was a moralist who detested sexual license, and that he intended to frighten the couple. "These sex horrors are the curse of Germany."

As he interrogated Boost, Kriminal Hauptkommissar Mattias Eynck recalled that in 1945, about 50 people had been killed near the town of Helmstedt, trying to cross from the Russian to the British zone. At that time, Boost had been in Helmstedt, acting as a guide to refugees who wanted to cross the border. When he had left Helmstedt, the killings had ceased.

While Eynck was interrogating Boost, a man named Franz Lorbach asked to see him. He was a nervous man with watery eyes, and Eynck recalled an entry he had found in Boost's diary: "Lorbach seems in need of another shot." Lorbach, he thought, looked like a drug-taker.

Lorbach was there to denounce Boost as the unknown sex killer. In 1952, he explained, he and Boost had teamed up to poach in the woods around Büderich. Boost was obsessed by courting couples, whom he seemed to hate. When they came upon a couple engaged in love-making, Boost and Lorbach would spy on them, then Boost would threaten them with a gun and rob them. These couples never reported the attacks. Then Boost graduated to rape. In a home laboratory he concocted narcotic substances and gases that could cause unconsciousness, and used these on courting couples. He and Lorbach would then rape the unconscious women.

Dr. Servé, it seemed, had been murdered by accident. Boost assumed the lovers in the car were male and female, and wrenched open the door, killing the man. Lorbach opened the other door and struck the young workman, ordering him in a whisper to pretend to be dead.

Lorbach went on to write a full-length confession, telling also how Boost had planned robberies; Lorbach had been in agony for months, trying to avoid taking any further part in Boost's crimes. This is why, as soon as he heard of Boost's arrest, he had hastened to the police; he was afraid that Boost might talk himself out of jail.

The revolver found in the woods proved to be the one that had killed Dr. Servé. In a laboratory in Boost's cellar, the police found materials for the manufacture of cyanide gas, and toy balloons, which Boost used to fill with the gas and release in the cars of his victims. At his trial, Boost was found guilty of the murder of Dr. Servé, and sentenced to life imprisonment; Lorbach received six years. If a perceptive forensic scientist had not noticed the menstrual bloodstains on the trousers, Erich von der Leyen might have been sentenced instead of Boost.

_____ 8 _____

So, by the end of the 1950s, the record of serology in the solution of violent crime was rather less impressive than that of fingerprinting or the microscopic examination of fibers. Even in cases where a bloodstain might have played a crucial part, it was often unidentifiable, either because it was too small, or was on material that confused the issue.

On 29 July 1950, the body of a woman was found lying in the road in south Glasgow; her injuries suggested that she had been struck by a heavy lorry. But when the police studied the scene of the accident, they began to have doubts. There were *two* sets of intersecting skid marks on the road, and it seemed unlikely that the victim had been struck by two vehicles. There were also signs of blood and skin tissue ground into the road for some distance from the body, as if she had been dragged under a vehicle. But there was no broken glass, or other evidence of an accident, near the body.

The woman was identified as Catherine McCluskey, a 43-year-old blonde who was the mother of two illegitimate children. She lived not far from the place where her body was found, and the police discovered that she had many male friends.

In the pathology laboratory at St. Mungo's College, the body was examined by Professor Andrew Alison. The first thing that struck him was the absence of the expected injuries on the woman's legs. Those who are knocked down by a car usually have some injury at bumper-level; lack of such injuries suggested that although the woman had been killed by a car, she had not been knocked down by one. And that combination of circumstances sounded like murder.

Interviews with Catherine McCluskey's friends suggested that one of her boyfriends included a policeman; she had told a woman friend that the policeman was the father of one of her children. Inspector Donald MacDougall of the CID made discreet inquiries, and learned that, on the night Catherine McCluskey had died, a policeman named James Ronald Robertson had told a colleague that he intended to take some time off from his beat to see a blonde. In fact, gossip indicated that Robertson was an enthusiastic pursuer of the opposite sex. And on the night of the murder, he had told the constable who shared his beat that he intended to take a short time off to run someone home in his car. In fact, he had been away two hours, and when he returned, seemed tense and agitated; his trousers were dirty and he told his fellow constable that his car exhaust had fallen off.

Robertson was arrested and his house was searched. There the detectives found a quantity of stolen property, including car registration books and a radio. Robertson's car, a large black Austin, was also discovered to be stolen. The number plates were found to be those of a tractor. Robertson admitted that the car was not his own—he claimed that it had been abandoned in a road near his home, and he had finally decided to "claim" it.

Robertson also admitted what the police experts soon confirmed: that his car had been the vehicle that caused Catherine McCluskey's death. His story was that they had quarrelled, and she had got out of the car to walk home. He relented, and reversed the car to pick her up; instead, he knocked her down and ran over her. He tried to drag her out from under the car, but her clothing was entangled in the propellor shaft. So he moved the car backwards and forwards until the body was free, then drove away...

There were two major objections to this story: first, that the lack of leg injuries indicated that she had not been knocked down accidentally, second, that the propeller shaft was boxed in, so it could not possibly catch her clothing.

Professor John Glaister—the man who had reconstructed the bodies in the Ruxton case—felt there was a more plausible explanation. When Robertson was arrested he had been carrying a cosh, and there was a bloodstain on it. Glaister believed that Robertson had used the cosh to knock Catherine McCluskey unconscious, then had deliberately driven the car over her, and reversed it over the body. Her injuries were consistent with this theory. Unfortunately, the bloodstain on the cosh was too small to test by the Lattes method—obviously, the evidence against Robertson would have been very strong indeed if the blood had proved to be of the murdered woman's group. In spite of which, it was bloodstain evidence that finally convinced the jury of Robertson's guilt—or rather, the completely inexplicable lack of it. If, as he claimed, Robertson had tried to drag the body free of the car, his trousers and cuffs would have become heavily bloodstained. There were no such bloodstains. It followed that Robertson had simply driven the car over the unconscious girl after he had struck her to the ground. Then he had driven away without touching the body. On this evidence, Robertson was convicted of murder—his motive, apparently, was to cease paying maintenance for his illegitimate child—and he was sentenced to hang.

The case is an example of the best kind of crime detection—

the combination of forensic skill with logic and common sense. If Glaister had been a slightly less old-fashioned pathologist, he might well have applied the latest serological methods to the bloodstained cosh, and perhaps succeeded in demonstrating that the blood was of the victim's group. Yet in the event, the forensic evidence about her injuries combined with the lack of bloodstains on Robertson's trousers built an overwhelming case for calculated murder.

Unfortunately, the combination was not always so satisfactory. Four years after the Robertson case, slipshod forensic work and a certain carelessness on the part of the police led to one of the most controversial murder trials of modern times. The defendant was a brilliant young neurosurgeon, Dr. Sam Sheppard, of Cleveland, Ohio. On the night of 3 July 1954, Sheppard's wife Marilyn was murdered in her own home, and her husband apparently knocked unconscious by an intruder. What actually happened is still—long after Sheppard's acquittal and death—a matter of controversy.

Sheppard's story—as told to the police—was that he had fallen asleep while watching television, although two dinner guests were still in the room. He was awakened, he claimed, by his wife's screams, coming from her bedroom. He rushed upstairs, only to be struck on the head from behind and knocked unconscious. When he woke up, he realized that his wife had been violently attacked. He ran to his son's bedroom, and was relieved to see that the boy was peacefully asleep. Then he heard a noise downstairs, and ran down to see a shadowy figure running from the back door towards Lake Erie. He gave chase, but was again knocked unconscious. When he woke up again he found himself half-in and half-out of the lake. For some reason, his assailant had pulled off his T-shirt. When he got back into the house he realized that his wife was dead, and rang the local mayor, who soon brought the police. Sheppard's brother Richard also arrived, together with the coroner, Samuel Gerber. They discovered that Marilyn Sheppard was dead, struck on the head repeatedly with a blunt instrument; she was clad only in a pajama top. The place was in chaos, with drawers pulled out and their contents scattered. Sheppard said that the "burglar" had been a big, bushy-haired man. But if he *was* a burglar, why had he apparently taken nothing, and even ignored money? Coroner Gerber quickly reached the conclusion that there had been no bushy-haired intruder; Sheppard had killed his wife during a quarrel, then tried to make it look like a burglary. His wife had died—according to medical evidence—at around 4 a.m., yet it had been another two hours before Sheppard had telephoned the mayor. His own account was that he had been dazed and unconscious much of the time; Gerber suspected that he had used the time to get rid of the murder weapon (if it was a blunt metal instrument, he only had to scrub it, dry it and replace it in the tool shed) and to set the scene of the "burglary."

In later accounts of the case, Gerber has come in for a great deal of harsh criticism; it is alleged that he was jealous of Sheppard's success and went out to "get" him. Yet anyone who studies the above account of the murder can see why he was suspicious. According to Sheppard, Marilyn had left him asleep in an armchair (wearing a corduroy jacket, according to the dinner guests) and gone off to bed. He sleeps on for between three and four hours—an unlikely contingency; most people who doze off in the armchair—particularly with the light on—wake up after half an hour or so and realize where they are. He is awakened by his wife's screams—an intruder has broken into the house, possibly walking past the sleeping man, and gone upstairs, where he proceeds to rifle drawers. When the woman wakes up, he attacks her to keep her silent—but does not content himself with knocking her unconscious, but goes on battering her with about 35 blows. Downstairs, the husband pauses to remove his corduroy coat and place it on the settee before he rushes upstairs to see why his wife is screaming. He is knocked unconscious by the intruder; but the intruder, instead of making off, goes downstairs and waits around until the husband again rushes down to pursue him out of the house. Yet again, the man somehow succeeds in knocking him unconscious, and he lies in the lake for a considerable period—perhaps an hour—before waking up, going indoors, and discovering that his wife has been murdered . . .

The whole story was highly suspicious. Why did the dog not bark when the intruder broke in? If Sheppard had been lying with his head on the beach, why was there no sand in his hair? Why was Sheppard's bloodstained watch—which he had been wearing presumably when he fell asleep—found in the garden, in a canvas bag he used on his boat? Sheppard explained later that the watch had become bloodstained when he felt for his wife's pulse; in which case, why remove it and put it in the garden? Gerber felt, understandably, that Sheppard had noticed the bloodstains while he was frantically trying to "stage" the burglary, and hid it outside.

By the time the inquest was convened on 26 July 1954, the investigation had discovered that Sheppard had been having an affair with a pretty technician at the hospital; she had moved to California, and Sheppard had been to stay with her a few months before. At the inquest, Sheppard declared indignantly that he had never had any sexual relations with the girl, Susan Hayes. Since the police knew this to be untrue, they must have found themselves wondering how many other things Sheppard was lying about. Four days later, Sheppard was arrested and charged with his wife's murder. The local newspapers were all convinced of his guilt, and announced it without regard to the laws of libel.

There were, of course, certain points in Sheppard's favor. If he had killed Marilyn with a bludgeon, he would have been sprayed with blood; but he had only one bloodstain on the knee of his trousers, and he claimed this must have happened when he was taking his wife's pulse. His brother had seen a cigarette stub floating in the lavatory; but Sheppard was a non-smoker, and Marilyn smoked filter tips; this was not a filter stub. Sheppard's medical bag had been up-ended, and an ampoule of morphine capsules was missing, which suggested that the intruder could have been a drug addict, crazed with the desire for a "fix." But then, Sheppard had had time to get rid of bloodstained clothes—perhaps rowing out into the lake, and weighting them with a stone. (This seemed a more likely explanation of the loss of his

T-shirt than that the ''burglar'' had taken it off him because his own was bloodstained.) The cigarette butt could have been thrown there by one of the policemen, or by one of the two dinner guests. (It vanished when a policeman flushed the toilet.) And he could have got rid of the morphine as easily as the clothes and the murder weapon. (A lake is a convenient item for a murderer to have at his back door.) Finally, the strange absence of fingerprints in the house could be interpreted in two ways—as an attempt by the intruder to destroy all evidence of his presence, or an another attempt by Sheppard to substantiate his burglar fabrication . . .

The prosecution rested its case after Susan Hayes had appeared in court and admitted to having an affair with Sheppard that started 18 months before the murder; she confessed that they had made love in cars and in a flat above the clinic. She also admitted that Sheppard had spoken to her about getting a divorce. After all this, the defense had an uphill task to depict Sheppard as a wronged innocent. On 21 December 1954, Sheppard was found guilty of second degree murder (because there was no evidence of premeditation) and sentenced to life imprisonment.

In June 1957, the Sheppard case became headline news again when a convict named Donald Wedler, serving a 10-year sentence for a hold-up in Florida, confessed to the murder. He claimed that he had been in Cleveland that day, and had taken a shot of heroin. Late at night he had stolen a car, then looked for somewhere to burgle. He had entered a big white house on the lakefront, seen a man asleep on the settee, and gone upstairs. A woman had awakened as he had been rifling her dresser, and he had beaten her with an iron pipe. Then, as he fled downstairs, he had encountered a man, whom he had also struck down with the pipe. Then he had flung the pipe in the lake and driven away. The story was obviously inconsistent with the one Sheppard had told—first, about being struck down from behind in the bedroom, and second, in failing to mention the struggle in the garden. Although a lie detector test seemed to indicate that Wedler was telling the truth, no further action was taken.

But in 1966, when Sheppard had been in prison for 12 years, an appeal finally succeeded—on the grounds that the newspaper stories had made a fair trial impossible. The conviction was quashed, and a new trial ordered. A young Boston lawyer, F. Lee Bailey, appeared for the defense. He embarrassed the police by revealing that their search for clues had been very casual indeed—they had not even tried to get fingerprints from the watch found in the duffle bag, as well as a key-ring and chain. Bailey accused Gerber of being out to "get" Sheppard through jealousy, and Gerber's angry reply made a bad impression on the court. But the turning point of the case was a photograph of Sheppard's bloodstained watch. The face contained specks of blood, such as would have been made if Sheppard had been wearing it when he battered his wife to death. Bailey noticed that there were also "flying" bloodspots *inside* the wristband, which indicated clearly that it had not been on Sheppard's wrist at the time his wife was battered to death, and that therefore the bloodspots had got inside the wristband after Marilyn was killed. This was the kind of Agatha Christie reasoning that impresses juries, and this time, they decided that Sam Sheppard was innocent.

Yet in retrospect, it is difficult to follow their reasoning. If there were spots of blood inside the wrist band, we have to suppose that the watch was lying beside the bed where Marilyn Sheppard was murdered. But it should have been on the wrist of her husband, who was just awakening downstairs. The only other logical explanation is that Sheppard went up to bed after the guests had left, leaving his corduroy jacket downstairs (whether it was on the settee or lying on the floor was a point of controversy at the trial), and removing his watch before getting into bed. We then have to suppose a violent quarrel, perhaps brought on by some talk of divorce, or perhaps by Sheppard's jealousy of his wife (who also seems to have had her admirers) and Sheppard's murder of his wife with a blunt instrument . . .

The fact that Marilyn Sheppard had admirers led one

writer on the case, the Chicago journalist Paul Holmes, to propound an extraordinary theory in his book *The Sheppard Murder Case,* written before Sheppard's final acquittal. Holmes suggested that one of these admirers had observed the light in the Sheppards' house, assumed the doctor was out on a call, and let himself in to enjoy a little hasty love-making. Unfortunately, he was followed by his wife, who battered Marilyn Sheppard to death . . . But this fails to explain why Sheppard failed to see the enraged wife when he rushed into the bedroom.

In his account of the case in *Cause of Death, The Story of Forensic Science,* Frank Smyth argues strongly in favor of Sheppard's innocence, as does Jürgen Thorwald in *Crime and Science.* Yet, as this re-examination demonstrates, the evidence of Sheppard's guilt remains highly convincing. All the same, the plausibility of Wedler's confession reminds us that the murder *could* have been committed by a burglar who was probably a drug addict. But if that is so, it only underlines the total failure of forensic science in a case where it might have been expected to reach important conclusions.

In 1963, while still in prison, Sheppard had announced his engagement to a wealthy—and beautiful—young divorcee from Düsseldorf, who had flown to America to see him. They married, but after his release she sued for divorce, alleging that he carried a heavy axe and a knife, and had threatened her. Sheppard subsequently became a professional wrestler, teaming up with a man named Strickland, and married Strickland's 19-year-old daughter. But it seemed clear that many people still believed he had killed his wife, and Sheppard's health began to fail; he died in 1970 at the age of 46.

———————————————— 9 ————————————————

What was becoming clear, in the 1950s and 1960s, was that in spite of the increasing skills of the forensic scientist, serology had not achieved the same pinpoint accuracy as other branches of scientific crime fighting. A criminal could be convicted by a single hair or a single cloth fiber, but seldom by a single bloodspot. In 1966, the newspapers announced the discovery of the "blood fingerprint" by Drs. Margaret Pereira and Brian Culliford; but they were not referring to some method of identifying the blood of a single individual, but only to new methods of increasing the likelihood that blood came from a certain individual by studying the rhesus factors. Such a method was invaluable in paternity disputes, but not necessarily to a "disappearing body" case in which the only clue might be a single bloodstain. Even cases involving dozens of bloodstains might still constitute a baffling problem in crime detection. Such, for example, was the case of Stanislaw Sykut, a farmer who disappeared from the remote Welsh farmhouse he shared with his fellow Pole Michial Onufrejczyc (pronounced Ono-free-shic) in December 1953. The two ex-soldiers proved to be poor farmers, and their financial problems became increasingly serious; things were made worse by Onufrejczyc's complaint that his partner was lazy, and on one occasion, Sykut complained to the local police that he had been beaten up. Sykut gave his partner notice that he wanted to leave, and asked for the return of the £600 he had paid for a half share in the farm. The last time he was seen alive was on 14 December 1953; when his mail at the post office remained uncollected, the police went to the farm to check up. Onufrejczyc's explanations left them more unsatisfied than ever, and they searched the farmhouse (which was at Cwm Du, near Llandilo, Carmarthenshire) and found the kitchen full of bloodstains—thousands of flying bloodspots which suggested that someone had been beaten to death. One of them even contained a small fragment of bone. Onufrejczyc claimed that Sykut had simply gone back to Poland, and that the blood came from rabbits. Forensic tests showed that it was human blood; whereupon Onufrejczyc changed his story and claimed that his partner had cut his hand in the hay machine.

For months the police searched for the body, with total lack of success. In September 1954, almost a year after

Sykut's disappearance, they finally decided to charge
Onufrejczyc with his partner's murder. At the trial in Swansea,
the defense poured scorn on the circumstantial evidence and
argued that there was no case to answer. There was no body,
which meant that Sykut might still be alive. The jury
disagreed, and found Onufrejczyc guilty of his partner's
murder. But in view of the doubts that still lingered, he was
sentenced to life imprisonment rather than to death. And in
spite of more than 1,000 bloodspots, all the skill of Britain's
forensic scientists was unable to resolve those doubts.

In 1981, the Hampshire police found themselves investigating a case in which there was even less evidence.
Twenty-seven-year old Danny Rosenthal was an intelligent
but highly disturbed young man who lived alone in a
bungalow at 7 Nordik Gardens, Hedge End—a suburb of
Southampton. He had turned his bedroom into a laboratory,
where he was trying to transplant chickens' brains into
fertilized eggs. He had a history of mild mental disorder,
and had been diagnosed schizophrenic. In a strange letter to
the FBI, he had accused his parents, Milton and Leah
Rosenthal, of committing serious crimes against him.

His parents had been separated since he was 12; his
mother lived in Israel, while his father, a retired UNESCO
official, had a flat in Meudon, a suburb of Paris. And in the
early autumn of 1981, it became clear that both his father
and mother had vanished. Leah Rosenthal had been staying
at a health farm in August 1981—she suffered from multiple
sclerosis and could walk only with the aid of crutches. Then
she had decided to go and see her son in Southampton; a
family friend, Dr. Hussein, had put her on the train. On 26
August, she had telephoned Dr. Hussein to say she was
worried about Danny—the implication being that she thought
he was going insane—and wanted to go and discuss it with
her husband in Paris. Dr. Hussein agreed to go with her. But
after that, he heard no more. A few days later, he rang
Danny to inquire about his mother, and was told that she
had returned to London. Dr. Hussein reported his worries to
the Hedge End police, who went to question Danny. He
repeated his story that she had left for London in a taxi. He

allowed the police to look over the house, and although the place was a shambles, with ivy growing down the wall in the living-room, there was no sign of anything suspicious. The police next tried to trace the taxi-driver. But neighbors had not noticed a taxi arriving, and no Southampton driver reported going to Hedge End to pick up a lady with crutches.

On 3 September 1981, Danny Rosenthal was taken to Bitterne police station, and detectives searched the bungalow. Again, they found nothing suspicious; but they asked the Home Office for a full scientific examination of the bungalow. Later that day, Dr. Mike Sayce and Dr. Sue Sims of the Aldermaston Central Research Establishment began their own search. They found the place looking like a rubbish dump, with books, papers, and clothing on the floors.

The police had found bottles of acid, which led Sayce to suspect that Mrs. Rosenthal had been disposed of in the same way as the victims of Haigh, the "acid bath murderer"; but the bath revealed no sign of acid damage. And in the outside drain they found a live frog, which indicated that no noxious chemicals had been flushed down recently.

In the bedroom, Sayce found traces of blood on the floor and skirting board. These could have been from the chickens, which Danny claimed he had killed; but tests back at the laboratory showed that they were human blood, and that its group was B. Danny's was O. And when Sayce examined a hacksaw found in a second bedroom (used as a workshop), he found human skin and muscle tissue, as well as bone. This left him in no doubt that Mrs. Rosenthal had been killed in the bungalow. They returned to search the bedroom, and this time found bloodspots on the legs of furniture, radiating away from the center of the floor. It looked as if Leah Rosenthal had been killed there, probably by a blow, and dismembered after she was dead. Bloodspots were no higher than nine inches off the floor, and if she had been alive at the time, the blood would have spurted higher—perhaps even to the ceiling.

There were also traces of blood on the bathroom taps, on

washed male clothing in the bath, and in a bucket beneath
the kitchen sink. It looked as if Leah Rosenthal had been
dismembered on a bedroom carpet, which had since been
destroyed, then the house had been thoroughly mopped.
Danny Rosenthal must have been certain that he had not left
the slightest trace of blood; the Home Office team showed
that this is far more difficult than it looks.

There was still no direct evidence of murder—Danny
could have alleged that his mother had died of a heart
attack, and that he had panicked and disposed of the body.
But by now, the police had tried to contact Danny's father,
Milton Rosenthal, in Paris, and learned from his housekeeper that he had also vanished. "Milton is dead—Danny killed
him" said Quibillah Shabbaz. She had reported her suspicions to the Meudon police on 17 August, but since she had
a record as a drug addict, they had ignored her.

It seemed that Danny Rosenthal had gone to visit his
father two weeks before the disappearance of Mrs. Rosenthal,
and that Milton Rosenthal had not been seen since. On 12
August 1981, the housekeeper had gone to Milton Rosenthal's
flat— she lived in the basement—to do some typing. Danny
had admitted her with obvious reluctance, and had retired to
the bathroom, where he had run water continuously for two
or three hours. That sounds like a cleaning-up operation.
After Danny had returned to England, the housekeeper had
found bloodstained paper and clothing, and plastic bags and
string in the flat.

Now Dr. Sayce went to Paris to search the flat. The French
police had already found traces of blood around a light fitting
on the bathroom ceiling, and a hacksaw. When Sayce arrived
he found that the bathroom was lit by an extremely dim bulb.
But he had brought his own lighting, and his soon showed
traces of blood on the bathroom floor, which someone had
tried to mop up—a bloodstained "squeejee" mop was found in
the kitchen. Cracks between the lino tiles in the living-room
also contained traces of blood, and there were drag-marks in
blood from the living-room to the . . . to the bathroom. Careful
examination revealed two fragments of bone. It looked, then,
as if Milton Rosenthal had been killed with a heavy blow in the

living-room—perhaps only minutes before the housekeeper had arrived—and had been dragged into the bathroom. Then he had been dismembered and put into plastic bags.

Study of the hacksaw again revealed fragments of human skin, bone, and muscle. There was now clear evidence that Danny Rosenthal had killed both his mother and father—possibly killing his mother when she announced her intention of going to see the father. He was charged with the murder of his mother by the Southampton police, even though an exhaustive search had revealed no sign of the body. Two weeks before his trial, in June 1982, the French police announced that some human remains had been found at Troyes, 100 miles south-east of Paris—the trunk, pelvis, and leg of a male of about Milton Rosenthal's age; they had been dismembered with a hacksaw. Dr. Sayce hurried over to view the remains. Since the head and hands were missing, identification was difficult. But from the long bones, Sayce was able to determine the man's height as just over five and a half feet, like Milton Rosenthal. The blood group was B, like Rosenthal's. As a final test, the hacksaw was used to cut wax, putting black powder on the blade to show the marks of the teeth. Comparing the wax with the bones revealed that the same hacksaw had cut both.

The plastic bin liners in which the remains had been found still bore the store label, and it was found to be close to the travel agent from which Danny Rosenthal had purchased his ticket to Paris. A final item of proof was a metal plate found in Danny Rosenthal's workshop; it bore the name "Zimmer", the manufacturer of Leah Rosenthal's crutches.

At his trial, Danny Rosenthal stubbornly insisted that his parents were still alive, but he was found guilty of the murder of his mother. His mental condition was found to be such that he was confined in Broadmoor.

10

For the forensic scientist, the most satisfying type of case is that in which he is able to help the police establish the identity of an unknown killer. This is what happened in 1983, the year that might be regarded as the centenary of *bertillonage*—for it was in February 1883 that Bertillon had first established the identity of a criminal through his system of measurements.

The Laitners were a wealthy Jewish family who lived in a luxury home in the fashionable Sheffield suburb of Dore. Basil Laitner, a 59-year-old solicitor, lived there with his wife Avril, his son Richard, who was taking a medical degree, and his youngest daughter Nicola, who was 18. On 23 October 1983, Laitner's eldest daughter Suzanne married an optician, and the wedding reception was held in a marquee on the lawn of the Laitner home. Unfortunately, the guests were unaware that they were being closely observed by a man who was hiding in the shrubbery, and that he was fascinated by the beauty of one of the bridesmaids— Nicola Laitner.

Late that night, Nicola was awakened by sounds of a struggle outside her door; as she lay there, wondering if this was a nightmare, she heard her mother's screams. Then, suddenly, her bedroom door opened; the beam of a torch fell on her, and a man with a "Geordie" accent ordered her to keep quiet or he would kill her. He told her that he had killed her mother and father, then added: "I don't want to kill you—I want to fuck you." At knifepoint, he forced her to get out of bed and go downstairs. On the way, they passed a body lying face downward, the head pointing downstairs—her father. The man, who was wearing a blood-stained blue T-shirt—took her out to the marquee on the lawn, and there raped her. He was dirty, smelt of sweat, and had cropped curly grey hair and an incipient beard. Like many rapists, he seemed to believe that his victim should enjoy it. "You've got to enjoy it or I'll kill you. That's where you mum went wrong—she made a fuss." When the rape was over, he took her back into the house—perhaps because she was wearing only a thin nightie and was cold—and in her bedroom, raped her twice more. Then he tied her up, and left the house at dawn, ordering her to "tell the police it was a black man". After a long struggle she succeeded in freeing herself from her bonds. The workmen who arrived early to take down the marquee were startled to be met by a weeping girl dressed in a bloodstained nightgown, who told them that her family had been murdered.

When the police entered the house, they found three corpses. Nicola's brother Richard had been stabbed through the heart as he lay in bed—the killer later admitted that he had entered the bedroom, seen a bridesmaid's dress hanging behind the door, and assumed that the figure in the bed was a girl. Hearing noises from upstairs, Basil Laitner—who had only just returned from an evening out—had run up to see what was happening; the man was lying in wait and plunged the knife into the back of his neck. Laitner fought hard, but the man forced him face-downwards over the banisters, and drove the knife into his back so hard that the point came out of his chest. Avril Laitner heard the sounds and came out of her downstairs bedroom to investigate; she was met by a blood-covered man who was wielding a knife, and who chased her back into her bedroom. The man's intention was probably rape—as his comment. "That's where you mum went wrong" implied—but as Avril Laitner fought back, he stabbed her again and again and cut her throat. Then the killer made his way up to Nicola's bedroom.

The investigators called in a team from the Home Office Forensic Science Laboratory at Wetherby. It was clear from the beginning that the man who would be at the center of the scientific investigation would be the man in charge of the serology laboratory, Mr. Alfred Faragher.

His problem, of course, was that there was too much blood, most of it—perhaps all of it—from the victims. But on Nicola Laitner's bed, there was one bloodstain that appeared more promising. It looked as if it was at about the knee level of a person lying in bed. And since Nicola Laitner had no cuts on her legs, it was a fair assumption that it came from the killer during the course of his rape. At this point in the investigation, the police had a list of about 200 suspects—men who, because of their criminal records, might well be capable of the crime.

Even by the end of the 1960s, so many new blood group factors had been discovered that the popular press was talking about the "blood fingerprint". This was a gross exaggeration, for there was no way of testing a bloodstain to determine which individual it had come from. Yet each new discovery helped to narrow the field: the new M and N factors, the P factor, the Rh and Hr factors. Sometimes, protein analysis of the serum could reveal a factor that was found in only one in a million of the population; others might be found in one in ten. It should be obvious that if a serologist can find the one-in-a-million factor in a blood sample, it can identify a suspect almost as reliably as a fingerprint.

In the case of the bloodstain in Nicola Laitner's bed, Faragher's team discovered a combination of factors that would be found in only one in fifty thousand of the population. And this combination was already familiar to Alf Faragher, since he had already encountered it in the blood of a suspect that had been sent to him for analysis a month earlier. On 28 September, a man named Arthur Hutchinson, a 42-year-old petty-thief, had escaped from the Selby police station by jumping out of a second-storey toilet window and then climbing a 12-foot wall topped with barbed wire. The offense for which Hutchinson had been arrested was not theft but rape. After hiding in the undergrowth of a garden in Selby, he had broken into the house when it was empty, and hidden in the roof space. The house was owned by a 45-year-old saleswoman who had recently come into an inheritance; it had been a newspaper report of this inheritance that gave Hutchinson the idea of robbing and murdering her—he had dug a grave in the undergrowth. During his two days hidden in the house, he had spied on the woman having bondage-sex with a young lover. And when the woman was alone, Hutchinson had walked naked into her bedroom, and raped her repeatedly at knifepoint. As he left her, he warned her not to contact the police; in fact, she telephoned them immediately, and Hutchinson was soon arrested. He had spent a month in custody when he escaped by jumping through the glass of the toilet window.

Fortunately, the police had taken a sample of Hutchinson's blood while he was under arrest.

Hutchinson was not known as a violent man, although he had served five and a half years in prison for carrying firearms and threatening his half-brother with a shotgun. Most of his prison sentences had been for minor offenses.

Rape is a serious but fairly common crime, so the hunt for "the Fox"—as Hutchinson was known—had caused little public stir. Nicola Laitner's description of the rapist-killer had led the police to suspect that it could be Hutchinson; but Hutchinson had no record of murderous violence. But Faragher's comparison of the bloodstain found in the bed with a bloodstain from the earlier crime left no doubt that Hutchinson was now a killer; the chances that the murders had been committed by another man with the same fifty-thousand-to-one blood combination were too remote. Televisions all over the country broadcast descriptions and Identikit pictures of Hutchinson, and his description was circulated to all hotels and boarding-houses. Hutchinson had a reputation for being able to live rough in "foxholes"—hence his nickname; in fact, as reports from boarding-house proprietors showed, he had a preference for comfort. In the 12 days after the Laitner murders, he stayed in York, Scarborough, and Manchester. Then he grew alarmed as he read reports that the barbed wire that had torn open his leg had been specially treated, and was likely to turn his leg gangrenous. In fact, the police knew that Hutchinson was inclined to call at hospital out-patients departments for treatment; he was captured in a turnip field on his way to a hospital in Hartlepool.

At the trial, which began on 4 September 1984, Hutchinson's defense consisted of the assertion that he had been invited to the house by Nicola Laitner, whom he had met in a pub with two girlfriends, and that the sex had been with her consent. The real murderer, he said, was Mike Barron, a crime reporter on a Sunday newspaper, who had entered the house after he, Hutchinson, had left. However, the jury also heard that Hutchinson had at first denied ever being in the Laitners' house. But a plamprint found on a champagne bottle found in the marquee left no doubt whatsoever that Hutchinson had been there. A piece of cheese in the refrigerator contained impressions of teeth, and a dental consultant, Geoffrey Craig, gave evidence that these matched impressions of Hutchinson's teeth, taken after his arrest.

It was at this point during the trial that Hutchinson changed his story, and alleged that he had returned to the house in the early hours of the morning—after having had sex with Nicola, with her consent—and found that Nicola had been raped and her family murdered. Nicola, he claimed, had named the killer as Mike Barron. The prosecution had no difficulty in convincing the jury that this version of events, like the previous ones, was a lie. The defense argument that, if Hutchinson had been the murderer, he would not have left Nicola Laitner alive, also failed to convince them. He was found guilty, and sentenced to three terms of life imprisonment, eight years for rape, and five years for aggravated burglary; the judge recommended that he should serve a minimum of 18 years in prison.

11

If the Hutchinson case is one of the most remarkable examples of serological detection, the Backhouse case of the following year is a textbook example of the collaboration of many forensic experts in the solution of a carefully planned murder.

Graham Backhouse had been a successful hairdresser before he made the mistake of turning to farming. By 1984, things were going badly at Widden Hall Farm, near the village of Horton—about 10 miles from Bristol. Two years of crop failures had left Backhouse £70,000 overdrawn at the bank. Moreover, some of his neighbors seemed to regard him with intense dislike. This became apparent on the morning of 30 March 1984, when Backhouse's herdsman discovered a sheep's head impaled on the fence, with a note that read: "You next." Backhouse told the local police that this was the latest incident in a campaign of harassment that had been going on for months, with threatening telephone calls and poison-pen letters, one of which accused him of seducing the anonymous writer's sister. This should have given Backhouse some clue to the identity of the writer; the problem was simply that, in the past 20 years or so, the 44-year-old farmer had seduced a great many people's sisters. Even after 10 years of marriage, he still had a reputation as the local Don Juan.

On the morning of 9 April 1984, Backhouse asked his wife Margaret if she would drive into town and pick up some antibiotics for the livestock. She climbed into her husband's Volvo—her own car was having starting problems—as the farmer went to the cowshed with the herdsman John Russell. As she turned the key, there was a loud explosion that came from underneath her, and the car filled with smoke. In agony, feeling as if her legs had been blown off, Margaret Backhouse succeeded in pushing open the door and falling out onto the ground. Her husband failed to hear her screams—there was a radio playing in the cowshed—but she was seen from a passing school bus, and rushed to hospital.

Forensic examination of the car revealed how lucky she had been. The bomb had been made from a length of steel pipe, which had been packed with nitro-glycerine and shotgun pellets; the detonator was exploded when the ignition switch was turned. It was virtually a miniature sawn-off shotgun, which fired upward through the driver's seat. Fortunately, the bottom of the Volvo had been weak enough to release most of the blast downward; as it was, Margaret Backhouse had lost half a thigh, and had to have thousands of pellets and fragments of shrapnel removed. Soon after she had been removed to hospital, the postman brought another threatening letter. This was passed on to Mike Hall, the Document Examiner at the Birmingham Forensic Laboratory. Hall realized that the handwriting would be practically impossible to identify—the writer had disguised it by "overwriting"—going backwards and forwards over each letter. But the original "You next" note was more interesting; on the back of it there was the imprint of some kind of doodle, which had been made on the next sheet of the writing pad; it suggested that the writer had been idly doodling with a ball-point pen while listening on the telephone . . .

Backhouse at first insisted that he had no enemies—at least, no one hated him enough to plant a bomb in his car (for it seemed obvious that the bomb had been intended for him rather than for his wife). On second thoughts, he was able to supply the names of a number of people with whom he had had unsatisfactory business deals or personal relationships. There was, for example, his neighbor Colyn Bedale-Taylor, a carpenter who lived close by; he and Backhouse had quarrelled violently about a right of way. Bedale-Taylor had been severely depressed since the death of his son in a car crash two years before. Another possible suspect was a man who worked in a local quarry, and therefore had access to explosives; Backhouse admitted to having an affair with the man's wife recently. But when the police began to follow up rumors of sexual irregularities in the village, they realized that Backhouse was not the only adulterer; wife-swapping seemed to be the local sport.

For nine days after the bombing, Backhouse was given police protection. This was withdrawn after he made an angry telephone call to Detective Chief Inspector Peter Brock, asking him to get his men off Widden Hall Farm. Brock had no alternative than to comply, but he warned Backhouse against taking the law into his own hands—he was aware that Backhouse kept a shotgun in the house. The farm remained connected to an alarm at the local police station.

This alarm sounded on the evening of 30 April 1984. Police who rushed to the farm found Backhouse covered in blood, and a dead man lying in the hall at the bottom of the stairs. Backhouse had knife wounds to the left side of his face, and a deep gash that ran from his left shoulder down across his body.

The dead man was Colyn Bedale-Taylor. Backhouse's story was that Bedale-Taylor had called to inquire about his wife, and he had invited him into the kitchen for a cup of coffee. Then, according to Backhouse, his neighbor had announced that God had sent him. When Backhouse laughed derisively, Bedale-Taylor grew angry, and accused Backhouse of being responsible for the death of his son. Backhouse claimed that Bedale-Taylor admitted planting the bomb, and declared that he would be successful next time. At this point, he pulled out a Stanley knife and slashed Backhouse's face, then his chest. Backhouse fled down the hall, and grabbed a shotgun that was standing on the stairs. As Bedale-Taylor rushed him, he fired two shots into his chest, killing him instantly.

The story sounded convincing enough, and seemed to solve the mystery of the car bomb. And when the police searched Colyn Bedale-Taylor's land, and found the rest of the length of pipe from which the "bomb" had been sawn, the conclusion seemed doubly certain. Then there was the fact that the Stanley knife found in the dead man's hand had the initials "B.T." scratched roughly on its handle. Yet this in itself planted the first seeds of doubt in the minds of the investigators. In Bedale-Taylor's workshop there were other tools with his initials; but these were all neatly engraved— for he was a man of meticulous habits...

Dr Geoff Robinson, the forensic biologist who studied the scene of the crime, had more serious doubts. There was a great deal of blood on the kitchen floor, but the spots were the wrong shape. They were all neat and round, as if they had dripped on to the floor—and furniture—by a man who was standing still. If Backhouse had been fighting for his life, many of the spots would have had "tails", as if flying. Moreover, Backhouse had no defensive wounds on his hands, which seemed extraordinary in view of his account of the struggle. And when Geoff Robinson noticed that there was no trail of blood down the hallway, although Backhouse claimed that he ran along the hall to escape his assailant, he became almost certain that Backhouse was lying.

The evidence of the forensic pathologist, Dr. William Kennard, confirmed that suspicion. Kennard was puzzled by the fact that the Stanley knife was still clutched in the dead man's hand, when it should have been lying on the floor.

There was a great deal of blood on Bedale-Taylor's shirt-front—far more than might have been expected. When this blood was tested, Kennard was surprised to discover that by far the larger part of it came from Backhouse. How had it got there in the course of a knife attack in which Backhouse was on the retreat? It looked as if Backhouse had stood over the body and deliberately allowed his blood to drip onto Bedale-Taylor's shirt . . .

All this left the police in little doubt that Backhouse's story was false. He had invited Bedale-Taylor to the house with the intention of murdering him, and after killing him with the shotgun, had then deliberately slashed himself with the Stanley knife. But although the evidence pointed in this direction, it was purely circumstantial. There was not enough to justify Backhouse's arrest.

Geoff Robinson came up with the most interesting clue so far. The envelope that had contained the first threatening letter had been sent to him for a saliva test, to see whether the man who licked the envelope had the same blood group as Backhouse. The letter had been opened with a paper knife, and when Robinson unsealed the flap, he found a tiny clump of wool fibers stuck to the gum. Under a microscope, he could see that they were probably from a woolen sweater, of the type Backhouse usually wore. The police soon obtained samples of wool from sweaters and jerseys in Backhouse's farmhouse. The comparison microscope left no doubt whatsoever that one of these was the sweater that the letter-writer had been wearing as he sealed the envelope.

Now certain they were on the right trail, the police made another search of the farmhouse, with Backhouse watching gloomily. In a drawer of stationery, a detective found a spring-backed notepad. And as he went through it page by page, he suddenly came upon the doodle that had pressed through onto the back of the "You next" note. Mike Hall, the document examiner, made blow-up photographs of the doodle and the impression; superimposed upon one another, it was obvious that they were identical. It was the final link in the chain of evidence that proved beyond all doubt that Graham Backhouse had written himself the threatening letters, and that this had all been part of a plot to murder his wife.

The motive became clear when it was discovered that, a month before the car bombing, Backhouse had increased the life insurance on his wife from £50,000 to £100,000. The murder plot had failed, and Backhouse had made the supreme mistake of trying to "close the case" by murdering his neighbor. A century earlier, a detective like Gustave Macé would have been helpless to establish the killer's guilt. In 1984, it took the aid of four forensic scientists—a pathologist, a biologist, a document examiner, and a bomb expert—to establish beyond all doubt that Graham Backhouse had murdered Colyn Bedale-Taylor and had attempted to murder his wife.

On 18 February 1985, Graham Backhouse was found guilty as charged, and sentenced to two terms of life imprisonment.

12

The most important single discovery in the history of serology, DNA fingerprints, was made by Alec Jeffreys, of the University of Leicester, in September 1984; this at last enabled the forensic scientist to pin down the identity of an individual from whom a blood sample had been taken. But before we speak of DNA fingerprinting, it is necessary to summarize some of the more important serological discoveries of the past two or three decades.

During the late 1940s and early 1950s, blood testing not only ceased to advance, but actually seemed to be slipping backwards—we have already considered the sad cautionary tale of the Werner Boost case. This was not the fault of the scientists so much as of the police specialists, who failed to grasp the importance of extreme precision and exactitude; the Uhlenhuth test, for example, could very easily yield mistaken results if the sample was even slightly contaminated. Yet in 1949, the Swedish scientist A. Ouchterlony had discovered a new and far more accurate method of applying the Uhlenhuth test to distinguish human from animal blood. It was he who discovered that gelatin could greatly simplify the process, since it will allow the serum to spread out in a circle around a hole punched in it. He covered a microscope slide with a substance called agar gel, made from seaweed, in which tiny holes had been punched around a central hole. The blood to be tested is placed in the central hole, and the various antisera in the holes around it; the slide is then placed for 24 hours in a moist chamber at 98° Fahrenheit. As the circles start to overlap one another, a horizontal line develops between the central hole and the antiserum of the same type. This not only saves a great deal of work with test tubes and pipettes, but means that a minute trace of blood can be tested. The same discovery—that antigens and antibodies would diffuse through the gel—led to the method known as gel electrophoresis, developed by Culliford, in which protein molecules are separated on an "electric racetrack".

Another important discovery involved the "rhesus factor" identified by Landsteiner and Weiner in 1940. This was discovered to be responsible for a percentage of stillborn babies. The rhesus factor is not present in all human beings; those who have it are called rhesus positive (Rh+) and those without it rhesus negative (Rh-). If the father was rhesus positive and the mother rhesus negative, the mother might develop a rhesus antibody, which could kill the baby by destroying its blood cells.

Anti-rhesus serum could reveal the presence of the rhesus factor in the father. But it proved far more difficult to find a way of revealing the presence of anti-rhesus factors in the mother, for it failed to cause "clumping" in many cases.

The problem was eventually solved—in a typically roundabout way—by the Cambridge immunologist R. R. A. Coombs in 1945. The trouble, it seemed, was that instead of "clumping" red blood cells, the anti-rhesus factors only coated them. The anti-rhesus factors consisted of proteins known as globulins (present, for example, in haemoglobin). The problem was to make the globulin visible. What Coombs and his colleagues did was to inject human globulin into rabbits, thus producing a serum that was anti-human globulin. Now let us suppose that the problem is to discover whether a wife who had produced a stillborn baby has anti-rhesus factors in her blood. The Coombs anti-globulin serum is added to a sample of the husband's rhesus positive blood, mixed with some of his wife's blood serum. If anti-rhesus factors had coated the husband's blood cells, the result is clumping as the anti-globulin serum attacks the globulin-coated cells.

But the process is not quite as straightforward as it sounds. It is not enough to add the Coombs serum to a mixture of the husband's blood and the wife's serum, for the mixture will contain other globulins which will clump spoiling the whole experiment. It is necessary to separate out the "coated" blood cells, and to add these alone to the Coombs serum; this is done by washing them in saline solution to remove all traces of the wife's serum. Like so many processes in modern serology, the Coombs test is a "fiddly" job. Yet its sensitivity made it invaluable. Moreover, it could also be adapted to the same purpose as the Uhlenhuth test. If a very small quantity of Coombs serum is contaminated with human protein, it fails to clump when anti-rhesus serum is added because its antibodies have already absorbed the human protein. So if a suspect bloodstain is added to a tiny quantity of Coombs serum, then anti-rhesus serum is added, it will instantly identify the serum as animal—by clumping— or as human—by not clumping. But again, it is an extremely "fiddly" process. Ouchterlony's gel method came as an immense relief to serologists, who could simplify the test by dropping tiny quantities of their sera into holes in the gel, and waiting for the "lines" to appear.

But perhaps the most important single discovery of this post-war period was a simple and reliable way of testing old bloodstains; it was invented by Stuart S. Kind, of the Home Office Forensic Laboratory at Harrogate, and was christened the absorption elution test. This came to replace the complicated Holzer method, using "dimpled slides," and which depended on finding out the exact amount of antibody that had been absorbed.

To simplify this explanation, let us think of the antigens in the blood cells as Yale locks, and the antibodies in the serum as Yale keys. Clumping occurs when keys combine with locks. The problem with old bloodstains is that some keys lose their strength sooner than others, so type O, with withered B keys and normal A keys would react like type A. But the "locks" in the blood cells retain their strength. So if locks from an old bloodstain are added to fresh serum, they will absorb some of its keys. And if the serum can be tested to find how many keys it has lost, then we shall know what type of lock the old bloodstain had. But Holzer's method, using a microscope slide with eight "dimples," was long and complicated.

In the 1920s, a colleague of Lattes named Syracusa saw another possible solution. If the antiserum, with its keys, is added to an old bloodstain, with its locks, some of the keys will combine with locks. Holzer's method was to try to *count* the number of keys combined with locks. Syracusa wondered whether it might not be possible to "discombine" the keys from the locks by heating them gently. He would then have a solution containing the original locks from the bloodstain, and the discombined (or "eluted") keys from his new lot of test serum. How could he go about testing these keys to find out whether they are A or B? Simple. Merely add fresh A and B cells to the liquid, and see if clumping takes place. If the A cells clump, then the keys were A, and the old bloodstain was A. If B cells clump, then it was B. It is obviously a highly ingenious method, which takes advantage of the fact that keys decay quicker than locks, and tests the stain by fitting it out with new keys.

Where Syracusa went wrong was in not being very clear about what to do with his solution full of newly discombined keys. He felt he ought to drain off the liquid containing the keys before he tried testing it with new cells. But during this complicated process the temperature inevitably dropped, and his keys recombined with the locks, aborting the whole process. So Syracusa finally decided his idea was unworkable.

Kind knew nothing about Syracusa's failure, and in what

he calls a "state of original ignorance," he decided not to bother with separating-off the liquid containing the keys. Instead, he divided the liquid—still containing the bloodstain—into two, and put A test cells in one lot and B test cells in the other. The result was that when the temperature was lowered, one of his samples would clump, revealing whether the original bloodstain was type A or B.

Why did this simple method work? Because although some of the keys recombined with locks from the original bloodstain as soon as the temperature was lowered, most of them would combine with locks from the new blood cells. To understand why this is so, we have to stop thinking about keys and locks for a moment, and recognize that what actually happens is that the antibody in the serum combines with the antigen on the surface of the blood cell. New blood cells have more surface than old ones, as a fresh pea has more surface than a dried one. So Kind's marvelously simple method worked, and saved the endless lengthy process of trying to count the keys on a dimpled slide. Kind's "absorption-elution" test is now the standard way of testing old bloodstains in all forensic laboratories.

For a brief period, it had a rival in a process known as the "mixed agglutination" method. This depended on a curious discovery first made by Wiener in the late 1930s, and rediscovered by Coombs, in the mid-1950s: that even when a key is combined with a lock, it still has two identical ends, so to speak. Coombs discovered that skin cells have blood group characteristics—they are, in effect, small locks. And if serum is added—anti-A or anti-B—they unite with the keys in the serum. Yet if the correct blood cells are added, clumping still occurs—as if, so to speak, the serum had two hands, and could hang onto the skin cell *and* the blood cell. Now obviously, this ought to be the simplest method of all, since it cuts out the intermediate step of "discombining" the locks and keys by heating them. Unfortunately the method proved to be unreliable. In his *Crime and Science*, Jürgen Thorwald remarks that "by August 1962 the mixed agglutination test was well on its way to acceptance by all the serological laboratories of the world''. In fact, the test has now been dropped by most laboratories, and replaced by Kind's absorption elution test—so that, for example, it was the Kind test that Faragher used to determine the ABO characteristics of the bloodstains found in Nicola Laitner's bed.

Yet in spite of these remarkable advances, the ultimate goal, the "blood fingerprint", continued to elude the scientist. And in 1984, Dr. Alec Jeffreys, of the University of Leicester, made the discovery superfluous when he stumbled upon a completely new method of "typing" an individual: the DNA fingerprint.

For readers whose knowledge of biology is minimal, an account of DNA fingerprinting should begin with the explanation that each individual is made up of about 100 million million cells, each of which consists of protein surrounding a nucleus; the latter is made of a substance called nucleic acid. In 1911, the biochemist P. A. T. Levene discovered that there are two types of nucleic acid, known as RNA and DNA, according to whether they contain a sugar called ribose or deoxyribose. Unfortunately, the cell nucleus was transparent, so it was hard to tell what was going on inside it, until someone discovered a method of staining it with dye. This showed that when cells divide into two—which is how they reproduce—the nucleus turns into a number of thread-like objects called chromosomes. There are 46 in all, 23 contributed by the father's sperm, 23 by the mother's egg. And the staining process revealed that the chromosomes appeared to be largely made up of DNA. In the 1940s, it became clear that DNA is the "transforming principle" in living things—the material which carries genetic information, and which determines whether you are born with red or black hair, an aquiline or snub nose, brown or blue eyes.

But if the DNA gives all these orders, how does it transmit them? The answer was, obviously, by means of a code—which could be compared to those plastic biscuits with notches along their edges, which housewives sometimes used for "programming" their washing machines. The DNA code, as everyone knows, was finally solved by

Watson and Crick in the early 1950s; they showed that the DNA molecule has a thread-like structure, and looks like two interlocked spirals—the double helix—held together by pairings of chemical building blocks as a ladder is held together by its rungs. The building blocks are four bases called adenine, guanine, cytosine, and thymine, and these are strung together in apparently meaningless permutations, such as ATTGGGTTCCC, and so on. This order of the bases determines the characteristics of a human being as the order of the notes of the scale determines a symphony. When the cell splits into two, the two spirals come apart, and each one attracts to itself various molecules—of adenine, guanine, etc.—that make it a duplicate of the original helix. This is the basic mechanism of the genetic code, and it explains why a human female gives birth to a human baby and not, say, to a dog or cat.

Now, obviously, long sections of this DNA (which is about three feet long) remain the same from person to person—since we all have heads, limbs and so on. But in 1980 it was discovered that there are stretches where the code differs dramatically in each individual—except identical twins, whose genetic material is identical. They were labeled "hypervariable regions," and were found to consist of short sequences of bases repeated over and over again like a stutter. The next question was to find out whether there was any molecular motif shared by these hyperactive regions. A simple analogy might help to make this clear. Imagine a Martian astronomer examining some newly built town on earth through a powerful telescope. He sees that it seems to consist of more-or-less identical straight roads with identical houses on either side. But every few streets he notices a church, which looks quite different from all the other buildings. The churches are of many different designs, and his problem is to study them through his telescope and see if he can find some basic building-block which is the same in all the churches . . .

Jeffreys made his discovery in 1984, when he was studying genes coding for myoglobin proteins, which carry oxygen in the muscles. He discovered a kind of basic building-block made of repeated sequences within the DNA, each 10 or 15 bases long.

Next he isolated two of these "blocks," and cloned them—that is, mass-produced them. The blocks—or genetic markers—were then made radioactive. Jeffreys wanted to see if he could use them as "probes" to detect hypervariable regions in other genetic material. (The blocks will tend to home-in on other blocks like themselves, like birds of a kind flocking together, and then wave a radioactive flag.) Jeffreys next obtained genetic material from members of a family, and set out to see whether his method could discover the relationships. The "fingerprints" of the hypervariable regions appear as dark bands on an X-ray film, so they look like long columns with a couple of black stripes of lines spread out against a white background. By placing the columns from parents and children side by side, Jeffreys was able to see that all the bands of the children derive from the mother or father and that the same applies to the parents and to their parents.

There was great excitement in Jeffreys's laboratory when this discovery was made. It was obvious, for example, that it could resolve the majority of paternity cases—to which all books on blood grouping devote a section. Blood factors can help to determine whether a certain man could or could not be the father of a certain child, but they cannot state beyond all doubt that it *has* to be a certain individual. Jeffreys's new method was almost as precise as a fingerprint. In one of his early cases, a Ghanaian boy who was born in Britain had returned to Ghana to rejoin his father. When he wanted to come back to Britain, the immigration authorities disputed whether he was the woman's son. The father was in Ghana, so he was not available for tests. But Jeffreys was able to get genetic material—from white blood cells—from the mother and three undisputed children. (Red blood cells have no nucleus, and so are not suitable for genetic fingerprinting.)

The process begins by separating the DNA from the proteins that surround the nucleus. Then the DNA is chopped up into a kind of genetic confetti with the use of an enzyme—a catalyst material (of which the digestive juices are an example)—and sorted into various sizes on the "electric racetrack" of gel electrophoresis, which separates them into bands. The bands are then stuck to a nylon membrane, and the radioactive "probes" added. All that remains is to place a radioactive-sensitive film over the membrane. The bands show where the probe has combined specifically with the "highly variable" DNA.

When this method was applied to the Ghanaian family, the boy's "autoradiograph" showed bands that were either present in the mother, or as paternal characteristics in the undisputed children: in short, it revealed unmistakably that the children all had the same mother and father. The Home Office was forced to admit that the boy had a right to enter Britain.

Soon after Jeffreys's discovery, his small daughter Sarah fell down in the playground at school and cut her face. Jeffreys was forced to cancel a lecture he had scheduled on his new technique to take her to hospital. The accident proved to be a remarkable piece of luck. If Jeffreys had given the lecture, the resulting public disclosure would have made it impossible to patent his process. As it was, it was licensed to ICI, and has proceeded to generate a considerable revenue, which Jeffreys has poured back into basic research. (ICI charge for each test performed, each one of which takes about three weeks and costs—at the time of writing—about £120.)

The new technique revealed its value as a tool of forensic science in a rape case that came to trial in November 1987. In January of that year a man broke into a house in Avonmouth, Bristol, where a 45-year-old disabled woman lived alone. After robbing her of jewelry, he raped her. Some time later, a laborer named Robert Melias was arrested for burglary, and was identified by the woman as the rapist. A year earlier, his defense might have argued mistaken identity. But when the semen stains from the woman's petticoat were sent to the Home Office Forensic Research

Establishment at Aldermaston, Dr. D. J. Werrett was able to compare them with Melias's own genetic material and show the DNA fingerprint to be identical. The chances of someone else having the same "fingerprint" were about four million to one—rather shorter odds than in the case of real fingerprints, but still 80 times greater than in the case of the "blood fingerprint" that convicted Arthur Hutchinson of the murder of the Laitners. On 13 November 1987, Melias was sentenced to eight years for rape and five years for burglary.

The case that excited nation-wide attention was heard in the following January. It had begun more than four years earlier, in November 1983, when a 15-year-old schoolgirl named Lynda Mann set out from her home in Narborough, near Leicester, to visit a friend in nearby Enderby. She took a short cut through a footpath known as the Black Pad. The next morning her body was found lying near the footpath; she had been strangled with her own scarf and raped. A lengthy police investigation led nowhere but—as usual in such cases—the rapist's semen stains were preserved.

Three years later, in July 1986, another 15-year-old schoolgirl, Dawn Ashworth, who lived in Enderby, failed to return from the house of a friend. It was three days before her body was found near another footpath, less than a mile from where Lynda Mann's body had been discovered. She had been battered to death and brutally raped; multiple injuries to her head, face, and genitals showed how violently she had resisted her attacker. A 17-year-old youth named Richard Buckland had been seen close to the murder site, and he was arrested and charged with the killing of Dawn Ashworth. But the police decided to check Buckland's DNA fingerprint at the University of Leicester, and Jeffreys was asked to undertake the task. His tests showed conclusively that Buckland could not be the rapist, and this was confirmed by the Aldermaston laboratory. So four months into their investigation, the police had to begin all over again.

It seemed probable that the rapist came from the small

area surrounding Enderby and Narborough, and including the village of Littlethorpe. The police decided to invite all the young males in this area to give blood samples. It was an immense task for the Aldermaston forensic team, involving 5,000 analyses. It was only possible to process such a large number by eliminating a large proportion of blood samples through conventional genetic markers, and then processing many others in parallel. (Most of the three weeks is spent waiting for the reaction to reach completion and X-ray films to develop.) The result was disappointing; although every young male in the area had volunteered a blood sample, the screening still failed to turn up the rapist's "fingerprint".

The testing was still going on when the police heard of a promising lead. A man having a lunchtime drink in a Leicester pub had boasted to a companion that he had "helped out" a friend by offering the police his own blood sample in place of that of his friend, who lived in Littlethorpe. The drinking companion reported the conversation to the police. A 23-year-old bakery assistant, Ian Kelly, was questioned, and admitted that he had acted as a "stand-in" for his friend and fellow worker Colin Pitchfork. A check with police records revealed that Pitchfork, of Haybarn Close, Littlethorpe, had a number of convictions for indecent exposure. According to Ian Kelly, when the police had asked for blood samples, Pitchfork had begged several workmates to impersonate him, explaining that, with his record for "flashing", he was afraid the police might "fix him up". He offered one man £50, and another £200. Kelly was finally persuaded to forge Pitchfork's passport and his signature, and to learn details of his family background by heart. The deception was successful; Kelly—who lived in Leicester—identified himself as Colin Pitchfork, and gave a blood sample.

Pitchfork was arrested, and a blood sample was sent to the Home Office laboratory; his "bar code" proved to be identical with that of the rapist. But by the time this was confirmed, Pitchfork had already admitted both murders. On both occasions he had been out looking for a girl to whom he could expose himself. On both occasions, the realization that the girl was alone and that there were no witnesses led to murder and rape. In the case of Lynda Mann he had taken his wife to night school, and committed the murder before picking her up again.

On 22 January 1987, Pitchfork pleaded guilty to both murders at Leicester Crown Court, and was sentenced to life imprisonment. His "stand-in" was given an 18-month suspended sentence.

—————————————————— 13 ——————————————————

On 9 May 1986—two months before the murder of Dawn Ashworth—Nancy Hodge, a 27-year-old computer operator from Disney World, returned home late to her apartment in Orlando, Florida. She was removing her contact lenses in the bathroom when she heard a noise, and found a man standing behind her in the bathroom doorway. She was able to see his face before she was pushed to the floor, beaten, and threatened with a knife. The man covered her face and raped her three times. Then he took her handbag and left.

It was the first of a series of break-ins and rapes—or attempted rapes; there were another 23 during the remainder of 1986. But now the rapist took care not to allow the victims to see his face, covering the woman's head with a sheet or blanket beforehand. One of his odder habits was to turn on the light several times during the attacks, presumably for visual stimulation. Another was to study the victim's driver's license, occasionally taking it away with him. On 22 February 1987, he broke into the home of a 27-year-old woman during the early hours of the morning, and raped her repeatedly, beating her and cutting her with a knife. Because her two children were asleep in the next room, she was afraid to make a noise. The man wrapped a sleeping-bag around her head to prevent her from seeing his face; but he was careless enough to leave behind two fingerprints on the window screen.

A police team studied the patterns of the rapes, and

staked out the neighborhoods where he was most likely to strike. In the early hours of 1 March 1987, a woman rang the police to report a prowler on Candlewick Street. A patrol car containing members of the surveillance team was there within minutes, and saw a blue car speeding away. They gave chase, and after two miles, the car—a 1979 Ford Granada—turned a corner too fast and crashed into a telegraph pole. The driver proved to be a 24-year-old, named Tommie Lee Andrews, who worked at a local pharmaceutical warehouse, and lived three miles from the scene of the original rape.

The next morning, at a photo line-up, Nancy Hodge immediately identified him as the man who had raped her. Andrews was charged with the attack, and with the rape of the young mother a week earlier.

Yet in spite of the victim's identification, the case was far from watertight. Nancy Hodges had only glimpsed him for a few seconds, and she could have been mistaken. None of the other victims had seen his face. The fingerprints left on the window screen proved that Andrews was the burglar who had raped the young mother, but this case would be tried separately. A sample of the accused man's blood was compared with semen taken from the victims, but the result was inconclusive; the result fitted Andrews, but it also fitted 30 per cent of American males.

In August 1987, the Prosecutor and Assistant State Attorney, Tim Berry, heard about the Pitchfork case in England, and about the new technique of DNA fingerprinting. The attorney who described the case also mentioned that he had seen an advertisement for a DNA testing service called Lifecodes, with a laboratory at Valhalla, New York. Berry rang Lifecodes, spoke to its forensic director Michael Baird, and agreed to send him the samples of the rapist's semen and blood samples from the accused man. The tests were carried out by Dr. Alan Giusti. And when the X-ray film was finally ready, in early October, it showed beyond all doubt that the blood and the semen came from the same man; their ''bar codes'' were identical.

Now the only problem was to convince the jury that a technique as new as DNA fingerprinting was trustworthy. At a pre-trial hearing, the judge agreed that the DNA evidence was admissible. And on 27 October 1987, Tommie Andrews stood trial on a charge of raping Nancy Hodge. She went into the box and identified Andrews as the man who had attacked her. Andrews's defense was that he had spent that whole evening at home, and this was supported by his girlfriend and his sister. But when the prosecutor was challenged to justify his assertion that the DNA evidence revealed that there was only one chance in 10 billion that Andrews was wrongly accused, he was caught unprepared; rather than venture into a specialized field beyond his competence, he withdrew the figure. This may have been one reason why the jury was split, and declared themselves unable to reach a verdict. The judge was obliged to declare a mistrial.

Two weeks later, Andrews stood trial on the second rape charge. This time, the prosecution made sure that the statistics were correct, and were ready for any challenge. Moreover, the case was bolstered by the two fingerprints found on the window screen, which were undoubtedly made by the accused. This time the verdict was guilty, and Andrews received a sentence of 22 years, the first man in the United States to be convicted by a DNA fingerprint.

At the retrial of the Nancy Hodge case in February 1988, the DNA fingerprint evidence again played a central role. Once again, Andrews insisted that he had been at home that night, and his evidence was backed by his sister and girlfriend. This time, there was no supporting prosecution evidence, except the victim's insistence that she recognized her assailant. Everything turned on the DNA evidence. The defense attempted to challenge it by arguing that not all the DNA molecule had been analyzed, only its hypervariable regions. Baird explained at some length that there would be no point whatever in analyzing the rest of the molecule, which contains human characteristics to be found in all of us—only the regions that differ. This time, the jury was convinced; after a 90-minute absence, they announced a verdict of guilty. Tommie Lee Andrews received a further 78-year sentence for rape, 22 years for burglary and 15 for battery, bringing his total sentence to over 100 years.

In the spring of 1989, two more British cases demonstrated the value of genetic fingerprinting as a "last resort" when all other resources of scientific crime detection had failed.

Between 1982 and 1988, a series of rapes occurred in London's Notting Hill area. All the victims were single women, living alone in basement or ground floor flats around a communal garden. In most cases the rapist broke in through French windows, and was waiting for the girl when she returned from work. She would be seized from behind as she entered the flat, and the intruder would assure her that he was a burglar and had no intention of harming her. Then, just before leaving, he would rape her.

On two occasions the police came close to catching the rapist, but he tore himself free and escaped. And when a 32-year-old ex-paratrooper named Tony Maclean was caught in the communal garden with anti-crime paint from the fences on his hands, he was released because of an error in the police records; the blood group of the rapist (determined from his semen) had been wrongly entered on the computer. Finally, a semen sample taken from a rape victim was sent to Alec Jeffreys in Leicester, and its genetic fingerprint determined. Meanwhile, a Notting Hill policeman, PC Graham Hamilton, had become increasingly convinced that Maclean was the rapist, and Maclean was asked for a second blood sample. Aware that the previous sample had eliminated him, Maclean agreed. But the genetic fingerprint of the new sample proved to be identical with that of the rapist's sperm—the chance of error was 2,750,000 to 1—with the result that, on 13 April 1989, Maclean received three life sentences for rape.

Even more remarkable was a case in which a man was convicted of murder although the police were unable to produce the body of the victim. On 9 February 1988, Helen

McCourt, a 22-year-old computer operator, vanished during the 300-yard walk from the bus stop to her home in Billinge, Merseyside. Ian Simms, the landlord of the local pub, the George and Dragon, came under suspicion when his name was found in Helen's diary. Three weeks later, her clothes were found in a plastic bin liner. And on a slag heap three miles away, police found bloodstained male clothing that proved to belong to Simms. But without Helen's body, the blood could not be proved to be hers. Then a forensic scientist, Dr. John Moore, saw the solution: that even though Helen was missing, blood samples from her parents could establish whether the blood on Simms's clothing was hers. Their genetic fingerprints established this beyond all doubt, and it was largely on this evidence that, on 14 March 1989, Simms was sentenced to life imprisonment. It was a historic legal precedent: the first murder conviction to be achieved with genetic fingerprints "by proxy".

3

The Craft of the Manhunter

1

The American equivalent of the great Vidocq was a Scottish-born detective named Allan Pinkerton. Like Vidocq, Pinkerton retired from the official police force to become a private detective, one of the first "private eyes" in the business. (In fact, the term private eye is probably derived from the Pinkerton symbol—an open eye bearing the legend "We never sleep".) But in the second half of the nineteenth century, the Pinkerton detective agency developed an efficiency that surpassed that of Scotland Yard or the Sûreté.

Allan Pinkerton was a radical, who fled from Scotland at the age of 23—in 1842—to avoid arrest. Working as a cooper in Dundee, Kane County, Illinois, he became an ardent advocate of the abolition of slavery, and helped to smuggle runaway slaves over the border into Canada. And in 1846, chance introduced him to his true vocation: detection. Walking in the woods on an island, he found the remains of a camp fire and trails in the long grass. Many men would have minded their own business; but Pinkerton had a social conscience. The local sheriff accompanied him back to the island, and decided that the camp belonged to a gang of counterfeiters. With Pinkerton's enthusiastic help, he uncovered a cache of fake money and arrested the gang. Only one of them escaped, and Pinkerton, flushed with triumph, offered to help run him down. He tracked the man, pretended to be a fellow crook, and succeeded in getting him arrested. The result was an overnight reputation as a detective.

On Lake Michigan, not far from Dundee, there was a new city called Chicago—although this little collection of wooden cottages and rooming-houses, with a population of 4,000, was hardly more than a town. Soon after his triumph with the counterfeiters, Pinkerton was asked to become a deputy in Kane County and Cook County, which included Chicago. Like Vidocq, he proved to be a born detective, with a phenomenal memory for faces and a sure instinct for the ways of criminals. But the Chicago police were poorly paid, and when the Post Office engaged Pinkerton as a special agent, he saw that there was more money in private work. This is why, in 1850, he founded the Pinkerton detective agency.

This new, fast-expanding America needed efficient detectives. A fast-growing economy needs to transfer large amounts of money and valuables, and in the wide empty spaces, coaches and railway trains were a great temptation to bandits. The railway came to Chicago in 1852, and the new crime of rail theft was soon costing the express companies and their customers enormous sums of money. In this vast country, Pinkerton often had to behave more like an Indian tracker than a policeman. In 1858, he was summoned to New Haven, where robbers had forced open the Adams Express car and pried open the safes with crow-bars, taking $70,000 in cash and jewelry. Near Stamford, Connecticut, Pinkerton found a bag containing $5,000, and knew he was on the right track. At Norwalk he heard of three men who had tried to hire a buggy, and tracked them down to a house where they had stayed overnight. When he learned that their host had been seen the next day on a train, carrying a heavy package that evidently made him nervous, he guessed that it contained the rest of the loot. He tracked the man to New York, but found that he had already left for Canada—but without the package. And under his questioning, the man's niece led him to the money and jewelry, hidden in the cellar. The gang was arrested, and Pinkerton completed the job by arresting the leader in Canada.

One early case from the Pinkerton archives is so incredible that it sounds like fiction. In 1855, a young bank teller named George Gordon was murdered late at night when working in his office; he was the nephew of the bank president. The bank vault was open, and $130,000 was missing. Gordon had been killed by a hammer blow dealt from the left. In the fireplace there were remains of burnt papers and clothing—the murderer had stayed on to burn his bloodstained coat. The only clues were two pieces of paper—a bloodstained page containing some penciled figures—found under the body—and a partly burnt fragment of paper that had been twisted into a "spill" to light the fire. When Pinkerton unfolded this, he found that it was a note for $927.78, and that it was signed Alexander P. Drysdale, the county clerk, a man of unimpeachable reputation. The bloodstained page contained a subtraction sum—$1,252 minus $324.22—the result being $927.78.

Pinkerton asked to see the bank balances of a number of prominent local businessmen whom Gordon might have admitted to the bank after hours. Drysdale's account showed a figure of $324.22. Now Pinkerton was able to reconstruct the crime. Drysdale had come to the bank in the evening to request a loan of $1,252. Gordon had agreed—but had subtracted from this sum the amount already in Drysdale's account. Then he had opened the vault. Overcome by sudden temptation, Drysdale had seized a hammer someone had left in the office and killed his friend.

Pinkerton was certain that Drysdale was the killer, but how to prove it? He began by finding an excuse to get Drysdale to write something, and noted that he was left-handed, like the killer. Next, he sent for three of his operatives from Chicago—an older man, a woman, and a young man called Green. They posed as visitors to the town, and began secretly investigating Drysdale's affairs. Green, a good carpenter, found himself a job in the local carpenter's shop, where all the old men gathered in the evening to gossip. The older detective, who was calling himself Andrews, learned by chance one day that young Green bore a close resemblance to the dead George Gordon. And when Pinkerton learned of this, he formulated an incredible plan. Not far from Drysdale's home was a spot known as Rocky Creek, reputed to be haunted. "Andrews," pretending to be interested in a local plot of land, got Drysdale to take him through Rocky Creek at dusk, and as they rode among the trees, a ghostly figure walked across the path, its hair matted with blood. Drysdale shrieked; Andrews looked astonished and insisted that he could see nothing.

The woman operative had succeeded in getting herself invited into Drysdale's home as a guest of Mrs. Drysdale, and she observed that her host was beginning to suffer nightmares and was prone to sleep-walking. Green, dressed as the ghost, kept up the pressure by occasionally flitting about outside the house when Drysdale was wandering around restlessly. Finally, Pinkerton appeared and arrested Drysdale, who protested his innocence. They took him to the bank, and when the "ghost" appeared from behind the teller's counter, Drysdale fainted. When he recovered, he still continued to protest his innocence, and it began to look as if Pinkerton's bold strategy had failed. But when Drysdale was shown the two scraps of paper proving his involvement, he broke down and confessed. The stolen money was found hidden in a creek near his home.

But most of Pinkerton's early cases demanded persistence and courage rather than this kind of ingenuity. His most remarkable feat of the 1860s was undoubtedly his break-up of the Reno gang, America's first gang of organized outlaws. The five brothers—Frank, John, Simeon, Clinton, and William—were the sons of an Indiana farmer who lived at Seymour, Indiana. John left home at 16—in 1855—and spent some time wandering around Mississippi, working on steamboats and learning to make a living by his wits. Back home, he propounded a scheme of amazing simplicity. The nearby small town of Rockford was prosperous and virtually unprotected. A series of arson attacks so terrified the inhabitants that they began moving elsewhere. Then the Renos bought most of Rockford at bargain prices.

During the Civil War, the Reno brothers served in the army; but most of them soon deserted. During the war, the bloodthirsty southerner William Clarke Quantrill led a band of guerrillas who were little more than robbers and murderers— it included Jesse James, "Bloody Bill" Anderson, and Cole Younger—and although most of the gang was wiped out in 1865, James and Cole Younger went on to become wandering outlaws. Meanwhile, back in Seymour, the Reno brothers formed their own outlaw gang, specializing in robbing county treasury offices. And in 1866, they invented a new crime—holding up trains. They boarded the wood-burning Ohio and Mississippi railroad coach as ordinary passengers at Seymour, then strolled down to the Adams Express car, forced the door, and held up the messenger at gunpoint. They pulled the communication cord, stopping the train, and rolled the safe off it. But they were still trying to burst it open in the woods when a posse drove them to abandon it. Nevertheless, John Reno had succeeded in seizing $10,000 in notes.

Pinkerton was asked to take on the case. The bandits had worn masks, but he had no doubt they were the Renos. A few weeks later, a new saloon was opened in Seymour—the amiable, round-faced man who ran it was really a Pinkerton operative called Dick Winscott—and the Renos soon became customers. Winscott even succeeded in persuading the brothers to allow him to take a group photograph—possibly the first time photography was used in crime detection. (Pinkerton had copies made and circulated.)

Seymour was an armed camp run by outlaws, and there was no chance of arresting the Renos on the spot. Allan Pinkerton enlisted the aid of Dick Winscott. The Renos were being sought for a bank robbery in Gallatin, Missouri, and had been identified by witnesses through their photographs. One afternoon soon after, the train stopped in Seymour, and Allan Pinkerton looked cautiously out of the window. On the platform he recognized the jovial figure of Dick Winscott, talking to John Reno. Six muscular men, accompanied by a sheriff from Cincinnati—another city that held warrants for the Renos—strolled casually off the train, surrounded John Reno, and hustled him aboard. Reno bellowed for help, but although the other Reno brothers commandeered another train and pursued the kidnappers, John Reno was handed over to the Gallatin authorities and sentenced to 25 years in jail.

In February 1868, Frank Reno—now the gang leader—led a raid on the Harrison County treasury at Magnolia, Iowa, which netted $14,000. Using his skills as a tracker, Pinkerton found them hiding in the home of a pillar of the Methodist church in Council Bluffs, and arrested them in a sudden raid. But the jail in Council Bluffs was not strong enough to hold them, and when the sheriff arrived the next morning he found the cells empty and a chalked inscription: "April Fool"—the date being 1 April 1868.

Local citizens were becoming enraged at the impunity the gang seemed to enjoy. The Reno brothers were not the kind of jolly outlaws who became folk heroes; they were bullies and killers. In desperation, some of the bolder Seymour residents formed a Vigilance Committee. The Renos heard the rumors, and made bloodthirsty threats.

After a train robbery at Marshfield, Indiana, which netted the gang $96,000, Pinkerton decided they had to be caught by cunning. He circulated rumors that $100,000 in gold was to be shipped via Seymour. The train's engineer pretended to agree to co-operate with the gang and tipped off Pinkerton exactly where the robbery would take place. And as the outlaws stopped the train and burst open the Express car, they were met by a volley of shots from Pinkerton's men. Most of the gang escaped, but the next day, three of them were captured in a thicket and arrested. But one dark night a few weeks later, the train on which they were being sent to their trial was stopped by men waving red lanterns; the three bandits were dragged off the train and lynched. A few weeks later, another three bandits who had been tracked down by Pinkerton were intercepted on their way to jail by a mob and lynched. The Reno gang left in Seymour began to fight back; members of the Vigilance Committee had rocks thrown through their windows; there were night raids, beatings, and mutilations. When Simeon and William Reno were arrested by Pinkerton detectives in Indianapolis, Vigilance Committee members received messages: "If the Renos are lynched, you die." The Vigilance Committee decided that if the Renos were not lynched, things would remain as bad as ever. The authorities decided to transfer the two Renos to the more secure New Albany jail. On 6 September 1868, there was a determined attempt by vigilantes to break into the Lexington jail, but the Renos had already been moved. They were joined in New Albany by their brother Frank, who had been arrested in Canada, together with a gang member named Charles Anderson. But on 11 December vigilantes surrounded the jail and burst their way in with a battering ram. The sheriff was beaten unconscious, and his keys taken. Then the Reno brothers and Anderson were dragged from their cells and lynched. As the vigilantes dispersed, prisoners watched from their cells and saw Simeon gasping for breath on the end of his rope; it took half an hour before he ceased to struggle.

The Vigilance Committee issued a notice, naming other members of the gang still in Seymour—including brother Clinton—and declaring that if they wished to remain as honest citizens, they would be welcome; otherwise they would meet the fate of the others. The gang accepted the ultimatum sullenly, and the outlaws ceased to be a power in

Indiana. Pinkerton was altogether less successful in his attempts to catch Jesse James. Like the Reno brothers, Jesse and his brother Frank came back from the Civil War, in which they fought for the South, wondering whether the methods of Quantrill's guerrillas could not be applied with equal success in peacetime. On 13 February 1866, 10 men rode into Liberty, Missouri, and robbed the bank; on their way out of town, one of them shot down an unarmed student on his way to college, then, whooping and firing pistols, the gang rode out of town. It was the first of many pointless murders committed by the gang led by this modern "Robin Hood." In December 1869, the James gang robbed the same bank in Gallatin, Missouri, that the Reno brothers had robbed two years earlier, and James shot the manager in cold blood.

The Pinkertons began trailing the James gang at about this time, but had no success. In February 1874, a Pinkerton operative, John W. Whicher, succeeded in infiltrating the gang, but was recognized and murdered. On 6 January 1875, the Pinkertons received a tip-off that Jesse was visiting his mother, Mrs. Zerelda Samuel; they surrounded the house and tossed in a "smoke bomb." It killed James's 8-year-old half-brother, and blew off his mother's arm. The incident brought much sympathy for the James brothers and indignant criticism of the brutality of Pinkerton. Jesse James was so angry that he spent four months in Chicago trying to get Pinkerton alone so he could kill him; he was unsuccessful.

On 7 August 1876, an attempt to rob the bank in Northfield, Minnesota, went disastrously wrong; the citizens all rushed outdoors with guns, and most of the bandits were either killed or wounded; James's cousin Cole Younger and his brother Bob were captured soon after and sentenced to life imprisonment. James formed a second gang, but it never met with the same success as the earlier one. On August 7, 1881, the gang committed its last train robbery, netting only $1500. Harassment by the Pinkertons was breaking their nerve. On April 3, 1882, Jesse James was planning another robbery with two new gang members, Bob and Charlie Ford, when Bob Ford pulled out his gun and

shot James in the back. He had agreed to deliver Jesse
James to the state governor for reward money and amnesty.
The murder of Jesse James—at the age of 34—made him
more of a folk hero than ever, and his brother Frank was
acquitted several times of crimes he had obviously committed (he died of old age in 1915). Allan Pinkerton died two
years after Jesse James, at the age of 65; but the agency
continued with unabated success under sons and grandsons.

—————————————— 2 ——————————————

By the 1880s, the day of the American badman was drawing
to a close—at least in the "wild west." But one of them
was still to achieve—briefly—some of the same notoriety as
Jesse James. Marion Hedgepeth was born in Missouri, and
became a cowboy in Wyoming, then a hold-up man in
Colorado. An exceptionally handsome man, he soon acquired the status of a folk hero when he began robbing
trains in Missouri, on one occasion blasting his way in with
dynamite. After netting $50,000 in Glendale, the "Hedgepeth
Four" (as they were known) moved to St. Louis and perpe-
trated a number of audacious robberies by daylight. Allan
Pinkerton's son William, now the head of the agency,
rushed to St. Louis to try and track down the gang. He
failed, but a little girl playing in a shed found a hole in the
corner, and discovered six-shooters and envelopes that had
contained money stolen from Adams Express. The gang had
left, but now Pinkerton had a lead; he tracked down the
expressman who had agreed to ship their effects—including
the loot—to Los Angeles. Hedgepeth's wife was arrested
when she went to the Express office to claim the trunks.
Hedgepeth escaped, but the Pinkertons knew he was associated
with a crooked attorney who was fond of billiards. The
attorney was watched, and one day when he had removed
his tailcoat to play billiards, it was searched; in the pocket
the detective found a letter to Hedgepeth which included the
address of his latest hideout. Hedgepeth was quietly surrounded
by detectives when out on a walk, and in St. Louis was

sentenced to 25 years' hard labor. In fact, he was released in 1908 with tuberculosis, and killed two years later in Chicago as he was trying to rob a barman of his takings.

But even in prison, Hedgepeth was to play an important role in criminal history; he was indirectly responsible for the capture of the worst mass murderer of the nineteenth century.

In June 1894, when Hedgepeth had been in prison for two years, a stranger with mild blue eyes and a gentlemanly manner was introduced into his cell. He introduced himself as Mr. Holmes, a druggist, who had sold a drug store that did not belong to him in St. Louis. Holmes was a man of 34, slightly built but with a winning smile and excellent manners. He asked Hedgepeth if he knew of a good—and not too honest—lawyer, and Hedgepeth recommended a man named Jephta D. Howe. Holmes, it seemed, needed a man who could be trusted, for he proposed to swindle an insurance company out of $10,000. Pressed by Hedgepeth, Holmes finally explained. He would insure the life of a friend called Benjamin Pitezel for $10,000, then arrange for Pitezel to be "killed" in an accidental explosion. In fact, a corpse obtained from an undertaker would be substituted for Pitezel. In exchange for securing the co-operation of Jephta D. Howe, Hedgepeth would receive $500 of the loot.

With the help of Howe, the soft-spoken Mr. Holmes was soon out on bail. And two months later, Hedgepeth learned that Pitezel had "died" in an explosion. But Holmes failed to send the $500 he had promised, and Hedgepeth, having nothing else to do in jail, brooded on it until he was filled with resentment. Accordingly, he wrote a letter to the Fidelity Mutual Life Assurance Company, which had recently paid out $9,715.85 to Jephta D. Howe, denouncing Holmes as a swindler. And William E. Gary of the Mutual Life Agency promptly hired the Pinkertons to find out whether there was any truth in this story.

What had happened, it seemed, was this. On 22 August 1894, a carpenter looking for work had called at a house in Callowhill Street, Philadelphia, hoping to obtain a job with a "patents dealer" named Perry. Instead, he had found the decomposing corpse of Perry on the floor of his laboratory;

he had apparently been killed in an explosion. An autopsy revealed chloroform in the stomach. Since no one claimed the corpse, it was buried in a public grave. However, before this happened, the St. Louis branch of the Fidelity Mutual Life had received a letter from Jephta D. Howe, saying that he had reason to believe that Perry was really Benjamin Pitezel, whose wife Carrie had insured her husband for $10,000.

The agent who had insured Pitezel was asked if he knew anyone who could identify him, and he named a Mr. Henry Howard Holmes of Wilmette, Illinois. Holmes was contacted, and he came to Philadelphia, together with Pitezel's 15-year-old daughter Alice. The corpse was exhumed, and proved to be badly decomposed; Holmes identified it as Pitezel, then the body was covered, all except for the teeth. Alice was now brought into the morgue and asked: "Are those your father's teeth?" She said yes and burst into tears. So the company paid up the insurance. And now, a few weeks later, the letter from Marion Hedgepeth suggested that the whole thing was a swindle arranged by Holmes, and that Pitezel was still alive.

Oddly enough, the insurance company was disinclined to believe Hedgepeth; they suspected him of inventing the story for his own devious purposes. Nevertheless, they asked the Pinkerton agency to find Holmes. The agency tracked him from Canada to Detroit to New York to New Hampshire, and in the meantime discovered that he had a number of aliases, and that his real name was Herman Webster Mudgett. Finally, Holmes was arrested in Boston; he strenuously insisted on his innocence. The police were unhappy about the evidence against him in Philadelphia— after all, there was nothing to tie him to the death of "Pitezel." When they learned that he was also wanted in Texas, they telegraphed Fort Worth and asked what he had done. The answer was that Holmes was wanted for horse stealing, and also for questioning about the disappearance of two sisters called Williams. When told about the horse stealing charge, Holmes proved unexpectedly co-operative— he knew that Texans were inclined to lynch horse thieves without trial. So he admitted to being guilty of fraud in Philadelphia, and was promptly returned to that city. Here he explained that he procured a corpse in New York—he would not say where from—and passed it off as Pitezel. Pitezel was then given his share of the insurance money, and sailed for South America with three of his children . . .

Holmes asked the Pinkerton detective to deliver a note to a woman called Mrs. Cook in Burlington, Vermont. The detective soon discovered that Mrs. Cook was Carrie Pitezel, and she was placed under arrest. She had been living with her eldest daughter Dessie and her baby son; she explained that Mr. Holmes had gone off with the other three—Alice, Nellie, and Howard. And although she trusted Mr. Holmes, she was worried about her husband and children . . .

Philadelphia detective Frank Geyer questioned Holmes, and soon decided that he was a born actor. He would talk with apparent candor, and his eyes would fill with tears; then, with a brave effort, he would master his apparently deep emotion and speak in a determined and forceful manner. And the more Geyer talked to Holmes, the more convinced he became that the children, like their father, were dead. But where were they? Geyer set out to track them down; he took with him photographs of Holmes and the missing children.

What followed was a masterpiece of dogged, old-fashioned "needle-in-the-haystack" detection. First Geyer went to Cincinnati, where the Pinkerton detectives had traced Holmes. Inquiries at dozens of hotels finally revealed that a Mr Cook had stayed at one of them with three children; the clerk recognized the photographs of the children. Holmes had stayed only one night in the hotel, so it seemed probable that he had taken a house. A round of estate agents finally revealed that Holmes had rented a house in Poplar Street, paying $15 rent in advance and giving the name A. C. Hayes. Neighbors had seen a man and a small boy getting off a furniture wagon, and noticed that one piece of furniture he brought was a large stove. The next morning, Holmes had told his neighbor that he had changed his mind about occupying the house, and that she could have the stove.

Apparently the curiosity of the neighbors had driven Holmes away. . .

The next stop was Indianapolis, where the Pinkerton detectives had found Holmes. There the usual search of hotel registers revealed that an "Etta Pitezel" had stayed there for four days in the previous September. Geyer reasoned that Holmes had left "Etta" (whom the clerk recognized from her photograph as Alice, the daughter who had identified her dead father) while he went to St. Louis to cash the insurance check. Geyer next tracked Holmes to Detroit, where he had stayed in a hotel with the two girls—a discovery that convinced the detective that the small boy, Howard, had never left Indianapolis alive. Mrs. Pitezel had also been in Detroit, apparently unaware that the children about whom she was so worried were staying in a hotel just around the corner, crying themselves to sleep with homesickness.

The Pinkertons had already established that Holmes had gone to Toronto. Geyer went to Toronto, and proceeded to make the round of estate agents, trying to find if Holmes had rented a house. When this brought no result, he called in the Press and told them the story. As a result, a man told him that he had leased a house to a gentleman called Holmes the previous October. This proved to be a false lead; after searching the property and digging in the cellar, they checked with the agent who rented the house; he looked at the photograph of Holmes and said it was not the same man. But by this time, another agent reported letting a house in St Vincent Street to a man who sounded like Holmes. The detective rushed to the house and persuaded its present occupant to let them dig in the cellar. Here, at last, they found what they were looking for—two naked bodies buried under three feet of earth. When Mrs. Pitezel identified them as her two daughters, she had hysterics and fainted repeatedly.

More patient research—particularly into letters written by the children—revealed that the boy Howard had almost certainly been killed in Indianapolis in October. Finally, an estate agent recognized Holmes's photograph, and his office boy remembered that Holmes and a small boy had gone to a one-story cottage at nearby Irvington. The place was searched, but Geyer could find nothing. Digging yielded no results. But after Geyer left, two children went on searching, and found a hole in the chimney; inside this they found pieces of bone and a set of teeth. Mrs. Pitezel identified them as the teeth of her son Howard.

Now, at last, the case against Holmes was complete. The corpse of the man found in Philadelphia had obviously been that of Pitezel, not some medical speciman purchased in New York. Holmes had persuaded Pitezel—a petty thief—to take part in the insurance swindle with a promise of half the proceeds. But he never had any intention of paying; instead, he intended to murder Pitezel, then kill his family one by one. Fortunately for Mrs. Pitezel, Hedgepeth revealed the scheme before it claimed its final victims.

But now Holmes's face had appeared on newspapers all over America, those who had known him in the past began to tell their stories. He had lived in Chicago, and built himself a large house on 63rd Street—a place so big it had become known as his "castle". Dozens of people went to the police to complain of having been swindled by Holmes, whose favorite method of raising money was to buy something on credit and sell it for cash the next day. And when the police went to investigate the "castle", they realized that it had been designed by a man whose life revolved around robbery and murder. There were secret rooms, trapdoors, rooms without windows which could be made airtight by closing the doors—one contained a huge safe with a gas-pipe running into it. But the most sinister discovery was a room lined with asbestos, with a gas-pipe that was designed as a giant blow-torch, in which a body could be incinerated. A large stove contained fragments of human bone, and in the chimney there was a bunch of human hair, a woman's. Chutes ran from the second floor down to the basement—chutes large enough to accommodate a human body.

Little by little, the full story of Holmes began to emerge, and even before it was complete, it was obvious that he was the most horrific mass murderer in American history. Born

in Gilmanton, New Hampshire, on 16 May 1860, Herman
Webster Mudgett had been a shy but brilliant child. He was
also timid, and when mischievous schoolfellows dragged
him into an empty doctor's surgery to confront a skeleton,
morbid terror began to turn into morbid fascination. So it
was perhaps inevitable that he should decide on a medical
career. He married at 18 but seems to have deserted his wife
at an early stage. During his first year studying medicine at
the University of Michigan, he went to Chicago, became an
agent for a textbook publisher, and absconded with the
funds. He practiced medicine in Moors Fork, New York,
but soon devised a method of making a quick profit:
insuring his life and then providing a substitute body. For
various reasons, the scheme fell through, but he returned to
it later in Minneapolis. Here, according to his later confession, he purchased a corpse from a medical college, insured
himself for $20,000, then transported the corpse to a lum-
bering area of northern Michigan. Holmes disappeared into
the forest, his "corpse" was found pinioned under a tree a
week or so later, and the insurance money was paid into
Holmes's bank account.

This tale seems to bear some of the marks of Holmes's
mythomania. What is undoubtedly true is that he moved to
Chicago in 1886, and married a girl named Myrta Belknap—
bigamously, of course—and that her family decided to break
with Holmes when he forged the signature of Uncle John
Belknap. Holmes invited Uncle John to go up to the roof of
a new house to discuss the matter; some instinct warned
Uncle John to decline.

Now he succeeded in obtaining a job as the assistant of a
widow, Mrs. E. S. Holton, who ran a drug store at 63rd
Street and Wallace in Englewood, Chicago. Business
prospered. But after a few years, Mrs. Holton and her young
daughter vanished; Holmes declared that she had sold him
the business. Now he purchased two vacant lots across the
street, and began to build his three-story "castle," using
borrowed money and money raised by petty swindles—one
furniture company succeeded in recovering its furniture
when a carpenter tipped them off about a secret room hidden

behind a false wall. Holmes also bought a vast safe, but failed to pay; when the safe company sent men to recover it, they realized that there was not a door or window in the house that was large enough to take it through. So Holmes retained his safe. He also took the precaution of sacking gangs of workmen every few weeks, so that no one knew too much about the place.

According to Holmes's later confession, his first victim was a doctor friend, Robert Leacock of Baltimore, Michigan, whom he killed for $40,000 life insurance money in 1886, but he offers no further details. Once the castle was constructed, he settled down to the serious business of paying off his debts with murder and robbery. The drug store opposite brought in a good income, but it was not enough. A room in the castle was let to a Dr. Russell, and one day Holmes killed him by striking him on the head with a heavy chair. He also killed a tenant called Rodgers, who had come to Michigan on a fishing trip, and a man named Charles Cole.

Holmes was an obsessive seducer, and he became involved with a woman called Julia Conner, whose husband Ned ran the jewelry section of the drug store. Ned Conner and his wife separated when it became clear that she was Holmes's mistress, and Mrs. Conner and her 8-year-old daughter Pearl moved into the "castle." They also vanished, probably around Christmas 1891. Holmes later said that Julia Conner had died as a result of an illegal operation, and that he had been forced to poison Pearl. At the time, he told acquaintances that she had left him to marry a doctor.

The next victim, according to Holmes, was a domestic named Lizzie, who had begun to have an affair with the caretaker of the castle, Pat Quinlan. Afraid that Quinlan—who was married—was planning to elope with Lizzie, Holmes suffocated her in the basement, after forcing her to write letters saying she was going out west.

A woman named Sarah Cook began to work for Holmes, and her niece, a Miss Mary Haracamp, became Holmes's typist. Sarah Cook became pregnant. One evening, they came into the "vault" (presumably the safe with its "blow-torch'') when Holmes was preparing his latest victim for shipment to the Medical School. According to Holmes, he slammed the door and gassed them both.

Some time in the spring of 1892, a beautiful girl named Emmeline Cigrand was lured to Chicago to work for Holmes; she had been employed at the Keeley Institute in Dwight, and Pitezel had been impressed by her when he went there to take a cure for alcoholism. It is typical of Holmes that Pitezel's descriptions of her led him to offer her a position as his bookkeeper and secretary. Her letter home to Dwight are full of descriptions of Holmes's kindness to her, and of how he often brought her flowers. She had one drawback; she was engaged to a young man in Dwight. Holmes claims that she became his mistress, but that was probably because he hated to admit failure. He became jealous enough to make plans to kill her fiancé, but these came to nothing. On the day in December when she came to say goodbye, Holmes pushed her into the vault, and offered to release her if she wrote a letter breaking off her engagement. He claims she did so, and that he then allowed her to suffocate. Since Holmes had no reason to want to get rid of her—unlike Julia Conner she had not become a nuisance—it seems probable that the motive was sexual: that this was his only way of possessing her.

The same probably applies to the next victim, another beautiful girl called Rosine Van Jassand, whom Holmes induced to work in his fruit and confectionery store. His story is that he "compelled her to live with him," then poisoned her and buried her in the basement; it seems more probable that she clung to her virtue and that Holmes killed her for this reason.

Holmes had employed a caretaker named Robert Latimer, who had learned about his insurance schemes. When he tried to blackmail Holmes, he was also locked in the vault. Holmes claims that he allowed Latimer to starve to death, and in fact, police found that some of the bricks and mortar had been torn away by someone using his bare hands. All this makes it clear that Holmes was not merely trying to shock when he claimed that, ''like a tiger that has tasted human blood,'' he began killing out of a sadistic mania. This also seems to be confirmed by his next murder, that of a Miss Anna Betts, a customer at the drug store, in whose prescription Holmes inserted poison. Since she died at her home, the motive could only have been the strange delight in killing that also motivated Niell Cream and George Chapman. Holmes claimed that he also inserted poison into the prescription of a girl called Gertrude Conner—presumably a relative of Ned Conner—but that it was slow-acting, and she died only after returning home to Muscatine, Iowa.

But the motive of the next murder was purely financial; he convinced an unnamed woman in Omaha that the time had come to sell her real estate holdings in Chicago. She came to Chicago to collect the money, then died in the vault, Holmes taking back the money.

Since 1889, Holmes had been associated with a man named Warner in an enterprise called the Warner Glass Bending Company. Warner, it seems, had invented a new process, which involved a large zinc tank that could be filled with a fine oil spray, which was then ignited, producing a temperature hot enough to bend plate glass. When Warner had finished building his patent over in Holmes's basement, he was pushed into it and incinerated. ''In a short time, not even the bones of my victim remained.'' The patent oven certainly existed. When police began investigating the ''castle'' in July 1895, they sent for a plumber to knock down a wall that sounded hollow; a stench of decaying flesh came out. The plumber made the mistake of striking a match, whereupon there was an explosion that filled the cellar with flames and disabled several workmen. When the wall was demolished, police found a cylindrical tank which was ten feet long and six feet high, and made of wood; inside this was a zinc tank, with numerous pipes running into it. The gas fumes overpowered a fireman who ventured inside.

Holmes's confession claims that he next went into partnership with an Englishman who was an expert in financial swindles. A wealthy banker was lured into the vault and forced to sign checks for $70,000, after which he was gassed; Holmes sold the body to the medical college. The motive of the next murder was also financial; he chloroformed a wealthy woman who lived above his restaurant, and presumably gained possession of her money.

The disappearance of the Williams sisters, for which Holmes was wanted for questioning in Texas, took place in 1893. Holmes had met Minnie Williams in New York in 1888, and in 1893, he offered her the job of secretary and bookkeeper. Minnie apparently had "an innocent and child-like nature," and was soon induced to give Holmes $2,500 in cash and to transfer $50,000 in real estate in Texas. Minnie had a sister named Nannie, and she was persuaded to come to Chicago on a visit. Nannie was pushed into the vault and gassed, and in her violent struggles she left behind her footprint on the vault door, where it was later found by police. He than took Minnie on a trip to Momence, Illinois, and rented a house, where he poisoned her and buried her in the basement. In the spring of 1894, Holmes and Pitezel went to Fort Worth, Texas, and built a store on the land once owned by Minnie Williams.

Another "business partner" was the next to die, Holmes having become disappointed with his business acumen. After that, Holmes found among Minnie Williams's papers an insurance policy on the life of her brother Baldwin, of Leadville, Colorado. This was too good an opportunity to miss, so Holmes hurried to Leadville, faked a quarrel with Baldwin Williams, and apparently shot him in self-defense. He was probably reckoning that in the wild west of the 1890s, no one was going to make too much fuss about a killing caused by a quarrel. Holmes's confession fails to explain how he induced the insurance company to pay him the money. The explanation of this discretion is probably that Holmes induced his latest "wife," a pretty girl named Georgina Yoke, to pose as Minnie Williams and claim the money; Holmes seems to have been genuinely in love with Georgina, and burst into tears when she gave evidence at his trial.

It was after the murder of Baldwin Williams that Holmes embarked on his plan to murder the whole Pitezel family for the $10,000 insurance money. In spite of his murders and swindles Holmes was apparently still urgently in need of money. But with his first encounter with the Pinkerton agency, his luck ran out and his arrest in Boston terminated three and a half years of murder.

At his trial in October 1895, Holmes was accused only of the murder of Pitezel. When Mrs. Pitezel told her story, even the judge was so deeply moved that he had to grope for his handkerchief. So the defense argument that Pitezel's death was suicide was virtually irrelevant; Holmes was really on trial for the murder of the Pitezel children. It took the jury three hours to find him guilty of murder. Back in prison, Holmes wrote his confession to 27 murders, which was syndicated by the Hearst newspapers. It was so horrific that many believe that Holmes was simply writing it for the $10,000 that Hearst paid him (and which went to Georgina Yoke). But his jailer observed that, after the confession, Holmes behaved as if a great burden had been lifted from his mind; he announced his conversion to Catholicism. He was firmly convinced that his career of crime had caused physical changes—a shortening of one arm and one leg and the "malevolent distortion" of one side of his face, which was so marked that he grew a beard to conceal it. That this was not entirely imagination is proved by photographs of Holmes reproduced in David Franke's book *The Torture Doctor*. In the November 1966 issue of *The Criminologist*, there is an article that discusses an old theory that the left and right sides of the human face reflect two different aspects of the character: that the left side is the "natural" character and the right the "acquired." (If a mirror is placed down the center of a photograph, so the face becomes two left sides or two right, an interesting difference often emerges.) The difference between the two halves of Holmes's face is marked enough to justify his assertion that "I have commenced to assume the form and features of the Evil One himself." The confession certainly reveals that, as in the case of the Yorkshire Ripper, killing became an addictive drug that literally turned Holmes into a monster.

Unpredictable to the very end, Holmes withdrew all his

confessions on the scaffold on 7 May 1896, and declared
that he had never killed anyone; Holmes always possessed a
strong dramatic streak, and probably felt that he owed some
last memorable gesture to the immense crowd that gathered
to see him hanged. Even his death was dramatic. When the
trap fell, it became obvious that the fall had not broken his
neck; his body swayed and contorted for at least a minute,
and two spectators fainted.

Holmes's celebrity had become so great that a number of
people made offers for his body—a man who offered Holmes's
lawyer $5,000 for it probably wanted to embalm it and show
it at fairgrounds. Holmes thwarted this by ordering that his
body should be encased in cement in its coffin; his lawyer
went one better, and had the coffin buried 10 feet deep, and
covered with a two foot layer of cement.

——————————————— 3 ———————————————

By comparison with the Holmes case, the murder of Henry
Smith, which occurred in London in the year of Holmes's
execution, has an old-fashioned, almost Dickensian air.

Henry Smith was a grey-bearded but vigorous gentleman
of 80, who lived alone in the north London suburb of
Muswell Hill. As a precaution against burglars, he had
screwed down most of the windows in the house, and his
gardener Webber had filled the garden with trip-wires connected to bells and detonating cartridges; these had already
discouraged one burglar. But when Webber arrived for work
on the morning of 14 February 1896, he found the kitchen
door wide open, and the body of Mr. Smith lying on the
floor. He was wearing a blood-spattered nightshirt, and his
hands and legs had been tied; there was also a gag in his
mouth. Death was due to blows on the head from some
blunt instrument. The old man had obviously disturbed two
burglars—two sets of footprints were found in the flower
bed outside the kitchen window, which had been forced with
a jemmy. The bedroom safe had been opened, and the house
thoroughly ransacked.

Chief Inspector Marshall of Scotland Yard was summoned to the scene by Inspector Nutkins of the local CID. They found only one clue, and that was a puzzling one: a child's toy lantern in the kitchen sink, together with a soaked box of matches. The neat way in which the trip-wires had been snipped, and the jemmy marks on the various windows, indicated that the burglars were professionals; but the toy lantern seemed incongruous—surely professional burglars would carry the real thing?

The crime looked insoluble; scientific detection—in so far as it existed in 1896—had no material on which to operate. The only possible approach to the mystery was the old-fashioned needle-in-the-haystack method, which had now become standard police procedure. For the next few weeks, Inspector Nutkins and his team went from door to door throughout the area, asking residents if they had noticed any suspicious characters around the time of the murder. Eventually, he found two witnesses whose stories sounded promising. A Mrs. Good had been accosted by two rough-looking men a few days before the murder, and asked the way to Coldfall Woods. They had also asked her about late night trains from Muswell Hill. But their most significant query was about whether certain gardens had entrances leading into the woods. They mentioned various houses, and Mrs Good thought they had included Muswell Lodge, the home of Henry Smith.

Another neighbor, a Mrs. Wheaton, had also seen two rough-looking strangers in a lane near Muswell Lodge two days before the murder; one of them turned and glared at her as though he thought she was spying on them. Their looks had terrified her.

Fingerprint classification did not exist in 1896—or at least, had not reached Scotland Yard. But there was another type of classification that might be useful. That remarkable sleuth Adolphus ("Dolly") Williamson had already started a file in which criminals were classified by their methods—their *modus operandi*. Here were two professional burglars who worked in tandem. Marshall checked the file and noted a number of possible suspects. And he also sent out a

directive to all metropolitan police stations to look out for
rough-looking burglars who worked together. This was read
by a detective named Ernest Burrell in Kentish Town, only a
mile or so down the road form Muswell Hill. Burrell noted
the suggestion that police should be on the lookout for
"ticket of leave" men—criminals on parole—who had failed
to report to police stations; he knew that when such men
return to crime, they usually stop reporting. One such ticket
of leave convict was Henry Fowler, a huge, brutal man who
looked like Dickens's Bill Sykes, and for some weeks now,
Fowler had been drinking in the company of a crook named
Albert Milsom. Burrell decided to check on Milsom, who
lived in Southam Street; he was met by a pale, tired-looking
woman, who said that her husband was away working, and
she had no idea of his address. Further checks in the area
revealed that neither Milsom nor Fowler had been seen in
their usual haunts from two days before the murder until two
days afterwards.

Later the same day, Burrell intercepted a letter written by
Mrs Milsom to her husband; it told him that the police had
been looking for him, and warned him that they were
looking for Fowler because he had failed to report to the
police station.

The police now had Milsom's address, but at this stage it
would have been pointless taking him in for questioning.
They had no evidence. Admittedly, Milsom and Fowler
sounded like the two men described by Mrs. Cook and Mrs
Wheaton; but even if the two ladies identified them, that
should still prove nothing. It was certainly tempting to arrest
them and try and force a confession, for the murder had
caused panic in north London. But while Marshall hesitated,
Milsom changed his address.

Marshall was already following another line of inquiry:
the stolen money. He talked to the old man's bank, and
learned that he had drawn out a £10 note shortly before his
death; and since £10 was a large sum in 1896—more than
twice the weekly wage of a detective—the clerk had
recorded its serial number. This note had been among cash
stolen from the safe, and its number was circulated to all

banks. Six weeks after the murder, the Bank of England reported that it had been paid in. Marshall traced it to a firm of tea merchants, who thought that it had been paid to them by a grocer in the East End of London. The grocer was able to remember where it had come from: a local publican had used it to pay his grocery bill. And the publican clearly remembered changing the note. He had been unwilling to do so, but the man who had presented it was a big, powerful-looking individual with an unpleasant glint in his eyes. That was a good description of Henry Fowler.

Meanwhile, in Muswell Hill, Inspector Nutkins had been following up the only real clue: the toy lantern. The Milsoms had two children, and Mrs. Milsom's younger brother, a 16-year-old named Harry Miller, also lived with them. Nutkins knew that if he asked the children about the lantern, he would be told nothing—they had obviously been brought up to regard the police as natural enemies. So Nutkins secured the co-operation of a local boy, one of Harry Miller's friends, and entrusted him with the lantern, with instructions to produce it casually. It worked; Harry Miller demanded to look more closely, and promptly claimed it as his own. How could he be so sure? Because the original wick had not burned properly, and he had fashioned another wick from a strip of red flannel, which was still in the lantern. Besides, he recognized other distinctive features, such as the cracking of a green glass panel, and a place where he had scraped away some varnish . . . At that moment, Burrell happened to wander by, and listened without apparent interest. He asked how Harry Miller had come to lose his lantern; Harry said it had vanished from the kitchen dresser. When asked what Milsom had been doing that night, he recalled that his brother-in-law had not come home until seven in the morning. And when Harry had complained about the loss of his lantern, Milsom had told him to tell anyone who inquired that he had broken it and thrown it away.

Now Marshall knew he had found his killers; but where were they now? The police intercepted a letter from

Milsom to his wife; it contained no address, but the postmark was Bow. It took some time to trace the pair in the Bow area of east London, and when they did, the wanted men had already left, saying they were going to Liverpool. This worried Marshall; they might already be on a ship to America. But in the dock area of Liverpool he picked up their traces again, and learned that they had been spending money freely—the old man's safe was said to have contained £700. From Liverpool the pair were traced to Manchester, then to Cardiff—by now they were using the names Taylor and Scott. In Cardiff, they had gone to see a phrenologist who was traveling with a fair, and "Professor Sinclair" had read their bumps. They told him they were seamen who were looking for work ashore, and were taken on as partners in Sinclair's waxworks business.

It was less difficult to trace the waxworks; it had moved to Swindon, then Chippenham, then Bath, and the police followed it to each of these places. They caught up with Milsom and Fowler—now calling themselves Stevenson and Walsh—in Monmouth Street, Bath. They had taken a room above a sweet shop, together with the "professor." That night—Sunday 12 April, eight weeks after the murder— the police burst into the room at 11 o'clock. Nutkins was carrying a loaded revolver. Marshall shouted "Hands up, we are police officers," and Milsom groaned "Oh my God!" But Fowler fought like a demon, and Marshall had to strike him on the head with his revolver before he fell to the floor and could be handcuffed. In the upholstery of the couch, the police found Fowler's loaded revolver.

At the local police station they were charged with murdering Henry Smith of Muswell Lodge; then they were separated. Fowler remained contemptuous and abusive; Milsom cowered and whined. Both denied the murder charge. Asked why, in that case, he had resisted arrest so violently, Fowler said he thought he was being arrested for failing to report at the police station. His alibi was that he was in a lodging-house in Kentish Town on the night of the murder.

The chief witness against them was the youth Harry

Miller, who had been placed in a special home in case Milsom and Fowler learned of his betrayal. In court, it was soon obvious that the case against them was damning. At this point, it struck Milsom that he might save his own neck by turning Queen's evidence. Standing beside Fowler, he told the court that he had nothing to do with the murder. According to Milsom, Fowler had planned the "job" with another crook, who had let him down at the last moment; on the evening of the burglary he had gone to Milsom's house, and finally persuaded him to join him. They had taken the toy lantern, and climbed into the old man's garden, carefully cutting the trip-wires. When it was dark, they broke in. The old man heard them and came downstairs with a light, shouting "Police, murder!" Milsom alleged that he was so alarmed that he ran away, expecting the neighborhood to be aroused. When all was silent, he went back and found Fowler standing over the old man's body. "It's your fault, you cur!" snarled Fowler, "for leaving a man on his own." They then ransacked the house and opened the safe with a key found in the old man's trouser pocket. After that, they went and hid in the woods until dawn, then walked home, with Fowler wearing Milsom's overcoat to hide the blood on his clothes. Later that day, he called at Milsom's house and gave him £53 as his share of the loot.

As Fowler listened to all this, he lunged at Milsom and tried to get his hands around his throat; the policeman who also stood in the dock dragged them apart. Then Fowler gave his own version. The safe had contained £112, he said, and he had given Milsom £53 of it; was that likely if Milsom had been a mere onlooker? According to Fowler, Milsom had stood with his foot on the old man's neck until he was dead. And the judge himself was to point out that two pocket knives had been found by the body—knives that had been used to cut up the table-cloth that had been used to bind the victim; this showed conclusively that Milsom had helped to tie the old man, and had therefore been present when he was killed.

For the second time, Fowler tried to kill his companion; this time he succeeded in getting a grip on his throat and hurling him to the floor; police filled the dock and tried to drag them apart; the glass screen around the dock shattered and the dock itself swayed. Fowler struggled to his feet, lashing out at the police who held him and kicking at Milsom, who was still on the floor. Then handcuffs were snapped on his wrists, and he was dragged out of court, still roaring defiance. The fight had lasted 12 minutes.

He was returned to court when the jury filed in; in the ruins of the dock, they heard themselves sentenced to death. In his cell, Fowler made two attempts to kill himself, but was prevented by guards. The two of them were hanged at Newgate, together with a man named William Seaman who had murdered an old man called Levy and his housekeeper; it is said that, as he stood between them on the trapdoor, Seaman remarked; "It's the first time I've ever been a bloody peacemaker."

---------------------------------- 4 ----------------------------------

The year 1898 saw the publication of two massive works on the history of crime and crime detection: *Mysteries of Police and Crime* by Major Arthur Griffiths, and *Murder in All Ages* by Matthew Worth Pinkerton, who was then the head of the Pinkerton detective agency. Both are heroic attempts to write a world history of crime, and both are now as readable as when they were written. And, as befits skilled criminal investigators, both have a note of buoyant optimism about the future of crime detection. Griffiths rightly singles out "the patient investigations of the medical expert, M. Bertillon of Paris" as the brightest hope for the next century. Pinkerton announces cheerfully that the increase in crime is only apparent, due to better "transmission of news," and states his belief that "a brighter era has dawned for mankind," due to the "wider dissemination of knowledge" and "the awakened conscience of thousands of men and women who are forgetting something of self that they may reclaim and elevate their fellows." He would have been saddened to learn that he was living in the dawn of a new "crime explosion."

France, the country of Orfila, Lacassagne, and Bertillon, undoubtedly led the world in scientific crime detection. Yet the recognition of their own pre-eminence could occasionally lure the French into truly monumental errors of judgement, which were sometimes—as in the Dreyfus case—complicated by a refusal to acknowledge the error. Such was the incredible affair of the "ogress of the Goutte d'Or."

In the Goutte d'Or, a slum passageway in Montmartre, lived four brothers named Weber, one of whose wives, Jeanne Weber, had lost two of her three children, and consoled herself with cheap red wine. Just around the corner lived her brother-in-law Pierre and his wife. On 2 March 1905, Mme. Pierre asked her sister-in-law if she would baby-sit with her two children, Suzanne and Georgette, while she went to the public *lavoir*, the 1905 equivalent of a launderette. Mme. Pierre had been there only a short time when a neighbor rushed in and told her that 18-month-old Georgette was ill—she had heard her choking and gasping as she passed. The mother hurried home, and found her child on the bed, her face blue and with foam around her mouth; her aunt Jeanne was massaging the baby's chest. Mme. Pierre took the child on her lap and rubbed her back until her breathing became easier, then went back to the launderette. But when she returned an hour later, with a basket of clean washing, Georgette was dead. The neighbor observed some red marks on the baby's throat, and pointed them out to the father, but he seems to have shrugged it off. Nobody felt any suspicion towards Jeanne Weber, who had behaved admirably and apparently done her best.

Nine days later, when both parents had to be away from home, they again asked Aunt Jeanne to baby-sit. Two-year-old Suzanne was dead when they returned, again with foam around her mouth. The doctor diagnosed the cause of death as convulsions. Aunt Jeanne appeared to be dazed with grief.

Two weeks later, on 25 March, Jeanne Weber went to visit another brother-in-law, Leon Weber, and was left with the 7-month-old daughter Germaine while her mother went shopping. The grandmother, who lived on the floor below, heard sudden cries, and hurried upstairs to find Germaine in "convulsions," gasping for breath. After a few minutes of rubbing and patting, the baby recovered, and the grandmother returned to her own room. Minutes later, as she talked with a neighbor, she once more heard the child's cries. Again she hurried upstairs and found the baby choking. The neighbor who had accompanied her noticed the red marks on the child's throat. When the parents returned, Germaine had recovered.

The following day, Jeanne Weber came to inquire after the baby. And, incredibly, the mother again left her baby-sitting. When she returned, her child was dead. The doctor diagnosed the cause as diphtheria.

Three days later, on the day of Germaine's funeral, Jeanne Weber stayed at home with her own child Marcel; he suffered the same convulsions, and was dead when the others returned.

A week later, on 5 April, Jeanne Weber invited to lunch the wife of Pierre Weber, and the wife of another brother-in-law, Charles. Mme. Charles brought her 10-month-old son Maurice, a delicate child. After lunch, Jeanne baby-sat while her in-laws went shopping. When they returned, Maurice was lying on the bed, blue in the face, with foam around his lips, breathing with difficulty. The hysterical mother accused Jeanne of strangling him—there were marks on his throat—and she furiously denied it. So Mme. Charles swept up her child in her arms, and hastened to the Hospital Brétonneau. She was sent immediately to the children's ward where a Dr. Saillant examined the marks on Maurice's throat. It certainly looked as if someone had tried to choke him. And when he heard the story of the other four deaths in the past month, Dr. Saillant became even more suspicious. So was his colleague Dr. Sevestre, and together they informed the police of this unusual case. Jeanne Weber was brought in for questioning, and Inspector Coiret began to look into her background. When he learned that all three of her children had died in convulsions, and that three years earlier, two other children—Lucie Alexandre and Marcel Poyatos—had died in the same mysterious way when in the care of Jeanne Weber, suspicion turned to certainty. The only thing that amazed him was that the Weber family had continued to ask her to baby-sit; they were either singularly fatalistic or criminally negligent. But then, the death of Jeanne's own son Marcel had dispelled any suspicions that might have been forming. When Examining Magistrate Leydet was informed of this, he found himself wondering whether this was precisely why Marcel had died.

The magistrate decided to call in a medical expert, and asked Dr. Léon Henri Thoinot, one of Paris's most distinguished "expert witnesses," second only to Paul Brouardel, the author of a classic book on strangulation and suffocation. Thoinot began by examining Maurice, who had now fully recovered. The child seemed perfectly healthy, and it was hard to see why he should have choked. Thoinot decided it could have been bronchitis. Next, the bodies of three of the dead children—Georgette, Suzanne, and Germaine—were exhumed. Thoinot could find no traces of strangulation on their throats. Finally, Thoinot studied the body of Jeanne Weber's son Marcel; again he decided there was no evidence of strangulation—for example, the hyoid bone, which is easily broken by pressure on the throat, was intact.

The accusations of murder had caused a public sensation; Jeanne Weber was the most hated woman in France. The magistrate, Leydet, had no doubt whatsoever of her guilt. Yet at her trial on 29 January 1906, Thoinot once again stated his opinion that there was no evidence that the children had died by violence, while the defense lawyer Henri Robert—an unscrupulous man who had unsuccessfully defended Gabrielle Bompard—intimidated the prosecution witnesses until they contradicted themselves. The "ogress of the Goutte d'Or"—as public opinion had christened her—was acquitted on all charges. The audience in the courtroom underwent a change of heart and cheered her. And Brouardel and Thoinot collaborated on an article in a medical journal in which they explained once again why Jeanne Weber had been innocent.

The public did not think so. Nor did her husband, who left her. Jeanne Weber decided that she had better move to some place where she was not known. She was a flabby, sallow-faced woman, who had little chance of attracting another male. And at that point, rescue arrived out of the blue. A man named Sylvain Bavouzet wrote to her from a place called Chambon—in the department of Indre—offering her a job as his housekeeper; it seemed he had been touched by her sad tale, and by the injustice that had almost condemned her to death. In the spring of 1907, Jeanne Weber—now calling herself by her unmarried name Moulinet—arrived at the farm of Sylvain Bavouzet, and understood that the offer had not been made entirely out of the goodness of his heart. It was a miserable, poverty-stricken place, and Bavouzet was a widower with three children, the eldest an ugly girl with a hare lip. What he wanted was cheap labor and a female to share his bed. But at least it was a home.

A month later, on 16 April 1907, Bavouzet came home to find that his 9-year-old son Auguste was ill. He had recently eaten a large amount at a local wedding feast, so his discomfort could have been indigestion. The child's sister Louise was sent to the local town Villedieu to ask the doctor to call. But Dr. Papazoglou gave her some indigestion mixture and sent her on her way. Hours later, Sylvain Bavouzet arrived, in a state of agitation, and said the boy was worse. When Papazoglou arrived, Auguste was dead, and the new housekeeper was standing by the bedside. The child was wearing a clean shirt, tightly buttoned at the collar, and when this was opened, the doctor saw a red mark around his neck. This led him to refuse a death certificate. The next day, the coroner, Charles Audiat, decided that, in spite of the red mark, Auguste's death was probably due to meningitis.

The dead boy's elder sister Germaine, the girl with the hare lip, hated the new housekeeper. She had overheard what "Mme Moulinet" had told the doctor, and knew it was mostly lies. Her brother had not vomited just before his death—so requiring a change of shirt. Precisely how Germaine realized that Mme. Moulinet was the accused murderess

Jeanne Weber is not certain. One account of the case declares that she came upon Jeanne Weber's picture by chance in a magazine given to them by neighbors; another asserts that she searched the housekeeper's bag and found press cuttings about the case. What is certain is that she took her evidence to the police station in Villedieu and accused Mme. Moulinet of murdering her brother.

An examining magistrate demanded a new autopsy, and this was performed by Dr. Frédéric Bruneau. He concluded that there *was* evidence that Auguste had been strangled, possibly with a tourniquet. (Doctors had found a scarf wrapped around the throat of Maurice Weber, the child who had survived.) Jeanne Weber was arrested. The new accusation caused a sensation in Paris.

Understandably, Henri Robert, the man who had been responsible for her acquittal, felt that this reflected upon his professional integrity. Thoinot and Brouardel agreed. They decided that the unfortunate woman must once again be saved from public prejudice. Robert agreed to defend her for nothing, while Thoinot demanded another inquest. He carried it out three and a half months after the child's death, by which time decay had made it impossible to determine whether Auguste Bavouzet had been strangled. Predictably, Thoinot decided that Auguste had died of natural causes—intermittent fever. More doctors were called in. They agreed with Thoinot. The latter's prestige was such that Examining Magistrate Belleau decided to drop the charges against Jeanne Weber, although he was personally convinced of her guilt. Henri Robert addressed the Forensic Medicine Society and denounced the ignorance and stupidity of provincial doctors and magistrates. Jeanne Weber was free to kill again.

History repeated itself. A philanthropic doctor named Georges Bonjeau, president of the Society for the Protection of Children, offered her a job in the children's home in Orgeville. There she was caught trying to throttle a child and dismissed. But, like Thoinot and Henri Robert, Bonjeau did not believe in admitting his mistakes and he kept the matter to himself.

She became a tramp, living by prostitution. Arrested for vagrancy, she told M. Hamard, chief of the Sûreté, that she had been responsible for the deaths of her nieces. Then she withdrew the statement, and was sent to an asylum in Nanterre, from which she was quickly released as sane. A man named Joly offered her protection, and she lived with him at Lay-Saint-Remy, near Toul, until he grew tired of her and threw her out. Again she became a prostitute, and finally met a lime-burner named Émile Bouchery, who worked in the quarries of Euville, near Commercy. They lived in a room in a cheap inn run by a couple named Poirot. One evening, "Mme Bouchery" told the Poirots that she was afraid that Bouchery meant to beat her up—as he did periodically when drunk—and asked them if their 7-year-old son Marcel could sleep in her bed. They agreed. At 10 o'clock that evening, a child's screams were heard, and the Poirots broke into Mme. Bouchery's room. Marcel was dead, his mouth covered in bloodstained foam. Mme. Bouchery was also covered in blood. A hastily summoned doctor realized that the child had been strangled, and had bitten his tongue in his agony. It was the police who discovered a letter from *maître* Henri Robert in Mme. Bouchery's pocket, and realized that she was Jeanne Weber.

Once again, the reputations of Thoinot and Robert were at stake (Brouardel having escaped the public outcry by dying in 1906). Incredibly, both declined to admit their error. They agreed that the evidence proved unmistakably that Jeanne Weber had killed Marcel Poirot, but this, they insisted, was her first murder, brought about by the stress of years of persecution. It is unnecessary to say that the French Press poured scorn on this view. Yet such was the influence of Thoinot that Jeanne Weber was not brought to trial; instead she was moved out of the public gaze to an asylum on the island of Maré, off New Caledonia in the Pacific. There she died in convulsions two years later, her hands locked around her own throat.

─────────────────── 5 ───────────────────

At the time of Jeanne Weber's death, another French
mass murderer had already embarked on the career that
would end under the guillotine. But in 1910, Henri Desiré
Landru was in prison for a series of pathetically amateurish
frauds. The latest of these had involved advertising for a
wife in a Lille newspaper, which led to an "understanding"
with a 40-year-old widow named Izoret. Landru handed
her his "deeds," and she handed over her cashbox,
containing 20,000 francs. Then he vanished. In March
1910 Landru was sentenced to three years in prison, his
fifth sentence in 10 years. He was released in 1913, and
within a year, had to flee from Paris to avoid prosecution
for embezzlement.

In May 1918, the mayor of Gambais, a village about 40
kilometers south-west of Paris, received a letter from Mlle
Lacoste, a domestic servant, inquiring about her sister Mme.
Celestine Buisson, who had gone to live in Gambais with
her fiancé, M. Fremyet, in the previous September. Since
then, her family had heard nothing from her.

The mayor recalled that he had received a similar letter
from Mme. Pelat, inquiring about her sister Anna Collomb,
who had also come to Gambais to live with her fiancé—a
M. Dupont—and disappeared. As the mayor considered the
two letters, he found himself wondering whether M. Fremyet
and M. Dupont might conceivably be the same person. Mlle
Lacoste had described the whereabouts of the villa—she had
once visited her sister there—and it sounded to the mayor
like the Villa Ermitage, owned by a M. Tric. He strolled out
and inspected the villa—it was locked and shuttered. Then
he spoke to the local shoemaker, who had given the keys to
M. Dupont. It seemed that M. Dupont was a small, bald-
headed man of 50 with a jutting beard, and he had been at
the villa with many ladies. Since this villa was plainly the
one described by Mlle Lacoste, it seemed clear that Dupont
and Fremyet *were* the same person. Back at the town hall,

the mayor dictated a reply, regretting that he was unable to help Mlle Lacoste, but mentioning that he had received . . . that he had received a similar query from the Pelat family, and enclosing their address.

Mlle Lacoste hastened to contact the Pelat family, who were a step above her on the social scale. And when she described M. Fremyet—the bald head, the beard, the piercing eyes—Mme. Pelat went pale and said: "That is certainly Monsieur Dupont."

On 6 April 1919, Commissioner Dautel of the Paris Préfecture of Police, summoned Inspector Jean Belin, and handed him the file of the disappearance of the two women. Belin soon established that M. Tric, the owner of the villa, had never met his tenant; Dupont had given an address in the rue Darnetal, in Rouen. But at the rue Darnetal, no one had ever heard of either Dupont or Fremyet.

Belin called on Mlle Lacoste, and was allowed to see her with some difficulty—servants were not allowed visitors. She was at first unwilling to speak to him but finally retold her story. In 1915, her sister, a widow of 44, had answered a matrimonial advertisement inserted by M. Fremyet, a rich land-owner; they met, she was fascinated, and became his mistress. But it was not until 1917 that she went to live with him at Gambais, and disappeared . . .

She could offer no further lead. Earnestly, Belin told her that if she happened to see M. Fremyet, she was to contact him immediately—he handed her his card. Then he went to call on Mme. Collomb, mother of the missing Anna. When he returned to the Préfecture, he was convinced that he had a murder case on his hands; his colleagues ridiculed the idea. But that evening at seven o'clock, just as he was preparing to leave his office, he received an excited telephone call from Mlle Lacoste. "Thank heavens you're still there. I've just seen him, in a china shop in the rue de Rivoli . . ."

Belin lost no time in joining her. She had, it seemed, been walking along the rue de Rivoli when she saw "Fremyet" walking arm in arm with a young woman. She had followed him into a china shop, "Lions de Faïence", and watched them choose a dinner service. He had paid a deposit and left his card. She had tried to follow them when they left the shop, but they had boarded a bus before she could reach them. Trying to jump on board, she had almost bumped into Fremyet, and he had looked straight into her eyes . . .

Belin's heart sank. Had he recognized her? If so, he may have already left his present lodgings. Belin hurried to the shop, and found that it had just closed. He obtained the manager's address from the night-watchman, and took a taxi there. It was out in the suburbs. The manager was unable to help him, but gave him the name of the assistant—he even offered to drive him there. The assistant was able to describe his customer—it was quite obviously Fremyet—but was unable to recall his name or address. Belin begged the manager and assistant to return with him to the shop. They searched . . . searched for the invoice, and found it with the card attached. The man's name was Guillet, and his address was 76 rue de Rochechouart.

Belin had to tread delicately. He had no warrant for "Guillet's" arrest; he had no proof that Guillet had been involved in any crime. Therefore he could not rush in and arrest him. Instead, Belin talked to the concierge, and was dismayed to learn that M. Guillet and his lady—a Mme Fernande Segret—had already left. They had not taken their belongings, but that meant nothing. If he knew he was being hunted, his quarry would lose no time in vanishing, preferably leaving no trace. Belin cursed his luck.

The next step was to get a warrant for Fremyet's arrest, in case he was traced. Then the house in rue Rochechouart was placed under round-the-clock surveillance. Since "Fremyet" was given to advertising, he instituted a search of newspaper columns, looking for the name of Lucien Guillet. They soon found one—a M. Guillet had advertised a car for sale at Etampes.

Belin set about cultivating the concierge, and soon gained his confidence. Meanwhile, like Simenon's Maigret, he sat round in local bars and cafés, keeping his ears open. And while he was sitting over his glass of white wine one evening, the concierge hurried in and whispered frantically: "*He's back.*"

Unfortunately, it was now after dark, and French law ordained that a search of a suspect's premises could not be conducted at night. So Belin stood outside Guillet's flat all night—at least the concierge allowed him into the building— and periodically placed his ear to the door. As the dawn broke, his colleague Inspector Riboulet tiptoed upstairs to join him.

At 9:30 he knocked on the door. There was no reply. Finally, a sleepy voice asked him what he wanted. Belin replied that he had come from Etampes about the car advertisement. The voice asked him to come back later. Belin said he couldn't. The key turned and the door opened a crack. Both men pushed it open, and grasped the small, dark-bearded man who stood there in his dressing-gown. He looked outraged. "What is the meaning of this?" "Police. We have a warrant for your arrest." (Belin hoped the man would not ask to see it, for it was made out in the name of Fremyet, and Guillet could have thrown them out.) At the mention of police, there was a scream from the bedroom and a thud; the policemen followed Guillet through the door and saw a beautiful naked girl sprawled on the floor. They tactfully withdrew as Guillet comforted her and for a moment their eyes met. Neither was certain that Guillet was Fremyet and Dupont; this could all be a terrible mistake. But as Guillet prepared to leave, Belin began to experience a sense that all was well after all. Guillet was singing an aria from Massenet's *Manon*: "Adieu notre petite table . . . ," the air the lover sings before he is forced to abandon his mistress. It was not quite what one might expect from an innocent man who expected to clear up the misunderstanding in half an hour. And as Guillet left the lovely Fernande Segret, he kissed her long and tenderly, as if knowing that this was the last time.

As Guillet was being driven off to the Préfecture in charge of Riboulet and another policeman, Riboulet observed that he was cautiously trying to extract something from his pocket, obviously thinking of throwing it out of the open window. Riboulet seized his wrist and forced from the tightly clenched hand a small black notebook. "I wonder why you were so anxious to get rid of this?" Riboulet asked as he slipped the book into his pocket.

Still in the flat in the rue Rochechouart, Belin was engaged in an illegal search (for he had no warrant). In an overcoat pocket, he came across an envelope addressed to

"Landru." It aroused a flash of nostalgia, for he had once used that name himself when on a "dirty weekend" with a mistress.

Back at the Préfecture, Belin glanced with interest at the small black notebook retrieved by Riboulet, and also at a smaller notebook found in Guillet's pocket. He glanced inside it, and saw two names that told him he had arrested the right suspect: they were Collomb and Buisson. But when asked about them, Guillet merely shrugged and said: "I have nothing to say." This man knew he was in a trap. He knew he would forfeit his head. His only hope was to refuse to admit anything, to leave it to the police to prove his guilt. Even at this early stage, Belin could sense this.

His next step was to search the files for a Landru. He found it without difficulty, and discovered to his delight that Landru was still wanted for a number of offenses committed between 1913 and 1914. This was welcome news, for it meant he could hold Landru without a more up-to-date charge.

"Guillet" made no attempt to deny that he was Henri Desire Landru, born in Paris in 1869; but when Belin mentioned murder, he shrugged and said that they would be unable to sustain that accusation.

Belin studied the black notebook. "I see that on December 28, 1918, you bought a single and a return ticket, costing 3.95 and 4.95 francs. I happened to know that these are the fares from the Gare des Invalides to Houdan, the nearest station to Gambais. Why did you take a return for yourself and a single for your companion?"

Landru shrugged. "It is too far back to remember."

The police went on questioning him in relays. They had to admit to a certain grudging admiration for the man. He did not bluster or whine or plead; merely remained completely cool and detached. He behaved like a man who is quite sure that he can never be found guilty. That thought disturbed Belin.

He left another officer questioning Landru while he went through the papers he had taken from the flat. Among these was a rent receipt for a garage in Clichy. He went there and found that it was used as a storage place for all kinds of odds and ends—furniture, bedroom junk, women's underclothes, even false teeth. But in a corner there were documents that bore the names Buisson and Collomb, including marriage and birth certificates. They only confirmed what Belin knew: that these women were dead. The problem was to prove it—and, if possible, to discover the remains.

The following day, Landru was taken around the villa at Gambais. It was uncomfortable and badly furnished, hardly a "love nest." In one room there was a trunk with the initials "C.L." Asked if it belonged to him, Landru said: "Of course—C.L. stands for Charles Landru."

"No. Your name is Henri Desiré Landru. This trunk belonged to Celestine Lacoste, or Madame Buisson—the label is from her home town of Bayonne. Where is she?"

Landru shrugged. "I gave her a few hundred francs to get rid of her."

"Where did she go?"

"I have no idea."

And this continued to be Landru's answer to all questions about the list of names—10 of them—that appeared in his notebook. There were many others—amounting to nearly 300—but these 10 were names of women who had disappeared.

But all attempts to find bodies, or evidence of murder, were a failure. Various stains on mattresses, walls, clothes, were examined, but they proved not to be bloodstains. Ponds were drained or dragged, but nothing was found. The likeliest possibility was that Landru had burned his victims in a huge stove he had had installed at Gambais—Belin tried the experiment of burning a sheep's head, and it was consumed in a quarter of an hour. In the stove installed in his basement by H. H. Holmes, women's hair had been found in the chimney; in Landru's stove, the forensic experts could find nothing that suggested murder.

Belin began the long task of trying to trace the 283 women mentioned in Landru's notebook. Landru himself flatly declined to discuss any of them. But, little by little, Belin began to piece together Landru's career. From the little notebook (*carnet*) it seemed that Landru had decided to embark on a career of murder after his release in 1913. That was logical. Landru had tried his most ambitious swindle so far—absconding with Mme. Izoret's dowry—and been caught because she had reported him to the police. If Mme. Izoret had not been alive to report him, he might well have escaped . . . Now Landru was determined to continue to pursue his career of seduction combined with fraud—it was so much more enjoyable than mere fraud. It suited his romanticism, his vanity, and his intense sexual drive. So he continued to advertise for lonely widows. In 1914, he made the acquaintance of an attractive widow, Mme. Jeanne Cuchet, who had a son of 17; she worked in a lingerie store. Landru introduced himself as Raymond Diard. In April 1914 they set up house together in the Paris suburb of Chantilly. Landru had introduced her to his two small daughters, but omitted to tell her that their mother Maria, whom he had married in 1893, was still alive; now, he claimed, he had sent the daughters to live with an aunt. He lost no time in transferring 5,000 francs of her money into his own account. Her relations instinctively disliked Landru. Endless delays in the marriage plans led her to storm out; Landru pursued her with love letters. Mme. Cuchet asked her sister and brother-in-law to help smooth things over, and they went to the villa at Chantilly. It was empty; but in a box they found letters that revealed unmistakably that "Diard" was a swindler and a seducer, as well as being already married. This should have been the end of the association. But Landru (she now knew this was his real name) presented himself at her door, told her he was unhappily married, and promised to get a divorce. Mme. Cuchet and her son moved back to the villa in Chantilly. By the end of March 1915, both had vanished, and neighbors had noticed an unpleasant black smoke issuing from Landru's chimney. The local police were called; Landru protested he was merely burning rubbish, and asked the gendarme to return the next day when his wife would be home from visiting relatives. The next day he wrote to the police, explaining that he had been called away on urgent business, and would be in touch with them as soon as he returned. The matter was not pursued.

Landru had developed his basic method, and he now stuck to it. Victim number three was a Mme. Laborde-Line, widow of a hotelier; she vanished about 26 June 1915, at his new villa at Vernouillet, only five days after she had moved in. Number four was a Mme. Marie Guilli, who possessed 22,000 francs; she moved to Vernouillet in August; a few days later he was selling her bonds and furniture. Now he moved to Gambais, and there disposed of a 55-year-old widow named Mme. Heon; she vanished in December. Anna Collomb, the cause of his ultimate downfall, already had a lover when she answered Landru's advertisement in May 1915; she moved to Gambais just after Christmas 1916, having presented Landru with most of her 8,000 francs. As usual, Landru bought a return ticket for himself and a single for her, saving 1 franc. In the *carnet*, Landru noted after her name: "4 o'clock."

Victim number seven was a 19-year-old servant girl, Andrée Babelay, whom he picked up on a Métro platform when he noticed she was crying. She was poor and unemployed, so the motive was simply "gallantry." In two months he had tired of her, and on 29 March 1917, she accompanied him to Gambais on a one-way ticket. Victim number eight was Mme. Célestine Buisson, whose sister's letter to the mayor of Gambais started the police inquiries; she died on 1 September, netting Landru a mere 1,000 francs. Next came Mme. Barthélemey Louise Jaume, a highly religious woman whose demise in November 1917 brought Landru less than 2,000 francs. Number 10 was a pretty divorcee named Anne-Marie Pascal who supplemented the income from her small dressmaker's business with prostitution. Like Andrée Babelay she was destitute, so Landru's motive must have been purely sexual. But the Pascal case offers one curious clue to Landru's method. After staying with him at Gambais, she rushed back to Paris, to pour out a strange story to her best friend. Landru had knelt at her feet and stared at her with such fixity that she had felt faint; she was unable to move, as though paralyzed. She became unconscious, and rushed back to Paris the next morning. But a month later, on 4 April 1918, she went back, and this time failed to return. Landru wrote "17h.15" after her name.

The final victim was a Mlle Marchadier, another ex-prostitute who had run a small brothel and saved 8,000 francs. Landru offered to buy her furniture, and had to borrow the money from his wife. By Christmas 1918, he was virtually destitute again, and persuaded her to sell her possessions and marry him. She moved to Gambais with her three dogs on 13 January 1919; on the following day, Landru paid several urgent debts. On the 18th, neighbors were disgusted by the stench of burning flesh issuing from the Villa Ermitage. The skeletons of the dogs were later found in the garden.

Ironically, Landru had by this time met the first woman whom he truly loved; Fernande Segret and a friend had been accosted by a "funny old man" on a tramcar, and she agreed to meet him the next day. Soon she was living with him. And in April 1919, their idyll came to an end when Landru was arrested.

This was the story as it was gradually uncovered in court. The courtroom was always crowded with women, who found Landru fascinating; one day, when some of them were unable to find seats, Landru rose courteously in the dock and said: "If one of you ladies would care to take my seat . . ." Yet the story that emerged was not of a demonic seducer but of a fool, a petty swindler who was permanently broke, and who made only about 3,000 francs per victim. Like many mass murderers, he could have made far more at any honest occupation.

Landru's defense council, the fiery Corsican *maître* de Moro-Giafferi, insisted that all the evidence against his client was entirely circumstantial, and he was undoubtedly correct. Many expected Landru to be acquitted, and if strictly legal rules had been applied, he might well have been. That he was, in fact, condemned to death may well have been due to his infuriating arrogance and cool disdain rather than to the evidence. There can be no doubt that if he had taken the precaution of destroying the *carnet*, the case against him would have collapsed. Fortunately, the *carnet* proved his guilt as certainly as 11 corpses would have done, and on 30 November 1921, he was sentenced to death.

The last act, on 25 February 1922, was described by a journalist named Webb Miller. Wearing a shirt from which the neck had been cut away, and a pair of cheap dark trouser, Landru was led out into the courtyard of the Versailles prison as the first streaks of dawn appeared in the sky. Since his condemnation, he had apparently lost interest in life, and spent hours gazing blankly at the ceiling,

On each side a gaoler held Landru by his arms, which were strapped behind him. They supported him and pulled him forward as fast as they could walk. His bare feet pattered on the cold cobblestones, and his knees seemed not to be functioning. His face was pale and waxen, and as he caught sight of the ghastly machine, he went livid.

The two gaolers hastily pushed Landru face foremost against the upright board of the machine. It collapsed, and his body crumpled with it as they shoved him forward under the wooden block, which dropped down and clamped his neck beneath the suspended knife. In a split second the knife flicked down, and the head fell with a thud into a small basket. As an assistant lifted the hinged board and rolled the headless body into the big wicker basket, a hideous spurt of blood gushed out.

An attendant standing in front of the machine seized the basket containing the head, rolled it like a cabbage into a larger basket, and helped shove it hastily into a waiting van. The van doors slammed, and the horses were whipped into a gallop.

When Landru first appeared in the prison courtyard I had glanced at my wrist watch. Now I looked again. Only twenty six seconds had elapsed.

_____ **6** _____

In France, the Landru case was the "crime of the decade," just as the Brides in the Bath case had been in England a few years earlier. But then, the murderers of England and France were old-fashioned and conservative in their habits, and criminals in general behaved much as they had in the nineteenth century. One consequence was that the crime rate in both countries remained low. Across the Atlantic, it was quite different. Society was changing so fast that the criminals had to change with it. The big cities bred a new type of businessman and a new type of crook—in 1916, one ingenious swindler named Louis Enricht persuaded Henry Ford that he had invented a method of running an automobile on water instead of gasoline, and parted him from $10,000, then took another $100,000 from the inventor of the Maxim gun for the same "discovery;" typically, Enricht stayed out of jail.

After the war, America made what was probably the greatest single mistake in its history and passed the Volstead Act outlawing alcohol; the result of Prohibition was an instant doubling of the crime rate, and it went on doubling every year or so. It enriched characters like Al Capone, Johnny Torrio, and Dion O'Banion; by the time it was repealed in 1933, it was too late, and organized crime held America in a grip like an octopus. In any case, America was now in the throes of the great recession, and Capone and Torrio had been replaced as "Public Enemy Number One" by men like John Dillinger, Baby Face Nelson, Clyde Barrow, and Machine Gun Kelly. The latter, who specialized in bootlegging and kidnapping, liked to boast that he could write his name on the side of a barn in bullets.

Kidnapping was a relatively new crime; America's first case had occurred in July 1874, when 4-year-old Charlie Ross was kidnapped from outside his home in Germantown, Philadelphia, and his father, a retired grocer, received a ransom demand for $20,000. But the ransom was never collected, and Charlie Ross was never recovered. In the

December of that year, two burglars were shot down as they crept out of the home of a rich New York banker, and one of them gasped out a dying confession that he and his companion had kidnapped Charlie Ross. They were Joseph Douglass and William Mosher, and their corpses were later identified as the kidnappers by Charlie's brother; but Douglass had no time to say what they had done with Charlie before he died.

In the bootleg era, kidnapping became a major criminal undertaking; now most of the victims were rich businessmen. The gangsters realized that they were as easy to kidnap as a child, and that it aroused less public indignation. But the most horrific case of the 1920s concerned a child, 12-year-old Marian Parker, daughter of a Los Angeles banker; the $1,500 ransom demand was signed "The Fox." On 17 December 1927, Perry Parker took the money to a shadowy street; a masked man at the wheel of a car pointed a gun at him and demanded the money. When Parker asked where his daughter was, the man pointed to a child on the seat beside him; he took the money, and told Parker that he would let Marian out at the end of the street. The child proved to be dead, her hands and legs hacked off, her body disembowelled, and the eyelids propped open with wire.

The following morning, a woman found a suitcase near the place where Marian had been left; it contained torn newspapers, towels, pieces of wire, and a writing pad, all soaked in blood. Laboratory examination established that the writing pad was the same one on which "The Fox" had written his ransom demands, and fingerprints were found. The towels were traced to a nearby apartment building off Sunset Boulevard, and the manager thought that a tenant named Evans seemed to answer the description of the kidnapper. He had now left. Milk bottles found in the apartment bore the same fingerprints as the notepaper, and laboratory analysis revealed spots of human blood on the bathroom floor; there were also traces of human flesh in the drain. A check with the criminal records revealed that the fingerprints were those of a young man jailed for forgery. His name was William Edward Hickman.

In Seattle a few days later, a haberdasher was struck by

the strange, haunted eyes of a young man who came in to buy clothes, and offered a $20 bill in payment; he contacted the police, and discovered that the bill was one of those paid over in ransom. A garage attendant who had taken another of the ransom bills noted that the man was driving an olive-green Hudson. The car—a stolen one—was soon picked up, heading back toward Los Angeles, and Hickman was arrested. Psychiatric examination established that he was suffering from delusions and hearing voices; he had chosen Marian Parker because he believed that her father was responsible for his imprisonment for forgery. In spite of his obvious insanity, he was hanged on 4 February 1928.

Even without the $20 bills, Hickman would undoubtedly have been caught and convicted on forensic evidence. In the most sensational kidnap case of the 1930s, forensic evidence was to play the crucial role in the conviction of the accused man.

March 1, 1932, was a rainy and windy day in Hopewell, New Jersey, and the family of the famous aviator Charles Lindbergh were all suffering from colds—which is why they had decided to delay their departure to the home of their in-laws by 24 hours. At 10 o'clock that evening, the nurse Betty Gow asked Ann Lindbergh if she had taken the baby from his cot. She said no, and they went to ask her husband if he had the baby. Then all three rushed up to the room where 19-month-old Charles Jr. should have been asleep. On the windowsill was a note demanding $50,000 for the child's return.

There were few clues. Under the window the police found some smudged footprints; nearby there was a ladder in three sections and a chisel. The ladder, a crude home-made one, was broken where the top section joined the middle one. There were no fingerprints in the child's room.

The kidnapping caused a nation-wide sensation, and soon Hopewell was swarming with journalists—to Lindbergh's anger and embarrassment: he knew that the furor would make it more difficult for the kidnappers to make contact. Crooks all over the country had reason to curse the kidnappers as the police applied pressure. Meanwhile, the kidnappers were silent.

The note offered few clues. It had variouis spelling mistakes, like "anyding" for "anything," and a handwriting expert said that it had probably been written by a German with low educational qualifications. It was signed by two interlocking circles, one red, one blue.

A week after the kidnapping, a well-wisher named Dr. John F. Condon sent a letter to his local newspaper in the Bronx offering $1,000 of his own money for the return of the child. The result was a letter addressed to Condon signed with two circles—a detail that had not been released to the public. It asked him to act as a go-between, and to place an advertisement reading "Mony is Redy" when he was ready to hand it over.

Lindbergh was convinced by the evidence of the two circles; he instructed Condon to go ahead and place the advertisement. That evening, a man's deep voice spoke to Condon on the telephone—Condon could hear someone else speaking Italian in the background—and told him the gang would soon be in touch. A rendezvous was made at a cemetery; at the gates, a young man with a handkerchief over his face asked if Condon had brought the money; Condon said it was not yet ready. The man took fright and ran away; Condon caught up with him and assured him he could trust him. The man identified himself as "John," and suddenly asked a strange question: "Would I burn if the baby is dead?" Appalled, Condon asked: "Is the baby dead?" The man assured him that the baby was alive, and said that he was now on a "boad" (boat). As a token of good faith, he would send Condon the baby's sleeping suit. In fact, it arrived the following day, and the Lindberghs identified it as that of their son.

On 2 April 1932, Lindbergh himself accompanied Condon when he went to hand over the ransom money; he clearly heard the kidnapper's voice calling "Hey, doctor!" But the baby was not returned. Lindbergh flew to look for a boat near Elizabeth Island, but failed to find it. And on 12 May, the decomposing body of a baby was found in a shallow grave in the woods near the Lindbergh home; he had been killed by a blow on the head—apparently on the night of the kidnapping.

The police investigation made no headway. The maid Betty Gow was widely suspected by the police of being an accomplice, but the Lindberghs had no doubt of her innocence. Suspicion transferred to another maid, Violet Sharpe, when she committed suicide with poison, but again there was no evidence.

Meanwhile, a wood technologist named Arthur Koehler was continuing his investigations into the ladder. He had written to Lindbergh offering to trace its wood, using the laboratory of the Forest Service in Wisconsin. Slivers of wood from the ladder had been sent to him for identification soon after the kidnapping. Now he spent four days studying the ladder microscopically, labeling every separate part. Three rails were of North Carolina yellow pine, four of Douglas fir, and ten of Ponderosa pine. The yellow pine rails contained nail holes, indicating that these pieces had been taken from elsewhere, and "rail 16" had square nail holes, and differed from all the others in that it had obviously been planed down from something wider. The whole ladder was "of poor workmanship," showing poor selection of wood and little skill in the use of tools. The microscope showed that the yellow pine rails had tiny grooves, which indicated that the lumber mill that had processed them had a defective knife in the planer. Koehler was aware that this was virtually a fingerprint; if he could find that planing machine, he would stand a good chance of finding what happened to this shipment of wood.

The investigation that followed has been called (in *The Trial of Richard Hauptmann*) "one of the greatest feats of scientific detection of all time." Koehler discovered that there were 1,598 lumber mills that handled yellow pine, and sent duplicated letters of inquiry to each of them. It took several months, but eventually he identified the mill as the Dorn Lumber Company in South Carolina. Between September 1929 and March 1932, they had shipped 47 carloads of yellow pine to East Coast lumber yards; Koehler and Detective Lewis Bornmann spent 18 months visiting yard after yard, and finally had to admit defeat; most of them had long ago sold their consignments of yellow pine, and had no records of the customers. Yet for some reason, they decided to revisit the National Lumber and Millwork Company in the Bronx, and there found a wooden bin which had been constructed of some of the pine they were looking for, with its distinctive planing. Of course, that was no proof that the wood of the ladder had come from that particular lumber yard; it could have come from 29 others. But it was certainly a triumph of sheer persistence . . .

The ransom bills—which included "gold certificates" which could be exchanged for gold—had all been marked (without Lindbergh's knowledge). Now banks were asked to look out for any of the bills, and in 1933 they began to turn up, mostly in New York, although some as far away as Chicago. This seemed to indicate that the kidnappers lived in New York or thereabouts. In early September 1934, $10 gold certificates began to appear in northern New York and the Bronx. In May of that year, Roosevelt had abandoned the gold standard, and called in all gold certificates; but they continued to be accepted by banks—and, of course, shops.

On 15 September 1934, a dark-blue Dodge sedan drove into a garage in upper Manhattan, and the driver, who spoke with a German accent, paid for his fuel with a $10 gold certificate. Because these had ceased to be legal tender, the pump attendant noted the car's number on the back of the certificate. Four days later, a bank teller noticed that the certificate was part of the Lindbergh ransom money, and saw that it had a registration number on the back: 4U-13-41-NY. The police were informed. They quickly discovered that the vehicle was a dark-blue Dodge sedan belonging to Richard Bruno Hauptmann, a carpenter of 1279 East 222nd Street, the Bronx. It proved to be a small frame house, and that night, police surrounded it. The next morning, when a man stepped out of the door and drove off, police followed him and forced his car over to the curb. Hauptmann, a lean, good-looking German in his mid-30s, made no resistance and was found to be unarmed. In his wallet, police found a $20 bill which proved to be from the ransom money. Concealed in his garage, they found a further hoard of Lindbergh money. Later, a further $860 of ransom money and a gun were found concealed in a plank in the garage.

The evidence seemed overwhelming—particularly when police discovered that Hauptmann bought his timber at the National Lumber Company in the Bronx located by Koehler and Bornmann. But Hauptmann protested his total innocence. The money, he explained, had been left in his care by a friend, Isidor Fisch, who had returned to Germany in December 1933, owing Hauptmann over $7,000, on a joint business deal. When Fisch had died of tuberculosis in March 1934, his friends in America—including Hauptmann—began looking into his business affairs, and realized that he had been a confidence trickster who had simply pocketed investments. Hauptmann and Fisch had been involved in a $20,000 deal in furs; now Hauptmann discovered . . . Hauptmann discovered that the warehouse did not even exist. In August 1934, said Hauptmann, he had noticed a shoe box which Fisch had given him for safe keeping before he left. It had been soaked by a leak, but proved to contain $14,600 in money and gold certificates. Feeling that at least half of it was his by right, Hauptmann dried it out and proceeded to spend it.

That was Hauptmann's story. It sounded too convenient to be true. And when Hauptmann's trial opened in Flemington, New Jersey, on 2 January 1935, it was clear that no one believed it. But the most important piece of evidence was the ladder. Not only was there a clear possibility that some of its timber had been purchased at the Bronx yard where Hauptmann bought his timber, but one of the rungs (16) had been traced to Hauptmann's own attic: Detective Bornmann had noticed a missing board, and found what remained of it, with the "rung" sawed out of it. The evidence could hardly have been more conclusive. Moreover, Condon's telephone number had been found penciled on the back of a closet door in Hauptmann's house, together with the numbers of some bills.

It was true that there was nothing conclusive to connect Hauptmann with the kidnap itself. The footmarks found outside the child's bedroom window were not Hauptmann's size; none of Hauptmann's fingerprints were found on the ladder. But a man called Millard Whited, who lived near

Lindbergh, identified Hauptmann as a man he had seen
hanging around the Lindbergh home on two occasions. And
Lindbergh himself declared in court that Hauptmann was the
"John" whose voice he had heard at the cemetery. All this,
together with the ladder evidence, left the jury in no doubt
whatsoever that Hauptmann was the kidnapper, and on 13
February 1935, he was sentenced to death. By October, the
Court of Appeals had denied his appeal. But when the
prison governor, Harold Hoffmann, interviewed Hauptmann
in his cell in December, he emerged a puzzled man, feeling
that Hauptmann's pleas of innocence rang true, and that the
case deserved further investigation. The truth was that
Hauptmann could easily have been "framed." Soon after
her husband's arrest, Anna Hauptmann had made the supreme mistake of moving out of the house, leaving it empty
for police and reporters to examine. It was after this that
Bornmann had discovered the missing board in the attic. But
was it likely that a carpenter, with plenty of wood at his
disposal, would prize up a board in his attic and plane it
down to size? Even the ladder itself gave rise to suspicion;
as Koehler pointed out, it was crudely made, and showed
poor judgment. But Hauptmann was a skilled carpenter . . .

For Lindbergh, Governor Hoffmann's attempts to prove
Hauptmann innocent were the last straw. He was totally
convinced that Hauptmann was guilty, and he felt that
Hoffmann was seeking publicity. He and his wife sailed for
England, and did not return for many years. He went to
Germany, was impressed by Hitler's revolution, and became
a frequent guest of the Nazis; later he tried hard to prevent
America entering the war on the side of the British.

But Hoffmann's efforts were of no avail, and on 3 April
1936, Richard Hauptmann was finally electrocuted, still
protesting his innocence.

Is it conceivable that Hauptmann was innocent? According to one investigator, Ludovic Kennedy, it was almost a
certainty. In the early 1980s, Kennedy took the trouble to
interview all witnesses who were still available, and to look
closely into the evidence—that which was presented in court
and that which was not. His book *The Airman and the*

Carpenter (1985) makes one thing very clear; that if all this evidence *had* been presented in court, Hauptmann would have been acquitted. Hauptmann came to America as a stowaway in 1924; he had a minor police record for burglary during the black days of inflation. But in America he prospered; he and his wife worked hard, and by 1926 he was in a position to lend money and to buy a lunchroom; the day after the Wall Street crash he withdrew $2,800 from his account and began buying stocks and shares at rock bottom prices. Hauptmann had no need to kidnap the Lindbergh baby; by modern standards, he was very comfortably off in 1932.

Kennedy's investigations revealed that Hauptmann's story about his friend Isidor Fisch was true. Fisch *was* a confidence swindler; he and Hauptmann were in the fur business together, and Fisch *did* owe Hauptmann over $7,000. His swindles were uncovered only after his death in Leipzig in 1934.

Then how did Hauptmann—or Fisch—come to be in possession of so much ransom money? The probable answer, Kennedy discovered, is that the Lindbergh ransom money was selling at a discount in New York's underworld—one convict bought some at 40 cents in the dollar. Nothing is more likely than that Fisch, with his underworld connections, bought a large quantity, and left it with Hauptmann when he sailed for Germany. Forsenic examination of the money showed that it *had* been soaked and dried out, confirming Hauptmann's story that he had left it on a top shelf in a closet and forgotten about it.

But Kennedy's major discovery was that so much of the evidence against Hauptmann was fabricated. When arrested, he was asked to write out various sentences; the court was later told that Hauptmann's misspelling of various words had been exactly as in the ransom note. This was untrue; he had spelled correctly the first time, then been *told* to misspell various words—"singature" for signature, "were" for where, "gut" for good. The court was also assured that handwriting experts had identified Hauptmann's writing as that of the ransom notes; Kennedy submitted the samples to two modern experts, who both said they were *not* written by the same man. Kennedy's investigation revealed that Millard Whited, the farmhand who identified Hauptmann as a man he had seen hanging around the Lindbergh property, had earlier flatly denied seeing anyone suspicious; he was later offered generous "expenses," and changed his story. As to Lindbergh himself, he had been invited to sit quietly in a corner of the room in disguise when Hauptmann was brought in for questioning; he therefore knew him well when he identified him in court as "John." As to the writing in the closet, Kennedy established that it was made by a reporter, Tom Cassidy, who did it as a "joke." Hauptmann had no reason to write Condon's telephone number on the back of a door; he had no telephone, and in any case, the number was listed in the directory. The numbers of bills written on the door were not, in fact, those of Lindbergh ransom bills.

The most serious piece of evidence against Hauptmann was, of course, the ladder. This constituted the "greatest feat of scientific detection of all time." Examined closely, it is seen to be highly questionable. Koehler's efforts established that some of the yellow pine was sent to the Bronx timber yard, and it may have been from this consignment that the rungs of the ladder were made. But this was only one of thirty timber yards to which the same wood was sent; the man who made the ladder could have bought the wood at any of them. Hauptmann rightly pointed out in court that he was a skilled carpenter, and that the ladder was made by an amateur. If the jury registered this point, they may have felt that he had deliberately botched it to mislead investigators— for, after all, was there not the conclusive evidence of the sixteenth rung, whose wood was found in Hauptmann's attic? But, as Kennedy points out, this plank was "found" when Mrs. Hauptmann had abandoned the house to the investigators. Was it likely that Hauptmann would go to the trouble of tearing up his attic floor, sawing out a piece of wood from the plank, then planing it down to size, when it would have been simpler to get another piece of wood? He was, after all, a professional carpenter. Kennedy quite clearly believes that rung 16 was concocted by Detective

Bornmann or one of the other investigators—he refers to the whole story as "Bornmann-in-Wonderland."

So in retrospect, it seems clear that the "greatest feat of scientific detection of all time" was based on false or suppressed evidence. The police firmly believed that Hauptmann was guilty, and they strengthened their case where necessary. Hauptmann may well have been guilty; but all the latest evidence points clearly to his innocence.

7

One result of the Lindbergh kidnapping was the "Lindbergh law" enabling the FBI to enter a case if the victim had been taken across a state line; the death penalty was also introduced in certain cases. It made little difference. In June 1933, a gang led by bank robber Alvin ("Creepy") Karpis, and including two of the gangsters who had taken part in the St Valentine's Day Massacre, kidnapped a wealthy brewer named Hamm, of St. Paul, Minnesota. They even took the precaution of having one of their men enroll in the local police force, in case treachery was attempted during the delivery of the ransom. Hamm was accosted outside his home and bundled into a car, driven by Karpis in chauffeur's uniform, then taken to the house of a postmaster in Bensenville, Illinois, where he was held. He was made to sign ransom notes demanding $100,000. When the police contact told the kidnappers that the police intended to hide a machine-gunner under the tarpaulin of the truck delivering the ransom, the instructions were changed. The $100,000 was duly collected, and sold to a dealer in "hot money" for $95,000, which was then divided between the gang members. The gang got clean away. But Karpis was finally arrested by J. Edgar Hoover in 1936, and spent the next 33 years in jail; during his latter days, he became the friend and mentor of Charles Manson.

Thomas Thurmond, a Californian, was 24 years old when he decided to turn to crime; with a friend named John Holmes, he intercepted Brooke Hart, son of the owner of a department store, and drove him to the San Mateo-Hayward bridge across San Francisco Bay. Hart was then knocked unconscious, wired to a lump of concrete, and thrown into the bay. He woke up and began to scream; the kidnappers fired shots at him until he sank. That same evening—9 November 1933—Thurmond rang Hart's father, demanding a ransom of $40,000, and warning him not to call the police. Hart contacted the police immediately. When Thurmond rang up again on 15 November, his call was traced to a San Jose garage, and police arrested him while he was still arguing with Hart senior about the pick-up point for the ransom.

When Brooke Hart's body was washed up nine days later, the enraged citizens of San Jose surrounded the jail—15,000 of them. The police sprayed the mob with hoses and tear gas, but they battered down the gates. Holmes fought frenziedly for his life, and his eye was dangling from its socket when he was dragged out. Thurmond's cell seemed empty—until one of the searchers looked up and saw him hanging from the water pipes. Both men were lynched in the park. Governor Rolfe of California went on record saying that the lynch mob "had proved the best lesson ever given to the country," and declaring that he would pardon any of them who were ever charged. No one ever was.

By 1933, Hoover had established what he called the "kidnap line"—a direct line to his office, so that anyone in the United States could call him the moment a kidnap had occurred. This happened on Saturday 22 July 1933, and the call came from Oklahoma City. That evening, a millionaire named Charles F. Urschel had been sitting out on the porch of his home, playing an after-dinner game of bridge with his wife and two dinner guests, Mr. and Mrs. Walter Jarrett. Suddenly two men appeared on the porch, one carrying a sub-machine-gun. "Which of you guys is Urschel?" When no one answered, the man said: "OK, both you guys on your feet." As the sound of the car died away, Mrs. Urschel ran to the telephone and dialed the "kidnap line"—a number that was familiar to most rich men in the country. A few hours later, as FBI agents were questioning the two women, Walter Jarrett walked in, looking exhausted. The gunman had halted 10 miles outside town and taken their wallets; Urschel's visiting card had identified him. Jarrett had been ordered out, and had to walk back to town.

Four days later, a family friend received a ransom demand for $200,000, together with a letter from Urschel; Mrs Urschel was instructed to place an advertisement in the *Daily Oklahoman*, offering certain farm property for sale. She did so, and received instructions to send the courier with the money to Kansas City, where he was to check into a hotel and await further orders. In due course, the courier received a telephone call ordering him to walk west from the La Salle Hotel. There a man approached and told him that he would take the bag. The "property deeds," he said, would be delivered within 12 hours. The next day, Charles Urschel returned home in a taxi.

For the investigators, Urschel proved to be a superb witness. He had paid minute attention to every waking moment of his captivity. In the car, his eyes had been taped, but the last thing he had seen before this was the power plant at Harrah. Through the open window—it was a hot night—he twice smelt the distinctive smell of freshly pumped oil and heard engines. He yawned and asked the time; one of his captors said it was 3:30.

The car halted, and he was made to get out and sit on the grass. Something bit his hand, and he caught an insect that was found in oil country. One of the men returned with a can of petrol, then they drove on for another hour. Dawn began to filter through the blindfold. The car stopped for a gate to be opened, then they drove into a garage or barn, where Urschel was transferred to another car; he smelt stable manure.

The drive continued for another 12 hours. Several times during the journey, it rained heavily. They pulled up for fuel at one point, and a woman with a shrill voice remarked that the rain was too late to save most of the crops, but might help the broom corn. When the car stopped again, he asked the time, and was told that it was 2:30. He was taken into a

house, where he was handcuffed to a baby's high-chair and
allowed to lie on a bed; a man and a woman talked, but one
of his captors taped cotton wool over his ears. Then he was
transferred to another house, about 20 minutes away, taken
into a room with musty blankets on the floor, and left there.
He could hear the sound of cows and guinea hens. He was
given water in a handleless cup; it had a strong mineral
taste, and came from a well on the north-west side of the
house; when the bucket was drawn up, the windlass
creaked.

He fell asleep, and when he woke up, he heard a plane
overhead; he asked the time, and was told a quarter to ten.
Later, he worked his blindfold loose enough to look at his
watch. Later in the day, when another aeroplane passed over
the house, it was 5:45. Thereafter, he noted the same
aircraft at the same time every day, for eight days, except on
Sunday. That day, there was a violent storm for most of the
day. Later that day, he was told that his ransom had been
paid, and he was free. The men drove him for hours to a
town called Norman, gave him $10, and told him to catch a
train home.

The investigators were delighted with this information.
Urschel's observations indicated that he had been driven
south, towards Texas. Reports from weather stations enabled
them to check the route the kidnappers had taken. But the
main clue was supplied by the aeroplane. Where in Texas
was there a morning plane at 9:45, and an afternoon plane at
5:45? In 1933, there were not so many airfields. American
Airlines had a flight from Fort Worth which left for Amarillo
at 9:15 in the morning, and returned from Amarillo at 3:30
in the afternoon. At 9:45 and 5:45 the plane would be over a
small town called Paradise, Texas.

An FBI team went to Paradise, posing as bankers willing
to offer loans to local farmers, and toured the farms. At the
farm of a man called R. G. Shannon, they found what they
were looking for—the house with the creaking windlass to
the north-west; when one of the "bankers" mopped his
brow and asked for a drink of water, it had a strong
mineral taste.

Further checks on the weather confirmed that this was the right place. There *had* been a heavy rainstorm for most of the day on Sunday 30 July, so that the pilot had turned north to avoid it. Investigations into Shannon's background revealed that his stepdaughter was the wife of "Machine Gun" Kelly, the bank robber, and that Shannon's son lived about a mile away—this sounded like the place where Urschel had been chained to a baby-chair. Urschel's description of the man who had handed him the $10 sounded like Machine Gun Kelly. Everything was falling into place.

At dawn on 12 August 1933, the police launched a raid and achieved complete surprise. Asleep in bed they found a gangster named Harvey Bailey, with a sub-machine-gun on the chair beside him. Urschel identified him as the man who had driven the car. Machine Gun Kelly's mother-in-law was among those arrested, and she mentioned that another gangster was involved in the kidnap plot, Albert L. Bates. Bates was later arrested in a brawl in Denver, Colorado, and found to be in possession of some of the kidnap money—whose numbers had been recorded. The home of Shannon's son Armon was also raided, and Urschel was able to see the baby-chair to which he had been handcuffed.

Eventually, 13 people were indicted for their parts in the kidnap plot, including a banker named Isadore Blumenfeld of Minneapolis, who was charged with "laundering" the ransom money. (The indictment against him was dropped, but two of his men received five-year sentences.) But Kelly and his wife remained at large. When the trial began, Urschel received a threatening letter from Kelly, ending "If the Shannons are convicted you can get another rich wife in hell, because that will be the only place you can use one." Urschel ignored the threat and gave his crucial evidence. A week later, as the trial was still going on, newsboys outside shouted: "Machine Gun Kelly captured!"

There was a curious story behind the arrest. In Memphis, Tennessee, a pretty 12-year-old girl named Geraldine Arnold confided to a playmate that she had some new parents; they had "borrowed her" for the sake of appearances. The playmate talked to a friend whose father happened to be a policeman. Soon afterwards, the little girl was met by a friendly FBI agent who bought her candy and asked her questions about her new parents. Her answers convinced him that they were Machine Gun Kelly and his wife. There was a dawn raid on 26 September. Kelly heard the noise and threw open the bedroom door, a revolver in his hand; a policeman pointed a shotgun at his heart and said: "Drop it Kelly." Kelly remarked: "I've been waiting for you all night."

The version concocted by Hoover was that Kelly whined: "Don't shoot, G-men," and that this is how the name "G-men" originated. The local Memphis newspaper of the day shows that this is untrue. In fact, the term "G-men" (meaning government agents) had been in use for some time.

Kelly and his wife received life imprisonment, and Kathryn Kelly was heard to murmur with disgust: "In this court my Pekinese dog would have gotten a life sentence." In fact, hers was well-deserved; it was she who had bullied the amiable but weak-willed Kelly into kidnapping Urschel, and she had tried hard to persuade him to kill the old man instead of allowing him to go free. Kelly's refusal cost him 20 years in Alcatraz, where he died of a heart attack in 1954; Kathryn Kelly was released in 1958.

***

8

***

There can be no doubt that detectives who have spent their lives hunting criminals finally develop an intuition that amounts to a "sixth sense." It was such an intuition that led Jean Belin, the man who arrested Landru, to the capture of his second mass murderer.

In 1937, the great International Exposition was held in Paris, and—like the Chicago World Fair, during which H. H. Holmes had flourished—it brought thousands of foreign visitors to the capital. One of these was a pretty American dance instructress named Jean de Koven, who was accompanied by her aunt, Mrs. Ida Sackheim. It was in mid-August that Mrs. Sackheim went to the police to report that her niece had vanished on 26 July. Two days before this, she had been sitting in the lounge of the Ambassador Hotel when she noticed a young man reading an English newspaper; when he put it down, she asked if she might look at it. The young man was handsome, and seemed to be rich; he called himself Bobby. Mrs. Sackheim suspected that her niece had accepted an invitation to tea from Bobby, but she had no idea where this was to take place.

Belin, who was now the chief of the Mobile Brigade, sent his men inquiring after Bobby in the places where he had formerly been seen, but could find no trace of him. But two weeks after Jean de Koven's disappearance, her traveler's checks were cashed by a young woman; the bank clerk had paid little attention to her, and could not say whether she was an American. Belin was inclined to believe that the charming Bobby was a confidence man, who had persuaded Jean de Koven to become his mistress for as long as her money lasted.

On 8 September 1937, the body of a private car hire driver was found near the Paris—Orléans road, shot in the back of the neck. He was Joseph Couffy, and his wife told the police that he had been hired by a man called Dushom to drive to the south of France via the Rhône valley. When Couffy had suggested taking a smaller car to save petrol, Dushom had said that he preferred comfort. The murderer had driven off in the car, and taken Couffy's money. Extensive police inquiries failed to find any trace of Dushom.

Five weeks later, a pedestrian in the rue des Graviers, in Neuilly, noticed that a car had been parked close to the cemetery for several days, and peered in through the window. In the back seat, he observed the naked body of a man whose hands and wrists were tied. The victim proved to be a young businessman . . . businessman named Roger LeBlond, and he had also been shot in the back of the neck. It seemed that LeBlond wished to start a theatrical publicity agency, and had advertised for a "sleeping partner" who would provide the money. A man named Pradier had come to see LeBlond at his apartment, and as they had left together, a servant had noticed that Pradier was returning his wallet to his pocket, and that LeBlond, who was accompanying him, looked well satisfied. It seemed that Pradier had driven to the cemetery with the young man, and had killed him—for what motive could not be ascertained.

Already, Belin noted the similarities between the three cases; a young man with a pleasant smile who seemed to have plenty of money. But he refused to allow himself to speculate about whether "Bobby," Dushom, and Pradier had all been the same man.

On 20 November 1937, the servant of an estate agent named Raymond Lesobre contacted the police to say that her employer had disappeared. All she could tell them was that Lesobre, who lived in St. Cloud, had taken an English client to see a villa called Mon Plaisir, with a view to buying it. The police called at Mon Plaisir and found it locked. They forced an entry, and found Lesobre sprawled across the cellar steps, lying face downward, and shot in the back of the neck. This time the motive was clear: he had been robbed.

Now there was a massive manhunt for the killer who shot his victims in the back of the neck. The newspapers gave the case a great deal of publicity. Belin was aware that he could, in fact, be looking for two killers; LeBlond had been shot twice, with two different revolvers, and from different angles, suggesting a left-handed and a right-handed killer.

In frustration, Belin decided to look up some of his old underworld contacts, men who in the past had been willing to slip him tidbits of information. But since he had been promoted to chief of the Mobile Brigade, these old contacts no longer trusted him; they excused themselves and hurried away. Meanwhile, the investigation was marking time. Belin's subordinates tried their own contacts in the Paris underworld, and also drew a blank. This was baffling. No one even seemed to be able to offer a suggestion about the identity of the killer. Could that be because he was an

Englishman, in Paris for the Exposition? Jean de Koven's "Bobby" had been reading an English newspaper; Lesobre had driven off with an "Englishman." Could that be why no one had heard of him?

One evening, Belin dropped into a bar near the Gare de l'Est to have a drink with a friend from early days, a policeman who was now in charge of that area. As they talked, two policemen who worked under Belin's friend came in. One of them, an Alsacien named Weber, was in an anxious mood. He explained that his nephew had not been seen for several days, and he was afraid that the young man had got himself into trouble. Belin asked why he thought so. Weber explained that his nephew, Fritz Frommer, had been in prison at Preugesheim, near Frankfurt, for his opposition to the Nazis, and that he had there made the acquaintance of a man named Siegfried Sauerbrey, who was in jail for robbery. When they were released, and returned to Paris, Fritz had continued to see Sauerbrey, although it was hardly appropriate for the nephew of a detective to mix with crooks.

Where does this Sauerbrey live? Belin wanted to know. Weber said that it was in a lonely house in the St. Cloud forest . . .

Belin had one of his intuitive flashes. Lesobre, the dead estate agent, had lived in St. Cloud. This Sauerbrey was a foreigner, just out of prison, and probably short of money. It was just possible . . .

"Do you have the address?"

"A villa called La Voulzie."

Back at his office, Belin made some notes about the case. When he returned the next morning, it was to learn that his superiors had taken him off it, and assigned him to investigate some right-wing secret society, suspected of plotting a coup. But he handed the case to a subordinate, with a recommendation to investigate Sauerbrey at La Voulzie. On 8 December, two Sûreté plain-clothed men, Bourquin and Poignant, called at the villa, and found no one home. As they were calling a second time, a good-looking young man came out of a side street, playing with a dog. He asked

the men if he could help them, and they told him they were
from the rates office. Poignant had meanwhile taken out his
wallet to offer his card, and then changed his mind; Bourquin
could tell that the sharp-eyed young man had seen the
inscription: Police. But he seemed perfectly at ease. Intro-
ducing himself as M. Karrer, he invited them inside. Bourquin
now asked to see his papers, and Karrer reached casually
into his pocket. A moment later, he was holding a gun, and
his expression had changed to one of fury. "Here are my
papers, damn you!" The first bullet struck Poignant on the
shoulder and knocked him onto the settee. Bourquin, who
weighed 17 stone, grabbed hold of Karrer's wrist, but the
man went on firing. One bullet grazed Bourquin's forehead,
while another went through his hat. Karrer had now turned
round in an effort to free himself, and was butting Bourquin
with his backside. Bourquin saw a small hammer on the
table, and hit the man with all his force. Karrer dropped to
the carpet. He was quickly secured, and Bourquin telephoned the local police station. Inspector Poignant proved to
be only slightly wounded, and helped Bourquin search the
grounds. They soon noticed that the steps near the front
door had been recently moved and replaced; when the police
arrived, these were moved. Buried only a foot deep, the
police found the body of Jean de Koven, fully clothed and
even wearing gloves. Investigation of the cellar revealed the
body of Weber's nephew Fritz Frommer. He had been shot
in the back of the neck.

Back at the police station, the arrested man seemed as
cool as Landru had been. With little prompting, he told
Belin that his real name was Eugen Weidmann. Equally
coolly, he admitted to murdering Jean de Koven—strangling
her while she was drinking tea—Joseph Couffy, Roger
LeBlond, and Raymond Lesobre. In fact, the car in which
LeBlond's body had been found was the one stolen from
Couffy; it had been repainted.

It gradually dawned upon Belin that he was talking to a
psychopath; it was impossible otherwise to account for this
absurd series of murders. Weidmann had been born in
Frankfurt 28 years before, and had served his first term in

reformatory for theft at the age of 14. His parents had sent him to Canada to make a fresh start—this is where he had learned his perfect English—but he was soon in jail again for theft. Back in Frankfurt, he had broken into a house and tied up two women; for this he had received a five-year sentence. It was during this sentence that he had met Fritz Frommer, who was a political prisoner. He had also met another two young Parisians named Roger Million—a slum boy—and Jean Blanc, son of a wealthy shopkeeper; they were serving time for currency fraud. Back in Paris, Weidmann, Million, and Blanc had gone into partnership in crime. Their first project was to kidnap a wealthy American named Stein, and hold him for a $25,000 ransom. With money provided by Blanc, they rented the villa at St. Cloud. But Stein became suspicious as Weidmann drove him back to St. Cloud at 90 miles an hour, and insisted on getting out of the car.

After this came the murder of Jean de Koven; her traveler's checks were cashed by Million's mistress, Colette Tricot. The murder of Couffy—also motivated by robbery—followed.

At this point in the questioning, Belin was interrupted by one of his subordinates. They had found a secret hiding-place in Weidmann's bedroom, and in it was a passport in the name of Jeannine Keller. Questioned about this, Weidmann admitted that she had been lured to Paris from Alsace with a promise of becoming a companion to an English girl who needed nursing. Weidmann had taken her for a walk in the woods near Fontainbleau and strangled her; then he and Million hid her body in a cave. (Weidmann led them to the cave, where the body was recovered.) The young man LeBlond had been shot by both Weidmann and Million, and according to Weidmann, Million had fired first. (Weidmann was the left-handed killer.)

Criminologically speaking, this is one of the most puzzling murder cases of the twentieth century. It seems clear that Weidmann fantasized about himself as a criminal genius and decided to form a gang consisting of men with whom he had been in prison; his aim was probably to dominate them entirely. (A curiously similar case had come to light in Stockholm the previous year, when a nerve specialist, Dr Sigward Thurnemann, had been exposed as the leader of a criminal gang whom he dominated by hypnosis and ordered to commit robberies and murders.*) In fact, Weidmann made so little from his six murders that it is tempting to look for some other motive. Was he, perhaps, a sadist like Peter Kürten, who derived sexual pleasure from strangling the woman and shooting men in the back of the neck? Unfortunately, there was no Professor Berg to study Weidmann as Kürten had been studied, so our knowledge is minimal. We know that Weidmann was bisexual, and that in the final year or so he had become entirely homosexual; this may explain why LeBlond was left naked. And it seems fairly certain that he tried to persuade Frommer to join the gang, and that Frommer was murdered when he refused. Otherwise, the case seems to belong to Locard's category of "crimes sans cause."

Weidmann was tried with his three companions—Million, Blanc, and Colette Tricot. He and Million were sentenced to death; Blanc and Tricot were acquitted. Later, Million was reprieved, and it was Weidmann alone who went to the guillotine on 18 May 1939.

Belin was modest about the flash of intuition that led him to link the disappearance of Inspector Weber's nephew with the other murders. But it seems clear that, but for that inspired guess, Weidmann would have continued his strangely haphazard career of murder for a great deal longer. The psychopathic killer has always presented the greatest challenge to the craft of the manhunter.

_____ 9 _____

Compared with California, the state of Oregon has a relatively low crime rate. But a case that occurred there in 1943 holds a unique place in the annals of crime detection.

*See my *Criminal History of Mankind*, pp.37–42.

On 21 June 1943, two fishermen discovered the body of a young girl, caught by the hair on a willow in the Willamette river; she proved to have died of drowning. But a bruise on her forehead suggested that she had been struck a blow which had knocked her unconscious, and had then been pushed into the river. The fact that one nylon stocking was missing, and the other dangling loose, indicated a sexual motive for the attack. This was confirmed by Dr. Joseph Beeman, head of the Oregon State Crime Laboratory, who said that rape *had* been attempted—there were fragments of skin under the dead girl's nails—but not completed. Richard Layton, the police chief of Sweet Home, who was summoned by the fishermen, observed that the girl's hands were soft and well-manicured, and pointed out that she was probably from a comfortable middle-class home—a student rather than a farm girl. In which case, a report of her disappearance should not be long in reaching the police. What seemed strange is that her body had been in the icy water for about two weeks, and yet no missing person report had so far been filed.

Police Chief Layton was due to retire within a few days, so a team of investigators was sent from Portland; it was headed by Captain Walter Lansing of the Oregon State Police. Dr. Beeman was able to tell Lansing that the girl had eaten a meal of beef soon before she died. When he returned to his laboratory, Beeman took the precaution of taking with him a sample of the girl's red-brown hair. Meanwhile, the corpse was moved to nearby Dallas, and newspaper publicity brought a stream of people to view it. And still no one was able to identify the pretty teenager. But as the body lay in the funeral parlour, Lansing observed two small marks on either side of the nose, indicating that she had worn glasses. A pair of glasses was placed on the dead face, and the girl photographed; but this still brought no identification.

The next problem was to try to find out where the girl had been killed. Captain Lansing and his assistant Sergeant C. D. Emahiser began to search both banks of the

Willamette river further upstream. Five days later, they found a glade on the riverbank, littered with beer cans and debris which suggested that it was used as a drive-in for lovers. Here they found the girl's missing nylon stocking and a broken pair of rimless glasses. The fragments of glass were carefully gathered; they were hoping that an optician could determine their prescription, so it could be circulated to opticians.

The glade was painstakingly searched, but recent heavy rains had washed away tire tracks or footprints. It ended in a steep drop to the river, and it seemed a fair assumption that the attacker had thrown the girl from there. As Sergeant Emahiser crawled among the pine needles, he found an unused bus ticket which had been issued on 7 June—two weeks before the body had been found. It would enable its holder to travel from Rickreall, a small town four miles east of Dallas, to Camp Adair, an army camp 20 miles to the south. Lansing contacted the Oregon Motor Stages Company, and had no difficulty in locating the man . . . man who had sold the ticket. He clearly recollected the girl, since she was friendly and talkative; she had mentioned that she was on her way to see a friend at Camp Adair. She had also mentioned that she had recently graduated from the high school at Independence, and was expecting to go to the University of Oregon in the fall.

The agent recollected something else. As they had been talking, a rancher named Ed Taylor had driven past, and recognized the girl; he was a friend, and offered to take her to Camp Adair. Since the ticket was already issued, it was too late to return her money; but the agent told her that if she mailed it to the bus company in Portland, they would give her a refund.

Lansing and Emahiser drove to the Independence high school. The students were on holiday, but the janitor was able to locate a copy of the school year-book. As soon as they turned to the senior class, they found the photograph of the girl who lay in the funeral parlor; her name was Ruth Hildebrand, and she was 17. School records also gave her home address on the outskirts of Dallas. Her mother, Martha

Hildebrand, was badly shaken to learn that her daughter was the widely publicized "sleeping beauty of Dallas" (as the newspapers had christened her). Ruth's father farmed near Camp Adair, and Ruth had gone off to see a schoolfriend at the army camp, saying that she would probably go on to visit her father. Mrs. Hildebrand had assumed that this was where she was.

The next person to be questioned was the rancher Edgar Taylor. But all he could tell them was that he had driven Ruth Hildebrand to Camp Adair and dropped her there.

The two policemen drove to Camp Adair, and there talked to John Macdonald, an 18-year-old private. He was shattered to learn that Ruth was dead. But all he could tell them was that she had arrived at one o'clock on the afternoon of 7 June 1943, and left at 9:30 that evening; a few hours before she left, they had eaten a dinner of steak. When she left, she had not made up her mind whether to return home or to go to see her father—it depended upon whether a north- or south-bound bus was the first to arrive.

The girl's father verified what they had already guessed: that she had not gone there. And the bus driver whose vehicle had passed the camp at 10 o'clock that evening recognized her photograph as that of a girl he had taken back to Monmouth. The bus was not going all the way to Rickreall that day, but the girl had decided that she could catch a shuttle bus or take a taxi for the rest of the way.

If Ruth had caught a shuttle, she must have gone to the booking office. The ticket agent remembered her. She had been too late for the shuttle. But someone had offered her a lift home.

"Do you know who it was?"

"No. He was a big man with a moustache—about 30. He wore a sport shirt but no jacket. Ruth looked bothered when he first talked to her, but he pulled out his wallet and showed her something. Then she got into his car—it was a Ford or Chevrolet."

The policeman called again on Ruth's mother and asked her if she knew anyone of that description. She shook her head. But she was quite certain that Ruth would never have accepted a lift from a stranger.

For the next few days, they questioned people throughout the area, asking if they knew a heavily built man who drove a Ford or Chevrolet; no one was able to help. Then one morning, as they sat eating breakfast in a Dallas café, Lansing suddenly gave an exclamation and pointed to an item in the *Portland Oregonian*.

"This has got to be it. Richard Layton, former police chief of Sweet Home, has been given a six months sentence for attempted sexual assault on a cannery worker."

Now, suddenly, the men knew what it was that the big man had shown to Ruth Hildebrand—it was his police identification card. That was why she had trusted a stranger.

The next stop was to interview the cannery worker who had been attacked; they obtained her name and address through the court that had sentenced Layton—it had been withheld in the news report. The girl told them she had accepted a lift on a hot day. Instead of taking her home, the driver had headed into the open country. The door had no handle, so it couldn't be opened from the inside. (In fact, both policemen had been in Layton's car when investigating the murder.) When he tried pulling off her clothes, she fought and scratched his face. In a fury, he went around to her side of the car and pulled her out. She clung to the seat, then let go, and he fell down. The girl jumped over a fence and ran into the woods. When she saw that the man was making no attempt to follow her, she crept back. As she expected, he turned his car and drove back the way he had come; as he passed, she was able to take down his license number. That was why Richard Layton was now in jail.

Layton's car was towed to the Oregon State Crime Laboratory, and studied by Dr. Joseph Beeman. His first interesting discovery was that the numbers on the engine block had been hammered out so they could not be read, but treatment with acid made them stand out. (Hammering the numbers would harden the metal, so it would become more resistant to acid than the metal around them, and would corrode less quickly.) The car proved to be one that had been stolen a year earlier.

With a small vacuum cleaner, Dr. Beeman went over the car's interior. From the back of the front seat, it sucked up a chestnut hair. Beeman still had the hairs he had taken from Ruth Hildebrand's head. They proved to be identical with the hair found in the car.

In an identity parade, Layton was picked out by the ticket agent as the man who had offered Ruth Hildebrand a lift. When Layton was shown the matching photographs of the two hairs, he knew that denial was hopeless. He described how he had encountered the girl outside the bus depot, where he had gone hoping to make a pick-up. He had taken her to the glade by the river and tried to undress her. She fought back furiously, scratching his face. Layton only succeeded in stripping off one of her stockings. Then, as with the cannery worker, he had opened her door and pulled her out. She broke away and started to run—but made the mistake of running towards the river, where there was a six-foot drop. As she continued to fight back, Layton punched her in the face, breaking her glasses; she fell backwards into the river. It was in flood, and should have carried her down to the Columbia River and out to sea. But her hair caught in the branches of the willow tree several miles downstream. Ironically, it was close to the town of Sweet Home, and Layton was summoned to examine the corpse . . .

Richard Layton was found guilty of first degree murder; on 8 December 1944, he was executed in the gas chamber at Salem prison.

---------- **10** ----------

The crime rate always drops during wartime, for the obvious reason that most of the professional criminals are in the army. In England, it began its slow rise in 1946, as large numbers of ex-military personnel returned to the relative anticlimax of the drab post-war world. But this increase was confined mostly to cities such as London; in rural areas, serious crime remained a rarity.

On 23 June 1946, there was a violent exception in the peaceful city of Warwick. PC Arthur Collins was about to climb into bed after a late night shift when he heard the sound of breaking glass; it came from a warehouse on the other side of Theatre Street. He pulled on his boots, seized his truncheon, and hurried downstairs. His wife—who had been asleep—went to the open window to see what was happening.

In the moonlight she saw her husband being attacked by five men, and beaten to the ground. The sound of a police whistle was cut off as someone struck it from the constable's hand. Mrs. Collins ran downstairs in her nightdress, and found her husband lying on the pavement, while a heavily built man leaned over him and struck him with his own truncheon. Mrs. Collins grabbed him by the lapel and tried to pull him away; there was a sound of tearing cloth, and she was hit with the truncheon. Mrs. Collins began to scream, and the attackers fled.

The police station was only 200 yards away, and her screams brought several policemen out to investigate; by the time they arrived, the men had gone. PC Collins was unconscious, and his pulse was so faint that it could hardly be detected.

The only clue was the piece of torn cloth. The following day it was shown to every tailor and clothing store in Warwick and Leamington. No one was able to identify it. Dustbins, rubbish tips, and vacant lots were searched for the suit from which it had been torn, and after 10 days, the Chief Constable of Warwick acknowledged that he needed the help of Scotland Yard.

The man who was sent was Detective Superintendent Robert Fabian, who was accompanied by his assistant, Detective Sergeant Arthur Veasey. The only clue the local police could offer was the piece of cloth. This proved to be most of a lapel, complete with buttonhole. Fabian had it photographed, and the pictures sent to every leading newspaper, with a request to publicize it. During all this time, Constable Collins still lay in hospital, and it seemed that the search might turn into a murder hunt at any moment.

Dozens of "tips" poured in; few sounded promising. Police vehicles with loudspeakers toured the streets, asking locals to go and see if they recognized the cloth. Half-way through the afternoon, a bronzed man with a military moustache came in, glanced at the lapel, and said: "I'm certain that's a bit of a demob suit."

Fabian's heart sank. Demobilization suits had been handed out by the million. Yet this lapel had a distinctive pattern. Fabian and Veasey traveled to the nearest Ministry of Supply depot, which happened to be in Birmingham. There a Civil Servant produced a huge book of samples, and quickly matched the lapel. "Pattern number DES 1012." He turned to another file. "Manufactured by Fox Brothers, Tone Dale Mills, Wellington, in Somerset."

Fabian and Veasey drove overnight. The manager of Fox Brothers consulted his records, and told them that the pattern was made under contract for a Royal Ordnance depot, and that 5,000 yards of the cloth had been woven. Most of this had been sent to Birmingham. But a small order of 900 yards had gone to a firm called Frazer Ross, in Glasgow.

Already, the case seemed hopeless. Many soldiers sold their demob suits to dealers waiting outside the gates, and they, in turn, sold them to cheap clothing stores. Nevertheless, Fabian went to call on the two Birmingham factories that had received the cloth. To his delight, neither of these had yet started to use their consignment. This left only the small order for Glasgow. Fabian and Veasey were on the next train. At the Frazer Ross factory, they spoke to the buyer. He told them that the cloth had already been made into suits, and took them into the workroom. There the supervisor studied the lapel and said: "That's Mac's stitching." He called: "Mac, come here a moment." A bent, elderly craftsman got up from his bench. "Is that your stitching?"

Mac studied it and nodded. "Aye, and there's nothin' amiss wi' it either."

Fabian asked anxiously: "I suppose you can't recall the suit it came from?"

"Aye. That lapel came from a suit specially made for a big man wi' a broad chest."

The order book revealed that a suit had been made specially for a man who was six feet two and half inches tall, with a 45-inch chest. It had been ordered by the special-size department of the Central Ordnance Depot at Branston, Burton-on-Trent. A telephone call to the depot established that the suit had been dispatched by registered mail on 10 January 1946 to Dominic Sutcliffe at an address in Birmingham.

By that evening, Fabian and Veasey were back in Birmingham and knocking on a door in a slum area. The big Irishman who opened it glared at them malevolently when they identified themselves as policemen. Fabian asked him what he had done with the demob suit despatched to him in January. Sutcliffe said he had sold it. When Fabian asked him who had bought it, he changed his mind and declared that he burned it. "It was too small for me."

Fabian shook his head. "That can't be true. It was specially made to measure by a Scottish craftsman. I'd like you to accompany us to Warwick."

Mrs Collins identified Sutcliffe as the man who had battered her husband to the ground—she had seen his face clearly in the moonlight. The four other men were soon tracked down, and stood beside him in the dock. Sutcliffe was sentenced to four years for grievous bodily harm, and the others to shorter terms. By that time— October 1946—PC Collins was back on his feet, although still unable to resume his duties; Sutcliffe had just escaped a murder charge.

—————————————— **11** ——————————————

Compared even with England, Japan has an exceptionally low crime rate; it seems typical that its Mafia—known as Yakuza—operate openly in buildings clearly labeled with their name, and that some citizens regard them as benefactors. When General Douglas MacArthur went to Japan in 1945 as the commander of the occupying forces, he expected to be received with hostility, perhaps with violence; instead, he was startled to be treated as a kind of father figure to whom the Japanese people owed respect and obedience.

This orderly and compliant aspect of the Japanese character is nowhere better illustrated than in the strange case of the poisoned teacups, whose solution, as we shall see, was also dependent on the typical Japanese virtues of efficiency and methodicalness.

At 3:20 on the afternoon of 26 January 1948, the Shiinamachi branch of Tokyo's Teikoku Bank was preparing to close its doors when a middle-aged man wearing an armband of the Welfare Department arrived and asked to see the manager. He was wearing a loose-fitting white cotton coat over a brown suit, and carrying a medical bag. The man's calling card was sent in to the manager, Takejiro Yoshida, and a moment later the Welfare official was ushered in. The card identified him as Dr. Shigeru Matsui, and he explained that he had been sent from General MacArthur's headquarters, with orders to immunize the bank employees against an outbreak of amoebic dysentery.

In fact, Mr. Yoshida was the acting manager that day because his superior had been stricken by a stomach ailment that morning, and had been forced to go home. He had also heard that one of the banker's customers was ill with dysentery. Therefore Mr. Yoshida summoned the staff of the bank, and told them that they were all to be given medicine. At this point, Dr. Matsui took over. Holding out an empty teacup, he explained that they would be required to take two drugs, one about a minute after the other. He then squirted liquid from a large syringe into each teacup, and handed out the teacups. At the command "Dozo" (please), everyone raised his cup and drank. Many began to cough and complain that the liquid burned their throats. "The second dose will make you feel better." He refilled the syringe from a second bottle, and once again squirted liquid into the cups. Again, they all drank. Someone asked: "May we gargle some water." The doctor replied: "Certainly." But as they lined up at the water fountain, one female bank clerk collapsed. Then the accountant fell down. Within minutes, the entire bank staff was writhing on the ground. The doctor watched them calmly, then scooped up 164,400 yen in cash and a check for 17,405 yen—a total of about £350 or $600—and walked out. It was an hour later that the alarm was given. By the time ambulances arrived, 10 of the victims were dead; two died later. Only four people survived, including Mr. Yoshida. When post-mortems were carried out, it was discovered that death was due to cyanide poisoning.

The totally ruthless nature of the crime—it still ranks as Japan's major post-war murder case—indicated that the killer was completely self-centered, indifferent to the lives of others. And the fact that he was a middle-aged man suggested that he should already be a known criminal. Yet no known criminal seemed to fit the description. The survivors told Inspector Shigeki Horizaki, head of Tokyo's Homicide Squad, that the robber had a mole on his left cheek and a scar under his chin. That also failed to provide a lead. The most important clue seemed to be the calling card. In Japan, the exchange of calling cards is as common as a handshake. This card presented by the killer had belonged to a real Dr. Shigeru Matsui, who lived in northern Honshu; but when Dr. Matsui called at the Tokyo police headquarters, it was perfectly clear that he was not the wanted man. It followed that someone had used his calling card, and had probably given his own in exchange. Fortunately, Dr. Matsui was a methodical man who filed all his cards. He recognized the card presented by the killer as one of a batch of 100, of which he had used 96, and taken 96 cards in exchange. The first task of the police was to interview every one of these persons.

Meanwhile, it was discovered that this was not the killer's first attempt. In the previous October, he had called at the Yasuda Bank in a Tokyo suburb and identified himself as Dr Matsui. And he had persuaded the employees to drink liquid from a teacup. No one had come to any harm, and the police suspected that this was intended as a dress rehearsal. But a week before the murders, he had called at the Nakai branch of the Mitsubishi Bank and handed over a card bearing the name "Dr. Jiro Yamaguchi" of the Welfare Ministry. When the manager asked to see more credentials, he had run away. Both cases had been reported to local police, but not to Tokyo's central police headquarters; the excuse was that, since no crime had been committed, it seemed unnecessary.

The day after the poisonings, the carelessness of a bank teller allowed the killer to escape again; he cashed the check for 17,405 yen at the Itabashi branch of the Yasuda bank by forging the endorsement.

One of the men assigned to the case was Sergeant Tamegoro Igii, who had been in the police force since before the war. Igii was something of an expert on calling cards—his colleagues even joked that he tried to foretell the future with them. He was among those whose task was to track down the 96 calling cards in Dr. Matsui's file. Igii made a personal vow to track down the killer.

Among the cards in Dr. Matsui's file was that of an artist called Sadamichi Hirasawa, who lived on Japan's northern island Hokkaido. His local police in Otaru had made a check on him, and reported that it was highly unlikely that he was the bank robber. He was a timid, gentlemanly sort of person in his 50s, and he had met Dr. Matsui on the Hokkaido ferry. Matsui recollected that Hirasawa was carrying a picture which he was going to present to the Crown Prince. He had been impressed by Hirasawa's position in the art world, as it emerged from the artist's conversation. In fact, the investigators discovered that many critics regarded Hirasawa as second rate. And he had been twice under suspicion for arson—he had collected insurance after fires at his second home in Tokyo—but had so charmed the police that he had been allowed to go.

By April, the investigators had reached a standstill, and decided to study all the evidence a second time, in case they had missed something essential. Again Hirasawa was interviewed by his local police, and again they reported that their investigation had cleared him completely.

Igii was a persistent man. Although he and his colleagues had now interviewed almost 8,000 people, he decided to go back to the beginning. In June, he set out to interview all the possible suspects again. In due course, he came to Hirasawa's name. Apparently the artist had left Tokyo for Otaru because his parents were sick. Through the artist's brother, a dairyman, Igii arranged to meet Hirasawa. On their way to the house, he asked what Hirasawa was working on at present. The brother replied: "Nothing." But when he was ushered into the presence of the artist and his parents, Igii noticed that the sliding door into the next room was open, and that there was a painting on the easel and paint brushes nearby, as if they had just been laid down. Igii was observant enough to notice that both the canvas and the brushes seemed dry. He concluded that Hirasawa wanted to give the impression of working hard.

Igii also noted that the parents seemed to be in the best of health, although Hirasawa had claimed they were both ill.

The first thing Igii noticed about Hirasawa was that he had a mole on his left cheek and a scar under his chin, and that he resembled the composite sketch that had been made of the bank robber. When he asked the artist what he had been doing on the day of the robbery, Hirasawa was able to offer an exceptionally full alibi. Igii pretended to be satisfied and took his leave. But a "hunch" told him that this was the man he was seeking.

On his return journey, Igii invited the artist out for a meal. It was apparently a social call, and the two men treated one another with smiling Japanese courtesy. But when Igii asked Hirasawa for a photograph, the artist said he had none. That struck Igii as strange, and he insisted on taking a few snaps "as souvenirs."

When he asked about the meeting on the ferry between Hirasawa and Dr. Matsui, Hirasawa remembered a detail that, if true, removed him from the list of suspects: he said that Dr. Matsui had written his address on the back with a fountain pen. Igii asked if he could see the card; Hirasawa said that it had been stolen soon after when his wallet had been taken by a pickpocket.

One more thing made an impression on Igii; for an artist, Hirasawa seemed to have an unusually wide knowledge of chemicals . . .

Back in Tokyo, Igii checked with Dr. Matsui about the writing on the back of the visiting card. Matsui denied it. "In any case, I never carry a fountain pen."

Igii felt certain that he had found his bank robber. He was therefore shattered by the news that his superiors had decided to suspend their inquiries into the case, which had apparently reached a dead end. Finally, they agreed to allow him to continue to work on his own, provided he did so discreetly. Igii even decided to mortgage his house to finance his investigation; fortunately, the police department came up with a small grant which would last for another 10 weeks.

Igii interviewed Hirasawa's daughter and his wife. Now he discovered the interesting fact that, only two days before the bank robbery, Hirasawa had been unable to pay even the smallest bill, but that soon afterwards, he had given his wife nearly 70,000 yen (about $200). He also discovered that Hirasawa was keeping two mistresses, and that they were probably the recipients of the rest of the money. Hirasawa suffered from a brain disease known as Korsakoff's syndrome, which involved amnesia relating to recent events; it was apparently the result of an anti-rabies injection. The disease had caused a deterioration in the artist's ability and a corresponding drop in income. But apparently he had told his family and mistresses that he had rich patrons and a large income—both statements being untrue. All this began to build up into a picture of a man driven into a corner by debt, who had decided to try and make a fortune with one desperate gamble. In fact, the robbery had brought only the equivalent of £350.

Igii's superiors agreed that there was now enough evidence to justify an arrest; on 20 August 1948, Igii journeyed to Otaru and charged Hirasawa with the Teikoku bank robbery. When the news got about, huge crowds waited at the railway stations to catch a glimpse of the suspected murderer of 12 people.

A search of Hirasawa's house revealed a brown suit and a loose-fitting white coat similar to those worn by the robber, as well as a leather case like a medical bag. Two of the survivors identified Hirasawa as the poisoner, although a third failed to recognize him.

Questioned about his income, Hirasawa told the story of rich patrons; but he was unable to name any of them. Asked about the money he had given his wife, Hirasawa claimed that he had received it from the sale of a painting to the president of a large industrial company the previous October; Igii, who had already checked this story, was able to state that the man had died in the previous August. Hirasawa looked shaken and admitted that he could not account for the discrepancy in his story.

Although the evidence against him seemed overwhelming, the artist continued to stick to his story, and to hint that Igii was "framing" him. Many people believed in his innocence, and he began to accumulate a large number of supporters. In prison, he attempted suicide three times. After the third attempt, he confessed to being the bank murderer, declaring that the ghosts of the people he had killed were haunting him; he also asked to be executed with a dose of potassium cyanide. At his trial—which began in Tokyo on 10 December 1948—his counsel insisted that the confession had been extracted from him under duress. But 15 months later, he was found guilty and sentenced to death. In fact, he was transferred to a prison cell to await execution, and remained there for the next 25 years, with many supporters attempting to obtain his release. Igii, who continued to have no doubt of Hirasawa's guilt, retired from the police force in 1964.

───────────────────── **12** ─────────────────────

If Tamegoro Igii had an equivalent at Scotland Yard—a man who combined intuition with sheer persistence—it was Detective Superintendent John Capstick, known admiringly to the criminal fraternity as Charlie Artful. The Blackburn fingerprinting case is an example of his persistence, but the case that best demonstrates the qualities that led to his nickname involved a double murder on a remote Welsh farm, and a killer who combined cunning and stupidity.

On 22 October 1953, the Carmarthen police received a report of the disappearance of a farmer and his wife. They were 63-year-old John Harries and his 54-year-old wife Phoebe; their farm, Derlwyn, was near the village of Llandinning. They had last been seen six days earlier, after attending a thanksgiving service for harvest; a neighboring farmer, R. W. Morris, had walked home with them and gone in for a cup of tea. While he was there, a young man had also paid a call; he was Ronald Harries, the nephew of the couple, who worked on his father's farm near the same village. When Morris left, Ronald Harries was still talking to his uncle and aunt. But when a neighbor called at the farm the next morning, he found it deserted, the unmilked cattle lowing indignantly. He called again a few hours later and found that the cattle had been milked, but the farm was still deserted. Meanwhile, Ronald Harries had been telling neighbors that his uncle and aunt had gone on holiday to London, and had asked him to look after the farm. It seemed strange that they had informed no one of their intention.

A local constable called at Derlwyn Farm, and there he discovered something that convinced him that John and Phoebe Harries had not gone to London: a joint in the oven, ready for cooking. No farmer's wife would waste a joint while she went on holiday, even if it had been a spur-of-the-moment decision.

Ronald Harries was questioned, and his story made the police even more suspicious. He claimed that he had driven his aunt and uncle into Carmarthen the previous Saturday to catch the London train. On the way, they had stopped at the Willow Café for tea, then gone to the station. But no one recalled seeing the trio, either at the café or at the station. Ronald Harries was now driving his uncle's car—although it had only third party insurance—and had transferred his uncle's cattle to his father's farm at Cadno, Pendine. The more the local police considered his story, the more suspicious they became. And the more they looked into the character and background of Harries—who was £300 in debt—the more certain they became that he had murdered his uncle and aunt and concealed their bodies somewhere. But a careful search of both farms revealed no evidence of murder. When the Carmarthen police requested the assistance of Scotland Yard, Detective Superintendent John Capstick was sent down, together with his assistant Sergeant Bill Heddon.

Harries told Capstick the same story: that he had left his uncle talking to Farmer Morris—although Morris insisted that *he* had left first—and that the next morning he had driven them to the station, then returned to the farm to milk the cattle.

By this time, another damning piece of evidence had come to light: a check for £909, signed by John Harries and made out to Ronald Harries's father; this had been endorsed by Ronald Harries and paid into his own account. But John Harries had only £123 in his account; consequently the check "bounced". According to Ronald Harries, his uncle had handed him this check—to pay off debts—just before he caught the train on the 17th. Forensic examination of the check at the Home Office Laboratory showed that the original date had been 7 October, and that the digit had been added; the check itself had originally been for £9.0.9d. Here, then, was an obvious motive for murder. But where were the bodies?

Capstick searched Derlwyn Farm and the Cadno Farm owned by Harries's father. He was looking for newly disturbed earth, or the sinking that might indicate bodies; he found nothing. He asked local farmers to search their own fields for any such signs, and 300 of them combined their efforts, all to no avail. Local rumor had it that the bodies had been taken to the sinking sands at Pendine, where Ronald Harries lived with his wife and baby. If that was so, there was no hope of finding them, and no hope of arresting Ronald Harries for murder. The gravest charge on which he could be arrested was forgery. On a remote off-chance, Capstick used every available policeman and soldier to search a rocket site at Pendine, but again the results were negative.

Capstick was never one to be discouraged. He firmly dismissed from his mind the possibility that the bodies were in the sinking sands, and asked himself where else they might be. The obvious place was on the farm belonging to the missing couple—surely no murderer would want to transport the bodies farther than he had to? Ronald Harries *had* been at Derlwyn Farm when Morris left at 9:15. But at 10 o'clock he was due to collect his parents from friends. He had arrived half an hour late, claiming that he had towed a neighbor's car. The neighbor denied the towing incident. All this meant that Harries would have had time to take his aunt and uncle to his father's farm, murder them, then go and collect his parents.

Capstick decided that his only hope lay in persuading the murderer to show his hand. He and his sergeant were staying in a Carmarthen hotel, The Blue Boar, which was also jammed with reporters, so everything they did was under constant observation. But at three o'clock in the morning, he and his sergeant tiptoed downstairs, and slipped out of a window—by arrangement with the publican. They drove to Cadno Farm, and spent half an hour tying thin green thread across every gate. Then they turned on the car's headlights and started its engine. Dogs began to bark in the farmhouse. As they drove away, the policemen saw that a light had come on; it was in the room they knew to be used by Ronald Harries when he stayed with his parents. Early the next morning, Capstick hurried back to the farm and checked all the gates. Only one had its thread broken: the gate that led into a field of kale.

Once again Capstick enlisted the aid of the local police, all countrymen who were as familiar with the fields as with the streets of Carmarthen. A line of them walked slowly down the kale field, requested to report anything that struck them as unusual. Half-way down the field, a sergeant called to Capstick, and pointed out that the kale plants in front of him were slightly yellow in color, and a few inches shorter than the rest; they looked as if they had been uprooted and replanted. Spades quickly uncovered the bodies of John and Phoebe Harries a few feet below the surface. Both had intensive injuries to the skull, suggesting blows from a hammer; John Harries also had a tear down his cheek, indicating that he had turned and fought before he was struck down.

Harries had so far been jauntily confident—one reporter described him as a "bumptious, verbose, even jocular" young man. Now his demeanor was more subdued. When told he was being charged with murder, he merely repeated the story he had already told. But his clothes were sent to the laboratory for study, and on one jacket there were traces of human blood inside the sleeve—suggesting that it was the jacket he wore to strike the blows. On another, there was blood on the lapel and inside the lining; this was probably worn when, later that night, he buried the bodies and replanted the kale. A few days later, a careful search of Cadno Farm revealed a hammer hidden in a hedge—a hammer that Harries had borrowed from a neighbor on the day of the murder, and later claimed that he had lost.

The trial was something of an anticlimax. Incredibly, Harries was convinced that he would be acquitted, and asked his parents to arrange a celebration party. The prosecution case was simple: that Ronald Harries had decided to solve the problem of his £300 bank overdraft—a large one for a farm laborer—by murdering his uncle and aunt. The idea had probably been suggested to him by the check made out to his father by John Harries 10 days before the murder. On 16 October, he had gone to Derlwyn Farm with some story about his parents wanting to see his uncle and aunt. He had taken them to Cadno Farm, waited until their backs were turned, then struck them down with a hammer. The medical evidence—the size of the holes in the skulls— suggested that the hammer was the one found in the hedge.

Harries's line of defense was to make wild attacks on all the witnesses, declaring that one was guilty of rape, another was insane, another was in the habit of seducing maids. The real murderers, he said, had dumped the bodies inside his gate to put the blame on him. Yet in spite of the obvious absurdity of these accusations, he seemed genuinely shocked when the jury brought in a verdict of guilty. He continued to insist on his innocence to the moment he was hanged at Swansea jail on 28 April 1954.

Postscript

A book on crime detection seems hardly the place for philosophical reflections. But even this grimly practical field can benefit from a wider intellectual perspective.

In the late 1930s, brain physiologists became aware that animal aggression seems to be associated with a part of the brain called the amygdala, or amygdaloid nucleus, an almond-shaped structure situated in the limbic system, the part of the brain that plays an important role in emotion and motivation. They discovered that if the amygdala of a highly aggressive ape is removed, it becomes good tempered and docile; when the amygdala of a sweet old lady was electrically stimulated, she became vituperative and aggressive.

But knowing the precise location of the "aggression center" fails to provide any real clue to the control of aggression. For it seems clear that the control of aggression depends largely upon whether a person *wants* to control it. Whether we like it or not, aggression depends, in the last resort, on "free will," Van Vogt says that the "Violent Man" *makes the decision* to be out of control.

This question of decision is an interesting one. Try a simple experiment. Ask a child to stand in the center of the room, then crawl towards him on all fours, making growling noises. His first reaction is amusement. As you get closer, the laughter develops a note of hysteria; at a certain distance, the child will turn and run—it is a good idea to have his mother sitting nearby so he can run into her arms. Now try the experiment yourself, getting a friend to crawl towards you growling; you will observe that you still feel a certain automatic alarm, which—being adult—you can easily control. It is an interesting demonstration that, although we consider ourselves to be rational creatures, there is still a part of us that stands outside our civilized conditioning.

It can, of course, be controlled. If you went on playing the game for half an hour, you would finally be able to watch your friend's approach without the slightest reaction. Moreover, if someone was rude to you within the next half hour, you would find that you had far less trouble than usual in controlling the rush of irritation.

It operates the other way around. If you respond to irritation by losing your temper, it becomes increasingly difficult to control your temper. The Panzram case is a classic illustration of how a man turns into a violent criminal simply by giving full rein to his resentment. At the same time, Panzram's rational self recognized that he was destroying the specifically human part of himself—after all, we use the word "humanity" to mean decency and kindness.

In an article on aggressive epileptics,* Vernon H. Mark and Robert Neville suggest that brain surgery—on the amygdaloid nucleus—could solve the behavior problems of many violent criminals. They go on to admit that this view will offend many humanitarians, who believe that violence is an expression of free will, and that brain surgery would have a "degrading effect" on human dignity. But they then make the important comment: "This view is particularly inappropriate, not because free will is to be denied, but because the quality of human life is to be prized. Many of the patients who come with focal brain disease associated with violent behavior are so offended by their own actions that they have attempted suicide." (This, of course, is what Panzram did.) They go on to argue that a brain operation could give a patient more rather than less control over his own behavior, and therefore increase his ability to express free will.

*In *Physiology of Aggression and Implications for Control*, edited by Kenneth Moyer, Raven Press, New York, 1976.

Theirs, it seems to me, is the sensible view. Human violence cannot be explained either in terms of free will or of physiological reflexes. It can only be understood as a *combination* of these two. Human evolution depends upon increasing control of the reflexes. This is why "the decision to be out of control" is always a mistake.

If we really wish to understand the issues involved, we must be prepared to consider them from a wider viewpoint than most scientists would allow themselves. In *A Criminal History of Mankind*, I suggested that they should be considered from the point of view of two opposing forces, which I suggest labeling Force T and Force C, the T standing for tension, the C for control. When a man badly wants to urinate, he experiences increasing tension; his heartbeat and blood pressure increase, his temperature rises. When a man becomes deeply interested in some problem, the opposite occurs; he soothes his impatience, focuses his attention, damps down his energies, until he achieves a state of inner calm. Some mystics—Wordsworth, for example—can sink into such deep conditions of calm that they achieve an insight into "unknown modes of being," and seem to grasp the workings of the universe. The criminal, with his tendency to lose control, has abandoned all possibility of such insights.

After publication of *An Encyclopedia of Murder*, many friends—and critics—expressed their perplexity about my interest in crime, which they seemed to feel indicated a streak of morbidity. One day when I was having dinner with the poet Ronald Duncan, and we were both in a pleasant state of alcoholic relaxation, he suddenly asked me: "Why are you *really* interested in murder?" He was obviously hoping that I would admit to a secret compulsion to rape schoolgirls or disembowel animals. When I explained that I saw it as a symbolic representation of everything that is wrong with human consciousness, he shook his head wearily, evidently feeling that I was being evasive. But I was also aware that the fault lay partly in myself, for failing to explain what I meant.

But as I was writing the section on Dan MacDougald in the final chapter of this book, I suddenly became aware that I was succeeding in saying *precisely* why the study of crime seems to me as important as the study of philosophy or religion. It was in the passage where, after explaining that Dickens's Scrooge is an example of what MacDougald calls "negative blocking," I go on:

> Now it is obvious that we are *all* in this condition, to some extent—for as Wordsworth says, "shades of the prison house" begin to close around us as we learn to "cope" with the complexities of existence. So we are all in the position of the criminal. But criminals do it far more than most people—to such an extent that, when we read of a man like H. H. Holmes, we can suddenly *see* that he was an idiot to waste his own life and that of his victims. As strange as it sounds, studying criminality has much the same effect on most of us that the ghosts of Christmas had on Scrooge—of making us more widely aware of the reality we ignore.

And there, I feel, I have succeeded in putting my finger squarely on the central problem—not only of criminal psychology, but of what I feel to be the essence of the human dilemma. This can be summarized in the statement that although human beings possess free will, they are usually unaware that they possess it. We *become* aware of it whenever we are in moods of happiness and excitement—what Maslow calls the peak experience. But under normal conditions, we are merely aware of the problems of everyday life, and these induce a feeling that we are fighting a purely defensive battle, like a man trying to prevent himself from drowning. Life seems to be an endless struggle, an endless series of problems and obstacles. And this condition produces a dangerous state of "negative feedback." As we contemplate the problems and obstacles, the heart sinks, and we lose all feeling of free will. And if our willpower is undermined, the obstacles seem twice as great. We *allow* the will to sink, until every problem produces a deep sense of discouragement.

On the other hand, when we are doing something we want to do, when we are carrying out some task with a deep sense of motivation, we are clearly aware of our freedom, and of our ability to "summon energy" to surmount obstacles. This has the effect of revitalizing us and recharging our batteries, which in turn deepens our sense of motivation, so that we actually enjoy tackling obstacles. In this state, we often observe that things seem to "go right," that obstacles seem to disappear of their own accord. This may or may not be true, but it certainly increases that feeling of zest and enthusiasm. We experience a kind of "positive feedback."

Now it obviously makes sense, on a purely logical level, to try to achieve these states of "positive feedback." No matter how serious the problems, it is obviously to our advantage to tackle them in a state of enthusiasm and optimism; it cannot possibly be to our advantage to sink into a state of discouragement. Unfortunately, we are not now dealing with a logical reaction, but with a purely instinctive one, like the child's desire to run away when you crawl towards him on all fours. And it is this negative reaction, this tendency to allow the will to collapse, and to seek the solution of the problem on a lower level, that constitutes the essence of criminal psychology.

Here is the paradox: that it is when we experience the feeling of helplessness, the sense that life has turned into a series of unfair frustrations and difficulties, that we are tempted to make "the decision to be out of control," to *restore the sensation of free will* by doing something absurd or violent or even criminal. This is the time when we lose our temper, or give way to a fit of self-pity, or take some dangerous and unjustifiable risk, like overtaking on a bend. Graham Greene has described how, as a teenager, he reacted to depression by playing Russian roulette with his brother's revolver, and how, when there was only a 'click' on an empty chamber, he experienced a tremendous surge of joy; he had *become aware of his freedom*.

But this is only half the story. The mechanism can be

studied even more clearly in Arthur Koestler's account of
how he came to join the Communist Party. In *Arrow in the
Blue*, he describes how he lost his money in a poker game,
then got drunk at a party and discovered that the car radiator
had frozen and the engine block had burst. He accepted the
hospitality of a girl he disliked and spent the night in her
bed. Waking up beside her with a hangover, he recalled that
he had no money and no car, and felt the urge to "do
something desperate" which led to the decision to join the
Communist Party. Here we can see that his misfortunes had
induced a sense of non-freedom that led him to decide to
renounce what freedom he felt he had left, and to take
refuge in a crowd. (This is, of course, the basic mechanism
of "conversion.")

We are all familiar with the same tendency. When our
energies are low, our freedom seems non-existent, and
everyday tasks and chores seem unutterably tiresome. Then
we slip into the vicious circle of boredom and loss of
motivation in which it seems self-evident that life is a
long-drawn-out defeat. This state of mind tempts us to take
"short cuts." And crime, of course, is a short cut. We can
study the same mechanism in Carl Panzram, who became a
killer after he had betrayed the trust of the prison governor and
decided that he was "worthless," and in Ted Bundy, who
became a Peeping Tom after his girlfriend had jilted him.

In this respect at least, crime is closely related to mental
illness. Maslow describes the case of a girl who had sunk
into such a state of depression that she had even ceased to
menstruate. He discovered that she had been a brilliant
student of sociology, who had been forced by the Depression of the 1930s to accept a job in a chewing-gum factory. The
boredom of the job had totally eroded her sense of freedom. Maslow advised her to study sociology at night school,
and her problems soon vanished; her sense of freedom had been
restored. Similarly, William James describes how, during a
period of anxiety about his future prospects, he also fell into
a state of depression. One day, entering a room at dusk, he
recalled the face of an idiot he had seen in a mental home,
staring in front of him with blank eyes, and was suddenly

overwhelmed by the thought: "If the hour should strike for me as it struck for him, *nothing* I possess could defend me from that fate." "There was . . . such a perception of my own merely momentary discrepancy from him, that it was as if something hitherto solid in my breast gave way, and I became a mass of quivering fear."

We, of course, can see clearly that there was far more than a "momentary discrepancy" between William James and an idiot suffering from catatonia; there was a vast difference in their capacity for freedom. But James had become *blind* to this difference because his depression had narrowed his senses. It is also significant that James began recovering from his period of mental illness when he came across a definition of free will by the philosopher Renouvier: that it is demonstrated by my capacity to *think one thing rather than another*. As soon as he became intellectually convinced that he possessed free will, he began to throw off his depression.

This is a point of central importance. Our free will is normally "invisible" to us, as a candle flame is invisible in the sunlight. We only become aware of it when we are engaged in some purposeful activity. Maslow made the interesting observation that when his students began to discuss peak experiences amongst themselves, and recall past peak experiences, they began having peak experiences all the time. The reason is obvious. The peak experience is a sudden *recognition* that we possess free will. It might be compared to discovering that the candle flame *is* there by putting your finger near it. Once the students became *aware* that they possessed free will, they kept on "recollecting" the fact with a shock of delight—the peak experience—like a man waking up in the middle of the night and remembering that he has inherited a fortune.

But *how* can we fall into this strange state of "unawareness of freedom"? The answer lies in a concept I have called "the robot." We all have a kind of robot in our subconscious minds which makes life a great deal easier. I have to learn new skills—like typing, driving a car, speaking French—patiently and slowly; then the robot takes them over and does it far more quickly than I could do it consciously. The trouble is that the robot not only does the things I want him to do, like typing, but also the things I *don't* want him to do, like enjoying nature, listening to music, even love-making. When we are tired, the robot takes control, and we lose all sense of freedom. We feel that we are merely a part of the physical world, with little or no power to "do." We lose our sense of our own value, and decide that the answer lies in compromise and seeking short cuts.

If we possessed detailed biographies of every criminal, we should almost certainly discover that most of them became criminals after such a crisis of "self-devaluation." But it is also interesting to note that some of the worst criminals—Henry Lee Lucas is an example—undergo religious conversion after they have been caught, as if the attention focused on them has restored their sense of personal value, so that they now become appalled by what they have done.

There is no obvious and simple method of restoring a criminal's sense of personal value, or of preventing him from losing it in the first place. But it may be worth noting the lesson of William James and of Maslow's sociology student: that as soon as the will is put to active use, the sense of personal value returns automatically. I have often day-dreamed of the idea of a prison where, instead of receiving remission for good conduct—which is at best a negative virtue—prisoners receive it for creative activity: a month's remission for a good poem or painting, three months for a promising story or article, two years for a novel or symphony... The idea may be unworkable, but I have a feeling that the approach is along the right lines.

These reflections also lead me to the unfashionable view that the social philosophy promulgated by our educational institutions also deserves its share of the blame. The old religious philosophy of earlier centuries was authoritarian and repressive, but at least it assumed that man has an immortal soul, and that our task is to surmount the problems of everyday life by reminding ourselves of that fact. As far as Western civilization is concerned, the great change began after the year 1762, the year Rousseau's *Social Contract* appeared, with its famous words "Man is born free but is everywhere in chains." Unfortunately, this is a half-truth, which can be far more dangerous than a downright lie. Freedom is a quality of consciousness, not another name for a man's political rights. To confuse the two leads to intellectual chaos,. which is the reverse of freedom. We all know people who ought to feel free because they have money and leisure, and yet who are miserable and neurotic. We all know people who ought to be miserable because they are poor and overworked, yet who remain remarkably cheerful. The very nature of freedom seems to be paradoxical.

As Rousseau's "Man is born free . . ." became part of the conventional wisdom, it became a justification for crime, as we can see in the case of Lacenaire or Ravachol. If I believe that I *ought* to be free, and yet I do not feel free, then I look around for someone to blame. And if I allow Rousseau and Marx and Kropotkin to convince me that the blame should be placed squarely on the selfish philosophy of Capitalism, then I have found the ideal excuse for ignoring my own shortcomings and indulging in childish outbursts of self-pity. Lacenaire believed he was combating social injustice by stabbing a "bourgeois" and pushing his body in the river. Charles Manson believed that society is so rotten that it is no crime to murder the "pigs." Carl Panzram went further and believed that life is so vile that to murder someone is to do him a favor.

We can see that this is merely unbelievably muddled thinking. But when so many academics and philosophers subscribe to it, we can hardly blame the criminals. Sartre is on record as describing the "Free World" as "that hell of misery and blood," and declaring that true progress lies in the attempt of the colored races to liberate themselves through violence. This philosophy inspired Italian terrorists who burst into a university classroom and shot the professor in the legs, alleging that he was guilty of teaching his students to adapt to a fundamentally immoral society. The same philosophy could easily be adapted to defend the activities of the Mafia.

In the Introduction to the *Encyclopedia of Modern Murder*, I pointed out that Albert Camus's book *L'Homme revoltè* (*The Rebel*) was designed as a final refutation of Rousseau. It sets out to demonstrate that all the philosophies of freedom and rebellion, from de Sade to Karl Marx, have led to tyranny and the destruction of freedom. The rising tide of violence in our society demonstrates that Camus was right and Rousseau wrong. And if Rousseau's idea could gain currency because a need for change was so urgent in the late eighteenth century, then the same applies to Camus's idea when there is an even more urgent need for change in the late twentieth century. That observation places the responsibility squarely on the shoulders of our educational institutions and on our "intellectuals." But this analysis of the nature of freedom should have made it clear that this is only part of the solution. The great "metaphysical" problem of the human race is that we possess free will yet are usually unaware of it. We cease to be aware of it the moment we allow tiredness and pessimism to erode our sense of purpose. We *become* aware of it by flinging ourselves into purposeful activity. The real enemy is the pessimism that arises when we contemplate the problems—for example, the serial killers and "motiveless murder"—in a defeatist frame of mind. For, as we have seen, it is that "invisible" element of freedom that spells the difference between failure and success. And since the history of crime detection has been a history of optimism and logic, it would be a total absurdity to abandon our most powerful weapon at this point.

This had been for me the major "lesson" of this book, and my justification in writing it. But I trust I shall not be condemned as too "metaphysical" if I also point out that is the general solution of the problem we all face every morning when we open our eyes. The problem of crime is the problem of human existence.

Coming soon from Warner Books!

Explore the minds and methods of criminals and those who hunt them— with Colin Wilson, author of *Written in Blood: Detectives and Detection*

WRITTEN IN BLOOD II:
The Trail and the Hunt
Coming in September 1991

WRITTEN IN BLOOD III:
The Criminal Method
Coming in January 1992